A Life Left Untold

GER GALLAGHER

POOLBEG

Published 2005
by Poolbeg Press Ltd
123 Grange Hill, Baldoyle
Dublin 13, Ireland
E-mail: poolbeg@poolbeg.com

1 3 5 7 9 10 8 6 4 2

A catalogue record for this book is available from the British Library.

ISBN 1-84223-252-5

Typeset by Type Design in Garamond 11/14.5
Printed by
Litografia Rosés S.A., Spain

www.poolbeg.com

About the Author

Ger Gallagher lives in Dublin with her husband and two daughters. This is her first novel.

Acknowledgements

This book would never have been written without the boundless enthusiasm of my dear friend Angela Fitzgerald who passed away before she could see my short story transformed into a novel.

My staggering ignorance of computers proved to be a massive obstacle when it came to writing this novel. I owe a huge debt to my husband, Paul Gallagher, for all the time and effort he put into bringing my manuscript to life. Thank you.

I extend a heartfelt thanks to the following: my teacher, Aine Millar, for showing not telling; Anne Raleigh, Vanessa Brady and John Daly who took time out to read my early drafts and gave me much valued insights; Dr. John McCusker, for his time and advice; my mother, sisters and brother, who urged me on with their support and encouragement; my daughters, Jessie and Eve, for the joy and happiness they bring to me every day.

Finally, a big thanks to my editor Gaye Shortland, Paula Campbell and all the team at Poolbeg.

Dedication

For my mother, Vera, and in memory
of my father, Billy.

Prologue

Bangor, Maine – 2003

Sometimes a person's death can unravel an entire family. That's what happened when my grandmother Lily died twenty years ago. She was the thread that kept us together, and when she passed away we fell apart.

My mother is an alcoholic. What more can I say? She lives alone, which is the only way she can exist. I stayed with her for a few years after my grandmother died, and in a way I think my presence only served to make things worse. I thought I was helping, but I became part of her disease, and in the end I realised the only thing left for me to do was leave. You see, my mother never wanted me. And in a perfect world, if I got to pick a mother, I certainly would not have chosen Grace. I never knew my father and I doubt he was ever aware of my existence.

My grandmother's name was Lily, and I loved her

dearly. She took the place of my mother, and the father I never knew – she was everything to me. When I was born, Grace, my mother, took me back to my grandmother's house and the three of us lived together. But Grace was more like a sister to me, and not a very nice one at that. I always called her by her first name, never "Mother". When I fell and cut myself, it was my grandmother that I ran to. In the evenings, it was my grandmother who read to me and put me to bed, and I never missed having a mother when she was around. Grace slowly withdrew from my life, and as I grew older we stopped talking altogether. It's strange, but the only time I miss not having a mother now is when I spend time with her.

Looking back, I don't understand how my grandmother could have watched her daughter fall apart, knowing she might have prevented it by telling the truth. I have sometimes wished that my mother's friend Sarah had never told me anything, but deep down I know she had no choice and knowing what happened helped me understand how Grace ended up the way she did. It would be easy to blame her for all that went wrong, but that would be unfair. Her path was mapped long before she was even born. Grace was just another casualty in my grandmother's quest to purge herself of the past.

Part 1

1

County Wicklow, Ireland 1931

One April evening, shortly before her eighteenth birthday, Lily Marsh was out in the back field. The evenings had become brighter with the arrival of spring, allowing her to go for walks after tea instead of listening to the wireless with her parents. When she reached the top of the hill behind her house she heard someone shouting. Lily turned to see her friend Sarah running up the hill towards her, waving her arms and screaming like a madwoman.

Lily could tell by the smile on Sarah's face that she had good news.

"What is it?" Lily asked when Sarah caught up with her.

Sarah was out of breath. She put her arms on Lily's shoulders to steady herself. "How would you

1

like to come and work in Dublin?" she panted.

"What are you talking about?" asked Lily, shaking herself free.

"I mean getting out of here!" Sarah shrieked. "Escaping!"

Lily put her hands on her hips and stared at Sarah closely. "Please explain."

"My Uncle Dan has opened a hotel in Dublin, and as soon as we finish school in June he'll have a job for us. We'll only be chambermaids to start with, but we'll get five bob a week, plus our room and board. And if we promise to go to secretarial school at night, Mam says we can go!" Sarah blurted the entire sentence without taking a breath. "But Lily, here's the hard part, she'll only let me go if you're with me. You have to talk to your parents, beg them, get down on your knees tonight and beg them to let you go!"

Lily's heart sank. How could she ask them? It would break their hearts if she left.

"Sarah," she mumbled – she could feel her cheeks reddening and turned away to hide her face, "how on earth could I ask them that? You know what they'd say."

"Oh Lily, for heaven's sake, you're seventeen! They can't expect you to live at home forever. You have to make a life for yourself. My mam's delighted."

"It's different for you. There are still the boys for her to look after. If I go Mammy and Daddy will have no one."

"They'll get used to it, Lily. We can come home every month to visit – please say you'll ask them! You're my only hope of ever getting out of here."

"You make it sound as if you're living in a prison," said Lily smiling.

"Well, I am! Slaving away day after day, picking up after those eejit brothers of mine, and if I wait around much longer they'll have me working in that bloody shop. Well, no thank you, I'm getting out while I still have my looks!" Sarah's face broke into a mischievous smile. "Come on, we'll have the time of our lives."

* * *

The day Elizabeth had been born was a day Mary and Michael Marsh thought they would never see. In their fifteen years of marriage Mary had suffered five miscarriages. Each pregnancy brought new hope and each miscarriage a devastating blow. Now as she approached the age of forty-five it seemed like a miracle to be blessed with a perfect baby girl. Mary knew women her own age who were already grandmothers, but she didn't care. She had waited so long for this child. They called her Elizabeth after Michael's mother who had died the previous year, leaving them the small farm where they lived in Wicklow. Their life was complete. They were a family now.

3

Michael called the child Lily and he loved her to the point of distraction. He had always been a quiet man who took little interest in the affairs of his neighbours. He kept his distance without being unfriendly. But when Lily was born he seemed to change overnight. Walking around the village of Redcross on a Saturday afternoon, he looked like a gentle giant from a fairy tale, as he clutched the tiny infant to his chest. He often called into the butcher shop to let the girls there have a look at her.

"Oh, Mr Marsh!" they'd shriek from behind the counter, wiping their hands on their aprons. "Can we hold her?"

Michael would hand the baby over, beaming with happiness as he watched his daughter being doted upon. When the child was handed back to him he would set off down the street, his chest puffed out with pride.

"He's gone soft!" the girls would giggle, as they watched him walk down the street like a peacock.

Lily was a good girl. She had no interest in school but was always ready to help about the farm. As she grew older Michael would sometimes let her skip school to help with a cow that was calving, and in the lambing season he always allowed her a few days off to help out. Lily loved nothing better than to run free around the farm, away from the boredom of books and school.

Sometimes her friend Sarah Lynch would come

over to play. Sarah's parents owned the local hardware shop, where most of the town gossip took place under the razor-sharp eyes of Mrs Lynch.

On Saturdays when the shop got busy Mr Lynch let Sarah and Lily help out behind the counter. The girls felt so grown up, taking money and counting out change, listening in on the idle chitchat of the customers. Mr Lynch got the girls to fill small brown paper bags with nails and screws. Fifty in each. For every twenty bags filled, he would give the girls a penny. Lily filled each bag, being careful to put the right amount in each time.

Sarah would nudge Lily roughly. "For God's sake! You'll take all night if you count every one like that. Here, do this!" And she'd grab a handful of nails and fling them roughly into a paper bag.

"But, Sarah," Lily would protest, "there's far more than fifty in those bags!"

Sarah would put her hand up to her cheek in mock surprise. "Well, some lucky customer is going to get more nails than he paid for! I doubt he'll be back to complain."

Lily would shake her head and continue to count her nails out correctly.

"Well, aren't you pair the best workers I've ever had!" Mr Lynch always said when he was locking up. "Isn't it a pity that I couldn't afford you full-time?" He counted out their pennies, and the girls would race down to Hackett's sweet shop just before it closed.

Lily was always careful to spend only half her money; Sarah made sure she spent the lot.

"What good is your money sitting at home in a jar?" Sarah would say, as she tore the wrapper off her chocolate bar. "Money is for spending, Lily, not saving."

"It's for spending and saving," was always Lily's sensible reply.

Sarah had five brothers, and the Lynch house was always bursting at the seams with the laughs and quarrels of the younger boys. Lily loved being there and wished that she was part of a big family and not always the only child. When she returned home after being in the Lynchs' it was like entering a convent. Her parents were older than Sarah's and they sat in silence every evening listening to the wireless. They never went to the pictures or out dancing like Mr and Mrs Lynch. Lily couldn't even imagine what her parents would look like dancing.

The girls were very different in lots of ways. Lily was dark-skinned and brown-eyed, and was shy and sometimes awkward with people she didn't know. Sarah had fair hair with pale freckled skin, and possessed a confidence that Lily envied. The fact that she had five brothers and was used to fighting her corner regularly had without doubt contributed to her supreme self-assurance. One thing the girls had in common was the fact that they both wanted to finish school and get out of Redcross as soon as possible.

* * *

That night, after Sarah had come up with her great scheme, Lily sat at the kitchen table, pretending to read. Michael was busy poring over accounts ledgers, while Mary sat in her usual spot beside the fire, her head bent at an angle towards the light as she darned one of Michael's socks. Each time Lily started to form a sentence she lost her nerve and sank back into the book that lay open before her on the table.

The following night she did no better. All the excitement that welled up inside her seemed to fade when she tried to find a voice. The words just refused to come out. Sarah was fit to be tied the following day. "Jesus, Lily, I'll go over tonight and ask them myself if you won't!"

"I'll do it tonight," Lily promised.

Lily couldn't eat that evening. Her stomach muscles tightened as she began to speak and, as she told them about Sarah's uncle and the jobs in Dublin, her cheeks began to burn.

The look of shock on their faces made her realise just how much she wanted to leave, and it filled her with shame. They had done nothing but love her so completely since the day she was born. They had covered her in their love until she felt she would smother, and now she needed room to breathe.

When she finished she looked from one parent to the other and waited for them to speak. Mary looked down at her hands, twisting her wedding band as she always did when she was troubled.

"Dublin," whispered Michael.

"Not yet. You're too young," said Mary.

"I'm seventeen, I'll be eighteen in three months. Lots of girls are working at my age."

"A chambermaid. Is it what you really want?" asked Michael.

"Yes, Daddy," said Lily choking back her tears, when she saw the look of devastation on his face.

Michael looked at Mary and shrugged his shoulders. "Well, I suppose it's your decision, Lily. We'll miss you sorely but if that's what you want we can't stop you."

"Michael!" protested Mary. "Is that all you have to say?"

Michael sat back in his chair and gave Lily a weak smile. "It seems she has her mind made up," he said.

Lily jumped up, pushing her chair out from under her. "Thanks, Daddy," she cried, hugging him tightly. Then she turned to face Mary, and with a little more caution she pleaded, "Please, Mammy, let me go. I'll come home often! It's not as if you won't see me at all!"

"It looks as if I don't have much choice in the matter," said Mary coldly.

Lily placed her arms loosely around her mother's

neck, knowing that Mary was always uncomfortable with any show of affection. She leaned in towards her, and their cheeks lightly touched. Then, trying desperately to contain her excitement, she charged towards the front door. "I'm just going over to tell Sarah. I'll be back later."

They stood at the window and watched their daughter rushing away from the house. Michael put his arm around Mary's waist and pulled her close to him. "We've lost her," he said gently.

"Not at all," said Mary, shaking herself free from his grip. "She'll be back before long. Lily's a home bird." The cups and saucers clattered together as she cleared them from the table. When Mary reached the sink she dropped the tray heavily on the draining-board. Michael turned and saw the look of bitter disappointment on her face. Mary threw her arms upwards in a gesture of hopelessness.

"I don't understand it. After giving her a good education and the best of everything. Why would she want to go running off to Dublin to work as a servant girl?"

* * *

Lily packed the last few things into her suitcase. They were catching the afternoon train from Wicklow town at two o'clock. She packed as slowly as possible, each garment folded meticulously and laid out with military precision. Lily wanted to stay in her room until it was time to go. She couldn't face going down to the kitchen where she knew her mother was waiting. Without saying very much, Mary had continued to make her disapproval clear. One word from her was all it would take, and Lily knew she would be back in her room unpacking. Sarah's parents were bringing them into town in Mr Lynch's new motor-car. At last, Lily heard the sound of the engine coming down the road, and ran to the window in time to see Sarah leaning over her father's shoulder to sound the horn. Lily waved down at them and rushed to her bed to close her suitcase. With both hands, she hauled it off the bed and dragged it downstairs.

Michael was standing at the front door and took the suitcase from Lily. "I'll put this into the car. You go on in and say goodbye to your mother." He walked out to greet the Lynches. Lily took a deep breath and prepared herself. When she walked into the kitchen she could tell that her mother had been crying.

Lily wanted to throw her arms around her, and say sorry a thousand times for causing her such grief, sorry for being such a disappointment, but she knew she couldn't weaken now. Instead, she took Mary's hand and gently squeezed it, and swallowed hard against the swell of tears. She kissed her mother on the cheek and said, "I'll write and I'll be home soon for a weekend," and giving Mary no time to reply, she walked quickly out of the room.

Mary sat at the kitchen table and listened to the excited chatter of Sarah and Lily as they said goodbye to Michael.Then her heart quickened as she heard the car door being shut.

"Goodbye, love, enjoy yourself! Don't forget to write soon!" shouted Michael over the noisy engine.

Mary sat perfectly still, until the sound of the distant motorcar was replaced by the ticking of the clock on the mantelpiece.

Michael stepped into the kitchen and stood behind her, putting his hands on her shoulders reassuringly. "The house seems quiet without her already," he whispered. Mary wiped her eyes quickly and stood up. Without looking at her husband she walked towards the door. "I think I'll go for a walk," she said, closing the door behind her.

2

Dublin - 1932

Lily loved Dublin, she loved her little attic room with the squeaky beds that she shared with Sarah. The work was hard and after almost a year they were still chambermaids. They had hoped to start their silver-service training by now but Mr Ryan, the manager of the hotel, still doubted their capabilities.

Lily didn't mind. She knew the day they expected her to wait tables was the day her job in the hotel was finished. She was all thumbs at the best of times, and was in no hurry to train as a waitress. Lily liked the solitude of being a chambermaid, having a certain number of rooms to do every day at her own pace. As long as her work was done well, no one bothered her.

Sarah on the other hand hated it, and moaned about it every day. "Feckin' slave drivers," she'd say every evening after her day's work. "If Uncle Dan doesn't have a word with that miserable git, Mr Ryan, I'm off to look for something better."

Lily always tried to look on the bright side. "Ah, Sarah, it's not so bad. We're making a few bob and we have our nice room."

Sarah was not so easily appeased. "It's just as well you like the room because we'll end up here till we're ninety, making beds every minute of the day. How in God's name will we ever meet some fellas?"

This made Lily laugh. Sarah had a different boyfriend every month. She was out almost every night, and never came home until late. Lily had to drag her out of bed every morning.

"You must have met every man in Dublin by now!"

"Well, I'm only making up for you. You're like a bloody nun. I thought when we moved up to Dublin we'd be out on the town every night, dancing till dawn. But look at us! We're no better than a pair of bloody skivvies!" said Sarah, as she examined her work-worn hands. "Listen, there's a dance tomorrow night across town. Johnny Boyle has invited me. Will you come?"

Johnny was a student who worked as a night porter in the hotel some evenings.

"He invited you, not me," said Lily.

"Well, he has a friend with a ticket and no partner – Johnny thinks you'd like him," said Sarah teasingly.

"No, Sarah, I'm not going out with someone I've never met."

Sarah would have given her back teeth to look like Lily. It just wasn't fair. Lily's pretty face was framed with beautiful glossy black curls that never seemed to go frizzy. Sarah would wrestle with her wiry hair every night before going out, damping and curling it, trying everything that might make it look less like a mop. It maddened her to see Miss Goody-Two-Shoes wasting her good looks – all she ever did was lie on her bed night after night reading books.

This time Sarah was insisting. "Lily, please, I'm *begging* you to come with us. You might even enjoy yourself."

"I've nothing to wear to a dance."

Lily's clothes were crushed into a corner of the wardrobe, which was filled with a mountain of Sarah's garments. Not only did Sarah take up most of the wardrobe space, she also had two trunks full of clothes under her bed.

"Well, step into my dressing-room, Miss Marsh, and we'll see if we can fix you up," said Sarah, diving under her bed to pull out a trunk.

Sarah took out a dark green satin dress her mother had bought her last Christmas. She held it up against Lily.

"Oh, I'm not taking that one! You haven't even worn it yet." Lily pushed the dress back towards Sarah.

"It's far too small for me. I'll tell you what: you can wear it as much as you like until I lose the bit of weight," said Sarah, knowing that day would not be too soon.

Lily pulled her chambermaid's uniform off, and stepped into the dress. It fitted her perfectly.

"Ah, Lily, it's just not fair!" wailed Sarah. "You look beautiful."

Lily stood up on her bed and tried to see what she looked like in the little mirror that hung on the wall. The rich shade of green suited her dark colouring, and it felt so good to be wearing a nice dress.

"This other fella who wants a partner, what's his name?"

"So you'll come?" squealed Sarah, clapping her hands.

Lily nodded, smiling. "Thanks for the dress."

"His name is Stephen Mitchell. I've met him a couple of times. He seemed a bit snooty at first, but I was talking to him the other night and he's very nice. Probably a bit shy. He's an engineering student at UCD. He was doing a line with a girl but they've split up. Johnny thinks a night out will cheer him up." With all that information out of the way, Sarah stood back and looked Lily over. "Now what will we do with your hair?"

Lily put her hand up to her hair. "What's wrong with my hair?"

Sarah began to rummage through a box on the dressing-table, until she found what she was looking for. She pulled out a pair of scissors.

"There's nothing wrong with your hair. It just needs to be tidied up a bit," said Sarah, moving closer. "Let me cut it up to your shoulders."

"No!" shrieked Lily, both hands shooting up to her head.

"Go on! If I cut a few inches off you can wear it down instead of pinning it up like an old granny."

"I don't know, Sarah. What if you cut it crooked?"

"Oh, for God's sake, with all those curls who'd ever notice? Go on out to the bathroom and wash it. I promise I'll make you look beautiful!" And she brandished the scissors with a menacing grin.

The following evening the girls sat with Johnny in Buswell's Hotel waiting for Stephen to arrive. Lily kept reaching for the ends of her hair, trying to get used to her new hairstyle. It was really quite nice. She could wear it down now without having it fall into her eyes, and with her mass of black curls nobody would ever notice the large chunk missing from the nape of her neck, where Sarah had got a bit carried away.

Lily's stomach was churning as they sat sipping their drinks.

"Stop biting your nails," ordered Sarah.

"Here he is," said Johnny, getting to his feet and beckoning to his friend.

"Lily, this is Stephen Mitchell."

"Pleased to meet you," she said, trying to stop her

face from going red, but she could feel that familiar flush as it invaded her cheeks. Sarah was right, he *was* nice. His fair hair was swept neatly back from his forehead and his deep blue eyes rested on Lily's face, causing her heart to beat rapidly.

"Sit in there," Johnny said, pointing to the chair beside Lily. Stephen stepped carefully over Lily's feet and sat down in the empty chair beside her. Johnny called a waitress and more drinks were ordered, giving Lily a chance to steal a closer look at Stephen. She noticed with relief that he seemed almost as nervous as she was. His knees jerked up and down anxiously as Johnny and Sarah chattered away to him. Lily maintained a frozen smile as she tried to keep up with the conversation whilst observing Stephen at the same time. His smooth pale skin and finely chiselled features gave him a delicate appearance. Lily noticed the perfect fit and fine quality of the dinner suit he wore which was in sharp contrast to Johnny's crumpled ill-fitting one. A sinking feeling gripped her as she looked down at her borrowed dress. Her hand wandered up to the back of her neck and she began to pull on the uneven curls. Whatever made Sarah think that he would like someone like me? She thought to herself. Lily tried to catch Sarah's eye to convey her doubts, but Sarah was too busy sharing a joke with Johnny.

"I hope you don't mind being lumbered with me

this evening," Stephen said, pulling his chair closer to hers.

"Oh goodness, no, not at all," replied Lily. Then silently cursed herself for sounding too eager.

"Well, thank you for coming," he said with a reassuring smile. "Do you work at the same hotel as these two?" he asked, nodding to Johnny and Sarah who were laughing uproariously at Sarah's punch line.

"Yes," Lily answered.

"Do you like it?"

Lily grimaced. "It's all right. The work gets a bit boring every now and again."

"Well, at least you get paid for it. God, I can't wait for the day that I am finally handed a pay packet."

Lily felt more at ease and ventured a question.

"Do you like college?"

Now it was Stephen's turn to grimace. "Apart from the study and exams, yes, I suppose I do," he said with a grin.

He had such an easy way about him that Lily felt her shyness gradually subside. When they had finished their drinks, Johnny pointed to his watch and suggested that they leave for the dance.

Stephen stood beside Lily and helped her with her coat. "Sarah tells me that you let her cut your hair," he said with a smile.

"Yes," answered Lily and, lowering her voice in case Sarah heard her, added, "I'm afraid it's not a very good job."

"Well, I think you look positively stylish," said Stephen, resting his hands briefly on her shoulders.

Later that night when they were dancing, Lily could feel the heat of his hand on her back as they moved closer. Stephen brushed his mouth gently past her ear, and her body shivered with a pleasure that she had never felt before.

They walked back to the hotel together. Lily felt so at ease with him that it took her a few minutes before she realised that he had slipped his arm through hers. When they reached the front of the hotel they stopped talking, and stood facing each other in awkward silence.

"Thank you for a lovely evening, Stephen".

"I really enjoyed your company," he answered, taking her hands in his. Then he leaned towards her and kissed her lightly on the lips. "Goodnight," he whispered.

Lily could feel her heart beating wildly as she watched him walk away.

It was after two when Sarah got in. Lily was still awake.

She sat up in bed, hugging her knees to her chest. "I'm so glad you're back. I think I'll burst if I don't talk to someone. I had the best night ever. Stephen kissed me, and I really like him."

Sarah staggered towards her bed, a little the worse for wear after too much gin. "About bloody time," she said kicking off her shoes. "Are you sure that's all he did?" A sly grin appeared on her face.

"Of course, it's all he did," said Lily indignantly.

"Almost nineteen years old and never been touched by a man – Lily Marsh, what will we do with you?" said Sarah, undoing her dress and letting it fall into a heap around her ankles.

Lily lay back on her pillow, too excited to sleep. She tried to imagine what she might have looked like dancing with Stephen.

"Sarah," she whispered, "am I a clumsy dancer?"

There was no reply, and a few minutes later Sarah started to snore.

3

The next day, Lily felt as if her whole world had changed. She could think of nothing but Stephen. She hoped he would ask her out again, but didn't dare say anything to Sarah for fear it would get back to him. The following evening as she was changing out of her uniform, Sarah burst through the door.

"Brush your hair and get downstairs, girl! Johnny's just told me that Stephen's waiting for you outside reception!"

Lily felt her heart leap inside her. "Oh God, Sarah, I'm shaking," she said, holding out her trembling hands. "What do you think he wants?"

"To ask you out, stupid!" said Sarah, starting to brush Lily's hair. "Only you can't this weekend."

"Why?" asked Lily in dismay.

"Because it's the last Friday. We're going home."

She pushed Lily towards the door. "Now get down to him quick – but don't let old Ryan catch you having visitors in reception or he'll send us packing."

Of course, it was the last Friday, thought Lily. She had completely forgotten. They went home for the last weekend of every month.

She walked downstairs slowly, hoping that by the time she got to reception her heart would stop pounding. Stephen was standing at the end of the stairs. He smiled warmly and took her arm, leading her outside.

"Thank you so much for the other night, Lily. I really enjoyed myself," he said, sliding his arm around her waist.

"So did I," said Lily in a half-whisper, her voice frozen with nerves.

"Would you come out with me again on Friday?"

"I can't, Stephen," said Lily, looking up at him.

The smile faded quickly from his face.

"You see," she went on hastily, "I go home to Wicklow at the end of every month. I wish I didn't have to, but my parents would be very upset if I missed a visit."

"You're not just saying that, are you? I mean, if you didn't want to go out again …"

Before he had finished his sentence Lily put her hand to his lips and lightly touched them with her fingers. He stopped talking.

"I do want to go out with you again," she said,

quickly withdrawing her hand when she realised what she had just done.

Stephen's smile returned. "Well, thank goodness, I thought you were giving me the brush-off. How about we make it for the following Friday?"

"That would be fine," said Lily with relief. She was aware of Johnny looking out from reception and waved in at him.

"Well, I won't keep you out here all night," said Stephen, kissing her quickly on the cheek. "See you next week."

Lily walked slowly through the reception area and nodded casually at Johnny. Then, taking the back stairs in twos and threes, she almost broke her neck rushing up to tell Sarah everything.

* * *

Michael and Mary were delighted to see their daughter every month. Mary baked until the kitchen could hold no more food. She always thought Lily looked far too thin. Michael always met her off the train, his heart almost bursting with pride when he saw the beautiful woman his daughter had become. They had learned how to live without her, but life was not the same. For the first few months it was as if she had died. The loneliness was unbearable, but, like any loss, Mary and Michael had slowly become used to it. For one weekend every month Lily returned to fill their lives with the joy they had taken for granted for so many years. On Sunday evenings before she set off for Dublin, the gloom descended, as if she were leaving for the first time. Mary had to accept that her daughter was quite capable of living without them. In fact, she had never looked so happy.

* * *

Lily began to see Stephen regularly, and loved every minute they spent together. They went to the cinema, or out dancing with Sarah and whoever she happened to be seeing.

Sarah was happy that Lily had at last decided to get out and enjoy her freedom, but she was not impressed with the big love affair.

"Don't go tying yourself down, Lily. Have a few on the go, keep them on their toes!"

Lily couldn't keep track of Sarah's boyfriends – they changed almost weekly.

When summer came and Stephen finished his exams, he sometimes borrowed his brother's car to drive out to the country for picnics. Lily began to dread the last weekend of every month as she wanted to spend all her free time with him. They were going steady now, and she would have to think about telling her parents about him soon. It was not something she looked forward to doing – a boyfriend would only be something else for them to worry about.

One Monday morning in late September, Lily was making her way up the back stairs with a basket of linen when she heard Sarah running up behind her. Lily knew immediately that there was something wrong.

"Lily?" Sarah said very quietly.

"What is it?" she asked, putting down the basket.

"Very bad news!" Sarah stared at Lily for a few seconds, unable to find the right words. Then she blurted, "Oh, Lily, it's your father. Mammy just rang from the shop. He collapsed this morning … he's dead, Lil."

Lily felt herself get dizzy, and put her hand on the banisters to steady herself. He couldn't be dead. He wasn't even sick. She had seen him only last weekend and he was fine. Her body began to shake, her legs grew weak and she wondered if she might be dreaming.

Sarah took her arm and pulled her gently. "You're in shock," she said. "Come upstairs and lie down for a minute."

4

Michael Marsh's funeral was a quiet affair. Mary and Lily led the small procession through the lonely graveyard. Lily felt numb. She tried to cry but her sorrow seemed to paralyse every nerve in her body. Mary wept quietly as they lowered the coffin into the ground. Lily put her arm around her mother's shoulder and felt her tiny frame tremble as if some invisible force was shaking her.

Lily took the rest of the week off work and stayed at home with Mary, but could find no words of comfort to offer her. Being there was the only thing Lily could do, and she couldn't even do that for very long.

The night before she returned to Dublin, Mary cooked Lily's favourite dinner; roast chicken with stuffing and roast potatoes. On the table the steam rose from the bowls of carrots and turnips, enough to feed a lot more than two people. It broke Lily's heart to think that her mother would have to cook for only one every evening from now on. Her husband's dinner had always been a source of great pride for Mary. It had been made with such love and care during all the years of their marriage. Mary sat down and blessed herself.

"I'll have to learn to make smaller amounts," she said sadly.

Every time Lily went to speak, she had to stop herself for fear of breaking down and bawling like a child. Mary looked at her daughter and knew just how badly she must be feeling.

"It's as well you're going back to Dublin. There's nothing for you here," she said, reaching across the table and taking Lily's hand.

"I feel like a bad daughter, rushing off when you need me most," Lily said, gulping back her tears.

"Jack Delaney has always wanted to lease the back fields but Michael wasn't interested. Well, now he can have them, and I'll have the rent to live on, and none of the worry of tending them. So you see, pet, there really will be nothing to do."

Lily looked at her mother with admiration. Always so practical, she was capable of making a level-headed business decision even at a time like this.

"Promise you'll tell me if it gets too lonely?" pleaded Lily.

"I promise," agreed Mary. "Now eat up."

* * *

Lily thought that getting back to work and seeing Stephen again would help her feel better, but it didn't. She could not help feeling that if she had never come to Dublin her father would still be alive. Every morning she woke with a heavy heart, and a sadness she did not recognise. In the seconds that followed she had to arrange her thoughts and remember that her father was gone, and another awful day was about to begin.

Stephen was so patient. They had hardly been out together for months. Christmas was even worse than Lily imagined it would be. Sarah's family had invited Lily and Mary to join them for dinner. Mrs Lynch did her best to cheer things up, and Mr Lynch sang Christmas carols after the boys were put to bed. When he sang 'O Holy Night', Lily could see her mother's knuckles turn white as she gripped the arm-rest of her chair and blinked back the tears. It had been her father's favourite carol.

Lily fell into bed that night, and took comfort from the fact that it would be a whole year before she had to face another Christmas without her father.

Stephen had given her a beautiful gold locket, and Lily promised him that when she returned to Dublin after the Christmas holidays, things would be better.

However, she didn't know how to make things better any more, for herself, or anyone else. The black cloud that hovered over her head seemed to grow bigger with each day, and she felt like she was losing the will to fight it.

Sarah was worried about Lily. It was now April, almost seven months since Michael's death, and Lily was still behaving as if he had died yesterday.

Sarah sat in front of the mirror on a rare night in, idly plucking her eyebrows. She turned to Lily who was lying back on her bed, and tried to pick her words carefully.

"Did Stephen ask you to the dance in the Yacht Club this Saturday night?"

"Yes," said Lily, staring blankly at the ceiling.

"Well? Are you going?"

"No." Lily swung her legs onto the floor and sat up, stretching her arms above her head.

"Oh, please say you will! His pal has invited me, but I'm only going if you are. I won't know anyone else."

"That never stopped you going to a dance before." Poor Sarah, thought Lily, she had tried so hard recently to interest her in going out.

"You haven't been out in weeks, Lily," said Sarah, her tone more serious.

Lily looked over at her. She could feel tears gathering behind her eyes. "I just couldn't face it," she said, lowering her head, not wanting Sarah to see her cry once again.

Sarah went over to her and sat down on the bed. "Lily, you have to start making an effort. You can't lie on your bed forever. I know it's been hard for you, but you have to get on with things. It's not fair on Stephen. He won't wait around forever, you know," she said pointedly.

Lily searched Sarah's face, and saw that she was trying to tell her something. "Did he say something to you?" she asked, wiping a tear from her cheek.

"No," Sarah lied. "It's just that a few people have asked me if it's all off between the pair of you."

Lily realised that she needed Stephen's friendship now more than ever. There had been a cooling in their relationship recently, which was completely her fault, and he had certainly every reason to be fed up with her. She wondered if Sarah was trying to tell her that Stephen had met someone else. "Are you sure he didn't say anything?"

"No. But please come. Please."

"I'll go," said Lily, forcing herself to make the decision.

Sarah hugged her.

"You're a great friend, Sarah," said Lily. "I'm so lucky to have you."

"Damn right you are!" said Sarah, delighted to get a glimpse of her old friend.

* * *

Lily was sorry she had let Sarah talk her into going to the dance. From the moment she woke on Saturday morning, she knew she had made a mistake. Sarah was so excited, making her try on dress after dress, chattering incessantly about her latest boyfriend and how great he was. She didn't have the nerve to back out and, besides, she couldn't disappoint Stephen either.

The feeling of constant despair seemed to cling to her skin all the time now, and she wished that it would leave her alone even for just one night.

It was such a beautiful night, so warm for April. Sarah had given her a lovely black crêpe-de-chine dress to wear. Then she pinned Lily's hair up loosely, and insisted that she wear lipstick. Lily felt like a rag-doll as Sarah primped and preened her.

"Now," said Sarah, standing back. "Didn't I do a good job on you!" She held up the mirror for Lily to see herself. "You're only gorgeous!"

Lily sat motionless and gazed at her reflection. She did look pretty, but no amount of make-up could disguise the sadness that filled her eyes.

That evening as she danced with Stephen, he kissed her neck and told her how lovely she looked, and to everyone else they seemed like the perfect couple. It felt good to be with him again, safe in his arms.

31

When the song ended, Stephen whispered, "Let's go." Before she could ask where, he was pulling her towards the door. Outside the Yacht Club, he took her hand. "Let's go for a walk. We haven't been alone for weeks."

As they walked down the wooden steps towards the beach, Lily inhaled the warm salty air. The breeze felt good against her skin, as if it was gently blowing her troubles away. She took off her shoes and felt the sand underfoot, still warm from the heat of the day. They walked away from the clubhouse, down towards the sea and stood motionless, gazing at the moon's reflection on the black water, both hypnotised by the pull of the tide. When they tired of standing, Stephen laid his jacket on the sand and pulled Lily down beside him. They moved close to each other until their foreheads touched, and he ran his fingers lightly across her lips.

"I've missed you," he whispered into her ear. The smell of whiskey from his breath was strong and sweet.

Lily put her mouth against his and ran her tongue across his teeth. He leaned over and kissed her slowly, resting his chest against hers. Lily could feel the rapid thump of a heart beating as they lay back but could not tell if it was hers or not. For those few moments, they seemed to share the same heartbeat. Stephen pulled her legs close to his, and she could feel his hardness pressing against her thigh. He whispered her name softly, and Lily was overwhelmed with a feeling of hope. All her anxieties dissolved as she felt the warm urgency of his body pressing against hers. The clawing feeling of despair was suddenly gone, and she immersed herself in a wave of pleasure and happiness. When Stephen entered her, Lily felt that he was pulling her back from the dark well of sorrow she had fallen so deeply into. With each thrust of his body, she felt alive again, and closer to salvation. When they had finished, Stephen rolled onto his back beside her, and they both gazed up at the starry sky. His breathing became heavier, and when Lily turned her head to look at him, he had fallen asleep. She propped herself up on her elbows and stared blankly out to the horizon.

The warm feeling was ebbing away, and she could feel the black chill seeping back into every corner of her being, like an ink stain. The sounds of the outside world gradually began to permeate her senses again. The breeze carried discordant notes from the music of the band, still playing in the clubhouse. Lily knew they would have to get back soon, before Sarah came out to look for them. Kneeling up quietly, she pulled the crumpled dress back down over her knees, and tightened the combs that had come loose from her hair. Stephen slept soundly beside her, and she leaned over to wake him. How she wished they could just stay like that, in the very same moment forever! She had made love to him in the hope that things would go back to the way they used to be, but now, looking into his sleeping face, she knew it was no good. She felt nothing.

* * *

In the weeks that followed, Lily spent much of her time alone. She went out with Stephen a few times, but they seemed awkward and uncomfortable with each other. Each time they met, the silence between them seemed to grow longer. Lily began to feel frightened. The sadness she felt every day had become a lot worse lately. It took all the strength she had just to get out of bed every morning and face another day. Everything seemed to be beyond her control, and as the weeks turned to months, she began to despair of ever feeling well again.

"You are depressed, Lily," Sarah said eventually. "It's normal to feel like that when you lose a parent, but you've let it get out of hand. I'm going to write to your mother if you don't make an appointment to see a doctor."

The threat had the desired effect – the last thing Lily wanted was her mother fussing over her.

The following week, Sarah made a doctor's appointment, and took the afternoon off so she could go with Lily.

As they walked through St Stephen's Green, Lily

slipped her arm through Sarah's and smiled nervously. "Thanks for being so kind."

"Don't mention it," Sarah said, brushing a piece of fluff from Lily's collar. "You probably just need a tonic to build you up again," she said reassuringly.

The doctor was a pleasant smiling man. "We'll have you sorted out in no time," he said.

After the examination, he invited Lily to sit down at his desk. She noticed that his smile had faded.

He picked up a pen and began to twirl it between his fingers. "Miss Marsh, do you know you are pregnant?"

The word hit her like a bullet in the chest. Her whole body grew limp. "No," she gasped and stared down at her hands.

"So, it's possible?" he asked, narrowing his eyes.

Images of the night with Stephen came rushing back. The one mistake she had made with him.

"Yes, it is," said Lily. A tear ran down her cheek, and splashed onto her hand.

"It seems you are about twelve weeks gone," said the doctor. "Is there anything you want to ask me?"

Lily jumped up suddenly and, after mumbling her thanks, she made her way outside to Sarah.

When they got out on to the street, Lily broke down, and told Sarah what the doctor had said.

"I suspected it," said Sarah, tears welling up in her own eyes. "That's why I made you go."

"Oh Sarah, what am I going to do?"

Sarah tried to force a smile. She put her arms around Lily's neck and hugged her tightly. "We'll think of something," she said faintly. But Sarah knew there was no one in the world who could help Lily now. She dug deep into her pocket and pulled out a handkerchief, and dabbed the tears from Lily's eyes. "Come on, Lily. Let's go home."

*　*　*

"You'll have to tell Stephen," said Sarah the following day, as they made up beds together.

"How can I tell him?" Lily's face looked as white as the sheets she was holding, her eyes puffed and red from crying all night.

"Do you think he'd marry you?" Sarah asked, trying to tread carefully. She knew Stephen had been out with other girls recently, but only because he was thoroughly fed up with the way Lily was neglecting him. Sarah was sure he would stand by her.

"Married!" The very word shocked Lily. But why should it? she thought. That's what girls in her situation did, if they were lucky. "Sarah, is that what I'll have to do? Marry him?"

"Yes," said Sarah. "It's the only way out of this mess. Now for God's sake meet him and tell him quickly."

It took Lily three weeks to find the courage to meet with Stephen. Every time they made arrangements to meet, Lily would lose her nerve and cancel. She felt so ashamed. He was about to enter his third year in engineering, and she had to give him news that would ruin his life.

They finally agreed to meet in a pub that they had never been to before. It was Sarah's idea.

"You don't want to run into anyone you know," she said.

* * *

Lily walked into the small pub and looked around self-consciously. Stephen was hunched over a low table with his back to the door. He turned around when he heard the sound of her footsteps on the wooden floor. Lily gave a strained smile, as she slid into a chair alongside him.

It was as if Stephen already knew. His greeting was cold and abrupt. He'd grown tired of Lily and her misery – he couldn't remember the last time he'd seen her smile.

"Well," he said, reaching for his whiskey, "to what do I owe this honour?"

Lily could tell he had been there for a while.

"Are we in good form this week?" he asked sarcastically.

"Don't," said Lily weakly.

"Don't what?" he said raising his voice. "You pick me up as you please, and then you drop me at a whim. I'm sick of it." He struggled to conceal the contempt in his voice. He knew what she was about to tell him. He'd been worried about it ever since that night on the beach, and now, looking at her pale face, the dark circles under her eyes, he knew.

"Stephen, I'm pregnant," whispered Lily. She stared down at her shoes, not wanting to see his reaction, but she could feel his eyes boring into the side of her head.

"How long?" he asked.

"About fifteen weeks now." She looked at him, and her heart softened when she saw the fear in his eyes. This is harder on him, she thought. He was hearing it for the first time. She had had weeks to get used to it. She put her hand on his. "I can't think straight since I found out …"

"How long has it been?" he asked again, pulling his hand away and reaching for his glass.

"Fifteen weeks."

"Fuck it, Lily, how long have you known about this?"

"I've known for a few weeks. I had to get used to the idea before I told you. What does that matter anyway?" Lily's face was burning. She hadn't counted on such a rebuke.

Stephen's fear had suddenly given way to anger. He gulped the remainder of his whiskey and, as he placed the empty glass on the table, he turned to her. "The reason you should have told me earlier is because the further along you are, the harder it is to get rid of it." His words were harsh and deliberate like a schoolmaster speaking to a tiresome child.

"Get rid of it?" said Lily faintly. She didn't understand.

"Yes. Look, I know a nurse who might be able to help."

"What are you talking about?"

"For Christ's sake, Lily," he muttered viciously, "I'm talking about an abortion! You'll have to get rid of it before it's too late."

Lily stood up suddenly. She felt as if Stephen had hit her.

"Sit down," he demanded.

"No, I won't sit down, and I won't be talked down to either. I'm sorry I took up so much of your time."

"Don't be like that! It's just that if we don't act now – "

She cut him off before he said any more. "How could you suggest such a thing? It wasn't easy coming here today. I needed you to . . ." She stopped, she didn't know what she was trying to say. Her legs felt as if they would buckle underneath her, and she gripped the back of her chair for support.

"Needed me to what?" he asked, looking at her. "To propose?"

They looked at each other in icy silence.

"Well, it's not the solution, Lily. I'll help you in any other way, but don't ask me to marry you."

"I am not asking you to marry me!" she spat. "And I don't need your help. You have done quite enough already."

In her blind fury she pushed her chair roughly towards the table, upsetting the empty whiskey glass. Stephen reached out and caught it before it hit the floor, and when he looked up again, he could see the back of her coat as she rushed out of the pub. He stood up, and made a feeble attempt to call her back, but she was gone. He slumped back down into his chair, and ordered another drink.

*　　*　　*

"Bastard, the little bastard!" was all Sarah could say, as she poured two more glasses of gin. She had once heard that gin caused miscarriages, so she had been buying it, and getting Lily to drink it without letting her know of the possible outcome, pretending they both needed it to relieve the tension. But nothing had happened. Instead, the swell of her stomach was beginning to become more noticeable.

"No more," said Lily, pushing the glass away.

"You have to make plans," said Sarah, as she sat on her bed, and picked up a pair of her precious black stockings which she was trying to mend.

"I know," sighed Lily.

"You're beginning to show," said Sarah gently. "You know as soon as they get wind of it here you'll be out on the street. Could you go home to your mother?"

The idea of having to tell her mother was making Lily ill every time she thought about it. How could she be such a selfish daughter? Her father's first anniversary was next week, and she had to break this news to her poor mother! It was so unfair, she didn't want to have a baby, and she certainly didn't deserve this after one night with a man.

"I can't go home. It would kill my mother," said Lily.

"Damn it!" said Sarah, as she pricked her finger with the needle. "Well, you'll have to think of something before people start talking," she continued, stretching over to lift Lily's glass. "And if you're not drinking that gin, I might as well have it."

* * *

Lily travelled home for her father's first anniversary. After the Mass, she walked back to the house with her mother. A hundred thoughts raced through her mind, yet she could not think of anything to say.

When she eventually got the words out later that evening, she saw a part of her mother die right before her eyes. Mary's tears should have been for her dead husband, and how she missed him every minute of the day. But, instead they were for her daughter, and the child she was carrying, and Lily hated herself for bringing such shame and worry on her mother. Mary twisted her wedding ring frantically, and rocked back and forth in her armchair, weeping openly. Lily had never seen her mother in such a state. Every time Mary looked at her daughter, she started to cry again. Lily sat opposite her, and bit on the knuckle of her finger until it started to bleed.

* * *

October was coming to a close. The wind that blew down Dawson Street had suddenly turned icy. Lily bent her head against the cold. Her winter coat was getting tighter every day, and although she hadn't told anyone in work, she knew she couldn't hide it for very much longer. The climb up the steep backstairs to the attic room made her breathless, and at the top she paused for a second and leant against the wall. When she opened the door, Lily was surprised to see her mother sitting in the room with Sarah. Mary looked up at Lily and smiled. She had turned into an old woman overnight, and Lily knew it was all her doing.

"Mam, it's lovely to see you. What are you doing here?"

Sarah stood up and walked towards the door. She looked upset. "I'll leave you to talk," she said, closing the door behind her.

Lily took off her coat and sat down beside her mother.

Mary took Lily's hands in hers, and drew her breath in sharply. "Lily, darling, we must make arrangements about …" She glanced towards Lily's stomach. "You've told me little about what happened, but I take it the father's not around any more." She held up her hand to stop Lily replying. "I don't want to know the details – just listen to me now."

Lily felt mortified to hear her mother speak so frankly about her shameful predicament, and she turned her face away while Mary continued.

"I've spoken to Father Casey, and he has arranged for you to go to a Home for unwed mothers, until the child is born."

"No!" gasped Lily. "Please don't send me away!"

Mary went on as if she hadn't heard Lily. "He will look for a suitable family to adopt the child. When it's all over, you can come home, and no one will ever know."

Mary sat and watched her daughter cry bitter tears. It broke her heart to do this, but she knew that it was for the best. If she allowed Lily to return home now, it would be without her dignity and she would be destined for a life of sneers and sideways glances.

This was something that Lily would have to go through alone, like every other fallen woman before her.

* * *

Sarah and Lily hugged each other tightly the morning Lily was leaving. She was going to a Home on the outskirts of Dublin, and would stay there until the baby was born. As Lily turned to board the train, Sarah looked at the shape of the bump under her coat, and shook her head. Poor Lily, she thought. It just wasn't fair.

5

Lily's new room was different from the cosy attic room she had shared with Sarah. She now slept in a dormitory with seven other girls, all in different stages of pregnancy, but each one in a similar state of disgrace. It was an ugly grey house on the side of a country road. Nearby were the big houses of Carrickmines and Foxrock, and it was in these houses that the girls from the Home were employed. Lily was sent to work nearby in a large three-storey redbrick house, called Willow Grove. It was the home of a wealthy Dublin solicitor, who had eight children, and a wife who worked her staff to the bone. Every morning Lily walked the short distance to the house and got to work, making up the eight bedrooms. When this was done, she helped out in the busy kitchen, taking orders from the lowest in rank. People treated her differently now. An unmarried pregnant servant had no place in respectable society. Lily didn't mind the work too much – she was used to making beds, and it kept her out of that depressing Home, away from those other girls with their swollen bellies. They were a constant reminder that she was one of them as well. The girl who slept in the bed next to Lily was no more than a child. At night Lily could hear the muffled cries that came from under her pillow. Her name was Patricia and she was fifteen years old. Her father did not know she was pregnant. He thought she had gone to work as a domestic servant in county Donegal. The order of nuns who ran the unmarried mothers' home had convents dotted all around the country. Many of the girls had close relatives who knew nothing of their unfortunate situations. Their letters were posted by the nuns to other convents, where they would be placed in a different envelope and sent back to the families at home, with a postmark from the county where the girl was supposed to have gone. Lily could only thank God that her father was dead. Seeing her like this would have broken his heart.

On Christmas Day, Lily worked all day and most of the night. As she prepared vegetables in the kitchen of Willow Grove, she could hear the excited screams of the children upstairs as they opened their presents from Santa Claus. After midnight, when the house was quiet, and all of the children had been put to bed, Lily scrubbed the kitchen floor, and left quietly to walk back to the Home. She had deliberately tired herself out, so she would not be able to think about anything else but sleep.

As she was dozing off, she looked around the room to see if anyone else might be awake. It was something Lily rarely longed for, but being Christmas Night, she really wanted someone to talk to. No one stirred. The only sound was the uneven rhythm of breathing from the other sleeping girls. Lily lay back and tried to remember other Christmas Nights, happier ones when her father was alive, before she had gone to Dublin. It seemed like a lifetime ago. A strong kick from the baby reminded her of what lay ahead. I'm the loneliest person in the world tonight, she thought, as she lay in the stillness of the quiet dormitory.

One morning in late January as Lily was doing the laundry in Willow Grove, her waters broke. There was a quiet pop, and warm water began to seep through her underwear. At first, Lily thought she had rinsed the shirts that were steeping in the sink too roughly, and made the water splash out onto her skirt. But when she looked down, she realised that the pool of water she was standing in had come from her. Hoping nobody would notice her taking leave without permission, Lily left the house by the side entrance. The walk back to the Home, which normally took five minutes, seemed like the longest walk Lily had ever experienced. As she approached the gate, a sharp pain shot through her stomach, which made her yelp loudly. Gripping the cold iron bars of the gate, she stayed rooted to the spot until the pain subsided, then slowly she made her way to the door.

As the night wore on, Lily was sure that she would die. Each time she passed out, she was revived by the rough hands of the head nun shaking and slapping her. After seventeen hours of severe pain, it ended with a sudden cry. Lily could see the tiny pink face of her newborn infant, as it let out its first cry.

"A boy," said the nurse, wrapping a sheet around the child. "You can hold him for a while."

"I don't want to," Lily said, turning to face the wall, remembering that the child was not hers to keep.

"Suit yourself," said the nurse, but as she headed for the door she stopped and walked back to Lily. "Are you sure you don't want to have a look at him? He's lovely."

Lily turned and gazed into the tiny beautiful face – she stretched her finger out and felt the soft flesh of his cheek. Feeling the warmth of his tiny hand made her heart melt. The desire to hold him overwhelmed her, but she stopped herself, knowing it would only make things harder. The nuns had told Lily that a home had been found for her baby, so she knew she would have no time with him.

"Do you want to name him?" asked the nurse. "Just for the registration papers. It will probably be changed when he's adopted."

Lily thought of her father, and wondered if it would be an insult to his memory to call her son after him. She closed her eyes and imagined she was a little girl again, walking up through the back field to meet him, at the end of a day's work. Michael would pick her up and put her sitting on his big shoulders. It was her favourite place in the world to be. How she wished she was back there now!

"I'll call him Thomas," said Lily.

"That's a nice name."

"It was my father's second name," said Lily.

"Will I leave him with you?" asked the nurse, holding the child out towards Lily.

"No. Take him now," said Lily, as she turned back towards the wall to hide her tears.

* * *

The child was taken, and Lily left the Home two days later when she was strong enough to walk. Mary welcomed Lily back home with open arms. She put her to bed immediately and made her stay there for a week. Lily had decided to move back home for good. She didn't want to go back to the hotel. She didn't want to face anyone she had known in Dublin ever again. Sarah had pleaded with her to come back, but Lily was determined to make things up to her mother. From now on she would be a good daughter and stay at home where she was meant to be. Lily's dark moods never fully left her, and at times she felt that the blackness would suffocate her. Then it would lift like a weight being taken away, and she would be able to cope again until it returned like a smack on the head, without warning.

Mary was delighted to have her daughter back home and, after the summer had passed, Lily began to look her old self again. The dark circles under her eyes gradually disappeared, and her pasty grey complexion was replaced with a healthy glow. It was so good to have someone around the house again, someone to talk to in the evenings. Mary knew that sending Lily to the Home to have the baby was cruel, but it was over now, and no one in the town knew about it.

If she had let her stay at home and keep the child, no man would have ever gone near her again. At least now it was over and done with. At twenty-one, she was still young enough to marry if she wanted to, and put the past behind her.

6

Lily found work in Sarah's parents' hardware store. Mrs Lynch was glad of the help. She still had all of Sarah's younger brothers at home, and there were never enough hours in the day. Lily missed Dublin, she missed the space and the freedom of living away from home, but most of all she missed Sarah. Sarah had met a new man, and only came home every six weeks because her mother insisted.

"*I only come home to see you, otherwise I wouldn't bother my arse,*" she wrote to Lily in one of her frequent letters.

Lily treasured Sarah's letters. They often made her laugh out loud. She carried them around and reread all of them until the next one arrived.

Sarah had left the hotel. Her Uncle Dan had no intentions of promoting her to the position of silver-service waitress.

"That daughter of yours is the laziest lump I have ever come across. And niece or no niece, she's lucky that I have kept her on this long," he announced to Sarah's mother.

Mrs Lynch thought it was about time that her daughter got a real job, and stopped making beds for a living, and made her sign up for a shorthand/typing course. Sarah moved into a flat with two other girls that she met on the course, and was now working in a solicitor's office. Her letters were mostly about how horrible her boss was, but reading between the lines Lily could tell that Sarah was having a ball.

For the two years that followed, Lily worked in Lynches' and apart from the weekends when Sarah was home, she led a solitary existence. On her days off she liked to walk into town to visit the library. Reading became a form of escape for her. She especially loved poetry and lost herself for hours on end in the stillness of the library.

Lily tried not to think about the baby, but some days she allowed herself a few minutes to imagine what he might look like, and every night she prayed to God that he was with a good mother who kept him safe and loved him.

*   *   *

It was a miserable wet evening in April. The rain had lashed steadily against the window all day. Lily was hanging up her apron, glad that the day had come to an end. The rain had kept people indoors, and there was nothing worse than a quiet day in the shop. She was preparing to lock up when she heard the sound of the bell over the shop door ring, and Jim Fortune walked in. He let the door bang behind him, and stood in the middle of the shop, brushing the drops of rain from the sleeves of his jacket. He pulled his cap off, and ran his hands roughly through his thick crop of sandy hair. Lily stood in the small stockroom and looked out at him. He was a regular customer. Every Wednesday he dropped in to buy supplies for his farm. Lily had always liked him. His gentle manner reminded her of her father. He had been the first customer that Lily had served on her first day in Lynches'. Jim had walked in, his huge frame seemed almost as wide as the counter. He had been quick to see how nervous Lily was on her first day, and chose to say nothing when she handed him the wrong change. Lily realised her mistake when he had left the store, and ran out after him with the money. When she had caught up with him, red-faced and out of breath, he had smiled and told her not to worry.

Jim had a farm just outside Wicklow town, where he had lived with his mother until her death three years before. She had been a widow and his two older brothers had left for Australia ten years earlier. His mother's death had been a terrible blow to him, and recently he was finding the loneliness hard to bear.

Every Wednesday for the past three months, he had entered the hardware store with the intention of asking Lily Marsh out, but the little bit of courage he possessed seemed to abandon him somewhere between the shop door and the counter. Every week he left with rolls of baling twine, and other paraphernalia that he had no use for.

This Wednesday he swore to himself that it was his last chance. He cleared his throat and walked towards the counter, his jaw set in tense determination. Lily walked out of the stockroom, holding her coat. Jim tried to smile at her, and felt his mouth dry up.

"Hello, Jim," she said with a smile. "I was just about to lock up."

"I was passing by, and it's such a wet evening I was wondering can I give you a lift home?" he asked, rubbing his hands together to stop them from shaking.

"That would be great, Jim," said Lily, buttoning her coat. Then it occurred to her that he had not asked for any provisions. "Do you need anything?" she asked, looking up at him.

"No, no, I'm fine this week."

On the way home, Jim tried to make conversation about the awful weather. He told Lily about his mare, and how she would be foaling any day now. Lily knew what was coming before he said anything. It had never dawned on her till now that he had liked her in that way. He was so much older, over forty anyway she guessed as she tried to look at him closely without staring.

Jim pulled up beside her house and Lily reached for the door handle and turned to thank him.

"Lily, I don't know if you'd be interested, but could I take you out sometime?" There, he thought with a sigh of relief. He'd said it.

Lily felt tongue-tied.

"Look, you don't have to – " he began.

"Yes, I would," she said, speaking over him.

His face softened into a smile of relief. "How about Saturday?"

"Saturday would be fine. Goodbye, Jim. Thanks for the lift." Lily's knees felt weak as she opened the front door. What on earth would her mother say?

Mary had heard the car, and was at the door as Lily walked in.

"What a night," she said helping Lily take off her coat. "Did Jim give you a lift?"

"Yes." Lily thought she might as well tell her straightaway. "He asked me out this Saturday, and I said I'd go."

"Good," said Mary. "You need a night out."

Lily stared at her mother, waiting for the questions to start.

Mary pulled her cardigan tighter around her body against the cold. "Isn't it a terrible evening?" she remarked, as she walked back into the kitchen.

*   *   *

To spare Jim the embarrassment of making small talk with her mother, Lily had suggested that he pick her up after work in Lynches', rather than at home. However, Lily hadn't realised that Sarah was home for the weekend. She had just changed into her good dress, and was brushing out her hair in the stockroom, when the door opened.

"Only me!" shouted Sarah.

Lily's stomach turned over. The last thing she wanted was Sarah hanging around when Jim arrived. Lily came out of the back room, and Sarah hugged her warmly.

"I didn't know you were coming home this weekend," said Lily.

"I only decided yesterday – your man's giving me a pain in the arse." She stood back to admire Lily. "Why are you all dressed up?"

Lily blushed, and tried to sound as casual as she could, but there was no fooling Sarah.

When Lily told her, Sarah's mouth fell open. "Big Jim Fortune?" she said, her eyes nearly popping out of her head.

"Yes," snapped Lily, "the only Jim Fortune we know."

"But, Lily ... "

"What?" asked Lily angrily. "What's wrong with him?"

"Nothing, except he's old enough to be your –"

Sarah didn't finish, because the door opened and before Jim could step into the shop Lily rushed over to him.

"No need to come in, I'm ready," she said, pushing him back out. She turned to Sarah and gave her a warning look. "Could you lock up, please?" she asked, holding out the keys.

"Of course," Sarah said, walking towards her with a huge smile. She took the keys and, as Lily turned to walk out, she muttered, "Go easy on him!"

Lily walked out to join Jim, banging the door behind her. How had she timed that so badly? Damn Sarah and her weekend home! For once Lily wished her friend had stayed in Dublin.

"Will we go for a drink?" asked Jim. He was relieved to see the door closing with Sarah on the other side of it. For a few seconds he thought that Lily had invited her along.

"Yes," answered Lily decisively. "Let's go to O'Dowd's." It was a dingy old pub on the road into town, a place that Sarah would never think to look, should her curiosity get the better of her.

"Are you sure you don't want to go somewhere livelier?"

"No. O'Dowd's is fine," said Lily, leading the way.

"Do you mind if we only stay for the one?" Jim asked.

Lily turned to look at him, slightly taken aback with this request.

"You see, the mare is about to give birth any day now, and I'm a bit concerned about her. I don't want to leave her too long on her own."

Lily's face softened into a smile. "Of course, Jim. We'll only stay a while."

They sat in a snug at the back of the pub. Jim took Lily's coat from her and hung it on a hook beside them. He went to the bar to order their drinks – a pint of Guinness and a glass of orange.

He came back with the drinks and set them carefully on the table.

"Thanks, Jim," Lily said, reaching for her orange.

Jim sank into the seat beside her. "Did you want to ask Sarah along?" he asked nervously.

"No," Lily answered hastily. "Not at all. I didn't even know she would be home this weekend."

"Well, she would have been very welcome to come along."

"I know, Jim. Thanks," Lily said as her eyes swept the pub for any sign of Sarah's arrival.

Jim drank his pint quickly and put the empty glass back on the table. Lily sipped the warm orange and ignored the glances from the old men sitting at the bar.

"I hope you don't think I'm being rude, rushing off. It's just that there's no one else there if anything were to happen tonight," Jim said, breaking the silence.

Lily turned away from the gawping men and seized the opportunity to engage herself in conversation with Jim. "You must be so excited. Can I come and see the foal after it's born?"

Jim smiled at her childish enthusiasm. "You come and see it whenever you like."

Some more men had entered the bar and sat opposite them. Lily could feel the weight of their unblinking stares boring through her. Jim nodded over at them and glanced down anxiously at the half-full glass of orange.

"I don't want any more," Lily said, pushing the glass into the middle of the table.

"Do you mind if we leave now?" Jim asked, hopping up from the seat

"Not at all," Lily replied, glad to get away from the stuffy little pub. O'Dowd's had been a bad choice. In her rush to get away from Sarah, Lily had forgotten how nosey the old farmers that drank in the bar could be.

As they drove out along the road towards home, Jim slowed the truck and turned to Lily. "Would you like a peek at her now?" he asked.

"I'd love to," she answered with genuine interest.

Jim parked the truck outside the farmhouse and, guided by the light from the moon, the two of them walked over the hill along the path that led to the stables.

Lily could see the silhouette of the horse as it

stood at the back of the dimly lit stall. Jim tried to coax her out of the shadows, but the mare stamped on the straw in defiance. She was staying where she was.

"She won't come out because she doesn't know you," he whispered to Lily.

"It's all right," said Lily. "I can see her from here. She looks beautiful."

"Yes, she is," he said with a bashful smile. Horses had always been his passion.

Lily could sense the love he felt for the animal, and was touched by his gentle nature. The two of them stood in an easy silence and gazed into the shadows, listening to the movements of the heavy mare. After a while Lily pulled her coat tightly around her as the night-time dampness began to creep around her.

"Come on," Jim said quietly. "Let's get you home."

When they reached her house, Jim asked if he could pick her up again next Saturday, and after a few seconds of hesitation, Lily agreed. Spending the evening with him had made her realise just how lonely she had become.

They began to see each other every Saturday evening, and as their relationship progressed they sometimes took in a picture on a Wednesday night as well. Lily looked forward to seeing him every week. It felt good to have someone to talk to. Jim had little experience of women. He had brought home a few girls over the years, but his domineering mother had made sure that none of them lasted too long. Lily was different, and Jim was sure that even his mother would have liked her.

Lily told him about Stephen, but not everything – she was too ashamed. Jim was an honourable, old-fashioned man and, apart from the usual kiss goodnight, there had never been any question of going any further. There was never a right time to mention what had happened to her, yet she knew that she couldn't put it off forever.

*   *   *

When they had known each other for eight months, Jim saw no reason to waste any more time. He knew that Lily was the girl for him, but he also knew that she was young, and could probably do a lot better, so he prepared himself for a refusal. It was the Saturday before Christmas, and they were driving home from town to Lily's house. Mary had invited Jim for dinner. The roads were icy, so Jim was taking it slowly.

"Do you mind if we stop for a while? I want to ask you something."

Lily's heart stopped beating for a second. Had he heard something? He couldn't have – only her mother and Sarah knew, and Sarah had sworn never to tell a living soul, not even her own mother.

Jim stopped the car and took her hands in his. She noticed how nervous he was. "Will you marry me?" he asked, almost crushing her hands between his.

She had to tell him now. She had rehearsed it so many times in her head. He had to know about the baby; she could not hide it any longer. This was her chance . . . but she knew she couldn't do it.

Jim's heart sank as he watched the panic spread across her face. He released her hands and turned back to the steering wheel, and ran his hand across his chin. "It's all right, Lily. You don't have to say anything."

The icy fog was descending on the fields, and she looked out into the darkness searching for the right words. She wanted to rest her head on his shoulder, and tell him everything, but the shame burned right through her, and instead she turned to him and said, "I would love to marry you."

Jim leaned heavily on the steering wheel, pressing the horn with his elbow, making both of them jump.

"Jesus, Lily. I thought you were going to say no." He breathed a sigh of relief, and threw his arms around her.

As they drove the short distance to Lily's house, Jim repeatedly looked from the road to Lily and back again.

"I must be the happiest man alive," he said, unable to contain his joy.

Lily swallowed hard and smiled back at him. She

could feel tears beginning to sting the back of her eyes.

* * *

The wedding date was set for February. Lily grew more nervous every day as it approached. The night before the wedding, she paced the floor of her bedroom, until she could stand it no longer. It had to be done, she told herself. He deserved to know. Pulling on her coat, she went downstairs. Mary had been working on the wedding dress for weeks, and was cutting loose threads from the hem when Lily walked in.

"I'll be back later – I'm just going up to Jim's."

Looking at Lily's worried expression, Mary sensed that all was not well. It was a look she had not seen on her daughter's face for a long time.

"Why are you going to Jim's tonight? Don't you know it's bad luck for the groom to see the bride on the night before the wedding?"

"Mother, he doesn't know anything!" she cried hysterically. "I never told him!"

Mary walked over, and taking Lily's face between her hands she looked her firmly in the eye. "Listen to me. He does not need to know anything," she said slowly. "You will achieve nothing by telling him. Do you want to condemn yourself to a life of loneliness?"

"But Jim should know. He'll understand and if he doesn't – "

"No man would understand," said Mary, growing impatient. "If you tell him you will ruin your only chance of happiness."

Lily looked into her mother's eyes and knew that she was probably speaking the truth, and without saying a word she took her coat off.

"Now dry your eyes and come over here – I need you to try it on one more time," said Mary, turning back to the dress.

Lily pulled off her skirt and blouse, and stepped carefully into the wedding dress. She turned around slowly while Mary checked the length of the hem. As Lily turned, she caught a glimpse of herself in the mirror and looked away in disgust.

Mary stood back and admired her. "You'll be a beautiful bride," she said, clutching both ends of the measuring tape that hung around her neck.

A beautiful devious bride, thought Lily.

7

The marriage certificate recorded that Elizabeth Marsh married James Fortune in the county of Wicklow on 7th February 1937. The bride was twenty-four years old, and the groom was twenty years her senior.

The farmhouse was big and draughty. It had been built by Jim's father, Joseph Fortune, the year he was married. At the time Joseph boasted that it was the biggest farmhouse in all of Wicklow. At the end of the lane that led up to the house was a large rock of granite, which had proved too heavy to move. Joseph decided to leave it there, and employed a local stonemason to engrave the words *Fortune's Farm* across the front of it. However, much to his disappointment, none of the local people had ever referred to the place as anything other than 'the farmhouse'.

"Lord above, he must have never washed a cup after himself," mused Mary as she surveyed the dirty kitchen on the morning Lily moved her things in.

They set to work scouring the range and scrubbing floors, throwing almost every piece of furniture out. Broken chairs and battered tables were piled one on top of the other, outside in the front cobblestoned courtyard, ready to be burned. Mary made new curtains, and the cracked cups and plates were replaced with a new dinner service that the Lynches had given them for a wedding present.

They had decided not to go on a honeymoon until the weather improved, the snow having made it impossible to travel. Their wedding night was spent in a hotel in Wicklow town. After the last guests had said goodbye, Jim let Lily go up to the room before him, while he sipped a last drink in the bar for courage. Lily put on her new nightgown and slid under the covers and prayed that she would be asleep before he came up, but minutes later she heard his heavy footsteps on the stairs outside. Jim came into the room and sat at the edge of the bed. He was unused to drinking so much stout, and his body swayed slightly.

"Are you nervous, Lily?" he asked, stroking her hair.

"A bit," she whispered, trying to stop her voice shaking. The sheets felt damp against her skin, and she wished she were back in her own warm bed.

Jim took her hand in his and patted it lightly. "I

won't hurt you. I'll be as gentle as I can."

He turned out the light and undressed in the darkness. Then he pulled the covers back and got in beside her. Lily moved over to make room for him, and the bed-springs squeaked under his weight. He pulled her nightgown up and ran his hands up each side of her body. His hands felt rough and cold. He felt the swell of her breasts and put his mouth to her hard nipples, groaning with pleasure. Lily bit her lip and tried not to make a sound as he thrust himself deep inside her. He came quickly, making a deep throaty sound as he did. Afterwards, too shy to talk, he ran his hand through her hair lovingly.

When he had fallen asleep, Lily got up and walked over to the window. The floor felt like ice on her bare feet. She pulled the curtain back and looked out at the snow falling heavily on the fields. It made no sound as it fell. Her heart felt heavy with the knowledge that she had started her married life so dishonestly. Her white linen wedding nightgown was unblemished and Lily felt a surge of panic as she thought of the coming morning, when Jim would awake and perhaps notice the absence of any evidence of a first-time sexual encounter. She tip-toed over to her case and stood still for a few moments, listening to the rhythmic nasal sound of his breathing. Satisfied that Jim was fast asleep, Lily pulled the nightgown over her head and replaced it with the long-sleeved flannel one her mother had packed. On opening the case earlier that evening, Lily had wondered why her mother had placed another nightgown in the suitcase when they were only staying one night. Now she knew why. Absorbed in her thoughts, she stood there until the cold air made her shiver. Then, silently, she walked back to the bed and climbed in beside her sleeping husband.

* * *

Lily tried hard to accept the path she had chosen. During the first few months of her marriage she would weaken at times and come close to telling Jim the truth. But as time went by she grew used to living with the guilt. It became a part of her.

In every other respect she was a good wife, and Jim was the best husband she could ever have hoped for. He worked long and hard hours on the farm and when his work was done he went up to the stables to tend to his beloved horses.

Lily longed to have a child and, although Jim had never said anything, she knew that he would be overjoyed with a son or daughter. Every month she prayed that her bleeding would not come, but it always did. One time it didn't. When they were almost three years married, her time of the month never came. Lily felt a familiar feeling enter her body and she knew that she was pregnant. It was exactly the same feeling she had experienced years ago in

Dublin, in another life. But it didn't last – three weeks later the bleeding started heavily with sharp twisting cramps in her stomach. Lily hadn't told anyone, and suffered the miscarriage in silence. Jim made her tea, and brought her a hot-water bottle. He wanted to call a doctor.

"Don't be silly," said Lily. "I'll be fine tomorrow. It's just women's problems, that's all."

* * *

Sarah got married three years after Lily. Her husband's name was Pat O'Brien and, being a garda, he was well able to handle Sarah. The first couple of years saw some spectacular fights and several times Sarah had her bags packed. They knocked the corners off each other, but Lily knew they were well matched.

Sarah's visits to Wicklow became less frequent as she made her new life in Dublin, and the girls missed one another terribly. So, when she suggested to Lily that they meet up every month for a day out, Lily agreed immediately. Once every month Lily would take the train to Dublin on a Saturday to meet Sarah. Sarah was always full of news and chat and would drag Lily into every shop in Dublin before they could sit down for lunch.

On one of these Saturdays Sarah didn't seem to be in great form. She was quiet and not a bit bothered about shopping which was unusual. After a while Lily suggested going for an early lunch. As they sat at their table Lily noticed that Sarah looked very pale.

"Are you sick?"

"Not exactly," said Sarah smiling wearily.

"Well, what's wrong?" asked Lily.

"Oh God, am I that obvious! I was hoping to keep it quiet for a bit longer but you might as well be the first to know." She lowered her voice. "I'm pregnant."

Lily gasped. "Sarah, I'm so happy for you!"

"Well, I'm sure I'll be happy too, once I get over the shock. We had intended waiting for a little while."

"But you're married three years already!"

"I know. I'm a selfish cow! I wanted as long as possible on our own."

"Oh Sarah, you'll be a wonderful mother! You're not a bit selfish! I bet once this baby is born there'll be no stopping you – you'll want another six or seven!"

"No bloody fear of that!" said Sarah "I'm not going to end up like my mother with a clatter of kids hanging out of me." She picked up a packet of cigarettes and snapped open her lighter. "And I'm not giving up these either," she said defiantly as she exhaled a long line of smoke. "You have the right idea, Lily. Wait as long as you can. Jesus, I wish I'd been more careful!"

Lily forced a smile and looked down at her plate. She gulped in a mouthful of air to try to stop her eyes from welling up.

Sarah realised she had said the wrong thing. "Lily, I'm sorry. That was a stupid thing to say – I wasn't thinking."

Lily blinked back her tears and reached her hand across the table to Sarah's. "No, *I'm* sorry. Spoiling your good news like this, it just – " Her voice broke off.

"What is it?" asked Sarah.

"I don't think I can have a child," whispered Lily, embarrassed by her lack of control. She pulled a handkerchief from her handbag and quickly blew her nose.

"How come?" asked Sarah.

"Well, we've been married almost six years and nothing has happened. I'm being punished for what I did." Her voice was thin and frightened.

"Lily, that's rubbish!" Sarah straightened up and stubbed out her cigarette. "Have you seen a doctor?"

"No." Lily dabbed her eyes with a napkin and tried to compose herself.

"There could be a problem from the time before." Sarah didn't want to say exactly what time she meant. They had never spoken about it. "What does Jim think?"

Lily shifted in her chair and looked around the dining-room. Hearing Sarah refer to the birth made Lily feel uneasy. She had never even told Sarah that the baby she had was a boy, and Sarah knew better than to ask. Now hearing her mention 'the time before' made Lily's blood run cold.

71

Sarah's eyes narrowed. "You didn't tell him, did you?" she said slowly.

Lily said nothing, but the veil of sadness that crept across her face was enough to answer Sarah's question.

* * *

As Lily approached her thirty-second birthday, she accepted that she would never be able to give Jim a child. He never complained, but Lily felt that she had failed him. Seeing Sarah with her new little baby boy, Patrick, had been even more difficult than Lily imagined it would be. Sarah had tried to be as sensitive as possible and after much thought she asked Lily to be godmother to the child. Lily was delighted to be asked, but every time she held the child during that first year, a lump would form in her throat.

Her nightly prayers became less frequent and a slow realisation began to dawn on her. God was not listening. She tried to stop anticipating the day that her life would change because she knew now that it wasn't going to. It could have been a lot worse. She thought of the girls in the unmarried mothers' Home, some of them only children themselves, with only a life of hardship ahead of them. At least she had a home and a husband to be thankful for, even if she had achieved them through deception.

8

Lily's mind was taken off her own troubles two years later when her mother became ill. At first it was only a cough, but as the summer wore on it became more serious. Lily argued with Mary about going to a doctor, but Mary would not hear of it.

"I don't need a doctor to tell me that I have a cough."

Lily knew that something was wrong but no matter what she said, Mary would dismiss her concerns with a wave of her hand.

It was a bright Saturday morning in late August and Lily had risen early in order to get the train to Dublin. She was meeting Sarah. As she checked the contents of her handbag, she heard a noise outside. Lily went to the window and saw a woman leaning with one arm against the gatepost. With her free hand she clutched a handkerchief to her mouth, coughing violently into it. It took a few seconds for Lily to realise that it was her mother. From a distance she looked like a frail old woman in bad health. Lily threw her handbag aside and ran outside.

Mary leaned against the pillar, beads of perspiration running down the side of her face.

"Mammy, give me your arm," said Lily, putting her mother's arm around her neck to support her. She put her own arm around Mary's waist and slowly walked her towards the house.

When they reached the front door Mary started to cough uncontrollably. Lily sat her down and ran to get some water. When she returned, Mary had stopped coughing. She was sitting on the chair with her shoulders stooped, trying to catch her breath. Lily stood behind her and saw the handkerchief that Mary had held to her mouth was covered in blood. Lily felt the colour drain from her face. She took a sip of water herself before putting the glass into Mary's hand, and she wondered how she had not noticed until now that her mother was seriously ill.

Mary turned to her and stretched out her hand. "Help me up, dear," she whispered.

They took the stairs slowly, resting on every third or fourth step so Mary could get her breath. Lily took Mary to the bedroom at the top of the house, the room she had decorated some years ago in the hope that their first child would sleep there. She gently lowered her mother on to the bed. Mary lay back and Lily pulled the covers over her. Then she went to get a doctor.

Mary had been diagnosed with TB two months earlier and it had advanced rapidly. As was her nature, she had told nobody. Frightened that she might infect Lily and Jim she had stayed away from them as much as possible in the weeks that followed her diagnosis. That morning she had called with the intention of breaking the bad news to her daughter, as she knew she did not have long to go. It never crossed her mind when she set out on her short journey that she would not make it home again. Mary begged Lily to take her back to her own house. She couldn't bear the thought of her daughter becoming infected, but Lily would not hear of it.

Mary lasted only another two weeks, and Lily, rarely leaving her side, watched her fade away piece by piece. Always around daybreak the coughing that had threatened to choke the life from her in the dead of night would abate, like a violent storm retreating. When the darkness began to lift Lily would rise from the armchair she slept in beside her mother's bed to open a window, and in the dim light of the dawn she imagined she could see tiny shards of her mother's soul leaving through the open window.

One morning Lily awoke from her sleep with a jolt. Her neck was stiff from sleeping in the chair and she moved it from side to side slowly. Dawn was breaking and the shadows of the night had not lifted completely. During the night Mary had put her hand upon Lily's, and Lily felt the coldness of the hand. She put her free hand on top of her mother's to rub some heat into it.

"Lily?" Mary whispered.

Lily leaned closer and saw that her mother was crying.

"Don't cry, Mammy," said Lily, gently wiping the tears from her clammy face. Mary tried to say something but her breath was ragged and she struggled to form the words.

Lily put her ear close to Mary's lips. "What is it? I'm listening."

Mary gasped like a woman drowning, frantically trying to gulp in air. "Your baby!" she cried. "I'm sorry!"

Lily sat up on the bed, and slid her arm behind Mary's back, pulling her mother close until her head was resting on her shoulder. "It's all in the past, Mammy. You don't need to be sorry, and everything worked out for the best." Lily tried to stop her own tears but it was impossible. She held her mother as tightly as she could, and both of them wept silently.

When Lily woke for the second time the birds were singing. The room was bright, and outside the sun burned through the greyness of a misty September morning. Mary's head still rested on Lily's shoulder, but Lily could feel that the life had left her body. Slowly she eased her mother back down on to the bed and whispered a prayer into her ear. Her mother was gone but so too was the suffering, and Lily felt a strange sense of peace inside as she folded Mary's arms across her chest. Then she opened the windows to let her mother's spirit take flight.

*   *   *

Lily felt sick for the first time on the morning of Mary's funeral. She had cooked a breakfast of bacon and eggs for Jim, but before the eggs were ready she had to run into the back yard to vomit. As she straightened up, taking deep breaths to control the nausea, Lily realised that she had not had a period for quite a while. Minding her mother had made her lose track of time and she had long given up counting the days of her cycle, being resigned to the fact that her chance to have children had passed. Jim appeared at the back door.

"Do you think the rain will hold off for the funeral?" he asked, looking across to the west with one hand shading his eyes from the early morning light.

"I hope so. Now come and have your breakfast." Lily took his arm and steered him towards the kitchen, hoping he wouldn't notice where she had been sick.

The rain did hold off for Mary's funeral. Sarah linked Lily's arm as they lowered her mother's coffin into the grave that held the remains of her father. As Lily looked around at the small gathering of mourners it struck her that her mother had so few friends. She wondered if, when the time came, she would have more loved ones to mourn her. After the burial the small crowd of distant relatives and neighbours went back to Lily and Jim's for tea and sandwiches. Mrs Lynch had made sure there was enough to feed everyone and Sarah helped Lily in the kitchen while her little boy Patrick played under the table.

Later, when all of the guests had left, Sarah suggested that Jim and Pat take a stroll down to Mulligan's for a pint. Lily was washing the last of the dishes while Sarah dried and put them back on the dresser.

Patrick was tired and Sarah picked him up and went to sit by the fire, wrapping a blanket around him in the hope that he would fall asleep before they left for home. He was almost three now and Lily adored him. Ever since the day that Sarah had asked her to be his godmother she had doted on him. "Let me take him," said Lily coming to sit beside Sarah. "You look tired, Sarah."

"So do you," said Sarah, handing the yawning child over. "Well, I have a good excuse – I'm expecting again."

Lily felt herself blush as she reached over and hugged Sarah. "Congratulations!" Bouncing Patrick on her knee, she whispered in his ear playfully, "Did you hear that, Patrick? You're going to have a new sister or brother!"

"Well, that's the reason I'm looking like shite," said Sarah. "But nursing your mother has taken its toll on you. You look so pale and drawn. Why don't yourself and Jim go off somewhere for a few days. You need to take a rest."

Lily hadn't intended saying anything until she was certain, but she could never keep anything from Sarah. "I think I might be pregnant too," she blurted.

Sarah jumped up from the couch. "Oh, Lily!"

Patrick became excited, sensing his mother's sudden burst of happiness. He began to clap his hands and mimic her. "Oh, Yily!" he laughed.

Lily put her hand up to silence them both. It was too soon for any excitement. There had been too many disappointments in the past. "Please, Sarah, not a word to anyone. I don't know for sure. I haven't been to the doctor yet. Just say a prayer that I'm right."

Lily was right. A visit to the doctor the following week confirmed what she instinctively knew. She was almost three months pregnant. On her way home she stopped off at the library, to give herself time to think. A million thoughts swam through her head and, although she had expected the diagnosis, she just could not quite believe it.

Miss Evers, who had been the librarian for as long

as Lily could remember, had developed arthritis and now as the years advanced she found it difficult to lift and stack books with her misshapen hands. Sometimes Lily would call in for a chat and help out for an hour or two. Today her own hands shook as she returned the books to their shelves. Thoughts of her stolen child came flooding back to her. He would be fourteen years old now. He was someone else's son – at least Lily hoped he was someone else's son. There were industrial schools she had heard about, where unwanted children were sent to live, and she hoped and prayed that her child had not ended up in one.

The thought of being able to keep this baby filled her with such strong emotions that she had to blink back the tears before Miss Evers saw her.

Lily waited until they were in bed that night to tell Jim. Her old feelings of deception had come back to haunt her. All day she thought of telling Jim what had happened before she met him, but deep down she knew she would not have the courage to do so. Afraid of how he would react, and fearful of ruining his happiness, she allowed her cowardice to win over. The guilt was written all over her face, and so she waited until they were in darkness to speak.

"Good night, love," said Jim as he turned over to his usual sleeping position.

"Jim, I have something to tell you."

He sat up and went to turn on the lamp beside the

bed, but Lily reached for his arm and pulled him back.

"There's no need to turn on the light."

Jim lay back and waited. "Well, what is it?"

"I went to see the doctor today. We're going to have a baby."

Jim gasped loudly and sat back up. "Lily, are you sure?"

"Sure," said Lily, feeling in the darkness for his hand. She found it and clasped it tightly.

He let his head collapse back on to his pillow. "My God! That's great news. I can't believe it! I never thought it would happen."

"I know." Lily could feel her face burning with shame. "Neither did I."

Jim put his arms around her and kissed her face. "You've made me so happy, Lily. I love you. I love you so much."

What should have been the happiest night of her life was tinged with the bitter reminder of her first child. The secret that had faded into the distant past now came rushing back to torment her. Lily listened to Jim's breathing get heavier as he fell asleep. She knew that the happiness she had brought him was fragile. If he knew the truth, and how she had cruelly deceived him, that happiness would be shattered forever. That night she passed the point of no return. No matter how many times she thought of telling him, from that day on she knew she had missed her last chance.

* * *

The following June, 1948, a baby girl was born. They called her Grace Mary after both their mothers. Lily haemorrhaged badly after the birth, and the doctor warned her that she would risk dying should she ever have another child.

9

Grace brought a joy to her parents that neither had ever dreamed of. She had a look of both of them. Her hair fell down her back in black glossy curls, the way Lily's used to when she was a young girl. She also had her mother's sallow complexion, but in her dark eyes Grace had an expression that was exactly like her father's. With her arrival came a closeness between Lily and Jim that had never been there before, and Lily wished that her own mother had lived to see their happy lives. On her sixth birthday Jim bought Grace her first pony, and taught her how to ride. His love of animals had passed on to his daughter and there were not enough hours in the day for both of them when it came to tending the horses. Jim was in his sixtieth year, and knew that he looked more like the child's grandfather than father, but when he saw Grace sitting on her pony his heart swelled with pride, and he felt like a young man again.

When the time came for Grace to start school, Lily counted the hours until she came home. Jim had installed a telephone in the farmhouse, and some days when Lily felt particularly lonely she would ring Sarah in Dublin. They would try to talk in between Sarah shouting at her boys to stop kicking ball in the house. Sarah now had four boys. In addition to Patrick, there was Andrew, Mark and John, and although Sarah was devoted to them, she was disappointed that she never got the daughter she had wished for. Every time she saw Lily with Grace she was reminded of how much she would have loved a girl.

"You're lucky, Lil. You have a friend for life," she said one day when Lily rang her.

"But you have your lovely boys," Lily protested.

"I know and I love them dearly. But in the end they're fellas and they'll wipe their feet on me."

"Sarah, that's an awful thing to say about your children."

"It might be awful, but it's true. I see my own brothers still treating Mam like a slave, and I know that one day my own will do it to me. They'll shag off with their wives and leave me on my own."

"You'll never be on your own, Sarah. You'll always have me."

Sarah laughed. "I suppose you will have to do."

On fine days Grace rushed home from school and ate her lunch while she scribbled her homework hastily. As soon as she finished she pushed the chair out from under her, wiping the crumbs from her mouth. Then it was out to the stables until dark. By the time she was nine years old, she had outgrown her pony, so Jim bought her a bigger one. Lily worried the morning the new horse was led into the back yard. It was a beautiful animal but Grace looked so small beside it.

"Jim, it's too big for her," whispered Lily while Grace jumped around the yard, unable to contain her excitement.

"He has a lovely temperament," Jim said, taking the reins in his hand. "Grace will do fine on him."

Grace ran up to Lily and put her arms around her waist. "I'll be careful, Mammy. I promise," she said, squeezing her mother tightly.

"Come on," said Jim, leading the horse out of the yard. "Let's take him up to the top field."

Lily stood in the yard and watched them walk away. Jim led the horse while Grace walked alongside him chatting excitedly. Lily blessed herself quickly and whispered a prayer asking God to keep her precious child from any harm.

*　*　*

When Grace started secondary school Lily found it hard to fill her days. Sometimes it was after four o'clock by the time Grace got home, so when Lily heard that Miss Evers was looking for an assistant in the library, she applied immediately. Miss Evers was only too delighted to give her the job, as Lily knew the place like the back of her hand. She worked three mornings a week, and was home in time to make the beds and cook the dinner, so nobody suffered.

"Well, I hope you don't end up like that frosty old cow," laughed Sarah when Lily told her. Sarah had never forgiven Miss Evers for telling her parents when she was caught smoking behind the library.

Lily still got up to Dublin to meet Sarah every month. They always had lunch in the Shelbourne Hotel on St Stephen's Green. Both women were now in their late forties and they had been meeting for lunch every month for close on twenty years. They treasured their Saturdays together; it gave them a chance to catch up with each other in peace. Lily felt a bond with Sarah that she had with no one else. As soon as they sat down their conversation flowed freely and they could talk about anything. Over the years they had become more like sisters than friends.

"Jesus," said Sarah screwing up her face as she lit a cigarette, "what possessed you to go looking for a job in the library? How old is that old cow anyway? She must be a least ninety!"

"I'll tell her you said hello!" said Lily laughing. Sarah never changed. She didn't hold back, and that's what Lily loved about her.

* * *

It was a perfect morning in the month of May that Jim died. It had rained for weeks, with no sign of spring on the way, then overnight the weather took a turn for the better. The sky was a brilliant blue with wispy white clouds dotted here and there. Lily threw open the big back door and set to work cooking a late breakfast. Jim and Grace had been up and gone hours before. The blacksmith had arrived at eight o'clock and they were up at the stables shoeing the horses. Lily could hear the faint clank of his hammer as she lifted a tray of scones from the oven. She looked at the clock. It was almost half past eleven. She would give them a few more minutes before walking up to get them. Lily hoped that the smell of baking might be carried up to the stables on the breeze and entice them down to the house, saving her the walk. She sat down and poured herself a cup of tea and thought about what she might get for Grace's birthday next month. It was hard to believe that her little girl would be sixteen soon. Grace was now as tall as her father, and her beauty was becoming more apparent every day as she grew into a woman. Lily had seen young men look at her when they walked through town, and although Grace was happier with her horses and showed no interest in boys, Lily knew there would come a day that she would lose Grace, and it hurt her to even think about it. She thought about how hard it must have been for her own parents when she moved away from them. She could never have realised the heartbreak they felt because they needed her so much more than she had needed them. It was something she would have to remember in the future when Grace wanted her freedom.

The sound of a car horn jolted Lily from her quiet reverie. It was followed by a distant roar. Immediately she knew something was wrong. Even before the horse galloped into the yard, Lily could sense that something terrible had happened. She jumped up from the table and ran outside. The new bay mare that Jim had bought last month had broken loose. Lily knew little about horses, but she could tell that it was frightened out of its wits. It reared up on its hind legs, its eyes rolling back with terror. Lily could hear Grace screaming in the distance, and as she turned to run towards the stables Mick Twomey, the blacksmith, ran into the yard.

"What happened?" Lily shouted, but he lifted his

hand, signalling her to be still.

He had a bridle in his hand, and slowly he approached the horse from behind. He spoke without taking his eyes off the animal.

"Mrs Fortune, call an ambulance," he said in a loud whisper, moving stealthily towards the horse that had backed itself into a corner. "There's been an accident."

Then Lily noticed a large stain on the front of his shirt that looked like blood.

"Who's hurt?" she pleaded.

"It's your husband," said Mick, throwing the bridle over the head of the petrified horse. "He was kicked in the head – call an ambulance quickly."

As Lily ran in to the telephone, Mick began to stroke the horse gently as he walked him back towards the stables. When Lily put the telephone down she realised that the sound she could still hear was Grace screaming. She ran out of the house and up the back hill to the stables. Grace was kneeling on the grass with Jim's head resting on her lap, her hands and face smeared with his blood.

"He's not moving, Mammy!" she cried hysterically, rubbing his face.

Lily felt her knees grow weak and she sank to the ground beside them. The blow had crushed the side of his head and Lily could see the large dent where the blood was spilling from.

The ambulance arrived and the men carefully

lifted Jim's lifeless body from the arms of his daughter. The blow to his head had killed him instantly.

Later on that evening, after they returned from the hospital, Mick Twomey called by to offer his condolences. Lily had sat with Grace for hours until her shock had turned to exhaustion and she had given in to sleep.

Lily led Mick into the kitchen. It all felt like a bad dream; the whole day seemed unreal.

"What happened, Mick?"

"It was all my fault," he said. "I'm sorry." He began to cry, loud choking sobs that he couldn't control.

At any other time Lily would have been filled with compassion to see a grown man break down in tears. But she was too numb with her own grief to try to comfort him.

"You said it was an accident, Mick," she said, leading him to a chair.

"You see," he said, wiping his tears with the sleeve of his jacket, "Jim was standing behind the mare and I went to the car to get my cigarettes and, as I was reaching over into the back for my jacket, I leaned on the horn … " His voice started to shake and he broke down once again. "The noise frightened her and she tried to bolt. The next thing I knew Jim was on the ground. She'd kicked him." He took a crumpled grey handkerchief from his trouser pocket and wiped his eyes. Then he stood up and went over to Lily. She took his outstretched hand. "If there is anything I can do for you, Mrs Fortune. I can't tell you how sorry I am." He gripped Lily's hand tightly, and started to cry again.

Lily could smell the drink from his breath and guessed that he had stopped into Mulligan's for a whiskey to steady his nerves before calling into her.

"It was a tragic accident, Mick. No one is to blame," she sighed, leading him towards the door.

"If I can do anything, anything at all."

Lily patted him gently on the shoulder and opened the front door, anxious for him to leave.

* * *

Lily tried her best in the months after Jim's death, but she could find no way into Grace's desperate sorrow. They both missed Jim so much that some days Lily just wished for night to come so she could draw the curtains and turn her back on another day. Grace suffered terrible nightmares in the first few months after the accident; the image of her father being kicked to death came back to haunt her when she fell into sleep. Some nights she woke to feel her father's head still resting in her lap, and she would crawl into her mother's bed shivering.

Lily was also haunted by her own dreams. In them, Jim would walk into the kitchen from the backyard and hang his cap on the peg beside the door. He would turn to her with a smile and say, "It was all a mistake, Lily. I'm not dead at all." Then she would wake and for a few seconds a warm feeling of relief would run through her, and she would try to remain as long as possible in that place between dream and reality. But that warm feeling would dissolve quickly when she turned to see the empty space in the bed where Jim had once slept.

Lily tried to manage the farm by herself for the first few months, but it proved too much for her. Jody Walsh was a local farm labourer who had worked for Jim two days a week. After much thought Lily decided to offer him a full-time job, and Jody accepted gladly. He was honest and obliging and didn't seem to mind the fact that Lily could not pay him very much. His thin strands of red hair and weather-beaten face made him look older than he was, but Lily guessed that he was not much older than Grace. Between them, they could manage the dairy herd, and Jody could help with the jobs Lily wasn't able for. The rest of the land she could sell or rent out.

Grace hadn't been up to the stables since Jim's death. Lily had tried to encourage her to get back to her riding, but she showed no interest.

It had been almost a year since the accident, and Jody was doing his best to look after the horses, but Lily knew she would have to make a decision. There was no point in keeping them if Grace wasn't going to help out. One morning as they were having breakfast Lily decided to broach the subject.

"Grace, would you not go up to see the horses today?"

Grace stared at her plate, lost for words.

"The poor animals are being neglected. We can't leave them up there forever, you know. If you don't want them any more, we can sell them."

Lily thought she saw a look of relief pass over Grace's face.

"Would you mind if we sold them?" asked Grace.

"Of course not, pet, I just want you to be happy. I never expected you to take them on. It's too big a job." Lily moved to where Grace was sitting and put her arm around her shoulder.

Grace looked up with tears in her eyes. "It's just not the same without Daddy. I wouldn't enjoy riding out on my own. We always went together."

Lily kissed the top of her head. "I'll get Jody to find them a home."

"Are you sure you don't mind?" asked Grace.

Lily smiled at her. "It's one less thing for me to worry about."

Two weeks later, Jody led the horses out of the stables. One by one the five animals were led through the yard and put into their new owners' boxes. Lily listened to the sound of their hooves on the cobblestones of the yard. It was a sound that she had once loved to hear. It was a sound that meant they were home safely. Now, listening to the clatter of metal on stone, it had an empty lonely ring to it. She listened from her chair at the kitchen table, but she did not go out to see them off. She simply didn't have the heart for it. Their movements sounded so slow, as if they were dragging a heavy load. Lily imagined she could see the horses wearing funeral plumes moving slowly across the yard pulling a carriage that carried the ghost of their master.

"Goodbye, Jim," she whispered as she went to the window and lifted the curtain to take a last look.

*   *   *

Things began to get easier as time passed. Lily managed to rent the land that they didn't use, and Jody proved to be worth his weight in gold. He was on the farm every morning before they woke and sometimes still there when they were going to bed. Lily wondered if he ever went home at all. Grace was studying hard for her Leaving Certificate. She was a good student and had made up her mind that she wanted to do nursing. Lily had always encouraged Grace to go to college – she wanted her to have a career of her own. The nineteen-sixties had brought big changes; women were becoming more independent and Lily felt it was important that Grace should have a good education.

Lily worried constantly about Grace. Ever since

Jim's death, Grace didn't seem to have much of an interest in anything. She didn't go out very much or have a large circle of friends. In fact she didn't seem to have any friends at all. Grace loved art, and seemed content to spend hours alone sketching and painting. So when she said she wanted to apply for nursing, Lily was pleased, even though it would mean Grace moving away. At least she would be mixing with other girls her age.

Lily still worked in the library. She loved the few hours she spent there every week. It had helped her get over Jim's death. When every day had seemed like an eternity, the library offered her the escape she needed. On the days when she had run short of patience with Grace's moping, the library had been her refuge.

* * *

Grace was accepted to train as a nurse at St Vincent's Hospital in Dublin. The training nurses were housed a short walk from the hospital in Leeson Lane.

On the day she arrived, Grace was greeted by Sister Charles, a tall thin woman who had little reason ever to smile. She put the fear of God in every training nurse that had ever been through her hands. She gave Grace and some other new girls a tour of the hospital, making sure they fully understood the enormous workload that was ahead of them. Later, as they unpacked, the nun explained sternly exactly what would be required of them. It seemed that training nurses were required to work until they dropped. At least that's the impression Grace got as she listened to the Sister drone on and on about the call of duty.

When Sister Charles was finally finished, she left the girls to have an early night. They were to start at 7.30 sharp the following morning. Grace slumped onto her bed and looked around, wondering what on earth had possessed her to volunteer for such drudgery.

10

1966

Lily missed Grace terribly. The days weren't too bad. She managed to fill the hours pottering around the house and working in the library, but the nights were so lonely. As winter set in she dreaded the dark evenings. Her nights felt like a long journey into an empty place. Lily went to bed early and rose with the first light, happy to have another night behind her.

Grace was getting on well in the hospital. She phoned a few times a week, but made it home only once or twice a month. Lily still went to Dublin to meet Sarah whenever she could, and sometimes Grace was able to join them. Lily was so proud of her. She knew the work at the hospital was tough, but she could see that Grace was thriving on it. Lily could see her daughter's confidence being restored. Living a life of her own had given her a sense of independence that she had badly needed and the discipline was good for her. Not that Grace would have agreed with her mother for one minute.

* * *

When Grace turned eighteen, Lily insisted that she come home for the weekend. Jody painted the outside of the house and tidied up the little side garden. He had planted some clematis against the old stone wall and it was just coming into bloom. Lily loved this time of year. The evenings had started to get brighter and there was a promise of summer in the air. Grace came home on the train and Jody collected her from the station. Lily dashed to the door the minute she heard the car pulling up.

Grace flung open the car door and ran to hug her mother. Lily only stood as high as Grace's shoulder now. Grace had inherited her father's height and Lily sometimes felt dwarfed beside her.

"Goodness, Grace, you haven't grown again, have you?"

"Maybe you're starting to shrink," laughed Grace, pulling her suitcase from the car.

That night they stayed in and had dinner. Lily opened a bottle of wine for the occasion. It was the first time she had ever had wine in the house and she had trouble trying to uncork it. They had dinner and watched the *Late Late Show* together. After a glass of wine Lily could feel her face getting flushed and she poured herself a glass of water, but to her surprise Grace continued to drink the wine until the bottle was almost empty. Lily decided not to say anything, but she hoped that Grace wasn't drinking on her nights out in Dublin.

The following night Lily brought Grace out for dinner to the Grand Hotel in Wicklow. Sarah travelled down for the celebration, and stayed the night. When the three of them walked into the hotel they were met by Sarah's brother Colm. He had stayed at home and taken over his parents' hardware shop.

"Now what's my big sister doing here on a Saturday night," he said, turning to wink at Grace. "Trying to meet a man, is it?"

"Hi, Colm," said Sarah kissing him. "I'm afraid my days of getting picked up are well and truly over. We're celebrating Grace's birthday tonight. You remember Grace, Lily's daughter? She's eighteen today."

"Of course, I remember Grace. Didn't she ride her horse through the village for years looking like a vision!"

Grace stared at the ground and wished it would open up and swallow her.

"Now let me buy you ladies a drink," said Colm, steering them towards the bar.

"Oh no, not at all," said Lily. "We'll just go on into the dining-room."

"Indeed you will not. I have to buy this eighteen-year-old her first legal drink." Colm ushered them into the hotel lounge, and insisted that they sit down while he went to the bar.

Lily looked around nervously. In all the years she had been married she had hardly ever set foot inside a public bar. Jim had always considered them to be a man's territory.

"Now here we are," said Colm, coming over with a tray. "Sherry for the old ladies, and a Babycham for the birthday girl!"

Grace forced a smile and accepted the drink. "Thanks."

"Thank you, Colm that's very kind of you," said Lily, raising her glass towards him.

"Now, I have a very important meeting in Mulligan's," he said, tapping his finger against the end of his nose.

"Would you stop your messing and go!" said Sarah, lifting her drink.

"Goodnight and happy birthday, Grace!" he shouted back as he walked towards the door. Some of the men who were sitting at the bar turned to look at Grace.

"Don't mind that loudmouth, Grace – he's only trying to embarrass you," smiled Sarah.

Grace drank her Babycham in gulps, and was finished before Sarah or Lily had made it halfway through their sherries.

"Would you like another one of those?" asked Sarah, nodding towards Grace's glass.

Before Grace could answer, Lily jumped to her feet. "No, don't bother, Sarah. Look at the time. We'll bring our sherries into the dining-room." Lily took her glass and started walking towards the door.

Sarah picked up her handbag and drained her glass. Then she gave a complicit smile and slipped her arm through Grace's. "I suppose we'd better do as we're told."

Lily had organised a birthday cake, and they sang 'Happy Birthday' to Grace. Sarah insisted on ordering wine and paying for the meal. It was her present to Grace.

Later that night when Lily was in bed she thought how lucky she was to have a friend like Sarah. Some people could live their whole lives without ever having such a friendship. When they were young they used to pretend they were sisters but now they were closer than most sisters that Lily knew.

Grace didn't seem to have a close friend. She had made lots of pals since she started nursing, but not a best friend. Lily worried about her; she knew that sometimes Grace came across as being aloof – she always seemed to keep people at arm's length. Lily wondered if it had something to do with the fact that they had spoiled Grace so much when she was younger. Jim had danced attention on her, giving in to her every whim. Lily turned restlessly in the bed.

Not used to eating so late, she found the heavy meal was keeping her awake. She turned to look at the picture of Jim on her bedside table. It was taken one morning up at the stables and Jim was smiling and shielding his eyes from the sun – Lily had always thought that he looked so handsome in it. She still missed him terribly, especially tonight. When they had sung 'Happy Birthday', Lily stole a glance at Grace, and without saying anything, they both knew what the other was thinking. They both wished that Jim could have been there.

Grace had drunk a lot of wine again with dinner. Lily let it go seeing it was a birthday celebration, but she hoped that Grace wasn't going wild – she knew that a lot of country girls who went into nursing lost the run of themselves when they moved to Dublin. Hopefully Grace would have the sense not to end up like them. Lily yawned and felt her eyelids begin to get heavy. She leaned over to turn off her bedside light, then she said her prayers and eventually fell asleep.

The next morning Lily woke early and crept down to the kitchen to start breakfast. She unlocked the back door and went out to feed the hens. The morning air had a chill in it and she pulled her cardigan around her. Lily loved her hens. Feeding them every morning and collecting the eggs was something that she had done since she had come to the house as a young bride. Apart from the dairy herd that was dwindling, the hens were the only creatures left on the farm. Lily hurried in with her basket of eggs and started to prepare breakfast. It was only eight o'clock so she baked some soda bread knowing she had hours to spare before the other two stirred. She lit the fire to warm the room, and turned on the radio to keep her company.

At half past ten Grace and Sarah appeared together.

"Good morning, sleepy heads," said Lily.

"Lily, you put me to shame, baking before breakfast," said Sarah, enjoying the wonderful smells that came from the bread.

"Oh great! White pudding!" said Grace looking into the pan. "You should see what they expect us to eat in that dump – pure poison!" she moaned.

"Well, sit down and eat up. It's the last decent breakfast you'll be getting for a while," said Lily. Already she felt her heart sinking at the thought of Grace going back that evening.

"I have to head back after breakfast," said Sarah. "Will I give you a lift to the station?"

"No, I'll take the evening train, but I'll take a lift into Wicklow with you. Old Miss Evers wants me to call in to her," said Grace, grimacing.

"You're not making her call up to that old prune?" Sarah exclaimed. "What did you do to deserve that, Grace?"

"Ah, the poor thing, she's so lonely, nobody ever calls to her," said Lily. "She's been asking about Grace for months." Lily saw the look on Sarah's face. "Sure maybe you'd drop in to see her too," she smiled.

"No bloody way," said Sarah, finishing her tea. "That was a grand breakfast, Lil, but I have to hit the road. I'm afraid those lads will burn the house down if I stay away too long."

Lily walked Sarah out to her car and gave her a loaf of soda bread to take home. Grace came out of the house, pulling on a jacket. Lily could tell she wasn't too happy about having to visit Miss Evers.

"Go on," she said, ruffling Grace's curls. "It won't kill you."

Grace rolled her eyes towards heaven and got into Sarah's car. The car drove slowly out of the front yard and as they drove down the lane away from the house, Sarah tooted her car horn twice. Lily stood outside the house and filled her lungs with the fresh morning air. She stooped to pull some weeds that had grown between the cobbles of the pathway. When her hands were too full to hold any more she walked back up the path towards the front door, but stopped when she heard the car coming back up the lane. She turned around expecting to see Sarah, she had probably left something behind. But the car that approached was not Sarah's. It was a red sports car and Lily could see a man behind the wheel.

Part 2

11

Greystones, County Wicklow – 1934

Maud Harrison's heart almost burst with the love she felt for the newborn baby when it was placed in her arms. Not giving birth to the child herself had filled her with worry of how she would feel towards him, but as soon as the tiny infant was put into her arms, she knew in an instant that she would love him forever. The child was only two weeks old. The adoption papers that came with him stated that he had been named Thomas by his natural mother. Maud had thought to name him Wesley, after her own grandfather, but when she looked at the papers, and thought of the girl who had given up her child, she decided to leave his name as it was.

* * *

Maud and William were childhood sweethearts. William had moved to Ireland with his family when he was a young boy when the family business, Harrison's Paper Mills of Bristol, had expanded their interests into Ireland. They had settled in Westfield, an imposing Victorian house in the seaside village of Greystones.

Maud had been a regular visitor during her youth, as her family had a summerhouse nearby, and she had fallen in love with William when she was only thirteen years old. It was many years before William fell in love with her.

The Harrisons were a family with an army tradition. William's father had been a general in the British army and, when the time came and the world was at war, William felt it was his duty to serve king and country. On the night before he left for France, Maud knew that she might never see him again. It was her last chance to let him know how she felt. The Harrisons had invited Maud and her parents to dinner and, after they had eaten, William asked Maud to take a walk in the garden.

"Why not?" Mrs Harrison said with a forced note of gaiety. "Off you go and get some air."

The adults looked on with sympathetic smiles as the young couple excused themselves. William kissed his mother and as he left the room she put her hand to the spot on her cheek he had kissed and said a silent prayer for his safe return from the war.

William and Maud walked out into the darkness and stood on the back porch, listening to the waves crashing against the cliffs. William was not in the mood for talking. He was preoccupied with thoughts of the journey ahead. His mind was crammed with images of horrible stories he had heard about the trenches. He felt that cowardice had begun to eat away through his courage and wondered if he would be man enough to face the hardships of war. He stepped off the porch and walked towards the end of the garden to where the cliffs began.

Maud walked alongside him in silence, and sensing his anxiety she slipped her arm through his. "I'll write every week. Promise you'll do the same?"

William looked at her and nodded. Theirs had always been an easy friendship. They had known each other since they were children. Their families had holidayed together in Italy. Maud had just been one of the younger ones, but recently William had begun to notice how pretty she had become. Her skinny boyish frame had filled out into womanly curves, and she now dressed like a young lady instead of a girl. Lately, William had found himself tongue-tied in her presence, trying to think of things to say that might impress her. The very large distance of four years between the two children had lessened almost overnight as they matured. When William was seventeen Maud had seemed like a child to him, but the past three years had seen her change into a woman, and William wished he had paid more attention to her. Now he was leaving and she would probably be married by the time he returned, if he ever returned.

"They say it will all be over soon," said Maud. "I really wish you weren't going." William looked into her face. Her pale skin glistened. The bright moonlight gave her an ethereal presence, and made her fair hair seem as white as silver. A few strands of hair had come loose from her combs and William gently brushed them behind her ear.

"Would you think it strange if I were to kiss you?" he asked.

Maud looked at him with her large blue eyes. That she had waited for this moment since she was thirteen years old was something she longed to tell him, but she said nothing and moved her face closer to his.

William kissed her. It was a long slow kiss that made her melt inside and, in the years that followed, the memory of that kiss kept their hope alive. When William went missing towards the end of the war and hopes of ever seeing him again were fading, Maud would think about that kiss and as long as she could imagine it, she knew he was alive. Sometimes when she was deep in prayer she imagined she could feel the warmth of William's breath on her face. Maud believed it was a sign from God and it was what kept her from going mad. If I can feel him this close, she thought, then he must be alive.

The same thought was with William as he lay on his bed in the army hospital, surrounded by the moans and desperate cries of the other wounded soldiers. He had lost his right eye and almost all of the flesh from his right leg. The small amounts of morphine he was given induced short periods of fitful sleep but in his waking moments he would look around and try to take in the horror that surrounded him. The men that had fought the enemy with such courage lay all around him, their bodies ripped open from the shells and grenades. Without the guns and uniform they were mere boys now, some of them even moaned for their mothers.

In his more lucid moments, William could feel a girl's presence. She floated above him like a ghost, so close that he could feel her sweet breath brush by him. When William tried to speak, a pain would shoot through his head, sending him reeling into another blackout. During his rare moments of recall, he tried to piece together what had happened but only small pockets of his memory survived. At first he recalled lying in the shell-hole with two others from his battalion. The blast had blown them backwards, and all three had landed at the edge of the hole. The faces were clear in his memory, but he could not remember their names. The younger one had pulled William further into the hole for cover, and poured water over his face to wash away the muck that had lodged in his eyes and mouth. The other one had pulled out his field dressing kit and tried to bind the remaining pieces of torn flesh on William's leg. The cloying smell of blood filled the air and William felt himself slipping away but was pulled back each time by the beautiful woman that hovered over him. With every fresh explosion she held his head gently in her hands and smiled down at him. He had stayed in the shell-hole for what seemed like days, drifting in and out of consciousness, with the deafening sound of machine-gun fire clacking in his ears. Most of his clothes had been blown from his body in the blast, and he had no identity tags. Infection had set in by the time he was brought to the hospital, but they managed to save his leg. The eye had been blown out of its socket.

As the fog that had clouded his mind lifted, William began to remember more. It was the two young corporals who had saved him: they had grabbed him under each arm and dragged him across no-man's-land. He remembered the excruciating pain as his mangled leg was bumped up and down over the bodies of dead soldiers that lay covered in mud.

On his third week in the hospital, he remembered who he was. He called a nurse over, afraid that the name would retreat into the margins of his mind if he didn't say it there and then. He took the nurse by the hand and whispered hoarsely, "I am William Harrison."

The name of the beautiful girl in his dreams came back to him too. It was Maud. During the long nights when the pain was too much to bear, her face had appeared to him like an angel and eased his suffering. As he became stronger, William realised that she was real. He remembered their last night in the garden. He could hear the waves breaking on the cliffs below, and could feel the soft touch of Maud's lips as they brushed against his. He clung to the memory like a lifeline and he prayed that he would somehow get back there again. But as he returned to full consciousness and his memory was fully restored, Maud's face seemed to evaporate. The clarity that was restored to his mind had blotted out her image. He couldn't remember what she looked like. He would spend long hours trying to summon her face from the deepest corners of his mind. Sometimes, during daylight hours when he drifted in and out of sleep, a perfect picture of her face would appear before him fleetingly. But when night came, and the cold black fingers of darkness gripped him, she was gone. It was during those long hours he was sure that he would die.

*   *   *

William was invalided out of the war. The army

had not much use for a man with only one eye and a leg so full of shrapnel it would drag behind him for the rest of his life. It was only when he got back to the comfort of his home and its familiar surroundings that he realised the extent of his injuries. In the army hospital William had seen men who had had their faces blown off – he had looked at them and recoiled in horror. His own injuries had seemed minor compared to the mutilation he had witnessed. However, now as he stood before the mirror in his own bedroom, far from the trenches and rotting corpses, he knew what others would think when they saw him. He could conceal the ugliness of his mangled leg with breeches, but the black and purple ball surrounded by ragged flesh that was all that remained of his eye could be hidden only behind a patch. He spent weeks pacing the floor of his bedroom with the help of a walking-cane, his dead leg dragging behind him. Every morning after breakfast he locked himself into his room and walked up and down in front of the mirror, determined to lose his limp.

One morning William stiffened his back and held his head up, took a deep breath and walked towards the mirror, trying not to lean too hard on his cane. He tried to imagine what other people saw when they looked at him. As he approached the mirror and stared into it he saw a tragic, almost comical sight. He remembered dressing up for a play in school when he was seven years old. He was a pirate with a peg-leg and a patch over his eye, a parrot resting on his shoulder. His parents had laughed when he limped out on stage, reciting his lines at the top of his voice. He felt a tear drop from his good eye. He wiped it on the back of his sleeve and in a fit of rage threw his cane against the mirror, shattering the reflection that he could not bear to look at.

* * *

Maud had steeled herself for their first meeting. Her parents had warned her of the severity of his injuries and she had prepared herself for the worst. Although she hardly recognised him, it was not his physical appearance that troubled her. It was the lack of any expression on his face that disturbed her most. If he were pleased to see her again, he certainly did not show it. There was no emotion in his voice as he greeted her. It was as if they had never met before. The Harrisons were hosting a dinner and had invited a few close friends to celebrate William's homecoming. Mrs Harrison did her best to appear bright and cheerful, but Maud could see the worry on her face when she glanced nervously in her son's direction. Maud sat beside William and tried to talk to him as best she could, but he sat looking sad and forlorn all night, barely saying a word.

Later on when everyone had moved into the drawing-room to hear William's mother play the piano, Maud realised that William had left the room without saying goodnight. Unable to hold back her tears, she backed out of the room and walked quickly down the hallway. She opened the kitchen door, hoping no one would see her and slipped out onto the back porch. Free from the worried glances of her parents and their friends, she broke down and cried.

Inside the house, the kitchen door slammed, and through the window she could see Stella the cook walking through towards the back door. Not wanting to be seen, Maud walked down the wooden steps from the porch and out into the garden, breathing deeply to control her loud sobs. The cold autumn air felt good on her face, and she stepped up her pace, walking further into the darkness. A faint glow appeared down low at the end of the garden. Maud stopped and looked at it and listened for a moment. It went dull and glowed again. She slowly walked towards it, and stopped when she realised it was William. He was sitting on an old wooden swing where they had played as children. The glow she had seen was his cigarette.

"Who's there?" he snapped.

"It's only me."

Maud walked over to him and sat down on the stump of an old cherry blossom that had fallen down in a storm last winter.

"Want one?" He held a cigarette packet out towards her.

She shook her head.

"I know I behaved horribly this evening," he said. "It was good of you to come and see me. I'm sure there were a hundred other things you would have preferred to do than spend an evening with a boring cripple." He took a deep breath. "I apologise."

"There's no need to. I didn't come out here looking for an apology. I thought you had gone to bed. I just had to get some air. I wasn't looking for you." She squeezed her eyes shut, hoping that he wouldn't see the tears in the darkness, but he had sensed them.

He flicked his cigarette away and stood up. He limped slowly towards her, and leaning on his stick he put his hand on her cheek and wiped away a tear.

"Don't cry, Maud," he pleaded. "They shouldn't have made you come tonight. I didn't want you to see me like this – it must be awful for you."

She stood up. "The way you ignored me at dinner tonight was awful. I've waited so long to see you again. I know you have changed. I've changed too, but I expected you at least to talk to me!"

They both stood still, neither of them knowing what to say next.

William cleared this throat. "I'm sorry I've upset you, Maud. I dreamed of meeting you again. It was what kept me from going insane, but now I realise it's selfish of me to expect anything of you. I'm an invalid now, and it's time for us to move on with our lives." He poked his stick into the ground and tried to smile. "I'm sure there are men lining up to take you out." He lit another cigarette and inhaled deeply.

"I kept all of your letters," she said softly then. "I still read them when I'm feeling lonely."

"Throw them away, Maud." His voice grew thin and he swallowed hard. "For God's sake, forget about me."

"I don't understand." She looked at him pleadingly.

"I'm not the man you used to know – he's gone, dead." He raised his voice with impatient anger. "I am a cripple with a patch on one eye. I drag my leg behind me like a simpleton. I can't dance with you any more. I'm not handsome. No woman in her right mind would ever –" He broke off, turned away and flicked his cigarette into the darkness. He kept his back to her but she could see his shoulders shaking. Maud moved closer and let her head rest between his shoulder blades. She put her arms around his waist and his whole body shook. He tried to stifle his sobs, and slumped to the ground, unable to contain the pain that he felt. Maud kept her arms around him and knelt on the ground beside him.

"I love you, William. I always have. Please don't send me away. I'm miserable without you."

He turned and took her face in his hands and kissed her. It wasn't the kiss of innocence they had shared the night before he went to war. He kissed her like a hungry animal, his teeth pressing into her gums, his hands searching for her breasts, tearing her blouse in his haste to feel her warm flesh.

Maud didn't stop him. It was not as she imagined it would be, a proposal on bended knee, being ravaged on a chaise longue while her parents were out playing bridge. Everything had changed so much in the two years that William had been gone, but Maud knew that her love for him had remained as strong as ever. The grass felt cold on her bare legs as she guided him between them. William pulled at her underwear in a frantic attempt to feel the warmth he had craved for so long. His movements were fast and furious, and as he reached a climax he groaned so loudly that Maud was afraid the guests would hear them. Afterwards they lay together in silence until the cold set in and they began to shiver. William got to his feet and helped Maud up.

"Christ, I don't know what got into me, Maud. I'm sorry, I shouldn't have done that."

Maud smiled at him and put her arms around his neck. "I'm so glad you are home." She brushed the damp grass from her skirt, and buttoned her blouse, then realised she couldn't possibly go back into the house looking so dishevelled.

"I won't go back in. I'll walk home. Tell Mummy I had a headache."

William looked at her blouse and brushed his

hand over the patch he had ripped, embarrassed by his clumsiness.

He picked his cane up and leaned on it. "I'll walk you home."

Maud walked slowly to keep the same pace as him. When they reached the front gate, he took her hand and kissed it. "Did you really mean it when you said you loved me?"

"Yes. I've always loved you, William."

"Are you sure? It's not just sympathy that you're feeling?"

"For heaven's sake, William! Do you think I would do what I just did if I didn't love you?"

They walked through the deserted streets until they reached her house.

When he got back the guests were playing cards. His mother looked up as he entered the room.

"All right, dear?" she asked with a worried frown on her face.

"Yes. Maud has a headache. I brought her home."

He said goodnight to the guests and went upstairs to bed.

The following day they were engaged to be married.

12

Five years after William and Maud married, they moved to Westfield. William's parents decided to return to Bristol, and William was given the house. He was left with the responsibility of running the family's paper mill in Dublin, an occupation that William found tedious and unrewarding but it provided him with enough money to live comfortably. The children that Maud had assumed would be born to her by now had not come, but she never abandoned hope, until the very end. William suffered greatly from his wounds, his leg was a constant source of pain and his headaches could last for days on end. Maud was as devoted to him as the day they had married. Her love for him never wavered.

William was ridden with guilt. He always felt the lack of children was a fault that most probably lay with him, a sign from above that he should never have been so selfish as to allow poor Maud to marry him. He could tell that not having children was more than she could bear, and as each year went by he could see the sadness etched into her beautiful face.

They had kept on Stella the cook who had been at Westfield when the Harrisons first moved there, but apart from her and the gardener who came every week during the summer months, Maud managed the house alone. She was a devout Catholic who went to Mass every morning in the village church, unlike William whose faith in God had diminished over the years. Maud looked after the flowers in the church and took great pride in ensuring that only the best blooms from her garden were used for her arrangements. Father Seán Melody, the parish priest, had married Maud and William, and Maud always made sure that he was a welcome visitor at Westfield. Maud always thought that the life of a priest was a lonely one, and she often invited him to dinner, especially during holidays when she knew he would be alone. He and William would sit up late into the night smoking and playing cards and, although William's faith had lapsed, Father Seán had never let it come between them. Sometimes when William had drunk too much whiskey he would ask Father Seán to hear his confession. The priest would sit at the card table with his head bowed and listen to William confess his sins.

Afterwards he would offer him absolution, making the sign of the cross as he did so.

One bitterly cold February evening Maud had invited Father Seán to dine with them. After dinner they pulled their chairs close to the fire to keep warm. They talked for a while but it wasn't long before tiredness set in and Maud tried to stifle a yawn.

"I think I shall go to bed," she said, getting up from her chair.

Both men stood. "Goodnight, dear," said William, kissing her forehead.

She smiled at the priest and left.

Then William looked at Father Seán and shook his head. "I'm such a lucky man to have her."

"You're both lucky to have each other."

"Maud's not lucky. The poor girl's been lumbered with me. For God's sake, I can't even give her children," he mumbled, knocking back what remained in his glass.

The priest had always wondered why it was they never had any children, but as neither of them had ever brought the subject up, he had thought it was not his place to ask. Now that William had mentioned it, he seized upon the opportunity. He couldn't have mentioned it at a better time – it was as if it was meant to be.

"Why have you not had children?" he asked, leaning forward in his chair.

"Don't know." William was staring into the fire. "I suspect it might have something to do with my injuries," he said with a twisted smile. "Wherever the problem lies, the fact is it just never happened. It doesn't bother me that much, but it hurts me to see Maud so disappointed. She should never have married me, you know. I told her so from the very beginning." He got up and poured more whiskey. "I suppose it's unlikely that anything will happen now, although Maud hasn't given up hope."

Father Seán took his chance to jump in. "How would you feel about adopting a child?"

William stood back in surprise. "Adopting? You mean taking a child from an orphanage? I don't think so – I mean, how would you know where it had come from?"

Their silence in the room was broken by the crack and hiss of the logs burning in the fire.

William realised how snobbish he had sounded. "I'm sorry, Seán. That was very unchristian of me."

"You're just being honest, nothing wrong with that. The child I'm talking about isn't in an orphanage yet. He was just born last week. He's with the nuns in a convent. They're trying to find a suitable home for him. He's from a good background. The father, an engineering student, got some poor girl from the country in trouble. When they asked me to make inquiries, you were the first couple I thought of. I wanted to see how you might feel about it before discussing it with Maud. Of course, if you don't think it's a good idea, I'll consider the matter closed."

"I don't know," said William sighing. "Can you love a child that isn't yours?"

"It's still an infant. I'm sure you could love it as if it were your own."

William was quiet. He stared pensively into his glass as he swirled the whiskey around. "What if I didn't get along with him?"

"Every parent takes that chance when they have a child. Just because it is born from your own flesh and blood does not guarantee you will get on together."

"Why don't you talk to Maud? If it would make her happy, then I'm willing to go along with it."

Maud was surprised to see Father Seán the following day. He rarely called without an invitation. They sat in the front room and chatted for a while. Stella prepared some tea and scones and carried them in on a tray. When she left the room Father Seán cleared his throat as if to speak but only reached across for the milk jug. Last night had been easier. William had practically opened the conversation for him and now without the whiskey to loosen his tongue he wondered if this wasn't a matter that William, not he, should be discussing with his wife. When the tea was gone and the usual pleasantries had been exhausted, he put his teacup down and cleared his throat again.

"Is there something you want to talk about?" asked Maud, sensing his unease.

"Yes. Yes, as a matter of fact there is." Thankful for her female intuition, he launched straight into it. "Maud, just hear me out, and please don't take offence at what I'm about to ask. I know it is a very intimate matter. I discussed it with William last night. He has given me permission to discuss it with you."

Maud was curious and somewhat alarmed. She sat up in her chair. "What is it?"

"How would you feel about adopting a baby?"

Not having children was a subject that she and William had always found difficult to talk about. Her mouth dried up and she brushed some crumbs from her skirt in an effort to gather her thoughts. "I have never thought about it."

"I have been asked to assist in finding a suitable home for a baby boy. He was born last week. The mother is unmarried and not in a position to keep him. In certain cases the nuns try to find a home for the child before it is put into an orphanage." Maud stared at the floor, feeling slightly hurt that William had talked this over with Father Seán before her.

"The poor woman," she said shaking her head. "I can't imagine what it must be like, not being able to keep your child." Her shoulders had slumped over with the weight of the commitment she had been presented with. "I suppose I'll never have any of my own now. I always imagined we'd have five or six children. Some days I get so sad about it."

"Will you think about it?"

"You said he was born only last week?"

"Yes."

"He must be so tiny. Is he healthy?"

"Yes."

"What did William say?"

"He said he would do anything to make you happy."

Father Seán stood and pulled on his overcoat. "Why don't you talk about it with William and let me know. Stay where you are, I'll let myself out."

He left the room. Maud heard the front door close, and sat back down. A single tear ran down her cheek as she thought of the children she had hoped for. Now it seemed that she must face up to reality and accept the fact that they would never be. She thought of the week-old baby in the convent with no mother to comfort him, and her heart filled with a longing for him. When William came home later that evening Maud told him about Father Seán's visit.

William had thought of nothing else all day, and had come to the conclusion that they had no business adopting someone else's child. He was sorry he had told Seán to talk to Maud about it.

"What would you like to do?" he asked as he lit a cigarette after dinner.

Maud spoke with a quiet determination. "Darling,

I think that after eleven years of marriage we can only assume that we will not be blessed with children of our own. I want to adopt this child."

William was slightly taken aback. Maud was never good at making decisions, yet she seemed so sure of this.

"Are you sure about this?" he asked pouring himself a drink.

"Yes. But only if you are."

William bit his lower lip and stared at the tablecloth. How could he deny her this, the one thing that would make her happy, after all she had sacrificed to be with him? "I only want what you want," he said, stubbing out his cigarette, trying to disguise his doubt.

13

Two weeks later Father Seán's black Ford moved slowly up the driveway of Westfield. In the back seat sat a nurse, and beside her was the Moses basket holding the infant boy. Maud watched from the bay window of the drawing-room. Her heart was beating fast and the palms of her hands had become moist with perspiration. William had promised to be home for the arrival of the baby, but there was no sign of him. Maud let Stella open the front door, as she felt far too nervous to leave the room. She heard Father Seán's voice greeting Stella, and the click of the nurse's heels on the tiles of the hallway. As the door opened, Maud moved towards the fire and busied herself by throwing on another log.

"Here we are, Maud," said Father Seán, carrying the Moses basket awkwardly.

Maud pointed towards the couch. "Put it down here."

Father Seán lay the basket down gently on the wide velvet couch. The baby was beginning to stir, his head turning from left to right like a small puppy searching for the comfort of his mother.

"He's due a feed soon," said the nurse.

The three of them peered into the basket.

"He's a little gem. There wasn't a peep out of him all the way." The nurse pulled back the blanket and his two little legs began to kick furiously.

"Goodness," said Maud, "he seems so tiny!"

The nurse lifted the child from the basket and cradled him in her arms.

"Would you like to hold him?" she asked, walking towards Maud.

Maud felt as if she were made of wood. She bent one arm and placed the other on top of it, looking carefully at how the nurse was doing it. The nurse placed the child in Maud's arms, and immediately all of her fears disappeared. It was as if she had just given birth to the baby herself. Tears of unexpected joy welled up in her eyes. "Is he really mine?" she whispered.

"He is indeed," said Father Seán. "Congratulations."

The nurse stayed for the afternoon and showed Maud how to feed and change the baby. He was to be fed every four hours, and winded during the feeds. He was to sleep in their bedroom for the first few nights until he settled, and then they could move him into the nursery. Maud had been busy in the weeks before he arrived, buying all the things a new baby would require. William's old bedroom had been converted into a nursery. It was beside their room so they would hear him if he cried during the night.

Before the nurse left, she handed Maud a large envelope. "These are some documents for you. The adoption papers and baby's birth certificate. The mother named him Thomas, but, of course, you can change that if you wish."

Maud looked at the infant sleeping peacefully in the crib and felt a pang of guilt as she thought of the mother. Who was she, why did she have to give up such a beautiful baby? Why did she name him Thomas? Perhaps it was the father's name? It was the least she could do, she thought, to allow him to keep the only thing his mother was able to give him.

"No, I don't want to change it. Thomas is his name."

William didn't come home that night until after nine o'clock. Maud could tell he'd had a few too many drinks but felt it was perfectly understandable. She knew how nervous he had been about this child. She took his hand and led him to the crib by their bed.

William peered in and stroked the sleeping child's hand. "He's a beauty," he whispered.

"Would you like to hold him?" asked Maud as the baby began to stir.

"Oh, not tonight, darling," replied William stepping back. "I had a few drinks earlier – don't want to drop him on his first night here!"

That night Maud lifted Thomas out of his crib when he started to cry for his feed. Not wanting to disturb William's sleep, she carried him to the nursery. As she sat in the rocking chair feeding him, listening to the unfamiliar sounds that come from a newborn baby, she prayed that they would be good parents to this child, their most precious gift.

The first few weeks seemed to fly by. Maud was exhausted. Becoming a mother overnight had given her little time to prepare for the demands of a new baby. She was thirty-eight years old and had never had to sit up half the night feeding a baby. Tom, as he was now called, was a full-time job. Sometimes it seemed that one feed just ran into another, giving Maud little or no time to herself, or William.

William was busy at the mill and dined out almost every night. Maud did not mind – in fact she was relieved when William rang to say he would be home late, as she was just too tired most evenings to wait up and have dinner with him. Most nights it was after ten when William came home and Maud would be sound asleep, until the baby's cries would rouse her for another feed.

One night Maud awoke with a start. She had

fallen into a deep sleep since putting Tom to bed that evening. The clock in the hall chimed to signal the hour. Maud lay still and counted five chimes. Immediately she knew that something was wrong, Tom had never slept that long without crying for a feed. Trying not to wake William, she eased herself from the bed and took her dressing-gown from the hook on the back of the bedroom door. Then she crept from the room, closing the door behind her noiselessly.

The first rays of dawn were breaking through the narrow chink in the nursery drapes, Maud pulled them open and the room was bathed in a dull grey light. She turned to take Tom from his crib, and almost fainted when she saw the child's face. His skin had turned purple, as if he had been strangled, and his breath was coming in short gasps.

Maud grabbed him from the cot and started to tap him gently on the back, but his breathing remained erratic. The nape of his neck felt wet and clammy and Maud instinctively knew that the baby was seriously ill. She ran in to William screaming, "Wake up!"

William had dined at his club in town that night and the brandy had sent him into a deep sleep.

Maud shook his arm violently. "William, something's wrong with the baby. Wake up please!"

William sat up and stared at both of them, his head swimming. "What's wrong?" he asked, reaching for a glass of water beside his bed.

Maud pulled him by the arm. "Get up and find a doctor. The baby is choking! William, I think he's dying!" she screamed. Maud was shaking Tom up and down in her arms, but still his shallow breaths came short and hard.

William pulled on his dressing-gown and stumbled downstairs. He would have to drive to Doctor Browne's house on the other side of the village. He cursed himself for not having a telephone installed in the house.

Maud walked halfway down the stairs, clutching the child tightly.

"Hurry, William! Find a doctor quickly," she pleaded in a thin frightened voice. William went to the hallstand and fumbled in his coat pocket for his keys. They weren't there. "Damn it," he mumbled. Then he hurried into the drawing-room and found them on the sideboard. "Don't worry, dear," he said, looking up at his terrified wife. "I'll be back in no time. Go back to the bedroom and keep warm." He walked outside, still feeling light-headed. The cold night air was sharp and helped to wake him fully. He sat into the car and lit a cigarette. Then he swung out of the driveway onto the deserted road.

When William arrived back with Doctor Browne, Maud was hysterical. Her eyes were wild with fear as she ran down the stairs barefoot, holding the baby tightly. "He's not breathing!"

The doctor took the child from her arms and William led the way into the drawing-room. He laid him on a rug beside the fireplace. The fire had gone out hours ago, but there was still a little heat from the smouldering embers. Dr Browne opened Tom's vest and began to massage his chest. "Hand me my bag, please," he said to William.

William got the Gladstone bag and opened it for the doctor.

"Don't worry, Mother. He's still breathing," the doctor said, not taking his eyes off the baby. He reached into the bag and took out a syringe. "Looks like he's had an asthma attack – this should bring him back." He quickly filled the syringe with the contents of a vial, and stuck the needle into the baby's thigh. Within seconds the colour returned to Tom's face and his breathing became more relaxed. He opened his eyes wide and started to cry.

Maud swooped down immediately and gathered him in her arms to give him comfort. She had never been so glad to hear him cry.

Doctor Browne asked William to fill a basin with boiling water. Then they stood at the kitchen table while the doctor showed Maud how to make a canopy with a blanket. He stood under the blanket with Tom in his arms and let him breathe in the hot vapours. After a few minutes he let Maud take over. She stood under the blanket and held Tom close as he gulped in the steamy vapours. Away from the eyes of the doctor and her husband, Maud kissed the top of her baby's head and whispered a prayer of thanks to God for sparing him.

"Give him some milk and keep an eye on him for the next few hours," said the doctor packing up his bag.

William reached over and patted the child's head. "What brought this on?"

The doctor shrugged his shoulders and sighed wearily. "Dusty environment, dampness, but in my experience asthma is almost always hereditary."

William frowned and glanced over at Maud. The doctor snapped the clasp of his bag shut. "Bring him down to see me tomorrow."

William drove Doctor Browne home and Maud took Tom back to her bed and pulled him close to her. His colour had returned to normal, but his breathing was still ragged and wheezy. Maud could feel his little heart pounding at the shock of what he had been through. She shuddered to think of what might have happened if she had slept any longer. "I'm sorry, my sweetheart," she whispered through her tears. His tiny hand gripped hers and she kissed it over and over again. "I will never let you out of my sight again."

From that night on, Tom slept next to Maud.

* * *

Tom had many bouts of asthma during his early years but none were as bad as the first attack. However, the trauma of almost losing him stayed with Maud. Every fall, every cut and graze was met with hysteria. A simple fall in the garden would be enough to have her running to the doctor. She lived in constant terror of something happening to him. No matter how William tried to allay her fears, she continued to fuss over him tirelessly.

William grew tired of them both. Maud rarely shared his bed any more as Tom refused to sleep without her. William began to spend more and more time in town. He had always liked to drop into his club at the end of the day to relax and have a drink or two. But now there hardly seemed any point in going home at all. When he did arrive home in the evenings, Maud had usually dropped off to sleep beside Tom, leaving William to eat alone. He preferred to dine at the club and stay on to play cards with some of the older members. Anything was better than going home to a silent house. In fact, there were times that William was sorry they had adopted the child. He had changed everything.

On the night before Tom's eighth birthday William returned from work early with a train set, which he assembled with great excitement in the attic room. It took him hours and the end result was magnificent. It was the type of birthday present he would have wished for when he was a boy. When

William entered the hallway the following evening he could hear no noises of birthday preparations. The house was completely silent.

"Hello, I'm home!" he shouted. "Where's the Birthday Boy?" He walked into the drawing-room and saw Maud sitting on the couch, looking pale and frightened. Tom was lying beside her, his head resting on her lap while she held a towel to his forehead.

"Oh, William, I'm so glad you're home! Tom fell out of the tree in the garden. I cancelled the birthday party. I think we should call the doctor. Look at the bump on his forehead."

William bent over and moved Maud's hand away. There was a small lump on his right temple.

"Well, that doesn't look too bad," said William, pushing himself between Maud and Tom. He put his hands under the boy's arms and gently propped him up. "Does it hurt?"

Tom began to wail, holding his arms out for Maud. William sat where he was, blocking Maud from getting to the boy. "Now look here, why don't you be a brave boy and stop crying and I'll bring you upstairs and show you your birthday present?"

"William, I don't think Tom wants his present just yet," said Maud. She moved around to the back of the couch and took hold of Tom's hand, putting the wet towel back onto his forehead.

"For God's sake, Maud, it's just a bump. I must have fallen out of every tree in that garden when I was a boy. It's what boys do. Isn't that right, buster?" He ruffled Tom's hair. "Now come with me, I have something to show you." William stretched out his hand for Tom to take.

But Tom became defiant and kicked William's hand away. "Go away. I want Mummy!" he cried, turning his head into Maud's hands.

"Why, you little horror!" said William, taken aback. He stood up, one hand leaning on his walking stick, and with his free hand he took Tom by the shirt collar and pulled him to his feet.

"William!" screamed Maud.

William swung around to Maud, almost losing his balance. "Stay out of this!" he shouted at her. Then turning to Tom, he steadied his voice and bent down so he was almost level with the boy. "Now then, you apologise and we'll forget all about your dreadful behaviour."

Tom stared at him. He hated this man with his funny limp and his ugly eye-patch – he wished he would go away and leave them alone.

William looked into the boy's eyes, and for the first time he saw the resentment that lurked behind them. "If on the other hand you don't apologise," he said straightening up, "you can go to your room without any supper and stay there for the rest of the evening."

"William, it's his birthday," whispered Maud.

"Yes, I know that. But we must never forget our

manners, even on birthdays. Now, Tom, what's it to be?"

Tom stood rooted to the spot. He stared hard at William for what seemed like an eternity. At last he spoke: "Sorry, Father."

"Good man," said William, moving towards the door. "Now let's see what's upstairs."

Tom ran into Maud's outstretched arms.

"Stay where you are, Mother. This present is only for boys," William said, opening the door without looking back.

Maud unclasped Tom's arms from around her waist, and pushed him towards the door.

William held his head high as he climbed the stairs. He didn't feel like giving Tom his gift after such an ugly confrontation. Boys need discipline, was what his mother had always said, and this boy was getting none. If William had ever dared to kick his father, he would have been given a good hiding and sent to his room.

William opened the bedroom door and tried to smile. "Happy birthday, Tom!"

Tom stepped into the room and looked at the train tracks. He walked around and looked at the little black shiny engines sitting motionless on the tracks. Then he stopped at the far side of the room and stood in the corner. William waited for the boy to say something, but Tom's face showed no expression.

William stepped over the tracks into the middle

of the train set, and knelt down awkwardly, throwing his cane beside him. He took hold of the controls and the train started to move.

"Come into the middle and I'll show you how to operate it."

Tom stayed in the corner, his back pressed hard against the wall. The train went around the tracks and William stayed crouched in the middle, his eyes never leaving the little black engine. They both held their positions without speaking.

After fifteen minutes had passed in silence, Tom stepped forward. "Can I go now? I need to use the toilet."

William gave him a withering look. "Aren't you even going to say thank you?"

"Thank you, Father," muttered Tom, gazing towards the window.

"Off you go," sighed William.

Tom ran from the room. William could hear his footsteps as he bolted down the stairs.

After a rather forlorn birthday supper, Maud sent Tom upstairs to bed. She made some hot milk for him, and carried it through the hall on her way up to read to him. William stood at the end of the stairs, blocking her way.

"Will you come to our bed tonight?" He slipped his arm around her waist.

Maud gave him a cold stare. "No, William. I'll stay with Tom. He seems very upset," she said, pulling away from him.

"Very well then," he said, moving towards the front door. "I'm going out."

* * *

Tom's birthday made William realise just how spoilt the child was, and he became obsessed with trying to discipline him. But every attempt of punishment ended with Maud's intervention.

"You're turning him into a damn sissy! Look at him, crying into his mother's skirt again!" William roared, following an argument about Tom not eating his dinner.

"For goodness sake, William," hissed Maud, "he doesn't have to eat it!"

After every argument it was the same. Maud would disappear with Tom, and William would sit out in the porch smoking one cigarette after another. He couldn't smoke in the house any more as Maud felt it was bad for Tom's asthma.

When Tom was nine years old, William raised his hand to him for the first time. It was a warm summer's day, and some of the neighbours' children had come to play in the garden at Westfield. The boys were playing football and the girls were helping Maud to make lemonade in the kitchen. William sat on the back porch in the shade, smoking a cigarette and watching the boys kick ball. He noticed an argument start up between Tom and one of the younger boys. He started to get up but sat back down again. He was too hot and besides they could sort it out themselves. The younger boy was teasing Tom by holding the football out of his reach. When Tom tried to get it, the boy moved away holding the ball behind his back. Tom made several attempts to grab the ball but the younger boy succeeded in keeping it from him. William sat forward in his chair, narrowing his eyes. He could see that Tom was becoming angry. Suddenly, Tom drew back and landed a blow to the child's face. The boy fell to the ground immediately.

William leapt to his feet. He grabbed his cane and made his way down the garden, as fast as his leg would allow him. When he reached them, the young boy was sitting on the grass looking dazed, blood streaming from his nose. Before Tom could open his mouth William had him by the earlobe, pulling him up the garden towards the kitchen door.

When Maud heard the commotion she ran out to the back porch in time to witness her son being dragged towards her. She clasped a hand over her mouth to stop herself from screaming. Tom reached out to her as they passed, but William pulled him away roughly.

"Go and see to that boy he hit!" His face was twisted with rage, and Maud could see pieces of spittle fly from his mouth as he barked the order at her. He then mustered all of his strength and caught Tom under his arm, and with great difficulty made his way upstairs trying to balance his weight on the cane, as Tom wriggled to get free. He hit Tom about the legs many times with his cane, and locked him in his bedroom for the afternoon. Later that evening as he sat out on the back porch drinking whiskey, William felt sick when he thought of the hiding he had given Tom. It wasn't the fact that he had hit the child that bothered him; it was the fact that he had wanted to do it for such a long time.

*　　*　　*

William's beatings became a regular occurrence, and as they did Tom began to despise his father. Whenever William was in the house, Maud noticed that Tom would do things to goad him deliberately. If William had a headache Tom would play with the noisiest toy he could find. If William was listening to the radio, Tom would bang away at the piano as loudly as he could. The tension was more than Maud could bear, and on the evenings when William rang to say he was staying in town, she would breathe a sigh of relief.

14

Tom attended the local junior school, but he was now approaching his eleventh birthday and further schooling would mean travelling away from home. Maud had always dreaded this day. Every morning she stood at the gate and watched Tom walk up the road towards the schoolhouse. It stood at the top of the hill in the village, beside the church. Maud could not bear the idea of sending Tom away to school. It would break her heart to be without him.

Maud did most of her thinking while she arranged her flowers on the church altar. During the summer months when the garden was in full bloom, the flowers from Westfield adorned the altar every Sunday. The time she spent alone in the stillness of the church gave Maud the peace she often did not find at home.

It was late one evening when William returned home. Maud was sitting in the drawing room with her embroidery. It helped to tire her when she was feeling restless.

William was surprised to see her up.

"Hello, dear," he said, kissing her cheek. "You're up late."

"I couldn't sleep. I thought I'd wait up for you, and have some cocoa," she said lifting her cup. "Would you like me to make you some?"

William walked over to the sideboard and opened a press. "I think I'll have something stronger," he said, pouring a glass of brandy.

"Stella left some food for you in the oven. I didn't know if you'd be home for dinner."

"Sorry, I should have called. I ate earlier."

William pulled an armchair over to the fire and sat opposite her. Maud put her needle and threads into the sewing-box on her lap, and rubbed her eyes.

"I think that's tired me out," she smiled.

William returned her smile. The evening light was fading and her face looked so delicate and beautiful in the shadows.

"It's been a long time since we've sat together like this," said William.

"Yes, it has." Maud was silent for a while. She had waited up with a purpose, but did not want to make it too obvious. They needed to talk about what school they were sending Tom to. Up until now every conversation had ended in an argument. William wanted to send him to the boarding school he had attended in England, Maud desperately wanted to keep him at home – "Toughen him up," William had said.

Tonight Maud wanted to put an end to William's notions.

She cleared her throat. "I spoke to Father Seán today," she said, brightening up.

"Oh yes, how is he? I must give him a shout one of these days," William said before draining his glass.

"He's fine. We were talking about Tom. He can make arrangements to get him into Blackrock College. He knows some of the priests there. I know we haven't enrolled him, but he thinks he'll be able to help us." She looked at William as he lit a cigarette.

"This again," he said exhaling a cloud of smoke. He rose to pour another drink. "Is that why you waited up for me?"

Maud looked down at her hands and, not wanting to lie, she said nothing.

William gazed into the fire thoughtfully. He finished his cigarette and flicked the butt into the flames.

"I'm sick of arguing about every little thing that boy does. He's yours, Maud. You've seen to that. Do what you like with him." He set his glass down on the table. "I presume you won't be coming to bed?"

Maud laced her fingers together until her nails

dug into the flesh on the backs of her hands. William leaned on his cane, looking down at her, then seeing he was not going to get an answer, he walked out of the room.

Maud sat still in her chair, and listened to the click of William's cane on the hall floor as he walked towards the stairs. When she was sure that William would be sound asleep, she crept upstairs to their bedroom but the bed was empty. Maud slipped between the sheets and felt guilty at the sense of relief that filled her. Tom would not be sent away to school. The battle was won, but her victory rang hollow when she thought of how she had sacrificed her marriage to obtain it. From that night on, William slept in the guest bedroom.

* * *

The winter of 1948 was a bitterly cold one. The rain was relentless and, as the days got shorter, it turned to sleet and then to snow. The older people of the village were cut off, not able to go outside their homes for fear of falling and perishing in the snow. Father Seán rallied the support of the more able-bodied parishioners, calling upon housewives to check on their nearest elderly neighbours and bring them food and any supplies they might need. Maud was glad of the opportunity to help. She and Stella spent hours in the kitchen cooking hot meals, and

Maud enlisted the help of Tom to deliver the boxes of hot food. He had started school in Blackrock College, but the railway line was closed until the snow stopped, so he was also housebound. Maud wore a coat belonging to William, as nothing she had was suitable for such awful weather. Her boots were not high enough to keep out the snow, so she pulled a pair of William's socks over them.

"My God, Mother," exclaimed Tom when he saw her, "you look like a tramp."

Maud laughed. "I suppose I do – now wrap up and help me."

Tom ran upstairs to get his coat and Maud stood in the hall and looked at him admiringly. How tall he had grown in a year! He was a young man now, his black curls that Maud had loved so much now combed down and tamed into a more mature style.

He raced back down the stairs, clutching his coat, and Maud put her hand on his cheek and kissed him. "My handsome boy," she smiled.

"Mother, please!" he protested, wiping the spot she had just kissed. Maud longed for the days when he used to climb on to her knee for hugs and kisses, but he was getting more independent now and her shows of affection embarrassed him. He bent down to pull on his galoshes.

Then, taking the boxes of food from the hall table, they set off into the snow.

They called to several neighbours. Maud insisted

on making tea and lighting fires in every home they visited, so they were gone all afternoon. By the time they got to the last house it was dark and Tom was sulking.

"Why can't you just hand in the food? That's all you were asked to do. Their houses are cold and dirty. I can't feel my toes I'm so cold."

"Now, Tom, that lady was too sick to light a fire. Doesn't it make you happy to know you helped her?"

"No," grumbled Tom, his hands thrust deep in his coat pockets for warmth.

"We won't take so long here," promised Maud as she knocked on the door of another cottage.

When they returned home that evening Stella had a fire blazing in the drawing-room, and she had made soup to warm them up. Maud was tired; she could still feel the cold in her bones even though she was sitting close to the fire.

When Tom came in to say goodnight she took his hand. "I want you to say a prayer tonight, to give thanks for all the things you have."

Tom rolled his eyes to heaven. "Yes, Mother," he sighed as she kissed him goodnight.

When he left the room, Maud sat staring into the fire and wondered what kind of home he would be living in now had they not adopted him. It had been on her mind a lot lately. Tom was growing up so fast, he would have to be told sometime soon. It hurt her to think she would have to tell him she was not in fact his real mother. No mother could ever love a son as much as she loved Tom. She shivered and stood up, pulling her shawl tightly around her shoulders. As she climbed the stairs she looked at the clock in the hall. It was midnight, still no sign of William. The snow began to fall again – she could hear it gently tapping against the windowpane of her bedroom as she undressed. She pulled the curtain back and looked into the garden. Everything was so still, covered in a thick mantle of snow. He'll probably stay in town tonight, she thought as she let the curtain slip from her fingers. Stella had put an extra blanket on the bed but Maud still felt chilled to the bone.

The following morning Maud woke early. She had slept badly, waking several times during the night with pains shooting up through her body. A cold sweat had made her hair stick to the back of her neck. When she tried to stand up she grew weak, black spots swam in front of her eyes and she fell back onto the bed.

Later that morning when Stella let herself in through the back door, she found it odd that Maud was not up and about. She had always been up before Stella arrived.

Tom came down a while later and Stella handed him his breakfast.

"Where's your mother?"

"Don't know," said Tom buttering his toast. "Maybe

she's gone visiting those old folk again."

"Not in this weather, she's not," said Stella looking out the window. The snow had turned to sleet and the sky was a dirty shade of grey.

"Go upstairs and see if she's in bed," ordered Stella.

"It's ten o'clock. She's not in bed."

"Go and check," insisted Stella, taking Tom's plate and placing it in the oven.

Tom stamped upstairs, cursing Stella under his breath. "Treats me like a bloody three-year-old," he muttered. He opened the bedroom door and the smell of stale air hit him immediately. His mother's room was always bright and airy, his father's room was the one that stank of bad breath and booze. He stepped into the room. The curtains were closed and it took a few seconds for his eyes to adjust. He walked over to the curtains and pulled them back a little. The sharp sound of the curtain rail caused his mother to shift in the bed.

Tom went over to her, and was shocked to see how pale she looked. Her skin was a sickly grey and her face was moist with perspiration. She tried to sit up but slumped back onto the pillow and started to cough, a deep hacking cough that racked her whole body. Tom grabbed a glass of water from her dresser and waited for her to catch her breath before handing it to her. She took a sip of water as Tom held the glass to her lips.

"Thank you, sweetheart," she said, slumping back on to her pillow. "I must have picked up a chill yesterday."

Tom looked at his mother's face, and knew immediately that she needed a doctor. He left the room and ran downstairs to the hall table. He flipped open his mother's black book and ran his finger down the column of numbers until he reached the doctor's. After several unsuccessful attempts at gaining a line out, he slammed the telephone down. "Back in a minute," he shouted to Stella from the hall, as he pulled on his coat.

It took him a while to track down Doctor Browne – it seemed everyone in the village was sick that morning. Tom finally caught up with him as he walked, head bent against the driving sleet, down towards the harbour. Tom saw the doctor's car approach slowly and he stood in the middle of the road to wave him down. The car came to a halt, the back wheels skidding on the slushy road.

"Hop in, I'm just on my way home," shouted Doctor Browne as he leaned over to open the passenger door.

Tom was soaked through and gladly climbed into the car. "Can you come by our house? My mother is very sick."

The doctor drove slowly towards Westfield. "How's the asthma?"

"Fine, hardly ever bothers me," said Tom

impatiently. "Look, can you drive a bit faster – she looked like she was dying."

The doctor leaned his foot a little harder on the accelerator, but the icy conditions made it impossible to drive any faster. He eased his foot back off the pedal, slowing the car back down to a crawl.

When they finally got to the house, Maud looked even worse.

Stella had a bowl of cold water and was sponging her forehead. "She's hardly conscious," she whispered.

The doctor washed his hands at the basin. "Can both of you leave the room, please, while I examine her?"

Tom and Stella went down to the kitchen.

"Will I make you another breakfast?" asked Stella.

"No, I couldn't eat," said Tom.

"She probably caught something from the folk she visited yesterday," said Stella, tidying away the breakfast dishes.

"I told her to just hand the damn food parcels in, but she wouldn't listen to me!" said Tom, pacing up and down the kitchen. "Some of them live in dirty hovels."

Stella turned her back on him and put the dishes into the sink. "There, but for the grace of God, go I," she muttered under her breath.

Doctor Browne entered the kitchen and set his bag down on the table. He took his glasses off and massaged the bridge of his nose with his thumb and forefinger.

"How is she?" asked Tom.

"There is a bad case of influenza going around. It looks like your mother has been infected. I've been treating cases all week. She is very weak at the moment but I have given her an injection that should help with the fever. Tom, if you could go to the chemist and get this prescription filled . . ." He scribbled on his note pad.

"Can I do anything?" asked Stella as she handed him his coat.

"Try to get some fluids into her."

"I'll go down to the chemist now," said Tom.

When he had left, Doctor Brown closed over the kitchen door.

"Keep an eye on her, Stella. Her temperature is dangerously high," he said quietly.

"Will she be all right, Doctor?" Stella was twisting a dishcloth in her hands.

"I hope so. I lost two patients to it last week. Hopefully her fever will break soon." He looked around the kitchen. "Where's William?"

"He stayed in town last night. He's probably at his office now. Should I contact him?"

"Yes, I think that would be wise."

Stella let the doctor out and went upstairs to sit with Maud. She looked so serene, lying there with her fair hair loose around her pillow. Stella stroked her hand. "Get well, Mrs Harrison," she whispered softly.

Maud stirred and opened her eyes. "Stella, where is Tom?"

"He's just run down to the chemist to get your medicine."

"Make sure he comes straight up to me when he gets in." Her voice was weak and Stella could see it was taking all her strength just to talk.

Stella sat with her until she heard the front door slam. She got up and tiptoed across the room. Tom came running up the stairs out of breath, and met Stella at the bedroom door.

"She wants to see you," said Stella. "I'm going down to the kitchen. Try to make her rest."

Tom entered the room and walked quietly across the carpet to the bed. He had never seen his mother looking so sick before. Maud opened her eyes, and he noticed how strange they looked, almost glassy. Her long slender hands patted the bed beside her. "Come and sit here," she whispered.

Tom sat at the edge of the bed and Maud put her hot clammy hand into his.

"I've wanted to tell you something for quite a long time," she said.

Her breathing was short, it reminded Tom of his childhood asthma attacks.

"Why don't you tell me later, Mother? You'll wear yourself out and you should take your medicine." He started to draw away but she caught hold of his arm, almost pinching him.

"I need to tell you this now," she said. "Listen carefully."

Tom moved closer, anxious to hear what was so important.

Maud seemed to gather all her strength. "You were born to another mother but she couldn't keep you because she wasn't married, so we adopted you." Her words were rapid, like gunfire.

Tom felt the hairs stand up on the back of his neck.

"I know this is going to be hard for you. I could never find the right moment to tell you. If anything should happen to me, I want you to know that I loved you the moment you were placed in my arms and I have never stopped loving you." Maud had propped herself up on her elbows as she spoke, but her arms were too weak to bear the weight and she slid back down until her head dropped heavily onto the pillows that Stella had arranged earlier.

Tom felt embarrassed by a sudden urge to cry, and he rubbed his eyes vigorously in an attempt to regain his composure. He didn't know what to say, so many questions were running through his head. He took hold of Maud's hand and stroked it tenderly.

"Who was my mother?" he asked flatly.

"I don't know, my love. I thought about her many times when you were a child, how she had given us the most beautiful son in the world."

"How did you get me?"

"Father Seán arranged it." Maud's eyelids felt heavy and she let them close, giving in to the frailty that had beset her.

Tom stayed with her and tried to piece together what she had told him. He shook his head in disbelief as he looked at his sleeping mother and tried to absorb what she had said. How could any other woman but her be his mother? It seemed impossible that what she had said bore any truth.

Until he thought of his father – then everything began to make sense.

*   *   *

That evening Doctor Browne called again. Maud's temperature had soared and she was talking wildly, saying things that made no sense to anyone. William had been informed of her worsening condition and had just come home when the doctor arrived. After Doctor Browne had seen to Maud, he went downstairs to the drawing-room where William poured him a drink.

"How is she doing?" William walked over with a glass of whiskey. As he got closer he could see that the doctor's kind smile had been replaced with a grave expression, one he kept for accidents and tragedies.

"William, she's bad, I can't seem to bring down

the fever. This influenza is spreading like wildfire. Someone will have to sit with her tonight, sponge her down with a cold cloth. Hopefully the penicillin will begin to work by the morning."

He took a large mouthful of whiskey and handed the glass back to William.

"Must be getting on, still have a few more calls to make. By the way, I treated a woman today who has a bad case of it too. It seems that Maud called in on her yesterday. It's probably where she picked it up."

William saw the doctor out to his car and then went upstairs to Maud. Tom was sitting by her bed. When he heard his father enter the room he stood up.

"How is she?" asked William.

Tom brushed past him and left the room without saying anything.

Maud turned her head to William. All of the colour had drained from her face. Even her blue eyes that usually sparkled had faded to a dull grey.

"I told him, William," she said, trying to lift her head. "He's upset."

William was confused. "Told him what?"

"About the adoption."

"Maud," he said taking her hand, "you just concentrate on getting better. We'll worry about things like that another day."

She lay back and slept again.

Later that night she woke again. William had

nodded off minutes earlier in the armchair beside her bed and she stretched out her hand to reach for him.

"William?" she said faintly.

He woke not knowing where he was for a second, then he heard the gasping breaths of his wife and fumbled about in the dark for her hand.

"William, are you there?"

"Here I am, dear," he said, moving his chair closer to the bed.

"William, I think I'm going to die," she gasped.

"No, Maud, *please* don't say that."

"I'm sorry for the way I treated you. I know I pushed you away. I don't know why I did it because I always loved you."

William could hear the panic in her voice. "Ssh," he whispered. She tried to continue, but he silenced her. "Maud, you don't need to say anything. You did what you had to do. I was the one who was impossible to live with. It's I who am sorry." He broke off and sobbed softly. "Sorry, my darling," he whispered.

But Maud had drifted back into unconsciousness.

William sat in the darkness and thought about the years of misery they had shared.

He was filled with a sickening guilt as he remembered the other women he had sought refuge with when he had tired of Maud's indifference.

"Forgive me, Maud." His hands shook and he got

up from the chair quietly, groping in the dark for his cane. He needed something to drink. He could hear the rattle in his wife's chest as he made his way towards the door. William went downstairs to the drawing-room and poured a large glass of brandy. He sat beside the dying embers of the fire that Stella had built up earlier, and drank in large gulps. He had never felt so miserable in his life. He remembered the time he spent in the army hospital in France and how he believed that things could never get any worse, but nothing he had experienced during those months could match the emptiness he was feeling now. He dozed on the chair for a while, and saw Maud tiptoe into the room and cross it until she stood before him. He held out his hand to touch her, but she smiled and stepped back out of his reach. William woke with a start, knocking the empty glass from the arm-rest onto the floor. He crept back up the stairs, but knew before he reached his wife's room that she was gone.

15

Father Seán tried to steady his voice as he prepared to address the large gathering of mourners. He had loved Maud dearly and found it hard to believe he would never see her again. He looked down at the first pew where William sat, his head bowed, resting on his walking cane. Tom sat a little away from him, wiping his tears with the palm of his hand. How the boy would miss her!

What a cruel God you can be, thought Father Seán as he began the funeral Mass.

The priest's voice faltered as he struggled to deliver the final words of the funeral homily.

William's mother had travelled from England alone for the funeral, his father being sick and too frail to make the journey. The days that followed the funeral were an endless procession of well-wishing neighbours and distant relatives whom William had never seen before.

Mrs Harrison stayed at Westfield for a week, but was anxious to get back to her husband. She arranged to leave on Saturday morning and William offered to drive her to Dublin in time for her to make the afternoon sailing. He woke early on Saturday morning after a night of broken sleep, and was glad to get out of bed. He washed and dressed in haste, and lit his first cigarette as he walked downstairs to breakfast. His mother was sitting at the breakfast table while Stella fussed over her. How strange, thought William, to see his mother sitting in the same chair that she had occupied every morning when he was a child.

Stella stopped talking when she heard him enter the room, making him immediately suspicious.

"Good morning, William," said Mrs Harrison. "Now put out that nasty cigarette and have some breakfast. We should be leaving soon."

William did as he was told. He opened the French windows and threw his cigarette out onto the rain-soaked terrace.

"I'll go and see if Tom wants some breakfast," said Stella, leaving the room.

"Some tea?" asked Mrs Harrison, pouring William a cup without waiting for his reply. She looked at him as she placed the teapot back on the stand. "William, darling, you look awful. Why don't I get a cab?"

"Mother, I'm fine," he said, trying to stir his tea without spilling it. He had been drinking far too much lately and it was beginning to show.

She stretched her hand across the table and patted his wrist. "Of course, you are. It's been a terrible shock. If only your father wasn't so sick I would stay for a while, but I really must get back."

William gave a weary smile. His mother was almost eighty years old and in no position to offer any help at all. She had worn him out over the past few days with her demands to be driven here and there, so he was quite relieved to see her go.

"Mother, you are needed at home. We'll manage."

"What will you do with Tom?"

This was a question that William had asked himself over and over since Maud had passed away. It would be so much easier now to send him off to boarding school in England. He could spend holidays with his grandparents and William would be free from the worry of raising him. But that would be going against everything Maud had wanted for him, and William couldn't bring himself to send the boy away.

"I've decided to board him in Blackrock College. I can't be here for him the way Maud was. It's the only solution I can think of."

"Do the two of you get along?" asked his mother.

William sighed. "No, not exactly."

Mrs Harrison had sensed the tension between the

two of them from the moment she had entered the house. It had been clear to her from the beginning that William had no love for the boy, but seeing the situation up close worried her.

After breakfast William packed his mother's suitcase into the back of the car. The light drizzle had given way to a steady rainfall. He slammed the boot shut, and walked back up the granite steps to the house.

"Mother, come on! We'll be late!" he shouted.

Mrs Harrison had gone back upstairs, to say goodbye to Tom.

"There you are," she said, entering the room.

He was sitting at the edge of his bed, still in his dressing-gown. His dark curly hair was dishevelled and in her opinion, getting a little too long. He looked so unlike a child that William and Maud would have had. This boy could have been a gypsy, with his dark skin and brown eyes, she thought, as she sat down on the bed beside him.

"You know, your grandfather has not seen you since you were seven."

"I don't remember him," said Tom.

"He's quite ill now. Will you come and see him soon?"

"When?"

"As soon as you like. Come for your summer holidays. We'd love to have you," she said taking his hands. "Will you?"

"Yes, I suppose so, if Father agrees." He tried to take his hands away, but she tightened her grip.

"Tom, I know how hard this is for you. I know we are old, but as long as we are around, your grandfather and I will always welcome you in our home. You only have to write and let us know when you want to come."

Tom smiled at her. He helped her up and walked her downstairs. When William saw them through the open front door he pressed the car horn twice and pointed impatiently to his watch.

William and his mother drove through the rain. William was quiet, and allowed her to do most of the talking. He smoked a cigarette, paying no attention to what she was saying.

"Well?" She had stopped talking, and was waiting for an answer.

"What?" asked William.

"*I was saying,* if you can't cope with things, Tom could always come to live with us."

"Don't worry, Mother," said William, trying to concentrate on driving. Recently the vision in his good eye had weakened, and driving had become almost impossible in bad weather.

"I'm sure you'll be fine," she said, sensing his irritability. "But do bear in mind he's only fourteen, William. It's been such a great loss for him."

William stared straight ahead, saying nothing.

He knew he would have to give up driving soon,

but he wasn't ready to do it just yet. He had never let his injuries get in the way of anything he wanted to do, but sometimes at night he felt as if he were driving with a blindfold.

They made their farewells brief. William promised to visit soon, but knew full well that he would not.

William arrived home just as Stella was putting her coat on in the hall.

"I'm off. Your dinner is in the oven." She rolled her eyes in the direction of the staircase. "His nibs hasn't been down all day. I've left dinner for him too."

William closed the door behind her and went into the kitchen. He took one of the plates from the warm oven. The roast beef looked all right, but a skin had formed over the mashed potatoes and the vegetables looked grey and soggy. William ate what he could without actually tasting anything. What he really wanted was a drink.

He went into the drawing-room and shovelled some coal onto the dying fire. He poured himself a large tumbler of whiskey and drank it back quickly. A good belt of alcohol was needed for what was ahead. He walked to the door and shouted Tom's name. A few minutes later Tom appeared at the top of the stairs, looking pale and tired.

"Come here, will you," ordered William, walking back into the drawing-room.

Tom entered the room silently. When William turned around after pouring another drink, he jumped slightly to see Tom standing behind him.

"My God, I didn't hear you come in." William tried to sound light and jaunty. He wanted this to be short and to the point. He signalled to the chair by the fire. "Sit down. We need to talk."

Tom sat down stiffly.

Damn it, thought William as he rested his cane against his armchair. He was at a loss for words.

"We haven't really had a chance to talk, what with all the comings and goings."

Tom remained silent.

William sat in the chair opposite him and hoped that Tom would say something, but he gazed into the fire, looking uninterested in anything his father might have to say.

"Now that your mother is no longer with us, there is no one here to look after you. Stella is getting on in years, and we can't depend on her. So I have made some arrangements."

Tom pulled his stare away from the fire and looked towards William. "Will you send me back to the orphanage?" he asked, barely disguising his sarcasm.

William tightened his grip on the glass he was holding. "What are you talking about?" he asked quietly.

"Mother told me before she died. I'm adopted. I was never your son." Tom leaned forward in his chair.

William could see he was being goaded, and tried to prepare himself for the impending confrontation.

"Yes, it's true we did adopt you, but it has nothing to do with what I want to talk to you about. I want you to board in Blackrock College." William's hands were shaking. He hadn't expected Tom to be so surly.

Tom remained perfectly composed, sitting very straight in his chair.

"You never really wanted me, did you?" he asked, looking into William's face, searching for an answer.

William pressed his back into the armchair. Tom's interrogation was making him uncomfortable.

"That's not true," he lied.

"Where did you get me from?"

William cursed Maud silently for creating this mess and leaving him to clear it up. "I'm not sure. It was Maud who arranged everything."

"I'll bet it was," Tom said with a snort. "I'd say you had nothing to do with it, did you?"

"No," said William getting up to pour another drink. He didn't like the way this conversation was going.

"Well, you must at least know where I came from." Tom's eyes followed William across the room.

"I really have no idea, Tom. Maud arranged it through Father Seán." He turned to face Tom. "It really doesn't matter now. We brought you up and cared for you."

Tom threw his head back and laughed forcefully. "But you never cared about me!"

"Stop that!" said William, trying to control his anger.

169

"You never cared about mother!" said Tom raising his voice.

William walked back over to his chair, his cane hitting the floor heavily with every step. He stared at Tom in disbelief. "Don't you talk to me like that. I cared a great deal about your mother. How dare you say such a thing!"

Tom jumped up from his chair, becoming more agitated. "Why didn't you ever come home and spend some time with her then? She might as well have been a widow for all the time you spent here!"

"That's enough," barked William, gripping his cane.

"What was so important that you could never come home? I suppose you preferred to stay out with some little tart!"

William couldn't listen to him any longer. He could hardly believe his ears.

He swung his cane around, hitting Tom across the side of his head. "Why, you little bastard!"

Tom fell back a few steps and put his hand on the mantelpiece to recover his balance.

"Get out!" shouted William.

Tom walked towards the door, feeling victorious. His head throbbed but he knew his words had hit the old cripple a lot harder. He stopped at the door and turned to face William.

"You know, the only good thing to come out of this is the fact that you are not my father. You cannot imagine how happy that makes me." Then he closed the door quietly behind him.

William slumped into his armchair, spilling whiskey onto his trousers. His heart was pounding in his chest. Tom's brutal attack rang in his ears. Had he been so indiscreet in the past that even his son knew about the other women? He knocked back another glass of whiskey and tried to control the anger that surged up inside him.

"Little bastard!" he roared as he hurled his glass at the hearth-stone, sending splinters flying into the air.

Part 3

16

Redcross, County Wicklow – 1966

Lily stood at the gate as the driver of the red sports car parked in the yard. The only car that ever drove up the lane was Jody Walsh's battered Ford Escort, so Lily gazed with curiosity at the stranger in his fancy car that had obviously taken a wrong turn.

A man got out of the car and stood looking at Lily. He had a thick crop of black wavy hair and, as Lily studied his face, she could feel her blood run cold. She dropped the bundle of weeds at her feet. "Can I help you?"

He closed the car door and walked towards her. As he approached, Lily gripped the wooden gate and leaned on it heavily. The ground seemed to be shifting under her feet. At first she had thought it was Stephen, but as her mind began to focus properly it dawned on her who he was.

He stopped before her. "I'm Tom."

"I know," she managed to say.

"I'm sorry I didn't write beforehand. If this is not a good time, I'll leave."

"No, no, not at all," said Lily. "I'm sorry – I'm just a bit shaken."

"I don't know what we're supposed to do," he said nervously. "It's very nice to meet you."

Lily was unprepared. Her limbs felt rigid, she lifted her arms mechanically and he leaned into her embrace. Her heart pounded as she thought of the last time she had held him, and she felt her body weaken with the weight of her emotion.

She stood back and looked at him. Lily had always imagined that her son would look like his father, but to her surprise he bore no resemblance. His dark hair and sallow complexion had come from his mother, but there was a look in his brown eyes that reminded Lily of Stephen Mitchell. "You look nothing like your father, but as soon as you stepped out of the car, I knew it was you."

"Is he here?"

"No." Again she could feel the blood drain from her face. "I never married your father, I never saw him after you were born."

Tom looked at the house. "This is where you live?"

"Yes," said Lily running a hand through her hair. "Please, come in." She led him into the front room. "I'll just go and make some tea. You sit down."

Tom sat, but stood up immediately when he saw she was leaving the room. "I'll sit in the kitchen."

"No, no. Please, it's a mess. Please sit down – I'll be back in a second."

Tom sat back down again.

Lily rushed into the kitchen and put the kettle on. She had deliberately left Tom in the other room to give herself time to gather her thoughts. Her hands were shaking as she poured the hot water into the teapot. Her mind had seized, leaving her incapable of thinking straight. She turned on the cold tap and cupped her hands together, letting the cold water fill them, then she splashed the water onto her face. She did this a few times until the panic began to subside. The cups rattled on the tray as she walked into the front room. She gripped the handles tightly for fear she might drop it. Tom was standing beside the fireplace looking at a photograph of Grace and Jim. Lily had taken the photo one day as they both sat proudly on their horses, smiling broadly for the camera.

"Is this your daughter?" asked Tom, putting the photograph back down.

"Yes, that's Grace and my late husband Jim."

"How many children do you have?"

"Just the one." Then she blushed when she realised how that sounded. "I mean one, apart from you."

"How old is she?"

"Grace is nineteen. She's doing nursing in Dublin." She handed him his tea. "What about you? Have you any brothers or sisters?"

"No, I was an only child."

"And your parents?"

"My mother died when I was fourteen. My father is in a nursing home. He's quite ill."

"Where did you grow up?" asked Lily.

"In Greystones."

"My goodness," Lily laughed nervously, "that's not far from here, is it?"

"No," said Tom smiling.

Lily looked at this handsome stranger and found it hard to believe that he was the baby she had given up all those years ago. Part of her wanted to cross the room and embrace the child that she had prayed for every night for years, but he was a grown man, a stranger in her home.

They talked for two hours. Tom told her about Maud and how devastated he had been when she died. He asked about his natural father and Lily had to tell him that she had no idea where he might be now. Lily told him about Jim's accident and how it had taken Grace so long to get over it. Tom said that he had always wanted a sister or brother, as being an only child had been a very lonely existence. He said it was a good feeling to know that he had a half-sister, and Lily felt the sinking feeling return. Grace would be back soon, and she was hoping that Tom would be gone, but he seemed to be in no hurry.

The dogs began to bark in the yard. Lily jumped up from her chair and rushed to the window in time to see Grace walking up the lane.

Tom walked over to the window and stood behind her. "Is this Grace?"

"Yes," said Lily turning to face him. "I never told them about you," she blurted.

"You don't have to tell her now," said Tom. "I understand. You need time."

Grace entered the room. She had seen the car outside and wondered who might be visiting.

As she stepped into the room, Lily could see Tom look at her admiringly. Her ponytail had loosened during the walk and her face was framed in tiny black ringlets. Lily noticed they had the same black hair and dark eyes, and her face burned as she introduced them.

"Grace, this is Tom. He just dropped in to say hello. He's Sarah's nephew."

Tom looked at Lily, but Lily ignored his stare. "He heard Sarah stayed here last night and he just popped in to see her. You had just left minutes before he came." Lily's hands began to shake again, and she gathered the cups and saucers onto the tray noisily.

"Hi," said Grace. "I think we saw your car pass us in the village this morning. Sarah didn't seem to recognise it though."

Tom smiled at her. "So you're the nurse." He spoke

in a polished upper-class accent, not at all like Lily and Grace.

"Mm," said Grace grimacing, "trying to be." She looked at the clock. "I'd better get my things together; I've a bus to catch."

"Well, you go on up and organise yourself. I'll see Tom out," said Lily, ushering Grace out of the room.

"Where are you getting the bus from?" asked Tom.

Grace stopped and shook Lily's hand from her arm. "Wicklow. It's leaving at four o'clock."

"I'll give you a lift in if you like."

Lily shot a glance at him, to which he did not respond. "Well, if it's no bother, that would be great. I was hoping Jody might take me but he doesn't seem to be around."

Lily could feel her heart racing. "That's not necessary. I'm sure Jody will be back soon. He knows what time your bus is."

"It's no problem at all. I'm going that way," said Tom coolly.

Grace ran upstairs to get her things. They both stared after her.

"Please don't tell her anything," pleaded Lily.

Tom looked at her with disdain. "Why would I do that?" he said curtly, and he turned to walk out to the car.

Tom helped Grace put her bags in the boot and before he got into the car he turned to Lily.

"Can I call again?" he asked.

"Of course," said Lily faintly.

As the car pulled out of the yard, Lily waved and tried to smile.

Tom smiled back, and for a split second she saw the same cold expression that she had seen on Stephen's face all those years ago when she had told him she was pregnant.

* * *

Later that day Lily phoned Sarah. Sarah could tell immediately by the tone of Lily's voice that something had happened.

"What's wrong?"

"Sarah, when you left today someone called to see me."

"Who?"

"He came back to look for me."

Lily's voice sounded weak and Sarah could hardly hear her.

"Came back? Who?" she asked.

There was silence.

"Lily, are you still there?"

"Yes."

"Who came back?"

"Thomas," said Lily.

"Who's Thomas?" enquired Sarah impatiently.

"The child I had, the child I gave up." Lily's voice broke again, and Sarah could hear her crying.

"I don't believe it." Sarah was unsure how to

react. For some reason she had always thought that the baby Lily had given up was a girl. Not wanting to sound too shocked, she tried to think of something appropriate to say. "Did you know immediately who he was?"

"It was awful, Grace came home while he was here. He ended up giving her a lift into town."

"Why was it awful? Was Grace upset?"

"No, no, not at all, it's just that . . . "

"What, Lily, tell me, what happened?"

"I lied, Sarah. I couldn't tell her. I feel so ashamed of myself but I just wanted him to leave. It's been so long. I couldn't tell Grace about it, not now."

Lily could hear Sarah lighting a cigarette.

After a few more seconds of silence Sarah said, "Jesus, Lily, who did you say he was?"

"Your nephew."

Another long silence followed.

"Say something," said Lily.

"Lily, who are you trying to protect? Grace can take it. I know she can."

"I can't tell her that I lied to her father for all the years we were married. She would never forgive me. Sarah, she's all I've got."

It was the first time that Sarah had ever heard Lily become hysterical. "Look, calm down, and think this through. Grace might have a few awkward questions but, believe me, I really think she'll understand."

Lily ignored Sarah's reasoning. "Will you please

back me up if Grace asks you anything? I'm sorry to involve you in this, but it won't be for long. He's going to England soon to look after the sale of his grandparent's estate. With any luck he'll stay there."

"So," said Sarah sighing, "you're going to continue lying to her?" It was a question that sounded more like an accusation.

"I'll handle it my way," said Lily firmly. "But I will need your help. Can I depend on you should the situation arise?"

"Yes," said Sarah sharply.

* * *

Grace rang that evening. It was something she always did when she got back to work, to let her mother know that she had arrived safely. Her mood was unusually cheerful, a little too happy for someone who had a week of night shifts ahead of her. Lily tried to make her questions sound casual.

"Did you make it to the bus on time?"

"Tom was coming up to Dublin anyway, so he gave me a lift all the way," said Grace.

"How nice of him," mumbled Lily, almost dropping the telephone.

"We stopped off at his house in Greystones. He had to pick up some things. It's beautiful, right beside the sea."

Lily felt her chest tighten. "You went to his house?"

"Yes," said Grace, laughing at her mother's surprise. "What's wrong with that?"

"Nothing, well – you hardly know him."

"For heaven's sake, Mum, he just gave me a lift. Why do you have to get so worried about everything?"

"Don't be silly, dear, I'm not worried," said Lily quickly. The last thing she wanted to do was sound alarmed.

"Anyway, there's someone waiting to use the phone. I'd better go. Goodnight, Mum."

"Goodnight." Lily hung up and sank down into the chair beside the phone.

What is he trying to do? she thought.

17

The second time Tom called to the house, Grace happened to be there on her weekend off.

It's as if he knew, thought Lily, as she watched him walk towards her with a bunch of flowers.

"Hi, there," he said, smiling broadly, holding out the flowers for her to take.

Lily took the flowers without looking at him and walked into the house, leaving the door open for him to follow.

"I don't have a telephone number for you, otherwise I would have rung." He looked around the room. "Is anyone else in?"

Lily turned the tap on and held a vase under it. "Yes. Grace is helping Jody with some lambs in the back field." She turned to look at him. "But she won't be back till this evening."

He sat down at the table, crossing his legs. "Never mind, I came to see you. How have you been?"

Lily set the vase down on the table across from him. "Look, Tom, you can't just call like this. I tried to explain to you last time. No one knows about you. I never told a soul. I couldn't tell Grace now, not after deceiving her father for so many years."

He looked at her in disbelief. "You mean you're not going to tell her?"

"Yes," said Lily, unable to make eye contact.

"You just want me to go away, is that it?"

Lily looked down at the floor, hoping her silence would answer his question.

He sat forward in his chair. "Tell me, did you ever think about me? Did you ever wonder where I was?"

Lily could feel her face getting hot, as she listened to the hurt in his voice. "Of course, I thought about you," she said in a whisper.

"Well, that's good," he said quickly. "Because I have dreamed about finding you since the day my mother told me I was adopted. I never fooled myself that it would end happily ever after, but I sure as hell didn't expect to be treated like a bloody nuisance."

"You don't understand," interrupted Lily.

"I think I understand perfectly. I'm not wanted here."

For a second Lily's resolve weakened. The pain she was causing him was hard to bear, but she couldn't live with the shame that would come with telling Grace that she had cheated and lied to her father.

Tom stood up and walked towards the door. "Do you want me to leave you alone?" he asked sourly.

"Yes," said Lily, and looked at him without blinking. Then she turned away.

He stood at the door and stared at Lily's back, but she did not turn around.

He turned and walked out of the house, and seconds later she heard his engine roar loudly as he pulled out of the yard.

"May God forgive me," she said, crossing the floor to the table where the vase of flowers sat. She picked up the hem of her apron and wiped the tears from her face, then, taking the flowers from the vase, she carried them outside and put them into the bin, stuffing newspapers on top of them, like a criminal destroying the evidence.

*   *   *

Grace came in through the back door that evening and kicked off her boots. Helping around the farm was something she hated, but it was hard to refuse Jody when he asked. She unpinned her hair, letting it tumble down her back and examined her face closely in the mirror. Then she pulled out the neck of her sweater and stuck her nose down into the gap. "I smell of muck," she remarked.

Lily walked into the kitchen with a basket of laundry. She had taken advantage of the mild weather to strip the beds and wash the sheets. The basket dropped from her arms onto the table with a loud thud.

"Was that Tom's car I saw earlier?" asked Grace, still looking in the mirror.

Lily shook out a sheet and tried to think quickly. "Yes, it was. He was in a rush and didn't stay long."

"He certainly didn't. I came down from the back field to say hello but his car was pulling out." Grace ran her fingers through her hair and looked at her mother through the mirror.

Lily could feel herself getting shaky. "It's a pity you missed him," she said casually. "He'll probably call again soon." She took the kettle from its stand and filled it. "Will you have some tea?"

"Yes, I'll go up and wash first." Grace knew that Lily wasn't overly fond of Tom and while she was curious to know why, she was just as happy not to take the conversation any further. She wasn't exactly lying, but she felt uncomfortable hiding things from her mother.

* * *

On the day Tom had driven her back to Dublin he had pulled up beside the hospital gates.

"Well," he said stretching his arm across the back

of her seat, "you must be back earlier than expected."

"Yes, I'm never back until eight." Grace had never met a man so good-looking and sophisticated. Everything about him was so perfect.

"How about a drink then?"

"I suppose I could. I'll just run in and change" Grace was sorry immediately. If Sister Charles saw her running in to change her clothes for a man in a sports car, she would have a thing or two to say about it.

"No, you don't need to change. We'll just go for a quick one," he said, pulling out onto the road.

They had gone to a pub nearby and after several vodkas Grace looked at her watch and jumped. The time had just flown. They had been talking for hours. Tom wanted to know everything about her and Grace had found it so easy to talk to him.

"You can leave me outside the gates. I'll walk in," said Grace as they approached the hospital. Tom looked at her. "I don't want Sister asking any questions," she said grinning.

Tom pulled up and shut off the engine. Grace could feel her heart pounding. They looked at each other without saying anything.

Then Tom leaned towards her and kissed her casually on the cheek. "Thanks for a lovely evening, Grace. It was nice to meet you."

He jumped out of the car to help her with her bags from the boot.

"I hope I didn't keep you out too late," he said, slamming the boot shut.

Grace smiled and took her bags from him. She stood beside the car, hoping he might ask her out again, but he turned and got back into car, waving goodbye as he pulled away.

* * *

Grace came back down to the kitchen. The comforting smell of her mother's baking filled the air. Lily had made a fruit cake and some scones.

Jody kicked his boots off at the back door and came into join them. He stood at the sink and washed his hands with a bar of Lifebuoy soap.

"That was a good day's work, Grace. Thanks for the help," he said, rubbing his hands dry on his trouser legs.

"Don't mention it," said Grace.

Lily brought a pot of freshly made tea to the table and pulled out a chair for herself. "Sit down, Jody, and have some tea. I've drawn up a list of things that need to be done around the place. I'll just go over it with you."

The three of them sat down and Lily read the list of jobs from her notepad.

Grace drank her tea and tried to follow what they were saying, but her head was filled with thoughts of Tom, and why he might have called.

18

Grace arrived back at work on Sunday evening after her weekend off, to find a note lying on her bed. One of the girls who shared her room had left it for her. Tom Harrison had phoned, but there was no message, or telephone number. Grace crumpled the piece of paper and threw it in the bin, wondering how she would make contact with him. She had begun to unpack her bag when the phone in the hallway outside the bedroom rang. Grace waited for someone else to get it, but nobody was around. Its shrill ring echoed down the empty corridor and she dropped her bundle of clothes on the bed and hurried to answer it. There was a sound of coins being dropped into a pay-phone. Then the voice on the other end of the line made her jump.

"Hello," she said, trying not to sound too excited

"I was just about to hang up," said Tom.

"There's no one around to answer the phone. I just got back a few minutes ago."

"Can I see you?" He raised his voice over the noise in the background.

"When?" asked Grace.

"Right now?"

"I suppose I could get out for a little while," said Grace, hoping that she didn't sound too available. But it had been three long weeks since he had given her a lift back to work, and she had given up hope of ever seeing him again.

"I'll come and get you right away," he said, and hung up without waiting for an answer.

Grace decided to wait for him outside. She paced the pavement outside the hospital gates and tried to calm the flutters of excitement in her stomach. Within a few minutes he pulled up beside her.

"Where did you ring from?" she asked as he pulled away from the kerb.

"I was just down the road in the pub," he said, looking at her with a smile. "How are you?"

"Fine," replied Grace. "I believe I missed you yesterday."

"What?" he said, with a look of surprise.

"Yesterday? When you called."

"Oh," he said looking back to the road. "She told you I called."

"Actually, I saw your car. Well, I saw the back of

your car as you were driving out."

Tom said nothing. He parked the car and jumped out, hurrying around to open her door.

They were back in the same pub he had brought her to the first night. Grace sat down at the same table, sliding into the banquette against the wall. Tom went up to the bar to order drinks and Grace watched him while he waited to be served. He hadn't asked her what she would like to drink. He stood at the bar jangling change in his pockets, looking very agitated. When he came back to the table he sat across from her and pushed a glass of vodka towards her.

"Thank you," said Grace. "Is something wrong?"

Tom looked at her suspiciously. "No," he said quickly, "why?"

"Well, you seem a bit edgy."

Tom said nothing.

"Aren't you going to tell me why you left so soon yesterday?"

A dark frown spread across his forehead and Grace immediately knew that she had said the wrong thing.

They both sipped their drinks, and said nothing for a few minutes. Tom flipped a beer mat through his fingers nervously. With a sudden jerk he tossed it aside and stood up. Grace thought he was leaving and looked up in surprise. He stared at her for a few seconds, then moved over to her side of the table and sat down on the banquette beside her.

"Did something happen yesterday?" Grace felt confused by his erratic behaviour.

Tom's knee bounced up and down nervously. Then, without warning, he leaned in towards her and kissed her on the lips. When he pulled away, Grace could feel the blood rush to her face and she looked around the pub to see if anyone was looking at them. Tom pulled her face back towards his and kissed her again.

"I have wanted to do that from the first moment I saw you."

Grace felt her heartbeat quicken. To be kissed in such a sudden and impetuous way gave her a rush of excitement.

"We have a problem," he whispered in her ear. "Your mother does not approve of me."

Grace opened her eyes wide and waited for him to continue.

"I called to see you yesterday, Grace, and when I spoke to your mother she told me in no uncertain terms to stay away. It seems that I am too old for you. You're still her little girl, and she's not prepared to lose you just yet, especially to an older layabout like me."

Grace felt embarrassed. "For heaven's sake, I'm eighteen," she said, trying to keep her anger under control.

"Don't be mad with her," said Tom, slipping his arm around her waist. "I probably shouldn't have told you."

"She had no right to say anything to you. Wait till I speak to her. I'm really going to let her have it."

"Now, that will do no good at all." His tone had become serious. "I don't want this to come between the two of you."

Grace looked at him and bit her lip. "What are you saying?"

"I'm saying that I will not be the cause of you falling out with your mother. How about you just don't tell her for a while? After all, you are an adult. She doesn't have to know everything that goes on in your life."

Grace forgot her anger and smiled at him. "You're right," she agreed.

"Just don't say anything to her for the time being. She's only doing what she thinks is the right thing for you." He moved closer. "It will be our secret."

Grace walked back to the hospital that night. She had drunk far too much and needed to get some air before she went back inside. Tom had wanted to drive her, but Grace insisted on walking back alone. Sister Charles loved to roam the corridors of the Nurses' Home at night to see who was keeping late hours. She had even written to some girls' parents expressing her concern about their daughter's social arrangements.

"If we're to keep this secret, we might as well start now," Grace said as they kissed outside the pub.

She walked towards home with a head full of mixed emotions. Tom had made it clear that he liked her and wanted to see her again and she certainly felt the same way. But her happiness was marred by the fact that her mother had tried to spoil it for her. Just because Tom was a few years older, thought Grace bitterly. It occurred to her how hypocritical this was – after all, her own father had been years older than her mother. Grace wished she could pick up the phone straightaway and ask her mother what on earth she thought she was doing? But she couldn't because she had promised Tom not to say anything for the moment. She just hoped that she could keep her mouth shut and her temper under control the next time she went home.

*   *   *

In the weeks that followed Tom's visit, Lily would hold her breath when she heard the sound of a car driving up the lane. At night she lay awake, overcome with feelings of guilt. Even her prayers brought her no solace. Her hours in the library did nothing to relieve the feelings of angst that would seize her suddenly, and send her body into a cold sweat. She knew that sending her son away so callously was unforgivable. But it had been her choice, and she knew she would have to learn to live with it.

19

Lily was sitting on the bus to Dublin. She rested her head against the window and let herself be rocked gently. It would be her first time to see Sarah since she had phoned her about Tom, and she was not looking forward to it. Sarah could be so intrusive with her endless questions. Why, Lily thought, did I involve her?

When they spoke the night before, Lily could tell that Sarah still disapproved of the way she had dealt with the situation. Nothing was said, but Lily knew Sarah well enough to feel her disapproval being transmitted down the telephone line.

Sarah was already sitting at their usual table when Lily arrived. They kissed and Lily arranged her handbag by her chair before sitting down.

"You look well," said Lily.

"Just got the hair done. I'd like to say the same about you – you look very tired," remarked Sarah, jumping in immediately.

"I've had a lot on my mind recently," said Lily wearily. "Let me order some tea before you start the sermon."

"I'm not going to go on about it, Lily. I'm sure you have your reasons. I just don't understand why you felt you had to lie."

Lily beckoned a waitress, and Sarah fell silent as she took their order. When she left, Lily took a deep breath.

"I made a decision not to tell Jim what happened with Stephen. As time went on I regretted that decision, but there was no going back. I feel so ashamed of what I did." Lily could feel her voice begin to break – she swallowed hard and continued. "I couldn't bear to tell Grace how I deceived him. I have to live with the guilt and shame for the rest of my life and that's punishment enough. But I will not tell Grace."

They were both silent while the waitress set the tea and sandwiches on the table.

Sarah sipped her tea and looked at Lily. Her annoyance gave way to sympathy and she reached across to give Lily's hand a tender squeeze.

"Why are you so hard on yourself?"

"Oh, Sarah!" Lily whispered. "I'll go straight to hell for what I've done. I deceived Jim for all of our married life, and now I'm doing the same to Grace."

Lily told Sarah how Tom had come back with flowers for her, and how she had sent him away.

"Was Grace there?"

"No, she was out in the fields helping Jody. She saw his car leaving, but I managed to make up a story."

"And do you think that's the end of him?"

"Yes. Oh Sarah, he looked so hurt! I can't believe it of myself, but I just wanted him gone. I feel so relieved that he won't be back."

Sarah felt shocked but tried not to show it. All her life she had thought she knew Lily inside out, but now she wondered whether she knew her at all. One thing Sarah understood was that Lily had made up her mind on this matter, and there was no use trying to reason with her.

"Is Grace going to join us today?" Sarah changed the subject, knowing she could say no more.

"No, she can't." Lily's mood lightened, with the mention of Grace. "Her social life seems to have taken off – she hasn't been home for three weeks."

Lily would normally be disappointed if Grace chose to stay in Dublin on her days off, but recently she didn't mind at all. It had made things easier that Grace wasn't around the farm, just in case Tom had showed up again. Grace had been pleasantly surprised by her mother's attitude when she had rung for the third time in as many weeks to tell her that she had been invited to another party, and Lily had actually encouraged her to go.

20

Grace's world had been turned upside down with the arrival of Tom. She seemed to spend her time waiting for him to appear, for that is exactly what he did: appeared and then vanished with no talk of when he would be back again. Grace did not have a telephone number for him as he had closed up the house in Greystones, and the electricity and telephone had been turned off. Tom had decided to sell the house and was staying with friends in town. Grace had not met any of his friends. Any time they spent together they were alone. When he dropped her back to the hospital, Grace would try to lead the conversation around to when she would see him again, but he always said the same thing, "I'll be in touch," and with a quick kiss he'd be gone. In the beginning he would always get in touch within a few days, but now she could never tell. It had been two weeks since she had heard from him, and since it was her weekend off she decided to go home rather than face moping around the hospital alone. Grace tried to put on a happy face for her mother, but Lily could tell that something was bothering her.

Suspecting that it had something to do with a boy, she chose her words carefully. Grace had always been guarded when it came to her feelings. One wrong word could sometimes be enough to make her clam up completely.

At breakfast, Lily stood at the cooker and broke some eggs into a pan. She looked across at Grace and smiled.

"I won't have any eggs," said Grace, pulling out a chair.

They ate breakfast and after a few minutes of silence Lily spoke. "You seem out of sorts this weekend. Is everything all right?"

"Of course everything is all right. What are you talking about?" she said, a little too quickly for Lily's liking.

"Well, you just seem a little preoccupied, that's all." Lily started to clear the dishes. Grace was going back later that day, and she was anxious not to end the weekend on a bad note. She watched her mother carry the dishes to the sink. Lying to her on the phone was one thing, but it was quite another when they were face to face. For a split second she considered telling her, but Tom had seemed so adamant that it would be better to do things his way.

"I'm just a bit tired these days," she said, getting up to help. "Things are hectic at work."

* * *

When Grace returned to the hospital that night there was a scrawled note on her locker. Turning it over in her hands she could just about make out the name: *Tom Harrison.*

"Damn it," she said, throwing her bag on the bed. Nobody in the house seemed to be able to take a simple telephone message – it looked as if it had been written with lipstick.

She went down to the kitchen where some of the girls were, but nobody could tell her who had taken the message.

* * *

Several days had passed and she had heard nothing from Tom. Feeling stiff with fatigue she climbed the stairs, after working a twelve-hour shift. All she wanted to do was fall into bed. As she kicked her shoes off, the telephone rang down the hall. Grace let it ring. Even though she knew there was a slight chance it might be Tom, she was too tired to answer it. The house was quiet, and whoever the caller was they were persistent. Grace let it ring out but, as she pulled back the bed sheet, it started to ring again. She heard footsteps in the corridor, and someone answered it.

"Grace!" called a sharp voice down the hall.

Grace stuck her head around the door. One of the nurses from her dorm stood with her hand over the receiver. "It's for you."

Grace ran down the corridor.

"Don't stay on too long," she said, handing her the phone. "Sister is on the warpath – she's giving out about personal phone calls."

Tom's voice sounded cold. "Where have you been?"

"I've been here, working."

"No, you haven't," he said sharply. "I rang you on Friday and you were out and again on Saturday."

"I went home."

There was a faint crackle on the telephone line. She could hear him breathing.

"Tom?"

"I was really disappointed you weren't there."

"But it's been almost three weeks. I thought you weren't going to ring."

"I've been busy. My father is very ill."

"I'm sorry."

"Can you come out tomorrow afternoon?"

"Yes," said Grace, her heart lifting. "I'm off tomorrow."

"I'll pick you up at lunch-time."

*   *   *

Grace spent the entire morning trying on clothes, then pulling them off again. She wanted to look good for him. As the morning progressed and the sun broke through the clouds, she opened the window and the smell of cut grass wafted in from the grounds below. She decided on a light cotton summer dress she had bought recently in Arnotts. It was light blue and had two satin ribbons which tied at the shoulders. It was a simple dress that fitted perfectly and showed off the curves of her slender body. As lunch-time approached she grabbed a cardigan and ran downstairs. As she walked out of the hospital she could see Tom's red car coming down the street towards her. He had rolled back the roof and as they drove away from the hospital Grace prayed that Sister Charles hadn't seen her. As they rounded the corner out of sight, Tom put his hand on her thigh and squeezed it.

"Hello, beautiful!" he shouted over the noise of the engine.

Grace noticed how tired he looked. There were dark circles around his eyes, as if he hadn't slept in weeks.

The car was noisy and they said very little as Tom drove out of town. They stopped at a traffic light and he turned to her, running his hand through her hair. The clips she had put in earlier had blown loose and Grace could feel her hair had turned into a wild mess.

"Where are we going?" she asked as he accelerated again.

They drove through Dun Laoghaire and along the coast road. When they reached the seaside village of Dalkey, he pulled over outside a large building.

Tom stopped the car and leaned over, kissing Grace on the mouth. He ran his hands down her arms, his thumbs stopping briefly over her breasts. Grace felt a shiver of pleasure run through her body.

"Would you like to meet my father?" he whispered.

"Where is he?"

Tom pointed to the grey building. "In there. It's a nursing home."

He got out of the car and went around to open her door. Grace now wished she had worn something different. Feeling self-conscious about her bare shoulders, she grabbed her cardigan and threw it around her. Tom led the way into the building, and they climbed a flight of stairs in silence.

"Don't worry. He won't bite," smiled Tom. "He can't talk since he had his stroke."

They entered a large dimly lit room. There was a tall bay window with heavy drapes that looked out to the sea. Three men sat in the room. Two were playing chess in the corner. The third man was sitting in a wheelchair by the window. Tom nodded in his direction, indicating that this was his father.

They stood beside the wheelchair and the man looked up at Grace. He had a patch over one eye and in his face there was such a look of sadness that Grace found it hard to meet his stare.

"Father, this is Grace. Grace is from Wicklow. She's a nurse." He shouted this quite loudly. The other two men looked over with some interest for a few seconds, then they turned back to their chess game.

Tom gave Grace a gentle push towards his father's chair, and her cardigan fell away from her shoulders as he did. "Isn't she lovely?"

Grace took the man's limp hand, which was resting on his knee, and shook it gently. She felt naked without her cardigan to cover her, but Tom held it in his hands. He went over to the other side of the room and dragged a chair over for Grace. She sat down, still holding the old man's hand. "Pleased to meet you," she said nervously. Tom sat down on the wide windowsill and tapped his fingers underneath it, then he began to whistle softly. He looked from his father to Grace with a wild expression on his face and Grace was sorry she had come.

"Nice place, eh?" said Tom looking around the room.

"Yes," said Grace quietly.

Tom continued to drum his fingers on the underside of the windowsill. Grace wished he would stop. It was making her uncomfortable. The old man didn't seem to notice their presence. He stared over Tom's shoulder towards the sea, his one rheumy eye hardly blinking.

After what seemed like a lifetime, Tom stood up and pulled Grace out of the chair.

"Well, that's it," he said, looking down at his father. "We're going now."

Again the old man gave no indication that he had heard him.

Tom nudged Grace towards the door and broke into a run on his way down the stairs.

They both squinted as they walked out into the sunshine. Grace's arms felt cold after sitting in the room. Even though they had only been there for a few minutes, the gloomy atmosphere had made her skin feel cold. They walked to a low wall beside the car and sat down.

Tom gently draped Grace's cardigan around her shoulders. "Thanks for coming with me. Christ, I hate those visits!"

"It must be difficult for him, not being able to talk any more," said Grace.

Tom exhaled deeply and looked at the ground. "We never got along."

Grace could see that the visit had upset him. "He looks sad."

"He is sad. He's going to die soon." Tom shuddered as if he had thought of something frightening, and stood up. "Let's have some lunch. I'm starving," he said, taking Grace's hand.

They got back into the car and drove to Greystones.

As they pulled into the village, Grace tugged at Tom's sleeve to get his attention. "Where are we going now?"

"I've had an idea. How about a picnic?" Tom pulled up beside a row of shops, and jumped out of the car. "Back in a minute," he said and disappeared into a grocery shop.

A few minutes later he came out carrying a bag of food.

"Do you mind if we go up to the house? I've been meaning to get up to it for weeks. It needs to be aired."

The gates of Westfield were closed as they approached. Tom stopped the car and got out. He opened the lock on the gates and pushed them open, flattening the large clumps of weeds that had grown up around them. The narrow tree-lined driveway that led to the house had been neglected, and the early summer growth sprouted masses of nettles that grew up through the gravel.

Tom parked outside the front door and got out of the car. Grace followed carrying the grocery bag. The house looked large and silent, all the shutters closed tightly as if it were sleeping. They stood in the porch and Tom fumbled through a set of keys until he found the right one and opened the front door. They stepped into the dark hallway.

"Wait here," said Tom.

He went into the room at the front of the house. Grace heard him open the shutters and a beam of light lit up a narrow strip of the hall. They went from room to room opening the shutters and windows. Grace thought the house was elegant. Most of the furnishings were covered with white dustsheets, but the few pieces she could see hinted at a splendour that her own home had never possessed. She noticed the huge empty vases that stood in each room, and imagined a time when they were full of flowers arranged in graceful bouquets.

Downstairs in the kitchen the air was musty. Tom took the shopping bag from Grace and emptied the contents on to the table. There was a loaf of bread, a few slices of ham and a bottle of wine. He entered a small pantry and ran his hand over the lintel of the back door until he found a key, then leaning his weight against the door he put the key in the lock and turned it slowly until he heard a click. He pulled the back door open, and a shaft of dust motes floated through the light that spread across the kitchen floor. The day had grown hotter and the back door felt warm to the touch.

"Now let's get to work – you make the sandwiches, and I'll open this," he said, rummaging through a drawer for a corkscrew. "I forgot to buy butter, so we'll have to rough it."

Grace found a knife and began to put the ham between the slices of bread. She opened some cupboards until she found the crockery. Then she piled the sandwiches on to a plate and followed Tom out to the garden. He eased himself onto a low granite bench, and rested his head against the wall behind him. Grace sat beside him and put the plate of sandwiches on the ground.

"I'm afraid it's a bit warm," he said, handing her a tumbler of wine.

They sat and ate, listening to the wood pigeons cooing in the trees at the end of the garden, and farther away the crashing of waves on the cliffs below.

After eating, they both leaned back against the warm wall. Grace tilted her head towards the sun. Tom poured the last of the wine and settled close to her.

"I'm glad you came with me today. I don't suppose I'll see this place again. You've helped me say goodbye. I spoke to an auctioneer this week. He thinks he's got a buyer for it."

"It's such a beautiful house. You must be sad to see it go."

Tom gave a sort of laugh. "Not really. It was never a very happy house."

Grace waited for him to continue, but he lifted his face to the sun again and closed his eyes. She looked at him and ran her hand along the side of his shirtsleeve.

"I'm glad I came too," she said softly, kissing his cheek.

Tom turned and kissed her, opening his mouth against hers. He ran his hand along her leg, under her dress until it reached the top of her thigh. He stroked her between the legs and Grace gasped, pulling him closer. Tom stopped and looked at her, then he stood up, took her hand and led her inside. They climbed the stairs together, Grace feeling warm and drowsy from the wine. Tom held her hand and led her gently into a room that they had not gone into earlier. The shutters were still closed and they walked slowly towards the windows, Grace holding his hand tightly as he led her around the furniture in the dark. Tom opened the shutters to let some light into the room, and then he pulled a white dustsheet from the large bed. He pulled Grace down on it beside him. Grace had never had sex before; she had never been with anyone special enough and wanted to wait until she was married. But Tom was special, and as she felt his breath on her neck all thoughts of waiting abandoned her. He ran his hands over the shoulder straps of her dress and untied them. The front of the dress fell down to her waist. Grace felt him stop suddenly, and mistaking his hesitation for shyness, she unhooked her bra and placed his hand on her breast.

He looked away and swallowed. "This isn't right," he said quietly.

"Yes, it is. It feels right," pleaded Grace, not wanting him to stop now.

He turned back to her and kissed her roughly, pushing her down on to the bed. He pushed her dress down further and undid his trousers with trembling fingers. He searched between her legs frantically, and entered her so quickly that Grace had to bite her lip to stop herself from screaming. It was over in seconds.

As soon as he had finished, Tom stood up and turned away from Grace as he fixed his trousers.

"Better get going," he mumbled.

Grace lay on the bed in a daze, confused by Tom's sudden rush to get away. The top half of her body was still naked and she pulled at her dress to cover herself.

When he left the room she sat up and smoothed her dress down over her thighs, then pulled the straps over her shoulders and tied them. Although it was her first time, she knew it shouldn't have been like that. Her feet dangled over the side of the bed and she heard banging downstairs as Tom closed the shutters. He appeared at the door a few minutes later, smiling casually as if nothing had happened.

"Ready?" he said moving towards the window.

Grace stood up. "Tom?"

He looked around at her.

"Was it all right?" she asked, looking at the floor, trying not to sound foolish.

Tom pulled the shutter closed, leaving them in darkness. "Yes, of course," he said, with a slight tone of irritation in his voice. "It's my fault . . . we should have done it somewhere else," he muttered. "This was my mother's room."

They said very little on their journey back to Dublin. The sun had gone in and the air had become damp and chilly. Tom put the roof back on the car and Grace pulled her cardigan around her for warmth. When they got to the gates of the hospital, he pulled in but left the engine running. He leaned over and kissed her lightly on the cheek. "Be in touch," he said with a smile.

Grace stood at the side of the road with a look of bewilderment of her face as he pulled away.

21

A week dragged by before Grace heard from Tom again. Each day seemed like a lifetime, waiting for the telephone to ring, checking the phone table and her bedside locker for messages that might have been taken, but nothing was. As each day passed, Grace began to feel cheap and foolish. She had given herself to him without knowing the first thing about his life. He had told her he was staying with some friends in Ballsbridge, but he had never brought her there. He was always very busy, yet he didn't appear to have a job.

When he finally rang, Grace was getting ready for work, trying to pin her hair under her white cap, a task she always found impossible. When she heard her name being called in the corridor she threw the cap onto her bed, and rushed out. Tom's voice filled her with a rush of happiness. Breathing a silent sigh of relief, she allowed her misgivings to vanish.

"How are you?"

"Great!" gushed Grace.

"How about a day out tomorrow? Actually a day and night. My friends are having a party at the flat in Ballsbridge. Will you come?"

Grace felt a weight lifting from her. An introduction to his friends meant that he must be getting serious.

"I'm working tomorrow," she said, panicking that she would put him off. "But, I'll be free at seven," she added quickly.

He thought for a few seconds. "We'll just have to forget about the day then. I'll pick you up at eight?"

"Yes. I'll wait outside."

"Look forward to it," he said, and to her annoyance he hung up before she could ask any questions.

Grace walked back to her room. She picked up the cap and started to pin her hair up again. He's just taking things slowly, she thought. All the doubts she'd had about him during the week seemed silly now. He was older and more experienced, she told herself. He'd probably had lots of girlfriends before her. Grace stared at her reflection in the mirror and decided she would have to be more sophisticated around him. The last thing she wanted to do was scare him off with her eagerness.

*   *   *

The following evening Grace was exhausted. Her shoulders ached – lifting patients from beds to wheelchairs was taking its toll on her back. Standing under the shower she let the hot water massage her muscles, giving her immediate relief. After that came the hard part. What to wear. Tom had given her no idea what kind of party it was. Grace decided on the same dress she had worn the last day she had seen him. It was what she looked best in, and it was the only thing in her wardrobe that was clean. The chilly evening air made her shiver as she stepped outside and she wondered if she should run back inside and change into jeans, but she could see Tom's car parked on the other side of the road. Her stomach tightened with excitement as she made her way across the road, all the time telling herself not to appear too eager. Grace eased herself into the car and Tom leaned over and kissed her.

"Let's have a drink on our own first," he said, kissing her again.

They drove to a rather gloomy-looking hotel in Dun Laoghaire. Tom parked outside and looked up at the blinking neon sign outside the door.

"Bit of a dump," he said looking at Grace. "Will I find somewhere else?"

"It's fine," said Grace, anxious to be alone with

him. "We won't be staying long."

They walked into the hotel and sat in a quiet corner by the window.

"Who's having the party?" she asked.

"It's Robert, the guy I've been staying with. I was in college with him, and he's been kind enough to let me stay at his flat while I sell the house."

"What did you do at college?"

"Accountancy," he said, pulling a face. "Very boring."

"Is that what you work at now?" Grace sat back, aware that she was firing too many questions at him.

"Not really. My father's family owned a paper mill, which has just about run itself into the ground. I'm winding it up at the moment."

"What are you going to do then?"

"Don't really know. My grandparents had some business interests in England that need looking after now that Father is ill. I will have to go over there at some stage." He lifted his glass. "Anyway, enough about my affairs – how have you been?" He leaned over and ran the back of his hand along her arm. "I've been looking forward to seeing you all week."

Grace smiled and sipped her drink, trying to look demure. If only he knew how many times she had rushed to answer the phone in the hope it would be his voice on the other end. A faint smile crossed her face, when she thought of all the praying she had done during the week, making deals with God so that Tom would ring.

He ordered more drinks.

"Have you said anything to your mother?"

"No," said Grace, pouncing on the opportunity to discuss the problem. "I really don't see why you're so worried about her. She'd come around, I know she would." Grace thought it was kind of him to think about her mum, but she'd have to be told sooner or later.

"Let's just leave it another while," he said tetchily. Suddenly his face became dark and troubled.

"It's good of you to think of her," said Grace, reaching across for his hand.

Tom stared into his glass, thoughtfully. He knocked back his drink and set his glass down on the table. "We'd better go," he said, standing up.

Grace looked at him. "Did I say something wrong?"

His mood had changed. It had happened several times before. He would suddenly become sullen for no reason at all.

"No," he said pulling on his jacket. "I just don't want to be late."

Grace almost had to run to keep up with him as they left the hotel.

They sat into the car and he put his arm around her.

"Sorry, I've got a lot on my mind right now. Maybe we'll skip the party." He kissed her neck and ran his hand along her leg and under her dress.

Grace pulled away and stopped him from going any further. "Let's go to the party for a while. I'd like to meet your friends." She straightened up in her seat.

He shrugged his shoulders. "It's up to you," he said, and started the car.

* * *

Robert's flat was in a large redbrick house on Lansdowne Road. The house had been divided into several flats, and they lived in the basement. Grace could hear the sound of the Rolling Stones as they walked down the steps to the front door.

It wasn't much of a party. There were about twenty people in the living-room, most of them sitting on the floor in small groups. Grace had never been around people who took drugs before, but she guessed that the pungent smell coming from the smoke-filled room was probably hash. A tall stringy-looking guy with wild matted hair came up to them.

"Grace, this is Robert."

Robert swayed slightly like a tree about to fall and put his arm around Tom's shoulders. "Hiya, Grace," he grinned.

A girl wearing a tie-dyed smock and a matching scarf around her head came running towards them. With slow intimate movements she put her arms around Tom's neck, as if she were about to dance with him.

"Tom, baby, where have you been?" she said, kissing him on the mouth.

"Here and there," he mumbled, turning to Grace. "Grace, this is Daphne."

The girl kept her arms around Tom's neck and nodded curtly at Grace. Then she started to pull Tom towards the opposite end of the room.

"Guess what, Norman's in the kitchen – he has something for you," she said with a girlish giggle.

Tom looked back at Grace with a helpless look on his face. "Back in a minute. Get yourself a drink." He pointed towards a table with some bottles of wine on it.

They left the room. Grace stood on her own and looked around self-consciously. Robert had moved over to some people in the far corner who were sitting cross-legged, nodding their heads to the blaring music.

Grace made her way over to the drinks table, and casually poured herself a large glass of red wine. Leaning against the table she gulped the wine, hoping that Tom would come back. When she finished, she poured another glass and looked around. There were two girls sitting on a couch in the corner.

Grace gripped her glass and walked over. In an effort not to appear too nervous, she forced a wide smile and sat down beside them. One of them was rolling a joint. Grace sat back as far as she could, not wanting to stare at what the girl was doing. From her place on the couch she could look around without seeming too conspicuous. She observed the other girls and saw how different and cool they looked. They were all wearing flared jeans with patches and woven belts. The girl beside her wore a T-shirt with an American flag shaped like a hand with two fingers raised in a peace sign.

Grace wished she had done what Tom had suggested and skipped the party. Instead, she stuck out like a sore thumb in her little sundress. I might as well have 'country training nurse' stamped on my forehead, she thought miserably.

The girl beside her offered her the joint. Grace looked at it, dumbly. Then realising that she couldn't possibly refuse, she took it between her fingers and took a tiny pull. The last thing she wanted to do was have a fit of coughing. After the third or fourth pull, she started to inhale little by little. The girl beside her gave her a nudge, and nodded to the joint.

Grace jumped and handed it back to her.

"Pretty good weed, eh?"

"Yes," said Grace, returning her smile. The girl's eyes were completely bloodshot. Within minutes Grace began to feel the effects of the joint. Her eyelids felt heavy and her mouth tasted stale and dry. She wanted to get up and find Tom, but her legs felt too heavy to carry her. She tried to strike up a conversation with the girl rolling the joints, but each attempt from Grace was met with a glassy-eyed vacant stare from the girl.

Almost an hour later, Robert came over and threw himself on to the couch between Grace and the joint girl.

"Where the fuck is Tom?" he asked, looking around.

Grace shrugged her shoulders politely.

"He's still in the kitchen, the bastard! Go on in and get him." He pointed to the door. Grace plucked up the confidence to stand up and walk out the door. Paranoia had set in and she felt as if everyone was looking at her dress. Earlier it had looked out of place, now she thought it seemed downright hideous. When she opened the door into the kitchen, the room was grey with smoke, and she could hardly make out where Tom was. There were about ten people sitting around a big wooden table, all of them laughing uproariously. As Grace moved closer they stopped laughing and looked at her.

"Hi," she almost whispered, scanning the table to find Tom. Then she recognised the giggling girl who had pulled him out of the room. They were sitting at the end of the table. The girl was sitting on his knee. Tom pushed her off and stood up.

"Grace, did you get a drink?"

"Yes."

Everyone looked at her. Grace saw lines of

powder set out in the middle of the table.

Daphne caught her eye and nodded to the powder. "Want some?"

"No," said Tom, moving towards Grace. "We've got to get going."

"Got to get Cinderella home before midnight," said Daphne, shooting a scornful look at Grace.

"Cut it out, Daph," said Tom curtly. He took Grace by the hand and left the room. When they walked into the other room, the joint girl was sitting on Robert's knee playing with his hair. The needle of the record player had got stuck on a Jimi Hendrix song, but no one seemed to notice.

Tom looked around. "Had enough?" His eyes darted about nervously.

Grace nodded her head and walked out past him.

They got into the car and he started the engine.

"Where to?" he asked.

"Home. I'm working tomorrow," Grace replied sharply.

Tom drove towards the hospital, saying nothing. Grace looked straight ahead, too annoyed to talk.

When they approached St Stephen's Green, Tom slowed down and turned the car into a quiet lane. It was a short narrow laneway with gates at the end, which were closed. They could go no further. Tom stopped the car and turned off the engine.

They sat there, saying nothing, until the silence became unbearable.

223

"You were the one that wanted to go to the bloody party!" he suddenly shouted. "I said let's skip it, but you were so determined to meet my friends." He stopped, and lowered his voice "Well, *now* you've met them, aren't they charming?" His eyes seemed to look right through her, and his tone became aggressive again as he continued, "Well, say something!"

Grace could see that this was turning into a drunken argument. "Bring me back to the hospital, please," she said quietly.

"No," he said, "not yet."

Another long silence followed.

Grace sat stiffly and stared at a mark on the windscreen. After a few minutes had passed, Tom placed his hand lightly on her shoulder as if he expected her to shrug it off.

She placed a hand on top of his. "Please, Tom, I just want to get back."

Tom leaned over and rested his head on her shoulder. "I'm sorry I was so rude."

"Forget it. Just bring me back to the hospital. I'm exhausted."

"A few more minutes," he whispered. He ran his hands through his hair and rubbed his eyes vigorously with closed fists. Then he turned to look at Grace, and for a moment she thought he was going to cry.

"You look so beautiful," he said.

Grace shook her head and tried to smile. "I don't

understand you," she whispered.

"Grace, I'm sorry. I was a complete pig tonight and I'm sorry. I've done something terrible. I've started something that is so wrong." He looked at her and Grace could feel a sense of panic well up inside her. "We can't see each other any more," he said, putting his hands on the steering wheel.

Grace bit her lip and tried not to cry, but as soon as she tried to speak she lost control. "Why?" was all she could manage to say.

"Because it's not right. Trust me, Grace. I'm no good for you."

"But I love you!" she said in a strangled high-pitched cry.

Tom shut his eyes tightly.

Realising how foolish she sounded, Grace tried to pull herself together. She took a deep breath through her nose and blinked quickly to stop the flow of her tears. She leaned in towards Tom and put her arms around his neck. Then she moved closer and kissed the side of his face while Tom remained rigid.

Her head felt foggy after smoking the joints and she knew that she should insist on him driving her back, but the thought of never seeing him again made her feel so desperate. Her arms felt dull and heavy as she tried to pull him closer to her.

Tom slowly turned his face to hers. She could feel his warm breath on her forehead. They kissed and she could feel the dark mood that had hung over him all night begin to lift. He buried his face in the dark curls that fell around her shoulders and sighed loudly. They kissed again and their passion overtook the feeling of anger and doubt that had pervaded just minutes earlier. Reaching across her lap, he pulled a lever that made her seat recline slowly.

Grace lay back and allowed him to climb over on top of her. This was wrong, she knew it was, but if it was the only way to keep him then she was prepared to surrender tonight.

"Forgive me, Grace," muttered Tom as they made love.

Grace felt weak, as if she were drifting in and out of a sleep. It was all happening in slow motion. When it was over, both of them lay still. The sounds of their breathing seemed to fill the car. Neither of them moved for a few minutes. Grace felt crushed with the full weight of Tom on top of her and her arms lay around his waist like lead weights, but she lay perfectly still, wanting the moment to last as long as possible. She slid her hand up to the back of his neck to pull him closer, but he immediately pushed himself away from her. Then lifting one leg over the gear-stick and then the other, he moved back onto his own seat and did his trousers up. He leaned over and put her seat upright again, and without meeting her gaze reached across and pulled her dress back down over her knees. Then he started the car and reversed back out on to the road.

22

Grace hated nursing more and more every day. She had no idea what had made her choose such a career and it was beginning to become apparent that she was not cut out for it. She was pulled up twice about her negligence at work. The first time it happened was when Sister Charles discovered that she had inserted an intravenous drip into the muscle of a patient instead of a vein. Grace had been summoned to Sister Charles' office and given a good talking to by the irate nun. In the days that followed Sister Charles was like a hawk, watching everything Grace did with her beady eyes. That was how she happened to catch Grace administering the wrong dose of morphine to an elderly patient. Just as Grace lifted the syringe to the old woman's arm, Sister Charles appeared from behind the partition curtain, as if by magic. Her white papery hand swooped down and snatched the syringe from Grace. Holding it level with her eyes, she looked at the dosage, and then threw Grace a murderous look. Placing it neatly back on the surgical trolley by the bed, she said, "Please follow me," and with a whip of her veil she was gone.

Grace felt her stomach turn over and she rushed behind trying to keep up. They went into her office at the end of the corridor and the Sister closed the door behind them.

"Sit," she commanded.

Grace eased herself down into a chair.

Sister Charles sat down and glared at Grace, her glassy blue eyes glinting with anger.

"Your work had been less than satisfactory of late, and that is not good enough. You are training to be a nurse, to care for the sick, and you are not doing a good job. What have you got to say about it?" She sat back in her chair and fiddled with the string of rosary beads which were attached to a cord around her waist.

"I'm very sorry, Sister. It won't happen again," said Grace dolefully.

"Well, it cannot happen again because the chances are that you will *kill* someone. Do you realise the importance of your job? Silly mistakes cannot be tolerated in this hospital, and neither can the nurses that make them. *Do you understand?"*

"Yes, Sister."

"Very well, get back to work, and have Nurse Kelly administer that woman's morphine. There are beds to be made up in St Brendan's ward."

Grace walked away from the office towards the linen room feeling miserable. She didn't care about being reprimanded – they could fire her for all she cared. What really worried her was that Tom hadn't been in touch for weeks. There had been no contact since the night of the party. Every time Grace thought about having sex in his car, she felt sick inside. She knew she should have insisted on him taking her home, but he had seemed so lost and genuinely contrite about how he had treated her that evening, it had made her want him more.

That evening Grace lay on her bed, willing the phone to ring. The sun came through the window blinds throwing lines of warm yellow stripes down her arm. In her hand she clutched a paper bag, containing a pregnancy test that she had robbed from the hospital stores. Her period was two weeks late. Her fear of being pregnant had stopped her doing the test for the past few days, but she knew it was time to find out. She couldn't put it off for much longer. Dragging herself from the bed, she took the test and pushed it up her sleeve, in case she met anyone on the way to the toilet.

A few minutes later she stood staring at it in horror. She had dropped the stick onto the floor of the toilet as if it had burnt her. Then hoping she had imagined it, she picked it up and examined it again. The line had appeared in the positive box. Pregnant.

Grace walked back to her room and stuffed the pregnancy test into the back of her locker. Her room was on the third floor of the nurses' house, and she went to the window and pushed it open. The drop to the ground below looked deep enough if she could bring herself to jump. She leaned out and let her waist rest on the windowsill. In seconds she could be sprawled on the ground below, her skull smashed and no one would ever know. Her mother would be spared the disgrace of having a daughter pregnant outside of wedlock. Grace let the top half of her body pull her further out of the window. The blood rushed to her head and she grew giddy knowing that with one small push it would all be over. But she did not have the nerve to make that final leap. Slowly she straightened and drew back inside the room, slamming the window shut.

Behind her locker in an empty suitcase was a bottle of vodka. Grace marched over and pulled it out. Ever since Tom's disappearance, she had missed the drinking that she had done with him. Not just the company and the social aspect – she had actually missed the taste of the alcohol. After the first few days of waiting for Tom's call, Grace had bought a bottle of vodka and spent her evenings alone, sipping from the bottle waiting for the phone to ring. She unscrewed the lid of the half empty bottle and, putting it to her lips, swallowed as much as her stomach would allow.

* * * *

Lily began to worry that something was wrong. She had phoned several times, but Grace was always too busy to talk. It had been six weeks since her last visit home. Lily lifted the phone one evening and dialled the nurses' home, just as Grace happened to be passing the telephone. Grace recognised her mother's voice immediately and went silent for a few seconds.

"Grace, is that you?"

Grace tried to gather her thoughts quickly; she couldn't face going home just yet. Tom would never try to contact her there, so she tried to manufacture another excuse that would sound plausible. "Yes, it's me. Sorry, I didn't recognise your voice."

"Well, I'm not surprised; it's been so long. Are you coming home this weekend?"

"I was going to ring you later." Grace tried to muster up the enthusiasm for another lie. "The girls are going to a dance and I said I'd go with them. Would you mind if I stayed here?"

"Whatever you like," said Lily sharply. "You will try to fit me in sometime soon?"

Grace tried to be light-hearted. "Of course, Mum.

I'm sorry. It's just that there seems to be something on every week."

"It's all right," said Lily softening up. "Promise you'll come down soon?"

"Promise," said Grace, putting down the phone.

Lily smiled to herself as she hung up. Perhaps she was feeling a little bit jealous of her daughter. Young pretty girls did not want to spend their time off sitting about farmhouses with their widowed mothers, and she knew she would have to get used to it.

Grace hung up and walked back to her room and wondered how long she could continue to hide it.

Deciding some air would do her good, she pulled on a pair of flat shoes and set out along the canal in the direction of Baggot Street. As she walked along the road, she tried to think of how she was going to tell her mother. If only Tom would ring, she knew she could persuade him that they could sort things out. Tom would be shocked at first, but she knew that they could make a go of it together.

Grace walked aimlessly along the path until her legs grew tired. As she approached a bend in the road, she slowed down and looked at the row of tall Georgian houses ahead of her. It was where she had gone to the party with Tom. All of the houses looked the same, and Tom's car was not parked outside any of them, but Grace remembered that the front door of the flat had been blue. Walking by each house slowly, she noticed that only one basement had a blue door. Grace gripped the wrought-iron spikes of the garden gate, and without allowing herself any time to think, she pushed it open and walked up the narrow garden path and down the steps to the flat. There was no bell so she made a fist and knocked on the small glass pane in the front door.

The breeze felt cold in the shade, and she stepped back into the sunshine while she waited for someone to answer. There was a sound within, and a few seconds later the blurry contours of a face appeared through the thick glass pane.

The door opened a crack and Tom's friend Robert stood there wearing only a pair of jeans. His hair was fuzzy and knotted and he gave a long chesty cough as he stepped out into the daylight. He put his hand up to shield his eyes from the sun and looked at Grace. He smelt like a mixture of stale smoke and sleep.

"What time is it?" he asked hoarsely.

Grace looked at her watch. "Two o'clock."

His eyes opened a little wider as he got used to the sunlight. "You got a ciggie?"

Grace shook her head. "Is Tom here?" She looked over Robert's shoulder as she spoke, trying to see if anyone else was inside.

Robert jerked his head back suddenly. "Ahh, now I remember you," he said smiling. "He brought you to the party."

"Yes, is he here?" she asked again rather quickly, not wanting to dwell on that night.

"Wish he was," said Robert shaking his head. "But he's split, and left some people pretty pissed off."

"Why?" asked Grace trying to hide her dismay.

"He owes people money all over the place. You know his old man died two weeks ago?"

Grace felt a swell of disappointment rising up inside her. "Died?"

"Yeah. He sold the house in Greystones and next thing I know he's done a runner. He owes me six months' rent. I don't know what he's playing at. All I know is that he's left a lot of bad debts behind him." Robert moved over to the windowsill and sat down. "Sure you don't have any fags?"

Grace ignored him. "Do you know where he went?"

"Nope," he shook his head. "My guess is that he went over to his grandparents' place in England, and no one seems to know where that is."

Robert opened his mouth and yawned loudly.

"You don't have any address?" she asked faintly.

"Nothing."

Grace stood, frozen to the spot as she tried to make sense of what he had just said.

"Listen," said Robert seriously, "it's none of my business, but you seem like a nice girl. Too nice for him. Take my advice and forget about him."

Grace stiffened. "What do you mean?"

"He's bad news."

"What are you trying to say?" asked Grace impatiently.

Robert cracked his knuckles and thought for a moment. "Tom is engaged to some girl in England. At least that's what he told me when he came to stay. He was selling up here to go back and get married."

Grace felt beads of perspiration begin to form on her forehead.

"Ah shit!" exclaimed Robert. "I'm sorry to be the one to tell you."

"No, it's all right," said Grace, turning to go. "Thank you."

As she walked up the garden path to the gate, Robert shouted after her, "He was full of shit! You're better off without him!"

Grace raised her hand in a wave without looking back at him, and walked away from the house as fast as she could.

When she got back, the dorm was quiet. She crawled into bed feeling miserable, and slept for a few hours. It was eight o'clock when she woke. Without getting out of bed she dragged her suitcase over and felt around until she found the bottle of vodka. Then she opened it under the covers and drank what remained of it. The telephone rang several times, and every time she held her breath in the hope that it was Tom, but she knew in her heart he would not be ringing again.

23

On her next visit home Grace knew she would have to say something. She had now missed two periods, and her waist had begun to thicken slightly. Jody was waiting for her as the bus pulled into Wicklow town. He filled her in on what was happening around the farm as they drove towards the house. Lily rushed out to the yard when she heard the sound of the engine. She beamed as she saw Grace emerge from the car, but as Grace stood out into the bright daylight Lily's smile vanished. As she got closer Lily could see how gaunt Grace looked, the dark circles around her eyes looking like bruises.

"You look so tired," she said as she kissed her daughter's face.

"I am a bit," said Grace wearily as she pulled a bag over her shoulder and walked towards the house.

Lily looked at Jody and he nodded his head towards Grace. "Working her too hard up there," he commented.

That night Grace had a bath and went to bed, saying an early night was all she needed. The next morning she still looked as bad. Standing in front of the mirror in her bedroom Grace smoothed down the thick jumper she was wearing. There had been a late spell of warm autumn sunshine and she had already started to sweat in the prickly wool. She stood sideways and wondered if the weight she had gained around her tummy was obvious to anyone else. Giving her jumper one final pull, Grace left her room and walked down to the kitchen.

"Good morning," smiled Lily, putting a large plate of eggs and sausages on the table.

Grace stared at the plate and felt her stomach heave.

"Morning, Mum," she said, pushing the plate away from her. "I think I'll just have some toast."

Lily frowned but said nothing; she knew that fussing over Grace brought out the worst in her.

"Would you like to come into town with me?" she asked, as she folded some clothes at the kitchen table.

Grace smiled weakly. "I think I'll just stay here."

"Do that," said Lily brightly. "Why don't you pull a chair out into the sun and relax. I'll be back to make some lunch at about one."

Grace watched Lily leave with great relief. Trying to pretend that nothing was wrong had worn her out. Grabbing the back of a kitchen chair she pulled it out to the back yard into the sun and sat down. The watery autumn sunshine warmed her and she tilted her head towards the sky and tried to think of what she would say to her mother. Whatever she chose to say, it would have to be done today. She couldn't go back to Dublin tomorrow without telling her. The more she thought about it, the angrier she became. If her mother hadn't interfered and run Tom off, things might have turned out differently. Grace began to feel sick. The sun had made her nauseous. She got up and went back to her bedroom. The curtains were still closed and she lay on her bed in the half-light and felt an overwhelming sense of exhaustion.

She woke with a start when she heard Lily's key in the front door. The clock beside her bed read one thirty, which meant she had been asleep for two hours. Trying to shake herself into wakefulness, she brushed her hair and went into the bathroom. The pillow had left a deep furrow down one side of her cheek and she splashed cold water on her face to make her feel more alert. Then she went downstairs to face her mother.

Lily unpacked the grocery bags and started to wash some lettuce leaves.

"Did you sleep?"

"Yes, a little," murmured Grace.

"Well, you look much better after it. Rest is what you need. It's a pity you can't stay for a few more days."

Grace set the table and tried to concentrate on what Lily was saying, but her thoughts were miles away. Lily stopped talking and looked at Grace with raised eyebrows, waiting for an answer to a question Grace hadn't heard.

"Well?" asked Lily.

Grace dropped the cutlery on to the table and without turning she hung her head and said, "I'm pregnant."

Lily fell silent. She walked over to where Grace was standing.

"What?"

Grace could hear the shock in her mother's voice. She turned around and took a deep breath. "I'm pregnant." She felt numb as the words tumbled from her mouth. Hearing herself saying it aloud made her more aware of her terrible situation.

Lily's hand shot up to her cheek and she took a step backwards, as if Grace had struck her.

"I'm sorry, Mum." Grace cast her eyes downwards in shame.

Lily straightened up and cleared her throat. "Who is the father?"

Grace stared at the floor.

Lily's voice hardened. "Who is he?"

"Tom Harrison." Grace kept her eyes averted and didn't see the look of terror that crossed her mother's face at that second.

"Oh, Jesus!" whispered Lily.

Grace couldn't hold back her tears any longer. "He's gone!" she cried.

"Gone where?" asked Lily flatly.

"He didn't say. England maybe. No one seems to know." Grace put her hands over her face and tried to stop crying.

Lily felt a tear roll down her cheek. "Does he know about this?"

Grace shook her head.

Lily pulled a piece of tissue from her sleeve and wiped her eyes. "This is my fault. I should never have sent him away," she said to herself, as if there was no one in the room.

Grace grabbed the back of the kitchen chair she was leaning on and slammed it into the table. "Why did you have to interfere? It was none of your business!" she cried.

Lily jumped. "I was trying to protect you."

"I am old enough to protect myself. Things could have been different. He might still be here if you'd stayed out of it, but instead we had to sneak around and lie to you!"

The tears ran down Lily's face, as she tugged and pulled at the raggy piece of tissue with a wild look of confusion in her eyes.

"I hate you!" shouted Grace.

Lily moved towards her and put a hand on her shoulder, but Grace shrugged it off and walked away.

"I'm going for a walk," she said and slammed the kitchen door behind her.

"Dear God," whispered Lily as she sank into a chair, "what have I done?"

* * *

Grace did not come down for dinner that evening. The following morning they ate their breakfast together in silence. Eventually Lily put down her knife and fork.

"What are you going to do?"

Grace pushed her food around her plate. "I'll work for as long as I can, then I don't know."

"I'll help you. Come back home when you're ready, and I'll help you in any way I can." Lily knew exactly how desperate Grace was feeling. The very least she could do now was make sure that her own daughter didn't experience the same hardship that she had during her first pregnancy. That the child she had been carrying all those years ago was the father of Grace's baby made Lily's skin crawl with fear.

A tear rolled slowly down Grace's cheek. "I don't want to have a baby," she sniffed.

Lily rushed to where Grace was sitting and put her arms around her. "It'll be all right. I'll mind you, and I'll mind the baby as well."

Grace put her head on Lily's shoulder and cried at her mother's reassuring words. She had been prepared for an argument, for insults and accusations, and in a way it would have been easier. But instead her mother's kindness had disarmed her. Grace felt an immense weariness descend on her. All the anger she had felt towards her mother yesterday had gone. The blame lay with her, Grace, and nobody else.

24

As Christmas approached, Grace could no longer hide her pregnancy. She had had to get a larger size uniform and already she could feel the middle getting tighter every day. Trying to conceal her swollen tummy was getting more difficult, and she hadn't got the energy to get her through a working day or night. Sister Charles seemed unusually sympathetic when Grace told her she would not be returning after the Christmas holidays. The nun opened her mouth slightly and her long yellow teeth rested on her lower lip, giving the impression of a forced smile. There were no questions or earnest requests to perhaps make Grace change her mind, and she wished her luck in whatever she might do in the future.

But as soon as Grace left the office, Sister Charles

reached for her telephone directory and ran her finger down the column of F's until she came to Fortune. Lily was cleaning the kitchen windows when she heard the telephone ringing.

"Mrs Fortune?"

"Yes, this is she."

"This is Sister Charles."

"Hello, Sister," said Lily, bracing herself for an interrogation.

"Grace has just been to see me, and I must say I'll be very sorry to see her go."

"It's very kind of you to ring, Sister, but I'm afraid Grace has made up her mind that nursing is not for her."

"Yes, I must say her unhappiness has been reflected in her work of late." An inquisitive note had crept into her voice. "Have you noticed that Grace seems a little depressed?"

Lily swallowed hard, giving herself time to think. "I think she's just tired, Sister."

Sister Charles hesitated slightly and then said, "This is difficult to say, Mrs Fortune, but I think you should know that Grace has been drinking. In fact, I think she may have a problem. I feel it's my duty to tell you, even though she is leaving us."

"What do you mean?"

"I have found bottles in her locker in the past. I didn't say anything. I may be a nun, but I have a pretty good idea what the girls get up to during their time off; they're only human after all. But with Grace it's different. Her drinking seems to be constant, and I strongly suspect that she has come to work under the influence of alcohol. To be perfectly honest, Mrs Fortune, it's for the best that she is leaving."

Lily stood rooted to the spot. Speechless.

"Thank you, Sister," said Lily after a few seconds, and hung up without saying goodbye.

The walls seemed to move towards her as she stood alone in the hall and she realised that this was not the end. Her lies had not lain dormant over the years. They had grown and festered and now her daughter was paying the price.

Christmas was miserable. Grace was constantly grumpy and made no effort to hide it. She wouldn't do any of the things that they normally loved to do together in the run-up to Christmas. They had always picked holly from the lane and made wreaths to hang on the gateposts, but Grace moped around the house and let Lily make them alone.

When Jody dragged in the Christmas tree and positioned it in the usual corner, Grace had gone upstairs complaining of a headache and left Lily to decorate it on her own. Lily pulled the string of silver bells from the box that Jody had fetched down from the attic and threw them carelessly around the tree. It was a ritual that she and Grace had always enjoyed, and without her it was just another chore. Lily heard footsteps on the stairs and she turned in time to see Grace walk through the hall.

"I'm going for a walk!" shouted Grace. Then the front door slammed behind her.

Lily had not mentioned the call from Sister Charles, but it had made her think that Grace's walks were not only to get fresh air. Lily was sure that Grace had no drink hidden in the house, but she could tell by the change in Grace when she returned from her walks that she had been drinking. It was probably hidden out in the barn, but she could never bring herself to check. It broke her heart to think that Grace was taking refuge in drink, but how could she say anything when their relationship was hanging by a thread?

*   *   *

Lily had put off meeting Sarah for almost two months. Sarah had been busy before Christmas and it had not been difficult to cancel their planned meetings. But Lily knew she would have to be told some time, and telling her was not going to be easy. Lily sat beside the phone one evening when Grace had gone for a walk. She dialled the first few digits of Sarah's number several times, but each time she stopped and put the phone down, afraid to go on. Finally she dialled the number and let it ring. Sarah answered, and after a few minutes of post-Christmas chat, Lily got to the point.

"Grace has given up nursing."

"That's a pity, Lily – she would have made such a lovely nurse. Did she get sick of the bedpans?"

"She's pregnant."

Sarah gasped. "Who is the father? I didn't even know she had a boyfriend!"

Lily tried to answer but her throat was dry and the words would not come out.

"Lily, are you there?"

"It's Tom Harrison," she said flatly.

Again Sarah gave an audible gasp. "I knew something was wrong. Do you know she rang me?"

"No," said Lily, shocked.

"Last month, she rang and asked me if I knew where Tom was. You know? Tom, my nephew?" A sharp tone crept into her voice.

"What did you say to her?"

"What could I say?" said Sarah, her voice rising with anger. "I told her one lie after another, as quick as I could make them up. But unlike you, I'm not very good at it. I told her we had no contact with him. I had to pretend we knew nothing about his father's death. Jesus, Lily, it was an awful position to put me in."

"I'm sorry. I had no idea she would ring you."

"Pregnant!"

"Yes," said Lily quietly.

For a few seconds they said nothing, then Sarah broke the silence with a loud groan.

"How could you let this happen?" she asked.

"They were seeing each other behind my back. Sarah. I had no idea," blurted Lily.

"He didn't tell her who he was. They had a relationship and. . ." Lily broke off, the words stuck in her throat.

"Dear God," whispered Sarah. Then her voice rose in anger. "He's her half-brother! And she's pregnant by him. What on earth are you going to do?" Sarah was becoming hysterical.

"We'll just have to wait and see," Lily whispered.

"I suppose she still knows nothing?"

There was a short pause.

"I think it's better if she doesn't. She's upset enough as it is."

"I'm sure she is, poor thing. Lily, what if there is something wrong with the baby?"

Lily closed her eyes. She couldn't bear to think that far ahead. Sarah's questions were beginning to make her feel queasy. "I don't know, Sarah. I'm just taking one thing at a time. We'll cross that bridge when we come to it."

Lily knew by the silence that followed that Sarah was finding it hard to contain her anger, and she wanted to get off the phone quickly.

"I'll never understand you, Lily," said Sarah icily.

"I know you're annoyed with me."

"I'm not annoyed," said Sarah. "Just disappointed."

Lily sat staring at the phone for a long time after

she had hung up. Sarah's harsh words were still
ringing in her ears.

25

As the pregnancy progressed, Grace left the house only when she had to. The poorly concealed looks of surprise, and the frenzied whispers as she walked by people in town, were more than she could bear. Lily on the other hand was perfectly calm. They had always kept to themselves, and so she felt they owed no one an explanation, and Father O'Sullivan, the parish priest, was no exception. When he called one afternoon to say he had heard of Grace's predicament, Lily offered him tea and chatted about the weather. When he asked what they intended to do about the baby, Lily assured him that the situation was under control. Grace sat across from them, biting the rim of her teacup. At least she had her mother to be thankful for. Most girls she nursed with would have been thrown out onto the street if they had gone home pregnant.

At night when Lily turned off her light, Grace would wait a few minutes to make sure she was asleep, and then slip out of her room. Her vodka was hidden in several places. One of them was an old outdoor toilet in the back yard that wasn't used any more. At first she would drink a few mouthfuls from the bottle and return it to its hiding place behind the cistern, but recently she needed more – she couldn't sleep without drinking large amounts.

Lily turned a blind eye at first. She knew Grace was scared about having a baby, but she was convinced that as soon as the baby was born things would get better. She just prayed every night that the child would be born without any afflictions. There was no one she could talk to about how the baby might be affected. She had looked up some medical reference books at the library but they contained nothing that might answer her questions. She missed Sarah. They had not spoken in months. Lily had hoped that she would mellow and perhaps feel sorry for her, but Sarah had not made any attempt to contact her since the night Lily had broken the news about Grace.

Grace thought Sarah's absence was strange as well, but she said nothing. She thought it was possible that Sarah was embarrassed by what her nephew had done. After the baby was born it would be easier to face her, but right now she was relieved that Sarah was keeping her distance.

Grace went into labour early one morning in April. By lunch-time her pains had grown worse, and Lily got Jody to drive them to the hospital. Lily stayed outside the delivery room for the seven hours it took until the birth. When the baby was born a nurse stepped outside and beckoned Lily into the delivery room.

Lily rushed in. Another nurse was wrapping the baby in a sheet.

"Is it all right?" she whispered nervously.

The nurse turned, letting Lily see the tiny face of the newly born infant. "It's a beautiful healthy baby girl!"

They put Grace in a room on her own. Unmarried mothers were kept isolated for their own good as visiting times often upset the single girls.

Grace sat back in the bed, exhausted.

"I'll go now. You need to get some sleep," said Lily, taking one last peep into the cot.

"Thanks for everything," Grace said smiling.

"A little girl, we won't know ourselves. Have you thought of a name for her?"

Grace propped herself up on one arm. "Do you like Iris?"

"That's a lovely name."

"Iris Lily," said Grace, lying back again.

Lily kissed Grace and left her to get some sleep.

26

Grace tried her best in the beginning. She loved her baby girl and was determined to be a good mother although sometimes that was difficult, with her mother always hovering over them, waiting for an opportunity to take over. Grace felt as if she could do nothing right. Lily would stand inches away from her as she tried to fold a nappy into the correct shape. If she hesitated for a moment, Lily would grab it from her and fold it correctly herself. If Grace couldn't manage to get the baby's wind up, Lily would place the tiny bundle across her shoulder, and minutes later the sound of a gentle burp would come from the infant's mouth. At night when Iris was sleeping in her crib, Grace held her breath and listened to the sound of her baby's tiny noises. Those little gasping breaths filled her with joy, yet broke her heart as well, when she thought that Tom was not with her to hear them. Then she would pull the vodka bottle from under her mattress and drink a little of it, just enough to help her sleep.

One night Lily woke to hear the baby crying. She lay still and waited to hear the sounds of Grace going down to the kitchen to heat a bottle, but no sound came from the room, only the furious cries of the hungry baby. Lily lay and waited until she could feel the perspiration break across her forehead. She had tried to stand back and let Grace find her way with the baby, but sometimes her daughter seemed so incapable.

It's because she's an only a child herself, thought Lily. There were never any younger brothers or sisters for her to look after.

As she lay there in the darkness the cries became more frantic. Lily couldn't listen to it any more. She got up and pulled on her dressing-gown. Opening the door to Grace's room she was surprised to find it in darkness.

"Grace?"

Lily turned on the light and Iris began to scream louder. Her little red face was soaked with tears. Grace was in bed asleep, her arm cradling an empty bottle of vodka.

Lily rushed to the crib and picked up the hysterical child. "Now," she cooed, rubbing the baby's back. Lily tiptoed downstairs, trying to comfort the crying child. In the kitchen she found a soother and the child sucked on it as Lily heated a bottle on the stove. Lily took the child back to her own bed that night, and the following morning she moved the crib into her room. Grace didn't try to stop her.

Shortly after Iris' third birthday, Grace got a job. She had applied for a position as a filing clerk in an accountant's office in Wicklow town, and to her surprise she received a letter asking her to start right away. Grace had never felt right living off her mother and not contributing any money to the running of the house.

Not that Lily had ever made an issue of it. In fact she never mentioned it, but one evening while they were having dinner Lily said brightly, "I've sold the back fields."

Grace stopped eating. "Why?"

"We don't need them any more. I have been meaning to do it for years. Jody can hardly manage the bit of land we use. It makes sense to sell it and I got a very good price." The back fields were a parcel of land that was not part of the original farm. Jim had bought them before they got married, and used them when he put the horses out to grass.

Grace didn't know what to say. She knew her mother had received offers over the years for those fields, but had always refused them, saying it would devalue the farm.

"It's because of us," she said, looking over at Iris

who was sitting in her high chair smiling.

"Nonsense," snapped Lily. "I shouldn't have told you. I just knew you'd hear it from someone else. Now, they're sold, and I don't want to hear another word." Lily pushed her chair out from under her and began to clear the table.

That was when Grace decided to look for a job.

Lily still worked a couple of hours a week in the library, but she was happy to give them up to look after Iris if it meant Grace could work. She had never suggested that Grace find a job for fear that she would take offence, and she had no problem supporting the three of them, but she knew that Grace would feel happier if she had her own independence.

Grace worked as a filing clerk for the first six months but, realising that she was going nowhere, she did a secretarial course at night and learned how to type. Sarah's brother, Colm Lynch, had a friend who had opened a small hotel outside Wicklow town and he arranged to give Grace a job as receptionist. Grace got through her work every day and left, doing no more or less than was required of her. The job paid for her drink, and whatever was left over went to Lily.

* * *

Grace took the day off work when Iris started

school. The three of them had breakfast together, and Iris was so excited she could hardly contain herself. She was a confident child, who behaved like an adult, because that was the only company she had ever known.

"It's such a nice morning I don't think we'll bother Jody for a lift. We'll walk," said Grace, looking out the window.

Iris put her head down and said nothing.

Grace looked at Lily nervously. "I'll get your jacket," she said, leaving the room.

Lily put her hand under Iris' chin and raised her head until she was looking at her.

"What's wrong?"

Iris turned her gaze downwards. "I don't want her to bring me," she whispered.

"Let her bring you, sweetheart. It's your first day at school – all the other children's mothers will be there."

"I want you to bring me," pleaded Iris, looking up at Lily.

Grace came back into the kitchen holding Iris' schoolbag and jacket. She began to put on her cardigan, but stopped when she saw their worried faces looking up at her.

"What?"

Lily looked over to Iris. "Come on, dear. Be a good girl and go with your mummy." Iris lowered her head again and kicked the leg of the table softly.

Grace took off her cardigan and sat down beside

Iris. She put her arm around her shoulders. "Would you like Gran to take you?"

"Yes," Iris whispered.

"Are you sure?" asked Lily, her face flushed with anxiety.

"Of course. I can take her another day. Isn't that right, Iris?"

Iris nodded.

"Well, you'd better go, or you'll be late."

Iris stood up and let Grace put her jacket on. Grace ran her fingers through her daughter's wavy black hair, and hugged her tightly. "Have a good time," she whispered.

Iris looked up at Grace, her hazel-green eyes full of sympathy. "You can come the next time," she promised.

Grace managed to keep back her tears until Lily closed the front door, then she sat at the window and looked at them as they walked up the lane. When they were out of sight she rushed upstairs to her bedroom and opened a bottle of vodka she had bought on her way home from work the night before. She put her lips to the rim of the bottle and swallowed furiously, letting it spill down her chin as she drank as much as her stomach would allow. Then she threw her head back and, screaming out loud, she hurled herself against the wall in a rage she had never known before, punching it with her fists and swearing out loud. Then she collapsed on to her bed and howled in pain like a wounded animal. Her crying was always saved for the stillness of night, stifling her muffled sobs under the blankets so her mother wouldn't hear. But this morning she didn't care any more. She lay back on her bed and cried until her throat hurt.

27

Sarah never fully forgave Lily for the way she had hidden so much from Grace, but she knew that if they were to remain friends she would have to remain silent on the issue. Ever since Grace had questioned Sarah about Tom, Sarah had always felt ill at ease talking to Grace on the phone in case the talk would turn to her fictitious nephew. Sarah felt that she had been made an accomplice, and it rested heavily on her conscience. She and Lily didn't see each other very often any more, but every now and again they broke the ice. One of them would phone the other and it usually resulted in Lily taking Iris up to Dublin on the bus to meet Sarah.

"Another girl in the family," Sarah marvelled. "You are so lucky!"

Both women were aware of how fragile their

relationship had become, and Iris created a much-needed diversion, her presence always helping to smooth things over. "How is Grace?"

Lily bristled at the mention of her daughter's name. "Fine," she answered tersely.

"I believe she's not working at the hotel any more," Sarah probed, hoping that Lily might open up a little and talk about things.

"No, that kind of work just didn't suit her," Lily answered, a little too quickly. "She's just too shy to deal with people."

Sarah let it go. Her brother Colm had told her that Grace had been sacked from the hotel because of her drinking.

Lily tried not to talk too much about Grace. She knew that Sarah was still angry, and whenever Grace's name was mentioned, Lily said as little as possible, warding off any unwanted comments from her friend.

Iris never asked about her father. When she did drawings of her family in school it was always of her grandmother and Grace. Lily would hang them up in the kitchen. "Another beautiful picture for me," she would say, handing Iris a chocolate biscuit for being such a good girl.

One evening Iris was sitting at the kitchen table. It was shortly after her eighth birthday. Lily had given her some paper and crayons to draw a picture while she made dinner. Iris was unusually quiet.

"What are you drawing?" asked Lily, stirring a pot of soup.

"My family," replied Iris, concentrating on her matchstick figures. "Gran?"

"Mmh?"

"Do I have a daddy?"

Lily stopped stirring and looked around.

"What makes you ask that?"

"Jane Kelly says I don't."

"Well, Jane Kelly is a silly little girl and you shouldn't listen to her," said Lily, turning back to the cooker to hide her dismay. Though she had known that Iris would eventually ask this question, she had managed to wipe Tom Harrison from her conscious thoughts in recent years. Grace never spoke of him, and hearing her granddaughter's question was like opening a wound that had never quite healed.

"Well, do I?" asked Iris, drawing big loops of hair onto Grace's figure.

"Of course, pet, everyone has a daddy." Lily wiped her hands on her apron and walked behind Iris to admire her picture. "It's just that some daddies don't live with their children."

Iris swung around on her chair. "Where does my daddy live?"

"In heaven, dear." Lily smiled stiffly.

"When did he die?"

"A long time ago, when you were a baby."

Iris turned, picked up another crayon and Lily

went back to the cooker.

"Will I make an apple tart for dessert?"

"Yes," said Iris, pushing her picture aside. "Can I help?"

"Of course you can, pet," said Lily, as she wiped the beads of perspiration from her brow.

* * *

On the morning of her First Holy Communion Iris stood before Lily and Grace in her white dress while Lily pinned her veil on. Jody said he would drive them but the rain that had fallen all night had stopped, and it was decided that they would walk to the church.

"Don't forget to say your prayers after receiving the Holy Communion," said Lily, holding the hairclips between her teeth.

"I won't," smiled Iris. "I'll say a prayer for all of us."

"Good girl," said Grace, taking her hand as they walked out the front door.

"And I'll say a prayer for my daddy in heaven."

Grace tightened her grip on her daughter's hand, and looked at Lily in horror. On the way to the church, Lily and Grace walked ahead exchanging livid whispers. Iris couldn't hear what they were saying, but she knew that Grace was being mean to Gran, and she knew it was because she had said she'd pray for her daddy. Iris hung back and looked at Grace giving out to her gran. She would say a prayer for her daddy and for her gran, but she wouldn't say a prayer for her mother because she spoiled everything.

After the communion ceremony, Lily took Grace and Iris out to lunch. Iris could tell that Grace was still mad with Gran. They weren't happy like all the other families in the restaurant. Iris looked around enviously at the other Communion girls. What she would have given to have a nice family like theirs, with sisters and brothers and happy fathers with big motorcars!

That night when Lily was putting Iris to bed, Grace asked Jody for a loan of his car. It had started to rain again, and she wanted to go into town. Keeping up the pretence of being a good mother all day had proved harder than she thought it would be. She needed a drink and there was no more vodka in the house. As Lily tucked Iris into bed, they heard the sound of Jody's car as Grace drove away.

Lily paced the floor till after midnight, but Grace didn't return. Later when she had given up hope and gone to bed she woke to the sound of the phone ringing. It was the hospital. Grace had crashed the car, they said. She was just badly bruised, but would have to stay in overnight.

The next morning Jody arrived in the car. He had been down to the police station earlier to pick it up. The back of it was badly battered and the exhaust pipe had broken, but he could still drive it. Lily and Iris walked out to the car where Jody was examining the damage. Iris climbed into the back seat and watched her grandmother deliver a sharp diatribe to Jody. Iris couldn't hear what she was saying, but she guessed it was something to do with Jody giving his car to her mother.

Grace was waiting at the door and walked out to meet them. Iris gazed at the purple lump on her mother's forehead and her swollen lower lip where she had bitten it when her head hit the steering wheel. Lily got out of the car and lifted the front seat, then she climbed into the back beside Iris. Grace slowly eased herself into the front seat, wincing as she did so.

Lily let a few moments pass until they were on the road again.

"Would you like to tell us what happened?" she asked in a clipped tone.

Grace ignored the question and stared ahead as if she had heard nothing. Jody fiddled with the knobs of the radio and the silence was broken with the crackled sound of the news headlines.

Lily had a framed photograph of Iris in her Communion Dress. It was kept on the dresser in the front room. Iris didn't like to look at it, and turned it face down whenever she passed the dresser. It was a feeling she could never put into words, but looking at that photo reminded her of the day that Grace stopped caring altogether.

*   *   *

Eventually Grace became incapable of holding down a job. Lily paid for all of Iris' upkeep, and every month she left sixty pounds on top of the bedside table in Grace's bedroom. She always waited until Grace was out, not wanting to embarrass her, but Lily knew that Grace had no income and what she did with the money was her business. Some months sixty pounds wasn't enough and Grace would rob money from Lily's purse, and though Lily noticed she never said anything.

Grace did her drinking late at night when Lily and Iris were in bed. Like a ghost that came to life when darkness fell, she roamed through the rooms of the house drinking in silence. By morning, she was gone, back to her room to sleep through the day. Lily always went up to Grace's room in the evening to bring her something to eat, but Iris could go for weeks without ever laying eyes on her mother.

Lily tried to give Iris as normal a life as she could but, unlike the other girls at school, Iris never brought any friends to the house. It broke Lily's heart, because she knew that Iris had purposely never become close to any of the girls in her class. All through her teenage years she never once left the school on Fridays linking arms with her best friend, making plans for the weekend. Iris liked the other girls in her class, but she knew there was no point in getting to know any of them too well, because she never wanted anyone to know about her mother. When Iris sang a solo in the school choir it was Lily who sat in the front row, dabbing her eyes with a tissue. When Iris got her first period, it was Lily she confided in. As Iris grew into a young woman, Lily was both mother and father to her. If she had ruined her own daughter's life, she made it up to Iris a hundred times over. And Iris never missed having a mother or father, as long as she had her gran.

*   *   *

One morning in late June, Lily opened her eyes and was surprised to see the room so bright. Outside she could hear the dull thud of hammering coming from the front yard. Kicking the tangled bedclothes away from her, Lily got out of bed and walked over to the window. She lifted the curtain back with one hand, just enough to see what the noise was. Below, Jody knelt on the narrow front path with his back to the house, replacing the garden gate, which had rusted free from its hinges. Lily looked at her watch and was startled to see that she had slept so late. It was half past ten. She had tossed and turned all night and woken early before it was fully bright, then drifted off to sleep again. Lily shuffled into the bathroom feeling dull and groggy. In the mirror she examined her face and in the unforgiving morning light she looked old and grey. At almost seventy-one years of age her hair still looked quite dark. She always wore it twisted into a coil at the back of her head. Now it fell loose to her shoulders and the yellow light that poured in through the bathroom window made the grey streaks shine like silver. Lily reached for her comb and twisted her hair into place, securing it with some V-shaped clips.

I'm getting old, she told herself, as the hot water filled the sink.

As she dried her face the pain shot through her arm, like a rapid bolt of lightning. She stiffened for an instant until it passed. It seemed higher up this time, almost crossing her chest. Leaning on the hand-basin, she breathed in slowly and the air seemed to push the wave of pain downwards. It was gone in seconds. Lily straightened up slowly. The pains had been coming and going for days now. They had bothered her in the past, but this morning's one had been different, sharper. Placing her comb back on the bathroom shelf, Lily promised herself that she would make another appointment to see the doctor about them.

Downstairs the kitchen was a mess. Usually Lily was first to enter the kitchen in the mornings and any mess left by Grace during her night-time wanderings was swiftly cleaned away by the time Iris was up. Lily opened the curtains and threw open a window to let in some air. Turning back she looked at the array of dirty dishes on the kitchen table. Beside an empty glass was an ashtray filled with cigarette butts. Grace had recently taken up smoking much to Lily's disapproval. Next to them was an empty cereal bowl with a few stray cornflakes floating in the remains of the milk – Iris' breakfast. Then Lily clapped a hand to her forehead as she remembered what day it was. Iris was starting her Leaving Cert exams.

"Poor Iris, no one to wish her good luck," she mumbled crossly as she cleaned away the dirty ashtray. What was wrong with her she wondered, sleeping in on such an important day? Bad enough that Iris had a mother who didn't care about her, now her grandmother was behaving the same way. Lily chastised herself as she clattered the dishes into the sink noisily. When the place looked tidy again, Lily went to the front door and walked outside to Jody.

"Morning, Mrs Fortune," he said, leaning his hammer against the wall. He shielded his eyes against the light and smiled up at Lily. The rough life he had led was reflected in the deep furrows that ran across his forehead. His ruddy skin had toughened like a piece of well-worn leather. He stood up and leaned a hand on the gatepost, his short fingers with deeply creased knuckles splayed out like a spade. With the other hand he took hold of the new gate he had hung and swung it gently open and closed.

"That looks a lot better," said Lily.

"It does. It will look even better when I paint it."

"I'm going to make some tea. Will you come in?"

Jody put his hands on the small of his back and stretched backwards in an arch. "I'd love a cup. I'll go over to the shed and get the paint first."

Back inside Lily lifted the kettle and walked over to the tap to fill it, but as she stretched out her arm towards the running water, it came again. This time the pain was so sharp that she dropped the kettle into the sink and gave a short gasp as she dropped to her knees. The pain raged across her chest in a tidal wave and she rode it until it got too big to fight. She could feel the cold kitchen tiles against her cheek and hear the sound of water rushing from the tap above her. Then she closed her eyes as the pain pressed down on her like a heavy blanket.

Part 4

28

My grandmother died in 1984. I was seventeen and that was when the second part of my life began. The first part was when I lived with her and she devoted her life to protecting me from any harm, namely my mother. The second part came after she died, and I was thrust headlong into a world of chaos.

I am Iris.

During the first exam of my Leaving Cert there was a knock on the door of the classroom and, as the supervisor opened the door I saw Jody standing there, and immediately knew that something terrible had happened.

At the hospital we walked in quick steps towards the room where they had taken Gran. Jody's thick workman's boots squeaked on the polished floors as he hurried to get me there, but we were too late.

Grace stood outside the room in the corridor being comforted by a nurse. She looked at me and tried to speak but nothing came out. The nurse left her side and came towards me, explaining that Gran was dead. Another nurse came and steered us away from the room. As we walked down the empty corridor, I was handed some tissues and a glass of water. Grace was utterly distraught, and I felt bad because I couldn't cry like she did. Her wails bounced off the thick hospital walls, creating a huge echo throughout. I noticed that she was still wearing her filthy dressing-gown and hoped that the nurse hadn't looked at it too closely. Even though we were sitting in the hospital and my grandmother was dead in the next room, I didn't believe it was really happening. I felt like I was hovering above the room, looking down at Grace and Jody as they tried to comfort each other.

Before she died my grandmother had made a will leaving everything she owned to me, but it was not to be mine until my eighteenth birthday. The year that followed her death was the worst year of my life. My mother became demented. She lost control and I could not look after her. We had very little money and I had no idea how to run a house. My grandmother had always done everything, cooked, cleaned and mended, and never asked for any help. It took me weeks just to learn how to light the Aga, which had been lit every morning before I got out of bed. I hardly knew where the ironing-board was kept. Once I reached the age of eighteen the house and land were mine to dispose of, but until then I had nothing. It seemed that my grandmother had kept quite a few things from us. Her doctor confirmed that she had suffered from dangerously high blood pressure in recent years, something we knew nothing about. Another thing she had chosen to keep from us was the fact that she had no money. The bank had advanced her a small loan, on the understanding that she would sell some of the land. We were broke. I tried to get a loan from the bank but I was turned down. The only money coming into the house was Grace's social welfare payment, which was not enough to subsidise her heavy drinking. I got a job in Doran's, the local supermarket that Grace had been fired from, and I hated every minute of it. But it was that or starve. If I left my purse lying around, Grace would take money from it for her drink. I allowed her to do this. I knew if she didn't get the money from me she would get it from Jody, even though she knew that I couldn't afford to pay him any more. Other people's circumstances didn't matter with Grace. There were times when I could have happily strangled her. In the mornings when I opened the kitchen door and saw her slumped in the armchair, I would hold my breath and secretly hope that she was dead, but then her head would move or her arm would twitch and a feeling of sick disappointment would seep through me. *Why wasn't it you?*

I left the house each morning, slamming the front door as hard as I could and set out to walk to the supermarket, which was almost a mile away, kicking every stone that came into my path. In work I would change into my yellow polyester coat and sneer at the irony of my name tag. Miss Fortune. How apt.

I suppose I could easily have ended up murdering Grace, or at least doing her some terrible injury had it not been for Sarah O'Brien, my gran's childhood friend. I had never really known her that well, but Sarah took me under her wing when she realised how bad things were.

One afternoon, a few months after Gran's death, she arrived unexpectedly. Grace was in a particularly ugly state, and the house was upside down, as it usually was in those days.

"Oh no!" I groaned, as I saw Sarah's car pull up.

Grace looked a fright. She hadn't washed for days and the dressing-gown she was wearing had something that looked like dried vomit stuck to the lapel. I opened the door and kissed Sarah, trying to make her feel welcome. I brought her into the cold untidy kitchen which had always been so cosy and full of food when she visited my gran. I spoke quickly and nervously, and apologised for the state of the place, but stopped when I saw the way Sarah was looking at Grace.

"Hello, love," she said, giving Grace a hug.

Grace ran a hand through the tangle of knots that had formed at the back of her head and looked about the room wildly. Then muttering something inaudible, she pushed her way past us and left the room. Sarah looked at me and shook her head in disbelief.

"My God, she looks terrible."

I nodded and said nothing. My grandmother had never talked about Grace and her drinking. It was always there in the background but it was never spoken about. I rushed to think of something to say that would cover up for her, but Sarah was too quick.

"Well, what's up with her?" demanded Sarah. "Is she drinking?"

The tears were falling down my face before I knew I was crying. What could I say? That she was drinking herself to death and there was nothing I could do about it? Actually that's exactly what I ended up saying. I don't know what made Sarah call that particular day. Any other day I could probably have lied quite convincingly and sent her on her way after a few cups of tea. But on that day I had reached my lowest point.

I told Sarah how Grace had stopped eating. Any time she did eat she got sick. All she could do was drink and I didn't have the power to stop her. My job at the supermarket wasn't enough to cover all the bills, and Jody could only do so much without being paid. Sarah listened to me without saying a word. She'd had no idea of the extent of Grace's problem. I don't think she could believe her ears. She insisted on staying the night, and the next morning when I got up, she had been to the shop and bought some much-needed groceries.

After breakfast, Sarah glanced about the kitchen. "You know, I don't think your gran would be too pleased at how her house is being kept!"

I looked about the place and threw my hands up in a gesture of helplessness. "I try, Sarah. I really do."

"Of course, you do, dear," she said, rolling up her sleeves. "You just need some help." We set to work cleaning the place. Sarah filled buckets of hot suddy water and mopped the sticky floor. Then she cleaned out the oven.

I was ashamed to see just how badly I had neglected the place. "You must think I'm a lazy slob," I said, hanging my head in shame.

Sarah sat back and stared at me in surprise. "You mustn't think that, Iris. You have been left to cope with a situation that no girl your age should have to deal with. I think you're doing the very best you can."

I shrugged my shoulders and gave her an uncertain smile. I was doing the best I could? By earning enough money to keep my mother permanently drunk? Her words of praise did not sit well with me. When we finished, we sat down and had lunch together. Grace remained in her room.

"What will you do with this place, Iris? It doesn't really make sense to stay on here with just the two of you." She stirred sugar into her tea and waited for my answer.

I had hoped that by ignoring the situation I was in, it might vanish some night, leaving me with no decisions to make. "I'll be eighteen soon and I'll be free to sell the place if I want."

Sarah nodded.

"But . . ."

"What?" she asked.

"Grace doesn't want to leave the house," I said quietly.

"Grace isn't in a position to make a decision on anything."

"I know that. I just don't want to be responsible for making things worse. If I sell the house and give her half of the money she'll drink it."

Sarah replaced her cup on the saucer with a solemn expression. "What will you do then?"

"Keep the house and try to sell the land. There's forty acres. If I sell that, we can spend some of the money making the house comfortable. Gran left everything to me which means I can control how much Grace spends." I bit on my lower lip to stop myself from saying any more. I had never spoken about Grace in this way to anyone.

"You're a wise girl, Iris. Your grandmother would

be so proud of you." A look of sadness passed over her face. "I miss her so much."

"Me too."

We sat without saying anything and listened to the sound overhead of Grace pacing the floor of her bedroom.

29

Sarah lent me five thousand pounds which eased things considerably. I continued to work at the supermarket, and being able to put food on the table and heat the house made life a little more bearable. Grace was very sick and, although there were times I found it hard to be in the same room as her, I came to acknowledge that she was now my responsibility. Looking at her lined and yellow face, it was hard to believe she was only thirty-seven years old. Her weight had become a cause for concern –, she was so thin that some days I thought her bones would poke through her skin.

For as long as I could remember the easiest way to scare Grace was to mention the word 'doctor'. It put the fear of God into her, and the doctor was only ever called when my gran felt that Grace's life was in danger. My gran had always called Dr Moynihan to the house, because she said he was 'discreet'. God forbid that anyone in town should know that Grace Fortune was a drunk.

A new woman doctor had moved into Wicklow town and I had heard people talking in the supermarket about how nice she was. Doran's was a hornets' nest of gossip, most of which went in one ear and out the other, but I took note every time this new doctor's name was mentioned and wrote it down when no one was looking. One night while Grace was vomiting in the bathroom, I pulled the phone into the front room, and pulling the piece of paper from my pocket I rang the number for Dr Jane Rice.

About an hour later she arrived. My hands were shaking as I opened the door. The first thing that struck me was how young she looked compared to the ancient Dr Moynihan. Her light brown hair was cut short, giving her a boyish appearance.

"Hi, I'm Jane Rice," she said, shaking my hand.

We went into the kitchen and I began to give some sketchy details of how Grace hadn't been well for a while, then realising there was too much to explain, I stood up and asked her to follow me.

We climbed the stairs quietly and approached Grace's room. The lion's den. I opened her door, turning the knob slowly so it made no noise. I hardly ever went into her room, and at first glimpse I was seeing it exactly as the doctor was. The air was cold, one of the window-panes had smashed from something Grace had hurled at it in a temper one night – I had completely forgotten about it. There was an acrid smell, like decomposing flesh. I looked around and shrugged my shoulders in despair.

Grace was lying on the bed with her face turned to the wall.

"I'll be downstairs," I whispered and walked away from the room, leaving the doctor standing in the doorway.

I sat in the kitchen for about thirty minutes and began to worry that I had done the wrong thing. What on earth was this doctor going to think of us, Grace lying in her own filth, suffering from God knows what and me, the hapless daughter, who had let her get to this stage without seeking help? I heard her footsteps on the stairs and jumped up from the table.

She opened the door and came in, walking around to the other side of the table. For a few seconds she stood facing me without say anything. Then she asked, "Do you know how sick your mother is?"

I nodded.

"She will have to go into hospital. Is that all right with you?"

I nodded again.

"They will run some tests on her. I suspect she

may have pancreatitis." She looked at me and her head fell to one side. "How old are you?"

"Almost eighteen."

"Will you be OK on your own? Do you have someone to stay with?"

"Yes. I can probably stay with some friends," I lied.

"Well, there's nothing I can do tonight, but first thing tomorrow I'll arrange for an ambulance to come. Can you pack a few things for her?"

I thanked her and pulled some money out of my pocket to pay her, but she pushed my hand away.

"Don't worry about that," she said, picking up her bag.

I saw her out to her car and thanked her again.

When she sat into her car she rolled down the window. "You did the right thing," she said. "I know it wasn't easy."

I tried to return her smile and lifted my hand dumbly in an attempt to wave as she pulled off.

The following morning I tiptoed into Grace's bedroom while she was sleeping and tried to find some nightclothes for the hospital. Her dressing-gown was too dirty to pack, but I found a nightgown that looked presentable. I folded it and put it into my gran's small suitcase, then I found some soap and toothpaste and wrapped them in a plastic bag and put them in with the nightgown. I picked up Grace's slippers from under her bed but they were as tatty as the dressing-gown. I went into gran's bedroom, and breathed in the familiar smell that had been uniquely hers. It still looked the same. I had left everything untouched, still waiting for the right time to clear out her things. I found her old blue slippers in her wardrobe and pulled them out. They were worn but clean, and I put them into the case. Grace lay in bed without stirring. Ever since I had been a child she would lie still whenever I came into her room, so I would think she was sleeping and leave. I leaned over to look at her face and with great relief I saw that she was definitely asleep.

When the ambulance arrived, I stayed downstairs and let them get on with it. Grace was too sick to object. As they carried her downstairs on a stretcher she looked around for a few seconds, then closed her eyes again. I stood watching as they loaded her into the ambulance and then clutching my gran's suitcase I climbed in after her. To my immense relief she slept again, making no explanation necessary. When we reached the hospital I was ushered into a room and given a pile of forms to complete. *Next of kin?* I supposed it was me. *Religion?* None. *Health insurance?* Definitely none. I stuffed them into my bag for Jane to look at.

When they put Grace in a bed, I was allowed to go in and see her.

I sat on a chair at the side of her bed.

She opened her eyes and blinked quickly like a frightened child.

"Grace," I said quietly, "you are very sick. The doctor who saw you last night said you may have something wrong with your pancreas."

She lay still, her eyes locked on mine.

"It's just for a few days. They want to do some tests. I'll take you home as soon as they're finished." I patted her hand in a feeble attempt to sound reassuring.

She looked at me in disgust and turned over on her side, dismissing me.

That evening as I searched the shelves of the kitchen presses for something to cook, I heard the sound of a car outside. I went to the window and saw Jane Rice get out of her car.

"Shit," I said, remembering what I had told her about staying with friends. I opened the door cautiously and let her in.

I said nothing and let her speak first.

"Are you staying here alone?"

"Yes," I said, deciding to come clean about it. If she was going to check up on me, there was no point lying.

She stepped into the kitchen and looked around. "It's very isolated. Aren't you nervous being alone?"

There was some tea left in the pot. I poured her a cup and set it down beside her. "No, I'm not nervous at all. I feel quite safe here."

She sat down. It was hard to know how old she was but I guessed her to be about thirty. I liked the way she dressed, kind of butch yet stylish, not at all like a doctor.

"Sorry, I don't have any biscuits to offer you."

"I've had enough biscuits today," she smiled.

I sat down and tried to think of something to say.

"How long have you been living around here?"

"Myself and my husband moved here last year from Dublin."

"Any kids?"

"Two girls, one and three, a bit of a handful at the moment," she said, raising her eyes to heaven. Then her voice became serious. "Look, I know you've been through a lot recently. I heard you lost your grandmother last year."

She had obviously been talking to Dr Moynihan and heard about our House of Horrors. I could feel the palms of my hands getting sweaty.

"I'm not here to pry," she said quickly. "I just want you to know that you can talk to me any time you feel like it."

I felt a lump form in my throat. It seemed that I could tolerate any amount of hardship without a flicker of emotion, but a simple word of kindness was enough to make me cry like a baby.

"My father was an alcoholic, so I have some idea of what you're going through." Her voice seemed to quiver for a moment.

I traced my finger over the pattern of the tablecloth, feeling lost for words. Did she really know what I was going through? It seemed impossible.

"Thank you," I said eventually.

She finished her tea and stood up.

I walked out to the yard with her and as she was getting into her car she turned to me. "You could come home and stay with me until Grace gets home. The children sometimes wake during the night, but if you don't mind the noise you are quite welcome."

"Thanks." For a few seconds I almost jumped at the offer, but I stopped myself. "I'll be fine here."

When she drove out I walked back into the house. I took comfort from her words. Perhaps she did know what I was going through, but I doubted it. I tried to light a fire unsuccessfully and gave up after a few attempts. In the silence I became aware of the kitchen clock ticking away on the mantelpiece above me. I was so lonely I even missed Grace.

I didn't go to the hospital the next day. It was raining heavily when I finished work so I cycled home and dried off. It was too wet to go out again, besides I was exhausted – I hadn't slept well the night before. I knew Grace had sleeping tablets somewhere, so I rummaged about through the debris of her bedroom in search of them. There were quite a few bottles of pills for her various ailments. I grabbed a load of bottles from her bedside table and found one that read: one or two to be taken at night. I twisted open the cap and examined the small white pills. They had an imprint on each pill of a closed eye, and I figured that these would do the job. I got into bed and opened the bottle again, emptying one pill onto the palm of my hand. Then I knocked it back with some water and waited for sleep to come. After a few minutes I began to panic. I didn't really know what I had taken. God only knew what kind of medication Grace kept in her room. But I soon relaxed when I felt my eyelids getting heavier, with a promise that sleep was not far off.

The following morning I woke feeling refreshed and clearer than I had felt in weeks. I went to work and asked if I could finish early. My plan was to go straight from work to visit Grace, but that wasn't necessary. I received a phone call from the hospital that afternoon: Grace had gone missing. I left work and cycled home swearing under my breath. When I reached the house I jumped off the bike and threw it in the yard. I had ridden so fast that my legs almost buckled when I tried to walk. Jody's car was in the yard and I immediately knew what Grace had done. My anger welled up when I walked into the kitchen and saw the two of them sitting at the table. They both had glasses in front of them and in the middle of the table sat a bottle of vodka. I stood looking at them with my mouth open. Grace kept her eyes locked on her glass, and Jody smiled nervously.

"Just having a quick one," he said.

I marched over to the table and pointed at the bottle, speechless with rage. "Who bought that?"

Jody shifted uncomfortably in his chair. "Eh me."

"And what are *you* doing here?" I said, turning to Grace.

Not looking up, she twirled her glass and glanced quickly at Jody, waiting for him to defend her. He stood up.

"I better leave."

"Do you know how serious this is?" I screamed. "How could you buy her drink and take her out of hospital when she is so sick?"

Jody put his hands in his pockets and mumbled apologetically.

"Shut up, madam," said Grace quietly. "I'll do as I please. You mind your own business."

I looked down at her in astonishment. "In case you haven't noticed, you *are* my business. I'm just trying to keep you alive, since you can't be bothered to do it yourself." I leant on the table, pushing my face close to hers.

Grace drew out and before I could see it coming she slapped the side of my face with a loud crack. I jumped back, putting my hand up to my stinging cheek. Stupefied.

"And who told you I wanted to be kept alive?" she said, standing up unsteadily, and putting the bottle of vodka under her arm she swaggered out of the room.

I stood like a statue with my hand pressed against my hot cheek.

Jody stared at me dumbly.

"You should go," I hissed.

He scowled at me and walked out of the house.

Jody had always worshipped Grace. He had come to work for my grandmother around the time that my grandfather was killed. Grace had been working with him the day he was kicked to death by a horse. Jody had seen how badly the accident affected Grace and he had treated her with a special kindness ever since. Grace was hurt that my grandmother had left everything to me in her will, and I know she had confided in Jody about it. I could feel their resentment.

It just amazed me that neither of them seemed to realise that my grandmother had a very good reason for doing what she did.

I went to the phone and rang Jane Rice to tell her that Grace was at home.

Three days later Grace collapsed on the kitchen floor. I found her when I came down for breakfast, and admitted her to hospital again.

30

They kept Grace in for three weeks and this time she made no attempt to escape. The day she came home was my eighteenth birthday. Sarah drove down from Dublin and collected Grace from the hospital. She was taking me out to dinner for my birthday. I had only visited Grace twice during her stay and both times we had hardly spoken. My heart sank as I heard Sarah's car pull into the yard. I went out to the front door and watched her help Grace out of the car. They walked in together, and for the first time in years Grace looked something close to healthy again. Her hair was down and it was clean and shiny, and the jaundiced look had gone from her face. I had been sure that Jody was smuggling booze into the hospital, but I was wrong, she had actually gone without a drink for three weeks.

Sarah put her arms around me. "Happy birthday!" Then she turned to Grace. "Lord, it doesn't seem so long ago since you were eighteen."

Grace smiled and reached over to hug me. "I never got you anything," she said.

I felt slightly dazed and stood still, rooted to the spot.

"Well, make us a cup of tea!" said Sarah, giving my shoulders a gentle shake.

Sarah had booked a table in the new Italian restaurant in town and Grace came too. She didn't drink anything but she smoked like a chimney. Her occasional smoking had escalated to help her cope with sobriety. I had taken up smoking after Gran died, mainly because there was little else to do in the evenings. I was bored one night and found a packet of Grace's cigarettes and decided I might as well smoke them.

I could tell from the overflowing ashtray that Grace was finding the night out hard to deal with. Sarah must have noticed too. As soon as we finished eating, she asked for the bill and we left.

Grace stayed off the drink for almost two weeks after she came home from hospital. We sorted out some legal paperwork and talked about selling the land. Now that I was eighteen the money from the sale would go directly to me.

"You know why Gran didn't leave it to you?" I asked her one evening as we were going to bed.

Grace sighed and nodded her head.

"It will be your money too." I had been trying to find the right moment to say something about it since the day we got a copy of the will, but I was afraid I might do more harm than good.

Grace chewed the inside of her cheek and looked at me. "Thanks," she said in a half-smile.

I opened my bedroom door and heard her whisper "Sorry," behind me.

But when I turned around she had disappeared into her bedroom.

I put the land up for sale. Our farm was made up of forty-two acres and a further ten acres where my great-grandmother's house was. I wanted to sell everything, make a fresh start but Grace insisted on staying in the house. God knows why – it was big and draughty and needed a pile of money spent on it, but she wasn't ready to move, so we kept the house. Within weeks I was offered a total of sixty-eight thousand pounds. Looking back now it seems like a very small amount for so much land, but in 1985 it was a king's ransom.

Unfortunately my elation at our new-found wealth was marred by the fact that Grace had started drinking again. This time she went at it with a ruthless ferocity. Gone were the discreet night-time drinking sessions, which she was so good at. Now it was a round-the-clock process of destruction with no respite. I don't know why I was so upset, but I was. I suppose the few weeks she had spent off the drink had given me some hope that we were finally getting ourselves sorted out. I felt cheated and let down, and slowly came to abhor her. I stepped over her body in the kitchen when she passed out, not bothering to check if she were still breathing. I let her drink herself back into the state she was in before, quietly hoping that this time she would finish herself off. It was the persistence of Jane Rice that finally brought me to my senses. At first I fobbed her off, telling her that Grace was doing really well. But she must have detected the uncertainty in my voice because she called by one evening on her way home from her clinic. My head jerked back in disbelief when I saw her car in the front yard. I started to grab dirty dishes and vodka bottles from the kitchen table in a wild panic. It would have taken days to straighten out the mess that lay in front of me. The place looked like a pigsty. It had become my way of punishing Grace, letting her live in her own filth.

I stood back and surveyed the hopelessness of the situation. I had about five seconds before Jane would knock on the door. Flinging the armful of bottles and mugs I had gathered into the sink, I trudged towards the door and answered it before she knocked.

She followed me into the kitchen and stood with her mouth open as she took in the squalor. I didn't know where to begin, so I decided to skip the explanations.

"You know where to go," I said, pointing towards the stairs.

I sat in the kitchen smoking a cigarette while I waited. It wasn't long before Jane came back down again, with a grave look on her face. She gave a long sigh and pulled out a chair, wiping it discreetly before she sat down.

"You're eighteen now?"

"Yes."

She paused for a second and then shook her head, quickly getting back to business.

"Iris, this is serious. She's getting worse."

"I know that, but there is nothing I can do about it."

"You can, you know," she said looking straight at me.

"Well, apart from committing her to a nuthouse, there is nothing else I can do."

Jane's stare grew more intense.

"Commit her?" I said wide-eyed. "Oh no, I couldn't do that! She's my mother."

"I'm not talking about a loony bin. St Paul's is a psychiatric hospital that deals with alcoholics, helps them to dry out. Iris, it's the only way she's going to do it. She's too far gone to help herself."

I lit another cigarette and tried to let her words seep in.

Jane stood up and eyed the sink full of week-old dirty dishes. "I know it's a tough decision. But it's the only chance she has of getting better. Think about it, but don't take too long. I'll ring you tomorrow."

"Maybe if I talk to her, she'll agree to go in." I knew she'd kill me with her bare hands rather than sign up for months without a drink, but I was grasping at straws.

Jane looked at me with a knowing smile. "Do you really believe that?"

"No," I said, squashing my cigarette into the ashtray.

"I'm sorry, Iris, but you're the only person who can do it. If I could help you at all, believe me I would."

I sat at the table, staring into a mug I had missed in the swoop. A brown furry substance had formed on the inside.

Jane picked up her bag. "I'll let myself out."

I sat at the kitchen table until my back grew stiff. I had run out of cigarettes, so I searched a few rooms upstairs but found none. I was exhausted but wide awake, so I took a sleeping tablet from the box I had taken from Grace's room and went to bed.

31

The next morning I woke from a night of fitful broken sleep. I dressed quickly and splashed my face with cold water. The immersion heater was broken and we had only cold water to wash with. I went down to the kitchen and opened a window to rid the place from the smell of stale smoke. Even though I was getting through a packet a day, I still couldn't stand the smell of cigarettes in the morning. I needed to talk to Sarah. She was well acquainted with my situation and I trusted her judgement, but phoning her from the house was too risky – the last thing I wanted was Grace to hear me. I opened the front door and stuck my head out. The clouds were grey and low and it looked like it could rain at any minute. I grabbed a jacket and wheeled my bike down the lane over the bumps and potholes until I was out on the road, then I cycled as far as the nearest phone box. I threw the bike down at the side of the road and entered the phone box, pulling coins from my trouser pockets. I balanced the receiver between my chin and shoulder and pressed a coin into the slot, but it stopped halfway. Jammed. I tried to pull it out but it was stuck. I hammered it with my fist, jamming it further.

"Shite!" I shouted, slamming the phone back down in a temper. I picked it up again, telling myself to calm down. There was still a line so I phoned the operator and made a collect call to Sarah and prayed that she would answer. She did, and without any small talk, I got straight to the point, telling her of Jane Rice's suggestion.

"What do you think? Am I mad even considering it?" I blurted.

For a minute I thought we'd been cut off. There was no sound on her end of the line.

"Sarah, hello?"

"I was your gran's best friend, but we didn't always agree with each other on certain things. And I certainly didn't agree with the way she handled Grace. Something should have been done a long time ago."

"So, do you think I should put her into hospital?" I asked impatiently. I wanted her to tell me what to do. Again there was another long pause. "Look, I'm sorry to throw this at you so early in the morning but I don't know what to do." I was beginning to sound like the one who needed psychiatric help.

"Would it help if I came down today?" asked Sarah.

I realised with a sigh of relief, that it was exactly what I'd wanted her to say. I couldn't do this on my own.

When I got back to the house the phone was ringing. It was Jane Rice. She asked if I had come to any decision and I told her I needed another day to think about it. She told me she had secured a bed for Grace in the hospital because she considered her to be an emergency.

I went into the kitchen and set to work cleaning. I scoured every cup and saucer until my hands were bright pink. The kitchen floor was almost dry when Sarah arrived late in the afternoon.

I rushed out to meet her and helped to carry in the bundles of food she had brought.

"Now," she said dropping the bags on the kitchen table, "will you unpack these, and I'll go up and see how Grace is." She didn't wait for me to answer and left the room, closing the door behind her.

It felt good to have someone else in charge, even if it was only for an afternoon. Sarah came back down a little while later and closed the door quietly behind her. She was clutching an old-fashioned lace handkerchief and dabbing at her watery eyes.

"For God's sake, ring that doctor," she said pleadingly.

That evening an ambulance arrived and took Grace away. Sarah insisted I stay in the kitchen, and I didn't argue. I heard the doors of the ambulance bang closed and I jumped from my chair and ran for the door. I almost knocked Sarah over as she came back in.

"Tell them to bring her back in!" I cried frantically. "I can't do it!"

Sarah put her arms around me and held me tightly. "You can and you must," she said sternly.

"I can't. I can't," I gasped, hardly able to get the words out.

Sarah took my head between both her hands and held it in a strong grip. "You are doing the right thing, Iris," she said, drawing my face close to hers. "You are doing what Lily should have done years ago."

My body felt limp and I let my head hang between her hands and sobbed loudly. Sarah put her arm about my waist and led me back to where I had been sitting.

"Sit down," she said pushing me into the chair and handing me a tissue. "I have something to tell you."

She lit the fire and started to make dinner. I watched from the armchair as she fiddled with the knobs of the cooker until she found the ones she needed. I knew I should be helping but I didn't seem to be able to move. The effects of last night's sleeping pill hadn't completely worn off. I stayed by the fire and stared at the flames as they grew higher, hypnotising me until my eyes closed. I dozed for a while and, when I opened my eyes, Sarah was standing over me with a plate and cutlery.

"Eat some of this," she said, putting a napkin on my knee. I smiled at her – she had even brought napkins. "It's just some casserole I made this morning."

I took the plate and began to eat. I had forgotten what real food tasted like, having eaten only frozen supermarket meals for months.

Sarah pulled up a chair opposite me and picked at her food. "I was never much of a cook!"

"Sarah, I don't know how I will ever thank you. I think we would have perished without you."

She held up her fork and waved it about. "Don't be daft. I did nothing."

"You did. You lent me money when I had no one to turn to, and today ..." I broke off and let my head fall back. "You'll never know how much this means to me. Thank you."

I felt a lot better after eating. Sarah took my plate away and brought me some tea before she sat back down again.

"Can I stay here tonight?"

"You don't have to," I said, reaching for my cigarettes.

"Yes, I do," she said, looking at me. She blinked a few times and turned her head towards the fire, sighing heavily. Her forehead was creased in a deep frown. "I probably have no right to tell you this, but I think you deserve to know. And it might help you make some sense of what has happened." She looked around the room as if she were making sure that we were alone. "Your grandmother tried so hard to protect you and Grace from the truth, but it made things worse. Poor Grace, it tore her apart."

I sat up in my chair and felt an odd sensation inside. I knew she was about to tell me something important. It was as if somewhere, in a dusty corner of my mind, I had been expecting it.

32

I sat and listened in stupefied silence, nodding at the right places to indicate my comprehension. Sometimes Sarah would stop and pause when she could see my mind was reaching overload. Then she would pick up and start again.

My grandmother had given birth to a son who she gave up for adoption. She then met and married my grandfather and never told him about the child. That much I could understand; it wasn't beyond the realms of possibility. But the rest of her story bounced off the walls of my brain like a rubber ball. I could hear her words clearly but when I tried to piece them together, they made no sense. *The son she gave up for adoption was my father.* He was Grace's half-brother, and Grace knew nothing about it. If she had been telling me about someone else's life I would have laughed at such a ridiculous story. I would have made wisecracks about how the poor child might have turned out, with the lunatic tendencies of the inbred. But I did not feel like laughing. This was my life she was talking about, and it sounded like a bad country and western song. This was the story of my grandmother and how she had lied through her teeth.

Eventually Sarah stopped talking and closed her eyes for a few seconds. "I had to tell you, Iris. I hope in time you will see that I did the right thing."

I couldn't think of anything to say. There were so many questions I wanted to ask but I was struck dumb. The most incredible part of her story was that my father might not be dead. What surprised me was that I had always suspected it. Perhaps it was the absence of any photographs of him. Or the way the mere mention of his name would result in hissing arguments and slamming doors. I learned to recognise the gloom that seeped into the house whenever I asked any questions about my father, and as I got older I learned to stop asking.

"What was my father's name?"

"Tom."

"I know that. His second name."

"Let me think," she said, trying to remember. "I ought to know – he was supposed to be related to me." She rubbed her forehead and squeezed her eyes shut. "Harrison!"

"Did you ever meet him?"

"No. I knew his father Stephen Mitchell. I never met Tom."

I wondered what he looked like. I had always had a mental picture of what my father would be like, but I had never told anyone. When I thought about him, the face of Andy Williams would appear before me. I think it was from an old record that my gran had. It was probably the only picture of a man in our house when I was a child, besides the pope and JF Kennedy. I used to gaze at the record cover and imagine that this man with the twinkling eyes and perfect American smile was my father.

"Did he look like Andy Williams?" I asked.

Sarah opened her mouth as if to answer me, but instead she started to laugh. I started to laugh as well when I thought of all the things I should have wanted to know. What a stupid question! The two of us sat by the fire and laughed as if I had told the funniest joke in the world. It was all we could do to diffuse the terrible strain we both felt. I could see that, by telling me, Sarah was shaking off the shackles of deception which she had been forced to carry around for far too long. And although I can't explain why, I felt an odd sense of relief. I had accepted so many lies in the past without questioning anything. It was the way I was taught to behave. Listening to Sarah's story of how everything had gone so wrong almost gave me hope. It was as if a light had been switched on and I could see things a little more clearly. My gran, Grace, my father, even myself all seemed to come more sharply into focus. Especially Grace.

After my outburst of laughter I wiped my eyes, and felt embarrassed. I had always found it difficult to deal with emotions. Usually my blank expression carried me through the toughest of situations, but this called for more than a vacant stare. The problem was that I didn't have the confidence to react in big gestures. As I grew older and was expected to have an opinion on certain matters, especially in school, I would study the face opposite me and mirror their expressions carefully, aping them. I didn't believe I was capable of forming an intelligent opinion.

Sarah stoked the fire and a rush of sparks flew upwards, but the flames had died.

I rubbed my hands together and shivered, all of a sudden feeling cold.

"I really don't know what to say," I said quietly.

"Don't say anything," she said, putting down the poker. "But someday before I die, tell me I did the right thing."

I brought her upstairs to my grandmother's bedroom. I had dragged a gas heater up earlier and the room felt muggy and warm. We both stood at the end of the bed.

"I hope you don't mind sleeping in her bed. It's the only decent room in the house."

"I'm so tired I'd sleep anywhere," said Sarah with a wide yawn. "I just hope she doesn't come back and smother me in my sleep!"

We hugged each other tightly and said goodnight.

I got into bed and tried to sleep but I couldn't – my mind kept wandering back to Grace, and everything my grandmother had kept from her.

33

The following morning Sarah had risen and left by the time I got down to the kitchen. There was a note on the table saying she'd ring later. I put the kettle on and cut some of the bread that she had brought with her. The phone rang and a shiver of anxiety ran down my spine. I picked up the receiver, expecting to hear Grace shouting at me, but it was Jane Rice.

"Just ringing to say that Grace is comfortable and you'll be able to see her in a few days."

"Oh. I was going to go up to her this evening."

"It's better if you leave it a few days. I'll keep you posted and let you know when you can see her."

I felt a guilty sense of relief. I wasn't ready to face Grace just yet.

"Iris, are you all right?" asked Jane. "I really am concerned about you. Is there anyone you can stay with? Grace could be gone for quite some time, you know."

I assured her I was fine. I was too preoccupied with last night's thoughts to start fibbing. I thanked her quickly, and said goodbye.

As I put down the phone I wondered why she didn't want me to see Grace. An image of my mother strapped to a bed, with a piece of rubber between her teeth swam before my eyes. I shuddered and went back into the kitchen to make my tea, but I couldn't sit down. I walked around the house from one room to another with my teacup in my hand. Apart from our bedrooms, there were also four large rooms upstairs that we never used. I went into each of them and looked around. The steam rose from my tea as the cold air wrapped around me. Rooms full of other people's memories, other people's junk, photos, furniture, toys, old clothes, possessions from our past, things that nobody wanted any more.

I decided to clear out the house completely. Throw everything out and have the place freshened up for when Grace came home. We had talked about it when Gran was alive, but never got around to doing it. I needed something to keep me busy, and for the next few weeks that is exactly what I did. Jody helped with the heavier things. He threw chairs and tables into his trailer and took them away. Some he burned, some he gave away. I didn't care what he did with them.

I don't know why I was shocked at the amount of empty bottles I found, but I was. They were hidden in every corner of the house. The spare rooms were like bottle banks. They were buried at the bottom of old tea chests that Gran had used for storage. The old free-standing wardrobes were heaving with them. When I opened the door of one I screamed as an avalanche of empty vodka bottles came tumbling out on top of me. I attacked every corner of the house, filling bags with empty and half-empty bottles. Grace had probably hidden the half-empty ones and then forgotten where she had put them in her drunkenness.

Every time Jody came to haul out another pile of junk, he would throw me a suspicious sideways glance. Ever since the day he had smuggled Grace out of hospital we had been on grunting terms only. I knew he was wondering where she was. In fact he was probably checking the sacks in his trailer to see if I had bundled her into one of them. To satisfy his curiosity and go some way towards making peace, I told him that she was in hospital. I didn't say where, for fear he would try to be her getaway driver again. He seemed satisfied with my explanation and didn't ask any questions. He stood twisting his cap between his hands, nodding his head respectfully. Ever since I had taken over the responsibility of running the house, my relationship with Jody had changed. I tried to be careful in the way that I asked him to do things, but in his eyes I was still the child of the house and there was always an air of resentment about him. It wasn't blatant, but I could tell that he was uneasy taking orders from me, and I was just as uneasy about giving them. However, he continued to work hard, and I know I would have been lost without him.

The house was emptied of so much that it seemed to float in the shadows of the dim evening light. I walked from room to room, my feet echoing on the bare floorboards in the rooms where I had pulled up the carpets. I opened the windows to clear the dust and let some air in. In my grandmother's bedroom, everything had been cleared out. Only a chair and a bottle of cologne remained. Her room looked out to the west. The last of the evening sun filtered through the windows and without the heavy drapes the warm light crept into every corner. I sat down on the chair and felt the thin wooden legs buckle under my weight. It should have gone out with the rest of the junk and I made a mental note to bring it down to Jody's trailer tomorrow. I ran my fingers over the almost empty bottle of *L'Air du Temps*, the only luxury my grandmother ever allowed herself. I lifted the bottle and sprayed some on to my wrists. The familiar scent wafted through the air and I closed my eyes and inhaled slowly. I let my head rest on the windowsill and felt the silky comforting warmth of wood against the side of my face. I stayed like that until it grew dark, breathing in the ghostly vapours of my grandmother.

34

I became obsessed with clearing out the house, performing a kind of ritual. My exorcism. Anything that held a bad memory for me got binned, and as every item left the house I was filled with a sensation of unholy mirth, as if all the rotten things that had ever happened to me were embedded in each chipped vase and sagging dust-filled armchair. Out they went, one by one. I stood at the door, clasping my hands with delight, as I looked at the tail-lights of Jody's trailer dragging away another load.

Grace had been in hospital for five days when Jane Rice rang. My heart sank when I heard the phone. I knew the time had come. I lifted the receiver slowly.

"Iris?"

"Yes."

"You can go in to see her today."

I played with the cord of the phone.

"Iris?"

"Do I have to?"

I could hear her take a sharp breath.

"Well, I think it would be good if you did. You know you did the right thing, and in time Grace will know that as well. The sooner you face her the better."

"Right," I sighed.

"Let me go with you. I'll wait outside. You might need someone to talk to afterwards."

"OK. Thanks."

"I'll pick you up at two o'clock."

I put the phone back down and felt weak. All my resolve had faded at the thought of actually seeing Grace.

*　　*　　*

I didn't talk much on the journey, my stomach felt sick and as we approached the hospital gates, I broke out in a sweat.

"Pull in," I said as I clasped my hand over my mouth.

Jane swerved the car over to the side of the road and I opened the door and jumped out. I fell to my knees and tried to vomit but nothing happened. When Jane came around to my side of the car, I was on all fours retching.

"It's just nerves, Iris. You're not going to be sick. Now stand up and breathe slowly."

I stood up and tried to regain my composure. Every inch of my body seemed to be shaking.

Jane turned me around and led me back to the car. "You must be strong if you want to see this through," she said gently as I sat back into the car.

I knew she was right. I couldn't weaken now. I had to show Grace that this was the only way. Jane sat back in and started the engine and we drove in through the gates. She pulled up outside the hospital entrance and turned to me.

"She's in St Joseph's Ward. I'll wait here. Take as long as you like."

I walked in through the automatic glass doors and entered a large modern reception area. It was different from what I'd expected. I had never been in a psychiatric hospital before but I had imagined it would have had bars on the windows, and staff with bunches of keys tied around their waists. This place was light and airy, more like a modern office building. Three members of staff were standing by the reception desk laughing at something in a newspaper. I walked up and asked for St Joseph's Ward.

"Who are you visiting, please?" asked the woman behind the desk.

"Grace Fortune."

She pulled out a clipboard and ran her finger down a list. She stopped halfway down and mumbled Grace's name.

"Ah yes," she said looking back to me. "Doctor Kelly would like a word with you before you leave. If you can come by on your way out – I'll page him for you. She's on the second floor – turn left when you get out of the lift."

I stepped out of the lift and a nurse pointed me in the direction of Grace's room. I passed some patients in the corridor and wondered if they could hear my heart pounding. When I found the room I poked my head warily around the door and saw that there were two beds, both empty. Grace was sitting in a chair by the window wearing my grandmother's dressing-gown. I walked into the room and cleared my throat, not wanting to startle her. She looked around at me, but I wasn't sure that she had seen me because she turned back towards the window again.

I walked up to her and leaned over to kiss her cheek, but changed my mind when I saw her flinch. I pulled a chair over and sat down, making sure to keep a comfortable distance between us. Still she continued to stare out the window. She appeared to look a little better. The yellowish hue seemed to have gone from her skin although she was still extremely pale.

"You look a bit better," I said breaking the silence.

She turned to look at me and I noticed how different her eyes looked.

"Do you think so?" she said sourly. "I'm so glad."

I gripped the underneath of my chair tightly. I hated when Grace was sarcastic.

"Do you need anything?"

She started to drum her fingertips on the arm-rest of her chair. Her nails were so badly bitten they looked more like knuckles. I sat there for several minutes and waited for her to speak, but it appeared that Grace was not going to say anything.

"I had to do it," I blurted awkwardly.

Grace swung around to face me, her glassy eyes riveted on mine. "You put me in here!" she spat. "You've locked me up!"

"You would have killed yourself! I had to!" I pleaded.

She batted my words away with her arm and again we sat in silence.

After a few minutes Grace spoke, but kept her back to me. "Why did you come?" she asked.

"To see how you are doing." I shifted in my chair. "Do you need anything?"

Grace said something but I couldn't hear her.

"What?" I said moving closer.

"Get me out of here," she said without looking at me.

"I–I can't. You have to stay until you're better," I stuttered.

Her shoulders drooped forward in defeat.

"Then get out!" she shouted.

318

I stood and looked at her back for a few seconds before turning to leave the room.

Once I was out of the room, I raced down the corridor, trying to at least hold back the tears until I reached the car. The lift took forever to reach the second floor and, as I waited impatiently, I heard footsteps behind me.

"Iris?"

I turned to see to see a man with white hair and a white beard. He looked like Santa Claus.

"Dr Patrick Kelly," he said, extending his hand. "I'm treating Grace."

I shook his hand and tried to blink back my tears. He guided me to a small office beside the lift and offered me a chair.

I collapsed into it and wept.

"Don't worry," he said, handing me a box of tissues.

He must be used to this, I thought, people breaking down on the first visit. It took me a while to dry up and speak coherently. Eventually I blew my nose and steadied my voice.

"I'm so sorry," I said.

He smiled at me. His face was etched with kindness. I liked him immediately.

"There's no need to be sorry. It's a tough time for you." He pulled out a chair beside me and sat into it heavily. "You really want your mother to get better. I know you do because you brought her to us, and

319

that wasn't easy for you."

I nodded, twisting the wet tissue into a ball.

"We will do everything in our power to ensure a full recovery. I want you to be sure of that," he said, reaching a hand over and patting my arm. "But it will be tough. Grace is very sick and it's going to take time and a lot of hard work from all of us, including you."

I looked at him questioningly. I thought I'd done my bit.

"Part of Grace's treatment is to make her realise how her drinking has affected the people she loves. You must let her know what it has done to your life."

I could feel my throat constricting and waited a second before I spoke. "She doesn't love me!" It was something I had always known, yet saying it sounded so pathetic.

"I'm sure she loves you very much, but her illness has stopped her from showing it."

I shook my head. "You don't understand. She never loved me. She never wanted me. She doesn't care how her drinking has affected me. We're not a normal family."

Dr Kelly gave a quick snort. "I'll let you into a secret. There is no such thing as a normal family." His eyes twinkled when he smiled, just like Santa's. "Now, Iris," he said, sitting forward, "I want you to do something for me over the next few weeks. I want you to sit down and write a letter to your mother telling her how her alcoholism has affected your life."

Now it was my turn to snort. A letter to Santa Claus. He looked at me and waited, and I realised he was serious.

"As far as she's concerned I've just locked her up in here. Now you want me to write her a letter and tell her how she ruined my life. I couldn't do that!"

"As the weeks go by she'll grow to realise that you brought her here to save her life. The biggest incentive for your mother never to drink again is to make her fully aware of the damage it has done to you. It's part of her therapy; she has to hear it. We'll wait until the right time. But for now I want you to write down anything that comes to mind, no matter how long ago it was. It's all relevant."

He stood up and led me out of the room. We took the stairs down to reception. He walked me to the door, then shook my hand and told me how brave I was.

Jane was reading the newspaper in the car when I got back out.

"Well?" she said, folding away the paper.

I shrugged my shoulders despondently. "Well, she hates me."

"Of course, she doesn't hate you. She's just angry right now. Give her a few weeks and she'll come round. She'll see you did the right thing."

"I hope you're right," I said.

"Was that Paddy Kelly I saw you talking to?"

"Yes, he's treating Grace."

"He's a great doctor. He treated my father."

We drove out of the hospital and headed for home. I wanted to ask Jane how her father was now, but I was afraid of what the answer might be.

35

I thought it best not to visit Grace until she had had a few more weeks of drying out. We didn't see each other for almost three weeks after my first visit. I spent a lot of time on my own in the house and I found the isolation unbearable. Sarah made curtains for some of the upstairs rooms and she came down to Wicklow a few times, to measure and then to hang them. The house looked nice, and so much bigger without all the junk but perhaps it just seemed big with no one to share it with. I left a pen and paper ready on the kitchen table. It was Jane's idea. Any time a thought came to me about Grace and her drinking I would write it down to use in my letter to her. My book of evidence. But every time I went back and read what I had written, I knew I would never have the courage to let her see it. I agonised over what to tell her. She had every right to know, and I desperately wanted to be done with all the secrecy of the past. But telling her that Tom Harrison, my father, was her half-brother, could also push her over the edge. I lay awake night after night weighing up the reasons why I should or shouldn't tell her. I had finished all of Grace's sleeping tablets plus another batch that Jane had reluctantly given to me, so most of my thinking was done during the night-time hours. There were times when I felt that morning would never come, and when it did I was usually just beginning to fall asleep, sometimes not waking until the afternoon.

My second visit to Grace was slightly better than the first. I stepped nervously into the room and saw that she was still sitting in the same chair by the window. There was a woman in the bed on the opposite side of the room. I braced myself for Grace's hostility, but instead Grace looked up from the book she was reading, and acknowledged me with a half-smile. The other woman sat up, smiling and nodding. I could tell by the way her eyes followed me across the room that she was desperate for someone to talk to. You drew the short straw, I thought, as I looked down at Grace. Her face was deliberately pointed away from the woman so she wouldn't be drawn into conversation. I think that sharing a room during those weeks was as tough for Grace as giving up drink. Her abhorrence of intimacy almost matched her chronic alcoholism.

"Hello," said the woman, looking from me to Grace.

Grace snapped her book shut and ignored her. I put a bag of new nightclothes on the locker beside the bed and kissed Grace in a jerky wooden manner. This time she offered her cheek and if she flinched she managed to conceal it.

"A visitor for you," said the woman, still nodding her head in our direction.

"This is Iris," said Grace, standing up. "And this is Maura – we're sharing a room." I smiled at her. I had barely managed to survive sharing a house with Grace, but to be stuck in a room with her while she was drying out must have been a sort of living hell.

Grace took my arm and steered me in the direction of the door. We walked down the corridor and I followed her into the lift. She pressed a button marked *"Garden,"* and we both stared ahead as the floor numbers changed on the digital display.

"You took your time," said Grace.

"I was waiting until you weren't so mad with me."

"You'll be waiting a long time for that," she growled.

The doors opened and I followed her down another corridor and out into a garden. It took a few seconds to adjust to the colour and brightness after the dim light of the hospital. It was early spring and although it was chilly, the sun was shining.

"This is nice," I said, taking in the different flowers and shrubs that were dotted about the place. Huge clumps of daffodils swayed in the breeze.

"I spend most of my time out here. I'm surprised I haven't caught pneumonia," Grace said, sitting down on a bench. She pulled a   packet of cigarettes out of her pocket and offered me one. We cupped our hands around the lighter as Grace lit them. Her nails were still gnawed to the bone, but she looked a lot better.

"What's your room-mate like?"

Grace shook her head and pulled deeply on her cigarette. "I'll hold a pillow over her face some night, if they don't take her away soon."

"Do you want me to start visiting more often?"

"Yes," she whispered.

I moved closer and rubbed the sleeve of her dressing-gown, all the time trying not to seem too patronising. "You're halfway there, Grace. Just a few more weeks to go."

She bit her lip and gave me a nod of agreement. "I know," she said, shivering suddenly.

I could think of nothing else to say.

The warmth of the hospital quickly evaporated from our bodies. We finished our cigarettes and hurried back inside to the heat. My visit was over and Grace walked me to the door.

"You know Dr Kelly has asked me to take part in your therapy?"

"Yes." Her eyes narrowed, and for a second I thought I saw a glimpse of terror that betrayed her outer calmness.

"I don't want to hurt you."

"I think that's the idea," she said, barely parting her teeth. "Just do whatever they want." Then she hugged me limply and walked away.

* * *

Some visits were easier than others. I could cope with sarcasm and insults, but when Grace gripped my wrist and pleaded to be taken home, like a child who didn't want to go to school, I almost reached breaking point. As I peeled her bony fingers off my arm, my teeth would chatter and I would be overwhelmed with self-doubt. Sarah lived near the hospital. On the days of the tough visits I would call to her afterwards, and she would fortify my spirits with words of encouragement, whilst offering me endless amounts of chicken soup.

I was approaching my nineteenth birthday and apart from looking after Grace, I had no life plan at all. Originally I wanted to be a schoolteacher and I had acquired enough points in my Leaving Certificate to get into teaching college, but that would have meant moving to Dublin. At the time it was simply out of the question. I couldn't have left Grace. Every time I went to Sarah's house she had another set of information leaflets on colleges and courses for me to look at. It worried her that I might end up spending my life caring for Grace. The truth is that I had no desire to do anything, and Grace was a convenient excuse for my lack of ambition.

36

When Grace had been in hospital for a month, Dr Kelly asked me to come in for a meeting. I had been to see Grace that week and was relieved to see that she was making good progress. She'd been to the hairdresser's and looked a thousand times better. The weight she had gained made her face look different and I could see the woman who had once been my mother.

When I entered Dr Kelly's office, both he and Grace were already there. He was sitting behind his desk holding my letter which I had sent through the post as planned. Grace was sitting opposite him with her legs crossed, the top leg jittering furiously with nerves. I smiled tersely at both of them and, without saying anything, sat down on the chair beside her.

Dr Kelly spoke for a few minutes about how well

she was doing, how she had come a long way since the treatment began. Whatever else he said was lost on me. My eyes were glued to the letter, which he seemed to wave like a flag as he spoke. I had to sit on my hands to stop myself from leaning over and snatching it from him. But that wasn't necessary, because when he finished speaking, he leaned over and handed it to me.

"Now, Iris. In your own time, if you would read what you have written."

I looked at him incredulously. "Me, read?"

"Yes." He rested his elbows on the arms of his chair and made a V with his two forefingers, then he leaned forward and waited for me to begin.

It was one thing being asked to write the damn letter, but being asked to read it out loud was quite another. I tried to convey my terror by throwing him a beseeching stare, but he looked away and settled back into his chair.

"Take your time," he said softly.

The air in the room was thick with tension. I had tried to be as honest as possible, but as I heard the words roll off my tongue, they sounded ruthless. I couldn't bring myself to look over at Grace as the accusations hit her like lumps of concrete, one after another.

Because of your drinking I have no friends.
Because of your drinking I hated my home.
Because of your drinking I have no confidence.

Because of your drinking I lost my mother.

And the list went on. I wrote of how I could tell how drunk she was when I walked into the house after school every day. I could sense it before I even saw her. When I finally finished, I handed the letter back to Dr Kelly, not wanting to bear the weight of its poison any longer.

Grace's head hung so low that I couldn't see her face, but I could see a tear splash down every few seconds, making a dark wet patch on the leg of her jeans.

I sat there in stony silence waiting to be thumped. Grace sniffled and made short gasping noises. The silence was deafening. Then something happened that I wasn't prepared for. Grace kept her head so low it almost rested on her chest, but she extended her arm, waving it around in the air, and searched for mine. I reached out and she took my hand and drew it up to her face. I could feel her wet tears.

"Iris." It came out in a sort of whine. "I'm so sorry." She started to cry again.

I knelt down and put my arms around her. "I didn't want to write it," I said, my voice cracking. "I didn't *want* to hurt you." I sobbed, full of regret at my accusations.

Grace turned to me and pulled me close until my head rested on her shoulder. Dr Kelly pushed himself away from the desk and left the room quietly. When we had cried ourselves out, I leaned back slightly until we were looking at each other.

Grace wiped my face with her tissue and stroked my cheek. "I want to be a mother to you. I just hope it's not too late." Her hand was shaking uncontrollably.

"Of course, it's not too late." I said, with uncertainty.

There was a moment of joy and optimism between the two of us, as if we were seeing each other for the first time, and I let myself be carried by it. *My mother was back.*

I had set out with the intention of telling her about my father when I wrote the letter to her, but in the end I couldn't do it. I was incapable of dealing another blow. I fooled myself into thinking that I was protecting Grace by not telling her, but in fact I was also protecting myself because the truth was too overwhelming, for both of us.

37

Jody was there to meet us at the train station. He came rushing over but stopped suddenly when he saw Grace, and his face broke into a wide grin.

"Welcome home," he said shaking her hand awkwardly. "You're looking well, Grace."

Although she was still skin and bone, her face had a healthy glow that had not been there for years.

"It's nice to see you, Jody," she said looking around, eager to move off before we bumped into anyone who might know us.

As we drove up to the house my heart was thumping with a mixture of fear and excitement. I so desperately wanted her to be pleased with what I had done, and yet I knew there was a good chance she wouldn't like it. Grace had never liked changes. I gave her the key and let her go ahead while I helped Jody take the bags from the boot of the car. I held back for a few minutes, then I walked slowly up the path and into the house.

Grace was in the front room. She stood at the dresser and ran her hand along the side of it, then she moved to the window brushing her fingers against the new curtains, like a blind person feeling her way in unfamiliar surroundings. Without looking at me, she moved into the kitchen. I stood behind her like a shadow, and her hand shot up to her chest in surprise as she took in the room and its contents. I had painted the walls a light shade of yellow and replaced the table with a smaller pine one that came with matching chairs. I had also installed a cooker. I had had to admit defeat with the Aga – it seemed that the only person who could light it successfully was my grandmother. But I kept it as a monument to her. I had ripped out the old linoleum and Jody had varnished the wooden floor that lay underneath.

Grace gave a girlish giggle and turned to me.

"You did this by yourself?"

"Jody helped, and Sarah made the curtains. Do you like it?" My head tilted to one side like a dog waiting to be patted.

Grace threw her arms around me in an uncharacteristic show of emotion. "You are the best girl in the world," she whispered in my ear. "I don't deserve you."

Jody shuffled about in the hallway, still holding her things.

"I'll put these upstairs then?"

"I'll take them, Jody." I wanted to be with Grace when she saw her room.

"Right. I'll be off then. See you tomorrow." Jody handed me the bags and looked at Grace. "Great to have you back," he said, nodding in her direction. "You're looking a million dollars." Then he pulled on his cap and left.

"I think he's in love," I said, looking at Grace.

"Poor Jody! What must he think of me?" she said, as we watched him leave.

We hauled the bags upstairs. Grace had left with only one small case that I had packed hastily for her, but over the two months she'd built up quite a considerable mound of clothes and books that were now stuffed into an assortment of plastic bags. Her bedroom looked airy and fresh in contrast to the hovel it had once been. I had painted over the floral-patterned wallpaper – the walls were now a plain shade of cream. I had pulled up the old threadbare carpet and Jody had varnished the floorboards, and put a rug on the floor by her bed to make the room seem warmer. He had also replaced the broken glass in the window. It was simple, but free from the chaos that she had lived with for so long. Again Grace walked around the room, slowly taking in the changes. She stopped at the window and looked over at me.

"It's a new beginning." She sank down on to her bed. "Thank you."

"I'll let you unpack," I said, closing the door.

I walked back down the stairs, feeling light-headed with sheer relief. She liked it! I was seized with an optimism that made me giddy with happiness.

Grace slept a lot when she came home. Jane Rice dropped by and explained her medication to me. It seemed that Grace had been suffering from depression for quite a while and they had put her on anti-depressants in the hospital, which is why she felt tired all the time. She was also on other medication that would have a nasty effect if she were to go back on the booze. It was important that she had no access to alcohol at any time. Our life was going to be so different, but no matter how hard I tried, I couldn't imagine a life with Grace not drinking.

I worried about money. We had never taken out any medical insurance so Grace's hospital bills had to be paid. I also spent more than I had planned to on sprucing up the house. There was still a lot of money in the bank, but neither of us was earning anything. I had given up my job in Doran's supermarket when the money came through. Grace was still very weak, and for all I knew she could be like that forever. It was up to me to find a job that would help to keep us ticking over. Besides, I'd had enough of sitting around the house. I got a job waitressing in the Italian restaurant in town, but left after three weeks. I don't know what made me think I could do that kind of work, when I didn't even know how to set a table correctly. That was followed by a brief stint in a shoe shop which almost bored me to death, and after selling a customer two left shoes, my boss decided I might do better elsewhere. I finally ended up back in the supermarket – the devil you know. It was close to home and because everything on the shelves was out of date, none of the locals ever went into it, therefore no brain power was required. Perfect. The place was empty most of the time so I could take as many cigarette breaks as I liked. In fact, if the weather was particularly foul I wouldn't bother stepping out the back. I would light up my smoke right there at the till and throw it into an ashtray under the counter if anyone came in. Some of the other girls would whine about how quiet it was. They said the day went quicker if we were busy. Not me. I was quite happy to read a book with the blow heater scorching my legs. A customer was nothing but a nuisance to me. After a few weeks the yellow polyester coat with the Miss Fortune name-tag felt like a second skin.

38

Grace did all right during the first few weeks at home. I stayed out of her way as much as possible and tried to give her the space she needed. She went to AA meetings twice a week, but rarely left the house for anything else. If the day was fine she would take a walk as far as the back hill and sit there for hours staring out at the land beyond that was no longer ours.

Jody usually gave me a lift into Wicklow town on Saturday mornings. He would go to the bookies while I shopped for the weekly groceries and anything else we might need. Sometimes Grace came along, but she would stay in the car. I didn't blame her – she still looked pretty bad and people made no attempt to hide their pitying stares when they saw her on the street.

One Saturday, when Grace had been home about a month, she decided to join me on my trip to town. At first she seemed undecided, but after dithering about over breakfast she said she would come. Jody arrived and beeped his horn in the front yard and we sat into the car. Grace sat in the front staring out the window, ignoring anything we said. I had become used to her long trance-like silences and accepted them as part of who she was. Jody shot worried glances at me through the rear-view mirror. He parked his car in a side street and turned to Grace.

"Will I get you a paper?"

"No, thanks," replied Grace, opening her door. "I'll go myself. I need a few things."

Jody and I looked at each other in surprise. Jody shrugged his shoulders and got out of the car, stretching his arms in the air.

"Right so. Give me a shout when you're ready to go." He walked off towards the main street.

I had paid Jody a few hundred pounds when the money came through, and I insisted on paying him a weekly wage as a retainer. Some weeks we didn't need him at all but he was always there when we did. He still looked after the garden and any other odd jobs that needed doing. He knew our land better than we did. He did his work and kept his head down, and anything that went on in our house never went any further.

I stood on the footpath with Grace, and leaned

against the car. It felt warm against my back. It was early June and the air was fresh with the smell of summer.

"Do you want me to go with you?"

Grace shook her head. "No. The car's open, I'll sit in and read the paper if I'm back first." Then off she went.

Where are you going? I knew better than to ask. She was the most secretive person I had ever known. Any questions, no matter how innocent, were taken as a personal affront. I watched as she walked off, and it took all my strength not to creep around the corner and follow her. When she was out of sight I walked slowly around the corner and saw Jody. He was waiting for me.

"Watch her, Iris. She seems a bit lost this morning," he said in a worried voice.

"Don't worry, Jody. I'll stay close behind her."

I rushed around like a madwoman, forgetting half of what I had come to town for, peering into every pub door and window to see if I could see her. As I made my way through the town I began to panic. She couldn't do it, not after all we'd been through. I put aside my trust in her and started to check the pubs one by one. Standing in the doorways furtively, I scoured the bar stools for her. By the time I reached the end of the town I had broken into a sweat. I turned wildly and started back, searching the bars that I'd missed on my way down. Then I saw her. She was walking towards me, smiling happily with a bag in her hand. Still sober.

"Where are you rushing to?" she asked.

I let out a loud laugh in an attempt to cover up my misgivings. "Nowhere."

"I'm going back to the car now – let me take some of those bags."

I handed her the grocery bags and she walked off, leaving me standing alone in the street. I wanted to fall to my knees and scream, "Thank you, Jesus!" Instead I stayed rooted to the spot, and let my heart-rate return to normal. I needed a drink myself.

When we got home Grace emptied the contents of her mystery bag onto the kitchen table. My curiosity got the better of me and I lowered my newspaper and leaned over to take a look. Tubes of paint, brushes and a sketchpad fell out of the bag. I looked at them with interest. That's what she had been doing.

Grace picked up a tube of paint and began to examine the label, and without lifting her eyes she said, "You'll have to learn to trust me."

"I'll try," I said.

But deep down, I knew that was impossible.

39

I never knew that Grace had loved to paint when she was younger. There was so much I didn't know about her. The pictures she painted were dark. All the years of silence and self-destruction came rushing from the paintbrush, as if it were a third arm. It was Doctor Kelly who had suggested she take it up again and after a while it became a form of therapy. For the first time in her adult life, Grace found peace.

Sarah had developed angina and couldn't drive down to us any more. I visited her regularly and stayed the night whenever possible. It was an opportunity to put some space between myself and Grace – living together again was tough going at times. There were days when Grace simply did not speak. We were polite to each other at all times, we never raised our voices or openly disagreed about anything. It's just that Grace didn't like to talk, and there were times when it did my head in.

Sarah, on the other hand, could talk all day and late into the night. Her husband, Pat, played golf almost every day and her boys had all left home, so my visits were warmly welcomed.

I had not managed to see her very much since Grace had come home from hospital, so when she rang to invite me to stay for a weekend at the end of July, I jumped at the chance. Grace was no company at all, painting in silence at night and sleeping most days and, besides, leaving her alone was a risk I was going to have to take sooner or later.

I took the weekend off work and got the bus up to Dublin. Sarah threw open her door and hugged me. Her eyes still had that youthful twinkle but she had aged in the few weeks since I'd seen her. For the first time ever she looked like an old woman.

"I know," she said as she read my expression. "I look like death."

"No, you don't." I protested, but it was no good – she could never be fooled.

"I'm bunched," she said as she led me into the hall. "It's the tablets. I was all right until I started taking them. Bloody poison!"

She had prepared lunch and we carried it out to a table in the garden. I told her how well Grace was doing and how her painting was helping to fill the days. Sarah seemed genuinely happy for us and

343

listened intently as I filled her in.

"Enough about Grace, what about you?" she asked.

I shrugged my shoulders. "Fine, I suppose."

"Still working?"

"Yes."

Sarah sighed softly. I could feel a talk coming on.

"Iris. What are you doing in a supermarket? You should be in college, not wasting your time as a check-out girl."

"I know. But it suits me for the moment and I won't be there forever."

"Well, make sure of that," she said, wagging her finger at me. "Remember 'just for the moment' can turn into forever very quickly."

A worrying image of me, sitting at a till in twenty years' time popped into my head, and I laughed. "Don't worry, Sarah, I'm not planning on making a career of it."

Sarah looked at me and moved her chair closer. "Have you thought of what you want to do?"

I looked at her blankly. I had no idea. My plans never seemed to stretch beyond next week.

"It's time you thought of yourself," said Sarah.

I shifted uneasily and the deckchair creaked underneath me. "I can't think of myself until Grace is better."

"Grace is as better as she'll ever be. You've done enough for her." Sarah put her hand up to her mouth and tapped her fingers against her lips. "Sorry, I'll shut up now."

I sat up. "Well, don't shut up now! Tell me what you think I should do?"

Sarah didn't waste any time and seized the opportunity. "Leave."

"Leave! How can I do that?" I asked, feeling an anger stir inside me at such a flippant remark.

Sarah leaned over towards me. "Leave, and make a life for yourself before it's too late."

I stared at her, bemused. "Sarah, you don't understand." I let myself fall back into the low chair.

"I understand more than you think I do. Are you prepared to bypass your youth to be your mother's keeper? You might say yes now, but believe me when you wake up some day and your life has passed you by, you'll regret it. And what's more, you'll resent Grace for the years she stole from you."

I had tried not to smoke all afternoon, but Sarah's words sent me diving into my handbag for my cigarettes and lighter. I lit up and inhaled a huge lungful of smoke.

"Have you anywhere in mind?" I asked sarcastically.

"Why don't you go to America?"

"America!" I laughed. "You couldn't think of somewhere further away?"

"Patrick and Andrew are over there. They could get you a job and help you find somewhere to live. It would be good for you."

Sarah's sons were both living in Boston. Patrick had married an American girl, much to Sarah's dismay, and Andrew worked for the Bank of Boston. It seemed like such an absurd suggestion that I just shook my head.

"It's a nice idea, but maybe in another five or ten years."

Sarah's eyes filled with tears.

"Oh, Sarah, I'm sorry. I didn't mean to swipe it aside like that," I said, jumping up and going to her.

Sarah quickly wiped her eyes and waved me back to my chair. "I promised Lily that I would take care of you if she went before me," she sniffed. "I can't bear to see you throwing your youth away, looking after your mother. You should be off with friends having fun, a lovely girl like you. You should have a boyfriend."

Well, I knew all that, but who was going to look after Grace, if I suddenly took off, as she was suggesting? No one, that's who. There was no point in arguing. Even Sarah, who I considered to be part of the family, wasn't close enough to understand.

We sat out in the garden until the sun moved off the patio and the evening chill began to set in, then we moved inside and had dinner in the kitchen. For the rest of the evening I was preoccupied with what she had said. It had never occurred to me that I might not be doing the right thing. Looking after Grace had never been a conscious decision. It just happened, and I had never questioned it. Sarah's husband, Pat, came in later that evening and showed us the Waterford glass trophy he had won in his golf competition. He was wearing one of those sweaters with diamonds on it, and practised his golf swing holding an imaginary club while he spoke to us.

After what seemed like an endless amount of small talk, I yawned loudly and said I was exhausted. Sarah showed me upstairs to the guest-room and then came and knocked on the door a little later, in her dressing-gown, to say goodnight.

I lay back in the unfamiliar bed and waited for sleep to creep up on me, but I wasn't one bit tired. Sarah's dismal prophecies had unnerved me, mainly because I knew she was right. I had never had the courage to plan a future. I had nothing. I had Grace to take care of, and that's where the road ended. A boyfriend! Now there was a thought. Who in their right mind would have me? Tears of anger rolled down my cheeks towards my ears. I put my face into the pillow to muffle my sobs, and cursed myself for not getting the bus home earlier.

The following morning I woke early, feeling horrible. I dressed quietly and sneaked out to use the bathroom. As I eased the bedroom door open and stepped out into the landing, I was surprised to see Sarah standing there in her dressing-gown.

"Have you been there all night?" I asked with a smile.

"Good morning. No, I haven't been here all night, smart Alec. Damn tablets have me up with the birds every morning. What's your excuse?"

Having been awake for most of the night, I had thought of a host of excuses to get away early, but now they all seemed pretty feeble. The truth was that I just wanted to go home. Sarah held up her hand before I had a chance to start explaining myself. I didn't have to say anything.

"You go and get your things together. Pat will leave you to the train station."

I think she guessed how I was really feeling even though I wasn't too sure of what I felt myself.

40

The rhythmic movement of the train had a hypnotic effect. My eyes began to feel heavy as soon as we left the station and within minutes I was asleep. I was woken by a man tugging at my arm roughly.

"Is this your stop?" he asked, pointing out the window at the Wicklow sign.

I quickly grabbed my bag and thanked him as I ran towards the door.

As I left the train station it began to rain. Great, I thought, pulling on a jacket. I hadn't bothered to phone Jody to tell him I was coming and I was faced with a two-mile walk in the rain. As I walked down the road, a car pulled up beside me. It was Larry Doran, son of my boss KP Doran, who owned the supermarket.

"Are you not working today?" he shouted out at me.

"No," I answered curtly and kept walking.

"Why not?"

"Day off."

"Well, hop in."

Normally I wouldn't have taken a lift from him. He thought he was a heart-throb in his stupid car. But the rain was getting heavier, so I swallowed my pride and jumped in.

He tried to strike up a conversation without any success, then he pushed in a cassette of ZZ Top and turned up the volume, until I thought my ears would burst. He pulled in at the end of the lane and went to open his door.

"I suppose a cup of tea's out of the question?"

"It sure is," I said as I jumped out of the car. "Thanks." I slammed the door and walked quickly towards the house. What a creep, I thought as I heard him screech off down the road.

I knew as soon as I stepped into the hall. Initially there was nothing to suggest it, I just knew. I gave the kitchen door a gentle push, trying to prepare myself for what I might find. The strange feeling that had tugged at the corner of my mind the night before, unfolded before me. The place had been trashed. Sketches and paintings lay in shreds on the floor, floating in a river of milk, which had been knocked from the table. The new cups had been smashed against the fireplace, and lying on the floor amongst the debris was the reason why I had come home early, an empty bottle of vodka. I had known it was only a matter of time before it would happen, but some part of my psyche would not let me believe it. I had acted as my mother's shadow ever since she had returned from hospital and as soon as I stepped away she had broken free of me and the restraints I had put upon her.

I spent at least an hour cleaning the place before I even thought of looking for Grace. I needed some time to think before I tackled her. I presumed that she was out cold upstairs, but when I went to look in on her, the room was empty. I checked all of the rooms but she wasn't in the house. It was still raining heavily. I pulled on an anorak and, swearing loudly, I went out to see if I could find her. I looked all afternoon, but she was nowhere to be found. I searched the farm, but there was no sign of her anywhere. I knew she couldn't have gone far with that much drink taken but I began to panic as evening approached. Jane Rice had warned us how sick she could get if she drank on top of the pills she was taking.

I ran back to the house, soaked to the skin. I peeled off my clothes and put on a dry pair of trousers and a shirt, then I sat on my bed and tried to calm down and think where the hell she might have got to. I needed Jody. It was half past six on a Saturday evening. He didn't have a telephone at home so I tried ringing Mulligan's pub in the hope that he might have had some luck with the horses that day and was in early to spend his winnings. He was there. I didn't say why I wanted him, I just asked him to come over and ten minutes later I could hear his car coming up the lane.

We searched town. We looked in every pub, but there was no sign of her. We drove back to the house and Jody followed me into the kitchen.

"I'm sorry for calling you out on a Saturday night."

Jody stood at the kitchen door, waiting to be invited in.

I went to offer him a drink and remembered that we had none.

"I'd offer you a drink, but she …" I broke off and put my hands up to my face.

Jody looked stricken. He came over and patted my back roughly. "Ah, don't cry, Iris. We'll find her."

"I'm sorry Jody," I whined. "I don't know what to do."

He led me over to the table and pulled out a chair for me. "Look, she's not in town, so she must be around here. There's a torch outside in the shed. I'll get it and have a good look out the back."

"But I looked!" I sobbed.

He patted my back again. "You make us a cup of tea. I won't be long." He pulled on his cap as he left.

I sat in the fading light and waited. The rain had stopped and the only sound was the heavy drips that fell from the branches of the trees outside the front door. The small voice inside my head had turned to a Greek chorus in the silence of the kitchen.

Leave. You can't help her any more.

About an hour later Jody burst into the kitchen with a wild look on his face.

"Call an ambulance!" he shouted at me.

He had found Grace in the old stable block, where she used to keep her horses, passed out behind some ancient bales of hay in one of the stalls. I had looked there but, in my panic, somehow hadn't spotted her.

The ambulance arrived and Jody led the paramedics to where she was lying. He wouldn't let me follow. They gathered Grace onto a stretcher and put her inside the ambulance, then drove back down to the house for me. I climbed in and sat on a bench opposite her. I reached over and took hold of her hand. It was frozen. The ambulance men had wrapped her in something that looked like tin foil. There was white froth coming from the corners of her mouth.

They whisked her off as soon as we reached the hospital. Jody had followed us in his car and insisted on waiting with me. We sat in the waiting-room and smoked in silence for what seemed like hours, until a doctor came in and explained that Grace was suffering from hypothermia amongst other things that I had never heard of. He told us she was still unconscious, and that there was no point in us staying any longer – she wouldn't come around for another few hours.

Jody drove me home, and as we approached Mulligan's he pulled in.

"I think we both deserve a drink," he said, pulling up the handbrake.

It was after midnight and the pub was closed, but Jody tapped gently on the window pane and a few seconds later the door opened. The pub was empty except for a few regulars at the bar, and a group of men playing poker at a table in the corner. They looked up and nodded at us and went back to their card game. Jody pulled out a bar stool for me, and sat up on the one beside it.

"What'll you have?"

I shrugged my shoulders. "Anything."

"Brandy. It's meant to be good if you've had a shock."

The funny thing was that I wasn't shocked at all. If I was shocked at anything, it was the fact that Grace had managed to stay off the drink for six months.

"A pint of Guinness and a brandy!" Jody called to the barman.

The brandy burned the back of my throat and I sipped it slowly, while Jody knocked back his pint.

He looked at me and shook his head sadly. "It's a terrible shame. Such a lovely woman."

I nodded in agreement.

"I think she misses your grandmother badly."

"She does."

"She'll be right as rain in no time."

"Jody," I said, twisting my glass around on the beer mat, "she'll never be right."

He straightened his back and looked at me. "Ah, don't say things like that, Iris. They'll fix her up in the hospital. She'll be grand."

My eyes had glazed over with tiredness and I nodded in agreement.

We finished our drinks and left. Jody drove me home.

He offered to sleep in the kitchen but I thanked him and said I'd be fine. I could hardly keep my eyes open as I climbed the stairs.

My overnight bag that I had brought to Sarah's was still on the floor beside my bed. I opened it and rooted around for my nightdress, and as I pulled it out an envelope fell out with it. I opened it and unfolded the three typewritten pages.

It was an application form. The heading read: *Application For Visa For United States Of America.*

Good old Sarah, I thought as I climbed into bed. She wasn't giving up on me too easily.

41

They kept Grace in the hospital for a month. The first time I went to visit her I had a sermon composed and was ready to shoot from the hip, but when I saw her forlorn figure propped up in the narrow bed, my accusatory mood dissolved into compassion.

I sank onto the bed alongside her, and she hung her head in shame.

"I messed it up," she said, searching my face for a reaction.

"It's OK," I said calmly. "You fell off the wagon. Isn't that what they say?"

She swallowed hard and struggled to smile.

"Do you think you can start again?" I asked, flicking my hair back nervously.

"Yes," she said, a little too quickly.

She had stopped going to her AA meetings because

there were too many local people attending them. Grace didn't want to believe that she might be the same as those sad broken people that she encountered in her group sessions. I can imagine the urge she must have felt to leap up off her chair and shout: "I am not like you lot!" But, the fact remained that she was no different from any of them and if she were ever going to succeed she needed to start attending them again.

"You'll start going to AA again?"

"Yes," she replied, brightening up, as if we were planning a holiday. Anything to make it up to me.

* * *

We started all over again. Grace came home and pottered about the house, and I went back to the supermarket four days a week. I tried to get her to go to the AA meetings, and she did for a while, but when I stopped nagging, she stopped going. I worried about her all the time. She didn't seem to eat at all. Her pancreas had just about packed in and she was never without a cigarette in her hand. At night when she coughed in her room, the whole house seemed to shake. Most evenings Grace would go up to one of the spare rooms and paint. I had bought her some paints and an easel for her birthday. Sometimes after work I went for a drink with the girls from the supermarket, but mostly I went home. I was always nervous about leaving Grace alone.

One evening I was leaving the supermarket when Larry Doran pulled up beside me, the music blaring from his car stereo. He leaned over the passenger seat and rolled down the window, his head bobbing up and down to the music. He wasn't bad-looking really, if he kept his mouth shut. The problem was he didn't. He bleated on and on about nothing in the thickest Wicklow accent I had ever heard.

"What are you doin' tonight?"

"Nothing," I said defensively.

"Will you come to the pictures?"

I wrinkled my forehead and stared at him for a minute. He was all dressed up in his Miami Vice suit. He'd obviously been stood up. Then I thought, what the hell? I was so bored and lonely that even Larry Doran was beginning to look attractive. I got into his car and we tore off down the road to downtown Wicklow. We were too early for the cinema, so we went for a drink. Larry talked and drank, while I sat and listened, trying to look interested in what he had to say. What I was really thinking was that I had never been kissed properly, had no idea what sex was all about, and I reckoned it was time I found out. As Larry chattered on about God knows what, I sat back and looked at him like a lab specimen. Imagining what it would be like to kiss him, that was if he shut up for long enough.

"So what do you think?"

I snapped out of my thoughts and sat up, reaching

for my drink. "Sorry, what did you say?"

"Jesus," said Larry nudging me in the ribs and moving closer, "do you ever listen? I was talking about the new supermarket we're going to build."

"Oh yes. Sounds great."

We sat at the back of the cinema and I let him do as he pleased. He came up for air every time the usherette passed by, shining her torch on us, then in he'd pounce again. He had sprouted at least four pairs of hands which found their way over every part of my body. When the film ended and lights came on, I pushed him away and looked around to see if I knew anyone. He drove me home and shouted over the music until I reached over and turned the volume down. My head was aching.

"Sorry, was it too loud?" he said, grinning.

I told him to stop at the end of the lane, in case he got any ideas about coming into the house. He went to get out of the car.

"I'm not inviting you in," I said, staring out the window. Grace's bedroom light was on, but she probably wasn't asleep yet. Larry's hand slid around my waist and he pulled me closer, but I'd had enough for one night and pushed him away.

"Thanks for a lovely evening," I said, stepping out of the car, trying to sound enthusiastic.

"Will you come out with me again?" he asked

"Sure," I shouted as I walked up the lane, not bothering to look back.

42

I suppose it's fair to say that we started going out together, even though the words 'love', 'girlfriend' and any other form of endearment were strictly forbidden. My feelings for Larry swung somewhere between ice-cold and lukewarm. There were days when I could barely tolerate him. I saw him when it suited me and told him to sod off when it didn't. I never mixed with his friends or accepted his mother's invitation to tea (she wanted to meet the check-out girl he had taken up with). I was never intentionally mean to him, but there were times when I wondered why he stuck around. There were lots of girls in town who fancied him, but human nature can be absurdly perverse, and my indifference became an aphrodisiac to him.

I told him very little about my home life, and he

pretended to know far less than he did. There was an invisible line at the end of our lane which he was not allowed to cross, and after we had been out a couple of times, he gave up asking to come in. He would sit in his car and watch me as I walked up to the house, no matter how many times I had told him not to do it. It gave me the creeps, having him sit there watching me, but he insisted.

"If you bring a girl out, you bring a girl home," he'd say as I rolled my eyes towards heaven.

Grace never asked any questions about Larry, and although we had been together for six months, I never volunteered any information. Her depression had worsened, and we spoke very little. I knew she lived in fear of the day that I would bring Larry home to meet her. I wanted to tell her it would never happen, but our inability to communicate was such that I could not even find the words to reassure her that I would never bring any friend of mine into our home. I could see the muscles in her face stiffen when she heard his car pull into the lane on the nights he came to pick me up, and then relax again as I ran out to meet him.

Grace managed to last through the winter, before her next disaster. I had sensed the warning signs but failed once again to act on them, perhaps because I knew what little difference it would make. Her sadness was smothering her.

It was a Saturday night in late April, and I had just

finished in the supermarket. I could see Larry's car parked outside and although I wasn't in the mood for a night out, I was glad to see him. I was loath to admit it, but we had become good friends. I could hear the pounding beats of his music as I approached, and he automatically reached for the knob to turn the volume down as I got into the car.

"Where to, sexy?" he said kissing me quickly, before I could pull away.

"Home."

"Ah, come on, Iris, it's Saturday."

"I don't care. Home please."

"I'll tell you what. A quick pint, then home."

"Whatever," I sighed.

We went to a quiet pub outside town, and after a drink or two my waspish humour mellowed. Larry was again jabbering on excitedly about the new supermarket his dad was building. Larry was going to run it for him. It would really be his shop, at least that's what he kept saying.

I couldn't think of anything more awful, but I tried to muster up some enthusiasm. "It'll be great."

"I think it's really going to work. You could come and work there if you like."

"Actually I don't plan on being there that much longer." I had made myself a promise to get out before the year was up.

Larry sat back in surprise. "Where are you going?"

"I'm not going anywhere. I just don't plan to

work in a supermarket for the rest of my life."

"What are you going to do?"

I hadn't thought that far ahead. "Mind your own business!" I snapped.

"Right. Let's go for a pizza." That is what I loved about Larry. My insults bounced off his thick skin leaving no marks of any ill feelings.

"OK, but then I'm going straight home. And if you won't bring me, I'll walk."

I had an uneasy feeling as we waited for the bill in the restaurant. I drummed my fingers on the table, trying to get the waiter's attention.

"Will you calm down," said Larry. "What's the rush?"

He leaned across the table and kissed my forehead and I smiled and tried to relax. I still couldn't decide whether he was attractive or not. His hair was somewhere between ginger and fair. He proudly referred to it as strawberry blond, and although he swore he didn't have highlights, I was never quite convinced. His eyes were pale grey and very intense, and he blinked a lot. I think what I found attractive about him was his openness. He spoke without deliberation and made no apologies for it.

It was about ten o'clock when we drove up the lane. Larry had moaned all the way back about how early it was to be going home on a Saturday night. He stopped the car and I noticed that all the curtains were still open in the house. Grace usually closed them at the first sign of darkness.

Larry put his arm around me and pulled me towards him. I kissed him quickly on the cheek and reached for the door handle.

"Great," he snorted. "Was it something I said?"

"Go home, Larry," I muttered under my breath and got out of the car.

I opened the front door and that familiar feeling of dread came rushing back to me. I had almost forgotten what it felt like. I looked around the downstairs rooms for Grace. There was no sign of her. The television was still on in the front room, and on the table stood a glass of what looked like water. I stuck my finger into the liquid and ran it across my tongue. It was vodka. Then I heard a loud thud on the floor above my head. I raced upstairs, and ran into Grace's room. It was empty. I could hear the sound of running water, and I ran to the bathroom. I tried the handle, but it was locked. I banged on the door with my fists, but I could hear nothing over the furious gushing of water.

"Grace!" I screamed. *"Open it!"*

I kicked at the door but it was shut fast. I rushed down the stairs, and screamed when I saw a figure standing at the front door that I had left open. It was Larry. He stood there, nervously jumping from one foot to another.

"What's wrong?" he asked.

I pointed to the bathroom door at the top of the stairs. "She's in there and it's locked."

Larry ran upstairs while I phoned an ambulance. A few seconds later he ran past me and out of the house, while I gave our address to the operator. When I finished on the phone I went back up and pounded on the door with my fists.

"Grace, please! If you can hear me, open the door!" I screeched.

Then I heard the sound of smashing glass, and realised that Larry had gone outside to climb up to the window. I could hear things on the windowsill being knocked to the floor as he squeezed in through the small opening.

"Oh fuck!" I heard him say as the noise of running water stopped.

"Larry, open the door!" I shouted.

"Don't come in, Iris," he ordered.

I paced up and down and listened to the sound of water lapping noisily against the bath tub.

"Larry, what are you doing?" I shouted, banging the door again.

I heard the key turn and he opened the door. His shirt was soaked and his arms were cut from the broken glass in the window. He raised his arms and blocked me from entering.

"Get a blanket," he said.

I tried to push him aside but he shoved me back roughly.

"Get a blanket!" he shouted. He was shaking violently and I decided to do as he asked.

He took the blanket and covered Grace's body before he let me into the bathroom. Nothing registered very quickly. I saw the last of the reddish water disappear down the plug hole. Grace was still lying in the bathtub. She looked dead but I knew she wasn't because her head was moving from side to side in jerky movements. There was a loud bang on the front door, and two ambulance men came charging up the stairs and into the bathroom. They stopped suddenly when they saw Grace.

"You wait out here, love," one of them said, and gently pushed me out onto the landing. We waited outside. I heard them say "One, two, three!" then the sound of their efforts as they pulled Grace's sodden body out of the bath and onto a stretcher. They carried her out carefully. The blanket had fallen away, and I could see the two gaping wounds on her wrists. It was only then that I realised she had tried to kill herself.

We followed the ambulance in terrified silence. Larry's arms were cut to ribbons and when we got to the hospital, a nurse put a dressing on them. We waited around and watched a Saturday night comedy show on the television in the waiting-room. The sound was turned down and we sat there looking at the screen like two zombies. The doctor came in and pulled a chair over beside us. He placed it opposite me and eased himself into it. "Grace is your mother?" he asked, giving me a sympathetic look.

"Yes," Larry answered for me.

The doctor leaned in towards me and adopted a reassuring tone. "Well, you did a great job getting her here tonight. She's had a lucky escape. Another few minutes like that and we would have lost her."

I feigned relief and tried desperately to disguise the thoughts that were crowding my mind.

Why was I in such a rush? Another few minutes and it would have been all over. She would have been out of her misery, forever.

Larry drove me home, and when we pulled into the lane he turned off the engine. We sat and stared at the house. It seemed so still and quiet in contrast to the scene of chaos only hours before.

Larry hadn't said much since leaving the hospital.

"Well, now that you've met my mother, you might as well come in for coffee!" I said, resorting to sarcasm.

He looked at me and shook his head.

I wanted him to come in, without actually having to ask. I got out of the car, but he sat there motionless.

"I don't want to be on my own, Larry."

He hesitated for a second, then he got out and walked towards the house with me.

We sat at the kitchen table and smoked some cigarettes. Larry was pale, but the soft white skin under his tear ducts had turned black. Once or twice he went to say something, but then stopped and stayed silent.

"I'm so sorry you had to be here for that," I said quietly.

"There's nothing to be sorry about." He forced a smile.

"Why did you follow me into the house tonight?"

He looked at me and threw his arms up. "I have no idea."

I stood up and held out my hand. "Will you stay with me?" I asked.

For a second I thought he was going to say no. It would have been so typical. He had been forcing himself on me for months, pressurising me to have sex. And now when I really needed him, he was backing down. Although, I can't say I would have blamed him.

He stood there looking at me and before he could say anything, I took his hand and walked out of the room towards the stairs, pulling him behind me. I'm sure the shock had something to do with it, but Larry for once remained silent.

I led the way up to my bedroom, and as I opened the door the strangest thing happened. Larry buried his face in my shoulder and started to cry. I held him tightly, and sat him down on the bed, keeping the light turned off. We lay back and I pulled the covers over us.

"Christ, I'm sorry," he whispered.

I felt for his face in the dark and pulled it towards me. "Thanks for staying with me."

We kicked off our shoes and lay close together. I drifted into a sleep full of strange dreams, and woke with a start a few hours later. The darkness had given way to a grainy half-light. Outside the birds had started their dawn chorus. Larry turned his head towards me and opened his eyes. We had both fallen asleep fully clothed, and the bed felt far too warm. He sat up and pulled his shirt off over his head. It was still stained with blood from the night before. Then he undid the buttons of my shirt and I sat up as he pulled it off. I undid my bra and slowly we undressed self-consciously, under the covers. Then with the frantic fumbling and clumsiness of first timers, we made love in the confines of my narrow single bed.

We must have dozed off again because when I opened my eyes it was nine o'clock. I lowered my legs gently over the edge of the bed and crept out of the room, dragging my dressing-gown behind me. I went into the bathroom and the cold air hit me like a wet cloth. There was glass all over the floor where Larry had smashed the window. I sidestepped it and walked against the wall over to the sink. I turned the taps on and washed my upper body with cold water. I reached for the towel and something in the bath caught my eye. My heart sank when I saw the dark rim from Grace's blood. It had dried leaving a reddish-brown tidemark halfway down the tub, and lying beside the plug hole was the blade that she had used to cut herself open. I shuddered at the thought of Grace alone in the bathtub hacking at her wrists, and rushed downstairs to get some detergent. I swept up the broken glass and scrubbed the bath until there was no trace of the previous night's events.

Larry came out of the bedroom, yawning loudly, wearing only a pair of jeans. He held his bloodstained shirt up and examined it.

"Can I borrow a top from you? I can't wear this home. They'll think I've been on a right bender."

I went into my room and rooted out a red sweatshirt from the wardrobe. He pulled it over his head and I helped him pull the sleeves over the bandages on his arms.

He grinned and patted his chest. "It's a bit girlie for me, but it'll have to do!"

He turned to check himself in the wardrobe mirror, back to his old self again.

I went downstairs and made some breakfast while he used the bathroom. He appeared a few minutes later. His hair, which was usually gelled and spiked to perfection, was limp and greasy and fell into his eyes. I could tell he was dying to get home to beautify himself.

"Do you want a lift to the hospital?" he asked, pouring himself some tea.

I accepted his offer reluctantly, and went to get some things together for Grace. I didn't really want to sit in a car with him and make conversation all the way to the hospital, but I had no other way of getting there.

It had started to rain and the only sound in the car was the rhythmic squeak of the windscreen wipers. Larry drove like a madman, which was not unusual, but his morning-after anxiety seemed to have given him a new edge. He pulled up at the hospital like a racing driver. I reached into the back seat to get the bag I had hastily packed for Grace and pulled it over onto my knee.

"Wait a minute," he said, turning off the engine.

I looked at him and waited.

He bit his thumbnail nervously. "Was it all right?"

"What?" I snapped, knowing exactly what he meant.

He jumped about in his seat. "You know. Last night. I didn't force you or anything?"

"No." I looked out the window, trying to disguise my embarrassment.

"You're all right so?"

"Of course, I'm all right," I snorted. "Why wouldn't I be?"

"Well, you know, I didn't use anything."

I tried not to smile. If this was his way of telling me he didn't use any contraception, it was a bit late. I rolled my eyes up to heaven. "Well, of course I know you didn't use anything. I'm not completely stupid. Luckily I did, so you can stop worrying."

I knew we would end up having sex some night, and not wanting to carry on the family tradition of getting pregnant on my first go, I had gone on the pill.

I opened my door and got out, slamming it behind me. Then a wave of guilt swept over me, as I looked back and saw his face. Why was I such a bitch to him, when all he ever wanted to do was please me? If he was a mean bastard who treated me like shit, I probably would have been head over heels in love with him. He began to pull away and I ran after the car shouting at him to stop. His brake-lights lit up and the car slowed down. I ran up to him, and he rolled down his window.

"Thanks for last night, Larry – not the sex, but for helping me with Grace. I really appreciate it."

The rain lashed down and I stood there getting soaked.

His face lit up and he leaned out and kissed a raindrop from the tip of my nose.

"See you later," he shouted. Then he drove out of the hospital like a maniac.

43

When I got into the hospital the first person I saw was Jane Rice. She was standing at the desk in reception. She smiled at me briefly, but immediately a look of worry spread across her face. She walked over and took my arm, leading me to a couple of plastic chairs in the corner.

"Sit down, Iris."

I sat down and she sank onto the chair beside me.

"How are you?" she asked, looking me over.

"I'm fine. I'm sorry I look a mess. I didn't get much sleep last night."

"Why didn't you ring me? I would have come over."

"I had someone stay with me." I didn't want to say who, so I changed the subject quickly. "How is she?"

Jane shook her head. "She'll be all right. It's lucky

you found her when you did. She was at death's door. Has she ever tried anything like this before?"

"No," I said, "it's a first."

Jane stared out the window anxiously.

"Is she awake?" I asked.

"She's coming and going, but not fully conscious yet."

"I'll pop in to her," I said, standing up.

"Iris. I think another stint in St Paul's would do her good. I know it's tough on both of you, but right now there isn't any other solution."

My heart sank like a stone into the pit of my stomach. "I couldn't do it to her again," I managed to say.

Jane gave me a sympathetic look. "It's for her own good. She's suicidal, Iris. She needs professional help."

"I know," I said faintly, trying to deal with the wave of nausea that swept over me.

Grace was in a small room on her own. She looked like a broken doll lying in the narrow white bed, her tiny wrists bound in thick dressings. The only noise in the room was the hissing of the ancient heating pipes underneath the window. I sat at the side of her bed and studied her face. There was a deep cut over her left eye that I hadn't noticed the night before. She had probably been struck by a piece of glass from the broken window. I ran my forefinger lightly over it, Grace's eyes fluttered open for a second.

"Why did you do it?" I whispered.

She lay perfectly still.

I stood up, pushing the chair away from me and walked over to the window, breathing deeply in and out, resisting the urge to cry out loud. I wanted to reach over and slap her until she sat up and talked to me. Talked about anything. I don't know if it was a hormonal side effect of first-time sex, or the delayed shock of seeing Grace lying in a bath of her own blood, or a fusion of both, but just at that minute I needed to talk to her to stop myself going insane. I rushed over to her bed and took her limp hand in mine.

"Grace, squeeze my hand if you can hear me."

Her hand didn't move.

"Grace!" I raised my voice urgently. "Damn it, I know you can hear me! Squeeze it!"

Then, I thought I felt the faintest movement of her hand in mine. I pulled my chair closer to the bed and started to talk.

"Why are you so sad, Grace? Is it because my father left? I know who he was, and you should too. Gran should have told you."

Her hand felt limp again, but it made no difference, I kept talking. I told her everything, leaving nothing out. I didn't skate around things to spare her feelings, I just told it like it was. I even paused now and then, waiting for her imaginary reactions. But there were none.

"Tell me you can hear me, Grace," I pleaded.

But she lay in a deep coma, unable to hear or see anything.

I got a taxi home that evening. The phone rang as I walked into the hall, but I was too tired to talk to anyone so I let it ring out. Jody must have been in earlier because the window in the bathroom was boarded up. I ran myself a bath and stepped into it, trying not to think of what had happened there the night before. The hot water lapped over my shoulders and I lay back and closed my eyes. The phone began to ring again and I listened to the shrill sound echo around the empty hallway downstairs. It was a lonely sound and I lay back until the water covered my ears and muffled the noise.

If there was a time in my life that stayed with me and moulded me emotionally, it is the night that Grace tried to kill herself. How it has stayed with me is hard to say. All I know is that what happened that night had a deeply disturbing effect on me. Even now, almost twenty years later, I can be momentarily paralysed by the memory of Grace and how she looked that night.

44

With the greatest of misgivings, I signed Grace in again. When she was well enough, an ambulance took her from the hospital directly to St Paul's, to begin another round of treatment. Her depression had deepened, and she was as low as a person can get. No one could get through to her, least of all me. I didn't go to see her very often and on the days that I did, I woke with a familiar tightness in my chest, and remembered it was my day to visit Grace. She never spoke. I tried at first, talking away to myself in the hope that she would say something, but as the weeks went by I gave up. What was there to say anyway?

Larry and I became close during that time. I gave up my job in the supermarket. Going out with the boss's son quickly changed the way the other girls treated me. I was no longer one of them. I spent a few weeks at home doing nothing – it was my favourite pastime in those days. I could quite happily drift from one day to another doing very little, and all of a sudden it would be the end of the week again. Larry called quite a bit, and although I always knew he wasn't right for me, I was lonely and enjoyed his company. The night we found Grace had created a bond between us that I had never had with anyone before, and it felt good to have a friend that I didn't have to hide my life from. Most evenings we would watch TV or listen to music, and when it got late Larry would beg me to let him stay, and I would push him towards the door, telling him to get out. He did stay at weekends, but always got up early and went home so his mother wouldn't know he'd been out all night. He bought me presents, opened doors for me, drove me wherever I wanted to go. I treated him so badly I don't know why he stuck around but he did.

Grace came home after completing a six-week period in St Paul's. That is, a person that looked like her came home. Grace never really returned. The scars on her wrists were still raw-looking and she tried to hide them by wearing long sleeves all the time. It was only when she reached for a sugar bowl or stretched an arm out to dip her paintbrush into water that I would catch a glimpse of the marks she had made. We never spoke about her suicide attempt. She never asked how I found her that night, and as always I was happy to let it pass.

Now that Grace was home again, I took the opportunity to cool things off with Larry. We had barely spent an evening apart since Grace had gone into hospital, and I was beginning to feel suffocated by him. He knew my house was off limits with Grace home so we had nowhere to hang out together. I had enjoyed having the house to myself and now with Grace back home I began to resent her. Life was so much easier when she was out of the way. I felt guilty for thinking like that. After all, she had tried to kill herself. Having had a glimpse of normality during the weeks she had been away made me realise that as long as we lived together, my life would always be a mess.

Larry began to grow impatient with our new enforced chastity. I refused to do it in his car, which only left his house on a Tuesday night when his mother was out at bingo, but I could never relax. The thought of her finding us doing it on her couch never failed to kill my passion.

* * *

Grace started to drink again immediately, but this time she was clever about it. She had stopped taking her medication because she knew it would make her sick, and so little by little she started to wean herself on to the alcohol again. It took me a while to realise that she had started, but when I did find out it had no effect on me. I had reached a point where I didn't care any more.

It was Valentine's Day and Larry was taking me out to dinner. Grace was in her room. I hadn't seen her for two days. We alternated from room to room but tried not to occupy the same space simultaneously, therefore not seeing each other for a day or two was not unusual. I burrowed into the depths of my wardrobe and pulled out everything I could find. I had gained weight since I had started taking the pill, and all of my clothes were too tight. I put on a pair of black trousers that had always been too big for me. They fitted perfectly. I heard Larry's car pull up outside and he blew the horn. I ran downstairs and went out to meet him with a face like thunder. I sat into the car and slammed the door,

"What's up?" he asked.

"Oh, nothing, c'mon, let's go," I grumbled.

"You look great."

"No, I don't. I'm getting fat from taking that bloody pill! None of my clothes will fit me."

He laughed and smacked my thigh. "You're a fine strappin' lass!"

I glared at him scornfully and we drove the rest of the way without speaking. Larry had been sulky ever since the sexual part of our relationship had abruptly ended, and it didn't take much to start a fight. We pulled up outside the restaurant and he took my hand.

"Let's not fight. It's Valentine's Day!"

I smiled and bit my tongue, trying not to say anything sarcastic.

We sat at a table that had a candle and a red rose at my place setting. Larry became quite excitable during the meal, chattering away like a demented monkey, only stopping to swallow his food in gulps. I relaxed and let him rant on. It was good to be away from the house for a few hours. As soon as he had finished eating, he threw his knife and fork together noisily.

"How about we skip dessert and go for a quick drink?"

"Fine," I said reaching for my coat.

He jumped up quickly and grabbed my coat from me. "Let me help the little lady," he said, sweeping the coat around my shoulders.

When we got out to the car, Larry stopped talking. He went to start the engine but then seemed to change his mind.

"Let's go," I said.

He sat there grinning at me.

"What?"

He slipped his hand into his inside pocket and pulled out a small black box.

I could feel the blood drain from my face.

"Happy Valentine's Day," he said, snapping open the box to reveal what was inside.

"Will you marry me?"

It was a ring. I looked down at the sparkling solitaire in horror. Then I reached over and snapped the box shut.

My mouth went dry and I struggled to find the right words.

"Larry," I gasped, "we can't get married!"

His smile began to fade.

"Why not?"

"Because we just can't. We don't know each other well enough."

"We've known each other for nearly a year."

I could almost hear the sound of his heart sinking. He looked crushed.

"Oh God, Larry, I don't want to get married."

"Well, what the hell are you doing with me!" he said in a high-pitched voice.

I looked out the window at the happy Valentine's couples tripping in and out of the pub, and wished I could have been like them. It would have been so easy to say yes, and for a split second I sat there and weighed up the pros and cons until I suddenly came to my senses.

"We're too young to think about marriage. We've got our whole lives ahead of us."

"Yes, and I want to spend my life with you," he whined.

There was no easy way to say it. "I don't feel the same way."

He leaned his head on the steering wheel and started to cry, big loud sobs like a child who'd had his sweets taken from him. I put my arm around his shoulder and tried to comfort him, but it was no use. The damage had been done. What I had said could not be taken back. We sat there for what seemed like days until Larry straightened up and wiped his face with the sleeve of his jacket.

"Sorry," he said quietly. "I'll take you home now."

The silence was painful, and for once I wished he would drive faster. He pulled into the lane and we sat there for a few minutes, still saying nothing. I tried to think of something that could possibly end the evening on a more positive note, but my mind was a blank.

Larry turned to me. "Iris?"

Oh no, I thought. He'd started to cry again.

"Will you think about it?"

The irony of the situation occurred to me, and I suppressed a wry smile as it would have been cruelly inappropriate. It was the first time I had ever tried to be nice to him. Unfortunately, I had to wait until I was giving him the elbow to show him that I was not completely made of stone. I took both his hands in mine and made him look at me.

"Larry – you deserve someone much better than me. We don't belong together. You know that."

He went to say something, but I put my finger to his lips and he stopped. I kissed him gently, and got out of the car before he could say any more.

As I let myself in the front door I could see Grace staggering up the stairs. She had heard the car and tried to vacate the kitchen with her bottle before I caught sight of her. I trudged up the stairs behind her and heard the click of her bedroom door closing. I went into my own bedroom and threw myself down on the bed. I lay there, staring at the ceiling for a while until I started to get cold. I got up and walked around and went to the window, pulling it open a crack. I sat on the windowsill and lit a cigarette and blew the smoke outside. In the darkness I could make out the shape of Larry's car. He was still sitting there. I moved away from the window, fearing a tragic Shakespearean scene and closed the curtains, then I changed into my nightdress.

I had let a pile of letters, mostly bills, pile up on the table beside my bed. It was too early to sleep, so I started to sort through them. A phone bill, an electricity bill, a hospital bill, and something I had completely forgotten about, the application for an American visa. I heard Larry start his car and drive off. He was probably going to the pub to get blind drunk. I could imagine the speedometer needle shuddering somewhere between eighty and ninety miles an hour, and I prayed he wouldn't do anything stupid. It was only fair that I should stop seeing him completely, but I would miss him. I wished he'd been a girl. He would have made a better girlfriend. I turned the visa application over in my hands and went to look for a pen. There was no reason in the world for me to hang around any longer.

The following morning I rang Sarah and asked if I could stay with her for a few days.

I knew Larry would be back. He could never take no for an answer. But I had made my decision, and I knew how easily he could talk me out of it.

45

I stayed with Sarah on and off for a few weeks until my visa and passport came through. Whenever I faltered, Sarah would urge me on, reminding me of how little I had to stay for. During the time I stayed with her, I made trips home to gather my things together little by little, and to check on Grace. She was drunk all the time. She got her drink by ringing a shop in town and ordering her weekly groceries along with all the vodka she needed, and Jody would collect it on a Saturday and bring it out to her. Unless I locked her up permanently, I had no control.

I bought my airline ticket, but the only person who knew I was leaving was Sarah. She had arranged for me to stay with her son in Boston until I got fixed up with a place of my own. I spent the weeks before I left in a state of anxiety, my guilt coiled around me like a string of barbed wire. Larry had left notes under the door at home, and had even left messages with Jody. But I never made contact. On one visit home I crouched behind the kitchen window while he hammered on the front door. I was so unsure of what I was doing that I almost wanted him to change my mind. I went home for the last time a week before I was due to travel. I stood outside Grace's bedroom and listened at the door for any sounds, it was quiet. I knocked as I pushed the door open. Grace stirred in the bed. The sour smell of stale alcohol filled my nostrils. Grace sat up and looked at me, then she let her head drop back on to her pillow.

"Hi," she croaked.

I walked over and stood at the foot of her bed. My legs were shaking and I put one hand on the bedpost to steady myself.

"Grace. I've come to tell you I'm leaving."

She raised herself up on one elbow and looked at me in mild disbelief. "Where are you going?"

"America."

She sat there blinking, trying to take it in.

My eyes filled with tears and all the conflicting emotions I had for her somersaulted through my head. I loved her. I hated her. I resented her. And now, looking at her lying on the dirty crumpled sheets, I mostly pitied her.

"I have to go," I said, looking towards the ceiling

in the hope that the tears would dissolve back into my eyes.

"For how long?" She looked dazed, and I wondered if she would remember this conversation tomorrow.

"I don't know. I'll write when I get settled."

Grace lay down and turned her back to me.

"Look, Grace, are you sober? I need to talk to you."

"Yes," she said in a whisper.

I moved towards the top of the bed and sat down beside her. "I'm going to take half of the money in the account. That leaves you with about twenty thousand pounds. You'll have to think about selling the house. Grace, are you listening to me?"

It was impossible to tell if she was freshly drunk or sobering up or somewhere in between. She sat back up again and her eyes fastened on mine.

"Will you forgive me?"

I gave a nervous smile. "Of course."

She grasped my arms with her bony hands, and I caught a flash of the angry red marks on her wrists.

"Really forgive me," she asked, as if her life depended on it.

We looked deep into each others eyes for a few seconds.

"I'll try my best," I said solemnly.

She pulled me to her chest and held me roughly and awkwardly, like a boxer with no strength left. When she released me, I got out of the room as fast as I could before she could see me cry. Then without taking a last look around, I ran from the house as fast as I could before I changed my mind. I didn't even wait around to say goodbye to Jody.

I stayed in Sarah's house the night before I left for America. I was so nervous that one of my eyelids had started to twitch. Jane Rice had given me some tablets to help me relax on the flight and I swallowed one as I packed my suitcase. I took Sarah out for an early dinner. As soon as I had finished eating I excused myself and went to the restroom to throw up, but I don't think she noticed. I felt like a prisoner, the night before the break-out.

I went to bed and felt the tablet begin to take effect. My legs felt tingly, and the twitch in my eye gradually began to disappear.

Jane had rung earlier and wished me well. She had promised to look in on Grace as often as possible, and I knew that she would. I had left a note for Jody in Mulligan's pub, and imagined his reaction as he read it, sitting on the bar stool, shaking his head. I knew he would think badly of me for abandoning Grace. I did the cowardly thing where Larry was concerned: I told him nothing. At the time, and for a long time after, I tried to convince myself that it was for his own good. Any kind of goodbye would have only upset him again. Now it seems nothing short of callous, that I didn't even bother to drop him a note.

I said my goodbyes to Sarah at her house the next

morning, preferring to take a taxi to the airport. Her angina had worsened and she really wasn't able for too much. We hugged tightly as the taxi-driver put my case into the boot.

"Mind yourself, my love," she said, as her eyes filled up. "Andrew will collect you at the airport in Boston.

When I got to Dublin airport I took another tablet, I needed to block out as much feeling as possible. I thought about ringing Larry, but decided against it.

I arrived in Boston on Memorial Day weekend in 1987.

I was twenty years of age and, although I was not aware of it then, I had changed the map of my life.

46

Andrew was at the airport to meet me. I knew straight away that he was Sarah's son, because he had the same smile. If I had met him before I had no memory of it. He moved to the States when he finished school sixteen years ago. He shook my hand and welcomed me to Boston in a clipped Irish American accent. He was almost bald and looked older than his thirty-five years. He lived alone in the Back Bay area, which was a really nice part of the city. I could only imagine what a pain this was for him, being forced to invite a stranger into his home.

As we pulled away from the airport and headed for the city I was anxious to let him know that I was not planning on staying with him long. I would rather have lived on the street than impose on someone I hardly knew.

"You picked a bad day to arrive. It hasn't rained for weeks," he said.

"You must be really pleased with your mum for making you do this." I tried to sound light-hearted, but I wanted to get the point across at the same time.

He looked at me in surprise. "Do what?"

"Have me stay with you."

"Not at all," he said warmly. Not a phoney warm – it was quite genuine.

"Well, I just want you to know that finding a place of my own is top of my list."

"You better make sure you like the place first," he laughed. "Honestly, feel free to stay as long as you like. I'm out from early morning and I rarely spend a night in."

His apartment was on a street that I had seen countless times in American movies. Old brownstone houses three storeys high with steps up to the front door. Andrew lived at the top of the house. I expected a more modest apartment , and imagined I might be sleeping on a couch, but when he opened the front door we stepped into a large hallway with high ceilings. The walls were painted white and almost every square inch was covered with paintings. I stopped to look at one. It was a woman with a black shawl over her head and thatched cottages in the background.

"That's my latest purchase," he said, his voice

straining as he hauled my case through the hallway. "Do you like it?"

The thick brushstrokes reminded me of Grace's paintings, and I felt a sudden rush of homesickness.

"It's a Markey Robinson. I collect Irish art," he said, brushing past me. "Here you go," he said opening a door at the end of the hall.

I followed him into the room and tried to suppress a gasp. It was the nicest bedroom I had ever seen. The bed had a leather-padded headboard, and was made up in beautiful white linen. The carpet and curtains were a light beige colour and looked brand-new.

"It's lovely," I said, trying not to sound too overwhelmed. I didn't want him to think I came from a bog-hole.

"Your bathroom is over here," he said, walking across the hall and throwing open another door. The marble and chrome sparkled, as if it had never been used. He showed me around the rest of the apartment: the art deco living-room, the white kitchen with no trace of food anywhere.

He stood on the thick white carpet of the living-room, both hands thrust into his trouser pockets, rocking gently back and forth on the balls of his feet. He was smart looking in a bookish kind of way. He wore black-rimmed spectacles that were geeky but trendy at the same time. I looked him over and noticed how well dressed he was. His trousers were casual chinos but well tailored and pressed to within an inch of their life. His shirt had one of those logos (a horse or a crocodile, I can't remember) that screamed preppie American.

I tried to cover a coffee-stain on my sweatshirt. Being surrounded by such style had made me aware of just how shabby I must have looked.

"Great place!"

"Thank you," he beamed. "Now why don't you freshen up and we'll eat."

"You don't need to cook for me," I protested.

He smiled at me. "You know, I've lived here for almost two years and I've never used the cooker. I meant eat out."

We went to a Japanese restaurant that night. I don't know how we hit it off so well, but we did, something to do with opposites attracting. I was his very antithesis.

It took me a while to realise he was gay. His friend Charles joined us for dinner one night and we ordered Chinese food to the apartment. As soon as he walked into the room the penny dropped. It was his partner. I had thought that Andrew had been staying with a girlfriend on the nights that he didn't come home, and wondered why he had been so slow to introduce her. When Charles left that night, Andrew came back into the living-room where I was clearing away the remains of the meal. He cleared his throat nervously.

"My mother doesn't know I'm gay," he announced.

"Well, she certainly won't find out from me."

"I'm just worried, if you're writing to your mom or anything."

I started to laugh. I had phoned Grace several times since I had arrived, but each time she seemed to be worse. Almost every time I rang Grace, she seemed to be incoherent. The only way of knowing how she was, was to ring Jane Rice, which I did regularly. "My *mom* doesn't know where I am, and we don't talk to each other about stuff like that. Even if we did, she wouldn't remember it the next day."

There was a long stilted silence between us. My outburst had made me feel stupid.

Andrew sat down and swirled his wine around his glass. "My mother told me a little about Grace. I guess you've had a rotten time looking after her."

"Yes."

We talked for a long time that night about our mothers. I told him how Grace was getting worse and how guilty I felt about being away from her. He talked about how isolated he felt, growing up in a family of boys, knowing he was not the same as them. It was reassuring to hear that someone growing up in a family like Sarah's could feel like an outsider too.

I found a job pretty soon after I arrived. It was in a fancy northern Italian restaurant (the northern bit

was important for some reason) on Boylston Street.
Andrew had offered to help me find a job. He had a
friend who owned a bookstore café in town, but I
thought it better if I found something myself.
Unfortunately it only lasted for one night. My big
mistake was lying about my waitressing experience.
On my first night I was introduced to the other staff,
and before the restaurant opened for the evening the
chef came out of the kitchen and recited the
evening's specials. Hundreds of them. Food I had
never heard of. Artichoke hearts. Poulet broiled in
apricot juice. Saltimbocca. Zuppa inglese. I broke out
in a damp sweat trying to scribble down what he
was saying, but then I noticed that none of the other
waiters were writing at all. They stood there listening
to him with slightly bored expressions as if they'd
heard it all a thousand times before. Maybe they had,
but this was my first time so I kept scribbling away
even though I couldn't spell most of it. The night
went from bad to worse very quickly. I didn't know
I would have to open wine at the table. The cork
broke in the first bottle. The second time I had to
hold the bottle between my knees and when the
cork came out I hit myself in the chin. People glared
when I came to the table trying to balance the plates
in midair, saying "The chicken?" The maitre d' took
me by the arm and pulled me towards a quiet alcove.
"Iris!" he hissed. "You do not wave the plates about,
asking who ordered the chicken! This is a high-class

restaurant, not a pizza parlour. Memorise your table plan!"

By ten o' clock that night my nerves were beginning to jangle. I cut through the kitchen and out to the back alley for a cigarette. Two of the Puerto Rican dishwashers were out there, and they introduced themselves in broken English. One of the guys offered me a joint, and not wanting to be taken for a square, I took it from him. I had smoked a few times before with Larry, and I thought it might calm me down a bit, the night had been so hectic. I can't remember how many puffs I had, but it was too many. What I do remember is feeling so stoned that I could hardly pronounce my name. The busy period must have eased off because three or four of the waiting staff came out for a cigarette break, but stood a few paces away from us. Obviously smoking pot with the dishwashers wasn't the done thing. I could hardly open my bloodshot eyes and I still had people sitting at my station who needed to be served. I went into the ladies' room to splash some cold water on my face. Then I looked at myself in the mirror and recoiled in horror. I was deathly white – even my lips had lost their colour. The whites of my eyes were a maze of little red veins, like an ordnance survey map. There was no way I could face anyone. I thought of my table with four people still waiting to be served, and panicked. Without making eye contact with anyone, I walked back through the kitchen and into the staffroom. Thankfully no one was there. I took off my bow tie and apron and stuffed them into an empty locker. I then grabbed my jacket, and keeping my head down, walked out into the back alley and ran.

The next day I met Andrew for lunch and told him what had happened. He bundled up his napkin and stuck it under his glasses to wipe the tears away. He thought it was the funniest thing he'd ever heard. I didn't find the episode as hilarious as he did. In fact I felt downright incompetent.

"Oh, don't worry about it," said Andrew, pouring me another glass of wine. "That place is a pretentious dump anyway. You did the right thing. Now, please let me ask Leon to give you a job."

I threw my hands up in surrender. "Fine," I conceded.

The bookstore café was perfect. Part bookstore and part café, serving only soup and sandwiches. Any idiot could do it. Leon was the owner, but he lived most of the year in France and two Australian sisters ran the place for him, Tina and Lisa Victory.

The day that I was due to start work I woke with a sinking feeling. I hated starting new jobs, all that standing around trying to fit in. I took as long as possible to shower and dress myself, but I still arrived far too early. I went into a small deli across the street and sat at the window, drinking coffee and smoking nervously. Andrew had offered to come with me but I thought it best if I went alone. I didn't want any special treatment. About thirty minutes and an ashtray of cigarettes later, I saw two girls get out of a car and walk towards the café. One of them took out some keys and opened the shutters. Slowly I got off my stool and made my way towards the door. I walked across the street, squinting in the early morning sun.

"Hi," I called to them before they shut the door behind them.

They both turned and looked at me. They didn't look at me the way the staff in the other restaurant did, the kind of look that starts at the feet and comes up slowly to meet your smile with a slight sneer. They had friendly open faces and one of them stepped forward.

"Hi there, you must be the new girl."

"I'm Iris." Not knowing whether to shake hands or not, I gave a sort of silly half wave. They were tall and blonde and very tanned, and looked as if they would be more at home on a surfboard than a city restaurant.

"Hi, Iris, I'm Tina and this is my sister, Lisa." Tina wore her hair in a short bob that she constantly tucked behind her ears. Lisa's was much longer and pulled back in a ponytail. They looked identical, and spoke with strong Australian accents.

They brought me in and showed me around. Apart from operating the coffee machine, there wasn't a lot to learn. Lisa worked in the kitchen making the soup and sandwiches and Tina served.

"It's been hectic," she said rolling her eyes up to heaven. "Ever since Kristen left, I've been working the floor myself."

Lisa shook her head sadly. "Kristen lived with us and worked here until last month. We really miss her."

"What happened?"

"Visa problems. She's gone home to try to sort something out."

"Our dad's American," explained Tina, "so we're legal."

"I hope I'll be OK," I said, nodding towards the tables. "You will tell me if I'm doing anything wrong?"

"Course, we will." Tina smiled reassuringly and handed me an apron.

I managed to get through the first day without any disasters. In fact, it was a lot easier than I had expected it to be.

I started at eleven o'clock every morning and finished at seven, so I had my evenings free. I was so happy that I had made the move to America. Grace and home, and the miseries attached to it, seemed like another lifetime. I wrote to Sarah and thanked her for making me come, because I know I would never have made the decision without her. Andrew was so good to me, but as soon as I got the job in the café I was anxious to get out from under his feet.

One evening as we were cleaning up, Lisa and Tina began to moan about the extra rent they had to pay since Kirsten's departure.

"We'll have to advertise for a roommate soon, Lisa, or I'll go broke!" wailed Tina as she took a handful of bills out of her bag. "I was just about making ends meet, but now, look!" she said waving the bills in the air.

"We'll do it tomorrow," said Lisa.

"I'll move in with you."

They both looked at me as if I had sprouted another head.

"But you live with Whatshisname," said Tina.

"I'm only staying with him until I find somewhere," I explained. Then realising that they may not have wanted to ask me, I said, "But if you would prefer someone else, I don't mind. I know we haven't known each other too long."

"Oh my God!" exclaimed Lisa. "You would be perfect. I didn't know you were looking for a place."

Tina kissed the bunch of bills in her hand. "Thank you, God!"

"I'm so glad, Iris. We were sick at the thought of sharing our home with a stranger."

So that was it. I moved in with them on the understanding that I had no idea how long I was going to stay.

They said I could move in straight away, so I went home that evening and started to pack my things.

When Andrew came home later that night and saw my bags lined up by the door, he seemed genuinely put out that I was leaving so soon. "You said you were staying for the summer," he protested.

"No, I didn't," I corrected him. "Your mother said that. I had no intention of staying with you for the whole summer."

He looked at my bags and then at me in a state of confusion. "But I'll miss you. At least stay for tonight – I don't feel like eating alone."

I laughed at his attempt to sound sad. "Of course, I'll stay tonight, but only if you let me take you out to dinner."

Since my arrival, Andrew had not allowed me to pay for anything. When we went out to eat he would slip the waiter his credit card before the bill came to our table. As the weeks went by I tried to beat him to it, excusing myself before the coffee was served and racing up to the cash desk, only to find that he had somehow managed to settle the bill again. That night we got dressed up and I picked a restaurant near Boston Common that I had heard Andrew talk about. It was very expensive, and full of gay men. Andrew was in his element.

"You know coming here and staying with you has been one of the best things that has ever happened to me," I said as we clinked glasses.

"Stop it. I'm getting choked up," said Andrew bashfully.

"It's true. Thank you for everything."

Andrew leaned over, almost knocking everything off the table, and hugged me. "It works both ways," he whispered. "I've really enjoyed having you stay."

47

Lisa and Tina's apartment was only a few blocks away from Andrew's. It wasn't quite as fancy, but I had my own bedroom, and the sisters were easy to live with. They missed their family, and whenever their parents phoned, one of them would end up in tears, usually Tina. They must have sensed that I had problems at home, because they didn't ask too many questions, and I never felt like talking about it. I didn't miss home at all. Sometimes I would wake at night in a panic, and get out of bed to check on Grace. Then the feeling would fade, like a fog lifting when I looked around my new room and realised where I was. But my relief was always mixed with guilt when I thought of where she might be. Jane Rice wrote often and assured me that Grace was no worse than when I had left. Needless to say she was also no better. Much to my surprise, I missed Larry more than anyone.

I had been working at the café for a month when I met Todd. He was so good-looking that I almost dropped the tray of coffees I was holding the first day he came in. He looked very American, dazzling white teeth and square-cut jaw. It took me a while to get beyond his good looks and when I did he was very disappointing. All the good stuff was on the outside. He hung around that first day until I had finished work, and then we went for a drink. I chose to ignore all the warning signs that were there from our first conversation.

"So where are you from?"

"Ireland."

"Your accent's cute."

He had a very annoying habit of nodding his head while he spoke.

"So … U2!"

"Pardon?"

"U2! D'ya like them?"

"Oh yes, they're all right."

"I stood in line overnight last fall for a ticket to their concert. They were awesome."

And so on and so forth. I could catalogue our relationship in little snippets like that. We started dating in July. He was a student at the Massachusetts Institute of Technology. His parents were very wealthy, so he got to bum around town for the summer holidays. The Institute was a college that required good grades to get into, and while I have no doubt that Todd was very technically minded and intelligent in the field he had chosen, his ignorance of the rest of the world was staggering.

He would say things like: "Do you have cars in Ireland?"

"It's somewhere near Sweden, right?"

"Man, I would never go near Europe again after that Chernobyl thing. The place is nuked!"

I didn't like bringing him back to the apartment. I got the feeling that the sisters weren't as crazy about him as I was. His parents had a house on Cape Cod, and on occasional weekends we went to stay there. It was an old clapboard house, with a swing out on the front porch, just like in *The Waltons*. At night we would sit on the swing and drink beer, listening to the ocean in the darkness. Did I mention that he smoked pot all the time? Well, he did, morning, noon and night. He spoke with his breath held most of the time, because he had just inhaled a big lungful of hash. But it didn't bother me one bit. I was smitten. I spent the summer in a kind of dreamy daze, serving customers with a smile I couldn't suppress, all the time thinking of what we'd do that evening. That was until September rolled around and I discovered what a rat he was.

One morning as we were opening up the café, he came by, looking a little rough around the edges. He stood at the counter, running his fingers through his hair.

"Can you come outside a minute?"

I looked at Tina and she nodded. "Go ahead," she said curtly.

We walked down the street and I waited to hear what he had to say. His hands were shoved deep down in his pockets, and he looked down at the pavement.

"We can't see each other any more," he mumbled.

I felt my face flush. "Why not?"

"I'm going back to college, and – "

"I know that, but we can still see each other!" I interrupted.

"I'm seeing someone," he blurted.

Yes, I know. You're seeing me. I blinked at him in surprise, waiting for an explanation.

"I've been dating a girl in college for like two years."

"Two years!" It was all I could say. I was stunned. It had never crossed my mind. How could I have been so stupid?

He opened his mouth again to say something, but I pushed him out of the way with all the force I could muster, which must have been considerable because he fell backwards almost losing his balance. That was the last I ever saw of Todd.

I went back into the café and burst into tears, feeling like a proper fool. The girls were ready, and armed with a mountain of insults they had stored up all summer. Lisa was particularly caustic in her outburst. "Fucking slimeball! I knew it all along. I knew he was no good," she said, handing me a tissue.

"He wasn't your type, Iris. You're far too intelligent for him." Tina was more sympathetic.

Lisa walked outside and looked up and down the street but he was gone, which was just as well. I think if he had still been there she would have smacked him.

I spent the next couple of weeks licking my wounds and feeling generally miserable. I came to the conclusion that men were bad news. I began to think about my father (uncle/father actually), and what a shit he must have been. I believe he had an affair with Grace out of spite. If he loved her he would have come back. He knew where she was. If I had got pregnant that summer by Todd, I probably would have had an abortion. Had things been different, Grace might have done the same with me and she probably would have had a much happier life. What Sarah had told me about my dubious parentage, I had swept carefully into the farthest reaches of my mind. I understood everything she had told me that night, but I never allowed myself to think about it. The reality was too grim. However, in the weeks after I was dumped by Todd, the truth about how I came to be began to invade my thoughts and unsettle me.

Andrew persuaded me to go home with him for Christmas. He hadn't been back to Ireland for nearly four years, and for some reason he thought it would make the trip easier if I went with him. I rang Grace and told her I was coming home, and spent the rest of the week sick with worry. I really wanted to see her again, but I was definitely not staying, and that was going to be hard.

"You look like you're going to a funeral," said Andrew as our plane took off from Logan Airport.

"Feels a bit like that." I smiled, thinking a funeral would be a piece of cake compared to what I had to face.

Dublin Airport was festooned with fairy lights and Christmas carols to welcome home the thousands of young Irish people who had moved away to England and America in order to get work. In the fifties it had been the builders and labourers who had gone, but in the eighties it was the doctors and lawyers, the Brain Drain.

Sarah and Pat were at the airport to meet us. Sarah cried and hugged us, and Andrew choked back the tears, not wanting to look like a sissy in front of his father. He had left his gay mannerisms on the other side of the Atlantic. I stayed the first night in Sarah's. She had invited Andrew's brothers with their wives and children around for dinner. The house could hardly contain them. It was funny to see Andrew change character for his family. I think he overdid it at times, slapping his brothers on the back and saying things like "Jaysus" all the time. He desperately wanted to fit in, yet knew he would rather die than be like them.

The following day was Christmas Eve. I took the bus home and as it pulled into Wicklow town I was surprised to see Jody waiting to meet me. He took my suitcase from me and shook my hand roughly.

"Good to see you again, Iris."

I didn't think he'd ever speak to me again because of the way I left Grace, but he seemed genuinely pleased to see me. He filled me in on all his news as we drove out of town. There was planning permission granted for twenty apartments on the land that we had sold. Mulligan's pub was for sale. Mick Doran, Larry's father, had almost completed the building of a big supermarket near Bray.

"How's Grace doing?" I tried not to sound too anxious.

"She's OK," he said flatly.

"That's good," I said looking out the window.

"I didn't agree with what you did," he said, cutting his eyes towards me sharply. "Running off like that without a word."

I braced myself for what was coming next.

"But now I know you did the right thing," he continued. "I just couldn't see it then."

"I did the right thing?"

"Well, she had to pull herself together. Don't get me wrong now, she's still drinking, but not as bad as before."

We pulled into the lane and there in the window complete with twinkling lights, was a Christmas tree. There hadn't been a Christmas tree in the house since my grandmother died. It felt like a scene from an old black-and-white Christmas movie. I expected the door to fling open and Grace to run out wearing a frilly apron saying, "Darling, you're home at last. We've missed you!"

OK, she didn't, but the tree was a nice touch. I could tell by the way Jody was smiling at me that he had been responsible for it.

I opened the car door slowly and walked up to the house, my heart almost bursting with nervous anticipation. The door opened and there was Grace. She looked different. Her hair was cut quite short and it made her look older, but she wasn't as gaunt as I remembered. We hugged in our usual wooden way, and the familiar smell of booze wafted from her breath. I followed her into the kitchen. It was warm and cheery. She had tried to light the fire but it hadn't taken, and the coals were still smoking in the grate. The kitchen looked a lot neater than when I last saw it. Grace lit a cigarette and took a long look at me.

"So, Miss American Pie. How have you been?" she asked, blowing smoke from her nostrils.

"I'm fine," I answered.

"It's good to see you again," she said smiling.

"It's good to see you too."

"Put your things upstairs and I'll dish up some food."

I picked up my case obediently and went upstairs. *Dish up some food!* I had hoped she would make an effort for my homecoming, have a wash, dress up, but cooking dinner far outstripped any expectations I might have had. I pushed open my bedroom door and looked around the room. I had been away for only eight months yet it seemed an age since I had slept there. I felt a strange sensation move through me, a mixture of pleasure and dread. Glad to be home yet frantic to get away again. I dumped my case on the bed and left the unpacking till later. I looked into the other rooms before I went back down again. Nothing had changed except the biggest spare bedroom, which I had completely cleared out, seemed to be full of junk again.

I turned on the light, and the room came alive with colour. Grace had turned it into a studio. There were two easels in the middle of the room, and all around the edges, leaning against the walls, were her paintings. I walked around the room and took a closer look. Most of them were landscapes, but not the sunny cornfield variety. These were bleak wastelands, rocky fields with misshapen trees painted in dark shades of brown and black and purple. They made me feel cold and I shivered and rubbed the tops of my arms as I walked from one to the other. When I reached the last one I stopped. It was different from the others, a portrait of a child. Then my mouth fell open when I realised who it was. It was me aged six in my Communion dress. I knelt beside it and ran my finger over the rough texture of the veil that framed my face, and a lump began to rise in my throat as I took in the detail. The misery of that six-year-old child came rushing back to me and I stood up quickly and took a step backwards as the picture threatened to suck me into it. I hadn't thought about that day for so many years. Now, being confronted with the image, I could remember everything about it, as if it was yesterday. I swallowed hard and tried to ward off the chilling thoughts that flooded my mind, making me feel as if I had never left.

I walked swiftly out of the room and pulled the door shut behind me. On the landing, I ran my fingers through my hair and gripped the front bits back into a clip, trying to pull myself together.

Damn this house, I thought as I went downstairs. I had only been home a matter of minutes, and already I was nervous wreck.

48

Our dinner on Christmas Eve was a cooked turkey that Grace had bought from a delicatessen in Wicklow. She fumbled awkwardly with a blunt carving knife, trying to cut the slices thinly.

"We might as well start on this now. There's enough to feed an army."

She had boiled some potatoes and put them in the middle of the table with a tub of coleslaw. I noticed a new addition to the kitchen in the shape of a microwave oven, and our turkey was heated in it. A good sign, I thought. She must be eating if she bought a microwave. It tasted better than it looked and I ate everything on my plate. Grace picked at her food slowly, until she saw me put down my knife and fork, then she pushed the plate away and reached for her cigarettes. She offered me one, but I declined.

Lisa and Tina had nagged me into not smoking in the apartment, and apart from the odd one in work and nights out, I had cut way back. Grace shrugged and took one out for herself and I started to clear away the dishes.

"Do you like it in Boston?" I could feel her eyes follow me.

"Yes," I said brightly. "It's really nice."

I kept my back to her as I washed the dishes and listened to her exhale loudly.

"If I drove you out, I'm sorry," she said.

There was silence. I stopped scrubbing a pot and turned around to face her. "In a way it was the best thing that could have happened to me. I really like it over there." My hands gripped the rim of the sink behind me. I had to sound sure of myself for fear that she would ask me to stay. "I'm *really, really* happy," I heard myself say.

Grace stubbed out her cigarette and smiled at me. "I'm glad for you."

I had expected the ashtray to come hurling across the room at me, and a tirade of abuse about how selfish I was – but a smile? It threw me, I could feel the adrenaline swishing around my limbs.

"I don't even have a phone number for you," she said quietly. It wasn't over yet.

"I didn't give it to you because I don't want you ringing when you're drunk."

Grace looked at me indignantly and a glint of

anger flashed in her eyes, but she must have remembered what time of year it was and composed herself quickly.

"It's too upsetting, when I'm so far away, to hear you like that." There, I'd said it.

Grace nodded her head grimly. "What if I promise not to ring when I'm like that?"

Like what, Grace? I wanted to ask. She couldn't even say the word 'drunk'.

"Then I'll give you my number. I want to keep in touch as well."

We said no more about it. Grace asked about my job and where I was living, I told her all about the Victory sisters and Andrew. She wanted to hear everything about my life over there, and it struck me that she had probably had no contact with the outside world since I had left.

At ten o'clock she stood up and said she was going to bed. As she walked by me she put her hand on my shoulder and gave it a squeeze, "It's good to have you back again."

"Thanks. It's good to be back," I said.

But it's only for a week.

I knew she was going up to her room to have the drink she had deprived herself of all night in order to welcome me home, but the fact that she had made the effort at all meant so much to me.

That night I woke. I thought I heard noises coming from somewhere in the house. I pressed a button on my digital watch which illuminated the face. It was 4.30am I needed to go to the bathroom, so I crept from my bed slowly, being careful not to bang into anything. I opened the door quietly and went out into the landing. The door to Grace's bedroom was open but she was not in there. I walked towards the bathroom and noticed that the light was on in the bedroom where I had seen the paintings earlier. I crept down the narrow corridor and up the short flight of stairs. The door was partly open and I could hear the swishing of her paintbrush on canvas. I looked into the room and saw Grace. A glass in one hand and a paintbrush in the other, oblivious to anything around her.

I slipped away quietly before she saw me and went back to bed.

The next morning I slept late. When I woke it was almost eleven. I pulled my dressing-gown on and went downstairs. Grace was already up and trying to light a fire. I didn't want to complain, but the house was like an icebox. I put the kettle on and waited for it to boil. "Happy Christmas," said Grace, throwing another match into the smouldering coals.

"Happy Christmas." I poured the boiling water into a teapot and stirred the teabags around. "Will I make you some toast?"

"No, I ate earlier," answered Grace. She stood up, brushing the sooty remains of last night's fire off the front off her trousers.

"I invited Jody to eat with us today, I hope you don't mind."

"No." My eyes opened wide with surprise. Every Christmas for as long as I could remember my gran would suggest inviting 'poor Jody' for dinner, but Grace always objected. I opened my mouth to remind her, but shut it again quickly. "That's a great idea!"

After breakfast I went back upstairs to have a bath, and listened to Grace banging pots and pans downstairs. When we finally sat down to eat later that day, I wondered what all the pot-walloping had been for. There was only the same turkey, coleslaw and potatoes again.

Jody arrived in the afternoon, scrubbed up in his Sunday best. He smelt of the many bottles of stout he had put away that morning, making his Christmas calls to friends. He was laden down with food. Thinking he would be alone on Christmas day, well-wishing neighbours had made him cakes and puddings. He even had a cooked ham. He set them all down on our table along with the gifts he had bought for us.

"Happy Christmas, Iris," he said, cutting straight to the chase and handing me my present. It had definitely been wrapped by him. I could hardly open it with all the tape that had been wound around it. With the help of a kitchen knife I finally managed to unwrap the set of three lemon-shaped soaps on a rope. Jody was crouched beside the fireplace rearranging the coals and screwing up pieces of newspaper to get a proper fire going. I went over and hugged him.

"Thanks a million, Jody. They're lovely."

"Don't mention it," he said, patting me on the back.

Grace came into the room carrying her Christmas presents. She had changed into a skirt with a hideous floral pattern and a white blouse which was far too big for her, but once again seeing her try so hard made me want to cry.

"Happy Christmas, Jody," she said, handing him his present.

"Well, be the –" he said, taking it from her and shaking it in his hand. "What's this?"

"Open it," said Grace, smiling at him.

I looked at this tender scene and my smile faded into a look of confusion.

The fire took immediately, and long orange flames licked up the chimney. Did he do that every day?

They're having an affair! I thought in shock.

Jody pulled the wrapping paper away to reveal a black Aran sweater. He put it up against himself and whistled. "That's a beauty," he remarked, turning the sweater around to examine it. "Thank you very much, Grace."

He handed her a present, which had been wrapped with the same care as mine. After much

419

pulling and picking, the paper came away to reveal the same gift, soaps on a rope. Grace thanked him and dangled the soaps in front of her nose to sniff the lemony scent. I ran upstairs to get my presents out of the case. My hands shook as I rummaged through the clothes to find them.

Could they be? Grace and Jody!

I felt the shapes of the gifts and pulled them out through the jumble of clothing that had been carelessly stuffed on top of them. A Boston Red Sox T-shirt and baseball cap for Jody. A hand-painted silk scarf and pearl earrings for Grace. I rushed back down to the kitchen, making lots of noise outside the door before I entered. They were standing by the fire, chatting in a casual manner. No jumping back or clearing of throats. Perhaps I was wrong.

"It's not very much, Jody, but Happy Christmas," I said, giving him the parcel.

I gave Grace a kiss and gave her the scarf, which was coming loose from its wrapping after the journey.

Jody gave a giggle as he put the cap on with the peak to the back. "Well, the lads will love this," he said. "Red Sox indeed! I'll be the height of fashion."

Grace pulled the scarf away from the torn paper and held it in both hands, feeling the fabric. "It's beautiful, Iris," she whispered, blushing. "I'll keep it for good wear." She folded it and put it on the mantelpiece, then she opened the box with the earrings and put them on. "You shouldn't have gone to so much bother!"

"They look nice on you," I said, feeling embarrassed at all this niceness.

Jody went to another bag he had brought, and took out a bottle of wine. "I brought this, to have with dinner." He held it out towards us. Grace quickly looked the other way.

"I'll start on the dinner," she said, moving towards the cooker and away from temptation.

I took the bottle and went to the cutlery drawer to find a corkscrew.

"That's a great smell of cooking, Grace," said Jody.

I looked at him to see if he was being sarcastic but his praise was genuine. He helped me open the wine. The corkscrew had seen better days and was bent at an angle. Jody put the bottle between his knees and pulled a few times until the cork slid out. Then he poured a glass for me.

"Grace, will you have a drop?"

Grace, still fussing around with potatoes, waved her knife in the air. "No, thanks, Jody. Not for the moment."

"What about you?" I asked, looking at his empty hands.

Jody quickly went to one of his bags and pulled a tin of beer from it.

"I'll stick to the hard stuff," he said and smiled as he pulled the ring of the can open. Grace took several breaks from the dinner preparations and retreated upstairs to her room. I felt like telling her to bring the vodka down and save herself the bother of the stairs, but I held my tongue. *Let her think I don't notice.*

It was torture to watch her make a complete mess of the dinner, but she refused to let me help. The turkey skated around the plate as she tried to cut slices from it. The gravy was abandoned. It seemed that no amount of stirring would break down the black lumps that had formed.

"I don't like the stuff anyway," said Jody, cracking open another can of beer.

When we finally sat down to eat I could tell by the look on Grace's face that she wanted to throw the contents of her plate at the wall and go to bed for the rest of the afternoon. But it was Christmas Day and we were halfway through.

"This is lovely," I lied, trying to swallow the barely warm pieces of turkey in one gulp without chewing.

"It is indeed," said Jody, emptying most of the butter dish into his potatoes.

Grace cut her food into tiny pieces but ate nothing. When she caught me eyeing her plate she sighed loudly. "I never feel hungry when I cook myself."

I can understand, I thought, as I gagged on the dried-up turkey.

We all dived for our fags as soon as the cutlery was put down.

Jody patted his stomach as he lit up. "Grand feed, Grace."

"Thanks, Jody," said Grace as she leaned across the table to take a light from him.

I looked sneakily from one to the other. *Were they?* They seemed so comfortable with each other. He was a good person, the only one I could rely on to take care of her. It should have been a load off my mind, but for some reason it shocked me. Jody stayed until seven o'clock, and then made his excuses, saying he was going to spend the evening in his cousin's house, but my bet was that he would be knocking on the door of Mulligan's. I said goodbye to him in the kitchen and let Grace walk him out to the door. I strained my ears, but could hear no signs of muffled endearments. I stood behind the door and heard him say goodnight, then I went back over to the fire when I heard the front door click.

Grace came back in and rubbed her hands together. "It's getting icy out there." She had made quite a few trips upstairs during the afternoon, keeping herself topped up. We watched television for a while, but Grace fidgeted, and grew restless. When the *Nine O'Clock News* came on, she jumped up from her chair.

"Do you mind if I go to bed? I'm exhausted."

"It's been a long day," I said. "I'm turning in soon myself."

She walked as far as the door and then stopped and turned around, slowly putting her hand up to her mouth.

"I never gave you your Christmas present," she said in a shocked whisper.

"It's all right." I waved my hand at her as if to say so what – she hadn't given me a Christmas present in years.

"No. I have one for you. I just forgot. Wait." She left the room and went upstairs.

A few minutes later she came back with a painting in her hands and propped it up against the leg of the kitchen table.

"I should have wrapped it."

It was the Communion painting. The face could have been any child's, but the eyes were mine. And in them she had captured an anguish that both of us recognised.

"It's haunting," I said quietly, trying not to get too emotional.

We both stared at it.

"It was a difficult one to do."

"I remember that day so well."

Grace jerked back, as if I had frightened her. "Do you?"

I bit my lip and continued. "I remember you got upset, because I wanted to pray for my daddy in heaven."

Grace went a sickly shade of grey. I lit up a cigarette and tried to appear calm, but the tidal wave of jangling nerves that were crashing about in the pit of my stomach resulted in my hands shaking.

"I remember it too," she said with a nervous sniff. "Iris, your gran did a terrible thing to you, and I never stopped her. I am as much to blame."

I pulled on my cigarette and listened hard, not wanting to say anything that would put her off.

"She told you that your father was dead."

I turned my head towards her so we were looking straight at each other. My stare was too intense for Grace and she looked away.

"He didn't die." Her voice was shaky. "His name was Tom Harrison. We went out together briefly. Then I heard he had moved to England. He took off before I could even tell him I was pregnant."

"Did you ever think of looking for him?"

"No. It would never have worked. Your gran didn't like him at all."

"Why not?"

"I don't know. Maybe she saw something in him that I didn't."

"Do you ever think about him now?" I asked.

"No. I only think about him in relation to you, and how I should have been more open about it. You had every right to know about him."

The two of us sat in silence. Grace hung her head and waited for my reaction. But I was unprepared, my mind racing back and forth as if my thoughts were trapped. Should I continue the story and reveal the details her mother deprived her of? The other side to her life, that she was never allowed to know. That her lover was actually her half-brother, that my father was also my uncle. What would she gain by being told? Maybe another few months in St Paul's. The opportunity dangled before me like a hypnotist's chain, and for a second I almost seized it. But I let the moment pass and remained mute.

"I'm sorry I lied to you," she said.

I reached out and took her hand. I wished she hadn't said that. What I was doing was just as bad.

"It doesn't matter," was all I could say. "Thanks for the painting."

Grace stood up and walked towards the door, and I realised that this might be the last time we would ever talk about him again.

"Sometime when you feel like it, maybe you'll tell me about him?"

"If you want," she said. But her face had closed down again. The moment had passed.

Grace didn't get out of bed the following day, and for the next two days she made only brief appearances. The weather was cold but it didn't rain, so I walked for miles each day, sometimes not passing a single person. It made me realise how much I had missed the stillness of the countryside. I didn't venture into town because I knew I would risk running into Larry, and I had had enough to deal with that Christmas without adding him to my list.

Unfortunately, Jane Rice had gone to the Canary Islands for the holidays. I should have called her before I made my travel plans – I would have travelled home a few days earlier. She was the one person I had looked forward to seeing.

On the morning I left, I crept around the house gathering my things together. Grace was asleep and I thought it might be better for both of us if I left it till the last minute to say goodbye. I went downstairs to make some tea, and on the kitchen table was a painting that I had admired. I had mentioned that Andrew would like it. It looked like one he had hanging in his apartment. It was two sunflowers in a vase that were withered and bent over, their petals strewn about on the table below them. Pinned to the painting was a note.

This is for Andrew. I hope he likes it. Grace.

I wrapped both of the paintings in a towel and put them in the middle of my suitcase. When I heard Jody's car in the lane I went upstairs and opened Grace's door gently. I could tell by her breathing that she was in a deep sleep. I tiptoed over to the side of her bed, but my presence did not wake her.

I leaned over and kissed her cheek and whispered goodbye. On the way out I left a note on the table with my address and phone number in Boston.

Jody insisted on driving me to Sarah's house where I had arranged to get a taxi to the airport with

427

Andrew. He looked very relieved to see me, his week of playing straight had worn him out completely. When we arrived at the airport and said our goodbyes, he grabbed my arm and started running towards the bar.

"Christ, I need a drink!" he exclaimed.

He ordered two brandies at the bar and we found a corner to stand in. The place was heaving with post-Christmas traffic. 'The Fields of Athenry' was being murdered by a group of hairy-looking rugby supporters.

Andrew looked around and shuddered. "God, I hate this country!"

I looked at him and raised an eyebrow, waiting for him to continue.

"I really wanted to tell them I was gay," he explained defensively. "I'm sick of hiding it. But I just couldn't do it. They'd label me a freak and things would never be the same again."

I couldn't argue with him, as he was probably right.

"Here's to my secret," he said lifting his glass.

"Mine too," I mumbled, as we knocked our plastic tumblers together.

49

I was glad to get back to Boston. Lisa and Tina had dinner waiting for me the night I arrived, and it felt like coming home. I experienced my first winter in Massachusetts. It was so cold that my lips were permanently blue and my teeth crashed together in audible shivers. Our apartment building was old and the heating seemed to become less effective the higher up you were. We were on the top floor, and at nights we would hug the pipes to keep warm. I didn't go home again for eighteen months because I had overstayed my visa and if I left the country, I would not be allowed in again. I applied for a Green Card. Some nice senator had lobbied for a visa lottery for the Irish, and a year after I applied I was granted one.

Grace rang about once a month. We never stayed on the phone for very long. After the initial greetings and weather checks, we didn't have a lot to talk about. I was just glad to know she was still alive.

I stayed working at the bookstore café, but I had become fed up with it. It paid the rent and stopped me dipping into the money my grandmother had left me. It's not that I had spent very much of it, but every time I went to make a withdrawal I would change my mind and do without whatever I was going to spend it on. I had, and still have although to a lesser degree, a fear of one day waking up to find that I have no money. At the rate Grace was drinking, I knew she would get through every penny I had left in the bank for her. If it wasn't gone already. In any case I felt better knowing that my money was still there, in case Grace got sick.

When my Green Card came through the first person I called was Andrew. He had put in a great deal of effort with the paperwork, calling in every contact he had to vouch for me.

"Guess what!" I whooped down the phone.

"What?"

"I got it. I'm a legal alien. I got the Green Card!"

"Great stuff! Well done!" His voice seemed to trail off into the distance.

"Want to come out and celebrate tonight?"

"Eh, yeh. Can I call you later?"

I knew by the rigid tone in his voice that something was wrong.

That night when we met, I was still walking on

air. Knowing that I could go home any time I wanted was a huge relief. I put Andrew's sombre mood down to the pressures of work. He had been complaining a lot about his job lately, how he was sick of being a banker. But when I reminded him of the pots of dough he brought home every month, he usually cheered up. That night was different. He remained morose and by the time our coffees came his chin was almost on the floor.

"Please tell me what's wrong," I demanded.

Andrew stirred his coffee, and a tear rolled down his cheek.

"Oh God, Andrew! What's happened?"

"I'm sick."

"How sick?"

"HIV positive."

My spirits came crashing back to earth with a thud. I sat there with my mouth open, unable to say anything.

"Do you know who gave – ?"

Before I finished, Andrew held up a hand to stop me. "That doesn't matter now," he said sadly.

"Does Charles know?"

He sighed heavily. "I'm no longer seeing Charles."

We walked home through Boston Common, my arm linked through his. Summer was almost upon us and the air was thick with the smell of lilac and cherry blossom.

"I'm sorry to spoil your Green Card celebration,"

he said with a smile.

I squeezed his arm. "Yes. It's very selfish of you."

Then Andrew stopped and looked at me. "You know you have become my closest friend?"

"I'm honoured," I said and kissed his cheek.

We walked on, linking each other tightly. Trying to be brave for each other.

"Let's go to a bar and get drunk," I suggested.

And that's exactly what we did.

* * *

I made two trips home that year, each one only lasting four days. Short spells made it easier to handle. Grace was still the same, no worse and no better. But the house was beginning to fall apart. Jody was still around. I often wondered about them but I never said anything. Who was I to question her? I had given up the right to do that the day I left. Grace seemed to have perfected the dosage of alcohol she could consume without actually killing herself. I went to visit Jane Rice as soon as I arrived. It was so good to talk to her again. She still kept a regular check on Grace, and gave her vitamin injections every few months. When I asked her how Grace was still alive, she threw her hands up into the air and shook her head. "Beats me!"

The second visit was for Christmas, and Andrew came home with me to tell his parents, not only that was he gay but that he was also HIV positive. We met up in the airport on the way home. I spotted Sarah and Pat before they saw me. I suppose it was the worry of her son being seriously ill, coupled with the fact that her heart was growing weaker every day that made Sarah seem so old and fragile. She hugged Andrew and told him how much she loved him. Pat stood back a few paces and studied the ground around his shoes, but I could see he was doing his utmost not to cry.

"Look after him," said Sarah looking at me.

"I promise I will," I said, squeezing her hand.

We watched them leave and Andrew groaned deeply.

"That was the pits."

"How did they take the gay bit?"

"OK, I suppose."

"Well, they're still talking to you," I said, brightly.

"Yes. It helped to follow up with the fact that I have a disease that may kill me. That upped the sympathy stakes no end."

50

When I returned to Boston after that Christmas I received a call from Jane Rice to say that she had persuaded Grace to do another stint in St Paul's. I was speechless. The fact that Grace signed herself into an institution where she would not have access to drink, the very thought that she wanted to do it, was unbelievable. The fact that she managed to complete four weeks before signing herself out, made me think that all was not lost. Just as I was reeling from that news, Andrew left his job at the bank. He was responding well to the drugs for his HIV, but they cost a fortune. His plan was to go to college and study something he had always wanted to do: garden design. I thought he was crazy, but it was good to see him so happy again.

I worried about how he would afford his medication.

"If I become desperate I can always sell the gin palace. I can live somewhere less flashy," he assured me.

He had reached a point where there was no turning back. He needed a life change to help him through his illness. As it turned out he did eventually sell the apartment. As well as needing the money, it no longer suited his image. During his first year in college he began to dress in more relaxed clothing. Gone were the Armani suits and designer spectacles that had been a part of his banking days. He began to dress like his fellow students, sometimes forgetting that he was twenty years older than most of them. However, I was always on hand with some blunt advice if he went too far. Like when he started wearing John Lennon specs.

"They're just not you!" I shrieked.

He took them off and put back on his black-rimmed ones. "Better?"

"Yes. Definitely."

He had traded in his sharp-cut suits and marine-style haircut for a more earthy image. His thin wispy hair had grown down almost to his shoulders. I told him that if he dared to tie it in a ponytail or wear Birkenstocks, I would not open the door to him. Like the hardy annuals and exotic hybrids he was studying, Andrew was also cultivating a new life for himself. Unfortunately it was a life that could only be lived from one season to the next. His medication made him weak and sick in the beginning and he lost a lot of weight, but what kept him going during that first year of living with HIV, was the happiness his new life had brought him. Chucking in his job was a gamble which could have gone terribly wrong, but it didn't. In fact, it turned out to be the best decision he ever made.

It was around this time that I met Robert. We threw a party for Lisa's twenty-sixth birthday, and invited everyone who had ever eaten in the café and told them to bring a friend. By midnight the place was swinging, the party had spilled out into the upstairs hall. As the night went on it got hot indoors, and people started moving downstairs. We had hung fairy lights across the hedge in the communal garden at the back of the house, and I had lit candles in jam-jars and dotted them about the place. It was a close humid night with distant rumbles of thunder. The heat in the apartment was stifling, so I took a beer from the fridge and went down to the garden, weaving a path through the groups of people sitting on the stairs. I opened the screen door and felt the warm air blow over me, and there he was, lying at my feet. I almost stepped onto his stomach. His arms were folded behind his head and he was smiling up at me. I stepped over him and sat down on a cushion beside him. He rolled over on to his side and reached over to shake my hand.

"Robert Miller."

"Iris Fortune."

He sat up cross-legged and pulled a packet of cigarettes from his shirt pocket.

"Want one?" he asked, holding the packet towards me.

I tried to concentrate on the cigarette, but I couldn't stop myself from staring into his good-looking face. It was like a magnet drawing my gaze towards it.

"Good party, eh?"

"Not bad," I said, looking around.

"When I find out who's having it, I'll be sure to thank them," he said, stuffing the pack of cigarettes into his shirt pocket.

I could tell that he was a bit older than me. He wasn't exactly what you would call confident, but he was comfortable in his skin. Somewhere I hadn't reached yet. He talked a lot, but I didn't find him boring. In fact by the end of the night I was in awe of him. He was eight years older than me, and had just completed his second novel.

Tina and Lisa had never ceased to amuse me with their endless conversations about men, and how you know when the right one eventually comes along. They could never explain how I would know, but they were pretty sure that I would recognise the signs when they presented themselves. I always thought it was a weird Aussie myth, but the night I met Robert I understood what they were saying. I just knew we were meant to be.

We talked until the last people left the party, and then he stayed and helped tidy up, which I took to be a good sign. If he was bored he could have left with the friends he had come with. It was getting bright as we carried in the last few bottles from the garden. I wanted him to stay so badly that I cleaned like there was no tomorrow. The apartment looked so neat it was hard to believe that there had been a party at all. We stood in the tiny kitchen like bashful kids, knowing the time had come to cross over that line. He pulled me towards him and we looked at each other for a long time. Our eyes were on the same level which felt good. I normally looked down at the men I kissed as they were always smaller than me. Robert was exactly the same height, his hair was brown and, while it was not straight, it wasn't curly either. His eyes were brown, and his front right tooth had a tiny chip missing from it, which seemed to add to his character. Within minutes we had made our way into my bedroom and between the sheets, our clothes still floating to the floor as we made love. He lived in Bangor, Maine, and three weeks later so did I.

Andrew gave him the thumbs-up, which was a big deal. I had given up on Andrew ever liking any guy that I dated. He was always very protective of me, and therefore felt he had to give my boyfriends the third degree. Not that there were very many of them.

This vetting procedure usually took place in a restaurant or bar where we would meet for dinner or a drink. When the victim would leave our company to use the men's room, Andrew would wait until they were out of sight and then pretend to stick his finger down his throat in a gesture that meant, no, he didn't like them. Or he would wait until they were out of earshot and say, "Are you sure he's not gay?"

But with Robert it was different. Andrew loved him. The three of us met for dinner and as I sat down to eat I realised how nervous I was. It was important to me that Andrew liked who I dated, after all he was the closest thing to family that I had.

But I didn't need to worry. As we left the restaurant, Andrew pulled me back.

"Marry him," he whispered a little too loudly.

"Shut up," I said out of the side of my mouth, embarrassed that Robert might hear.

"You're blushing," Andrew teased.

I stuck my nose into my handbag and pretended to look for something.

"Andrew, piss off!" I hissed.

"Iris is in love!" Andrew sang under his breath as we walked towards the door that Robert stood holding for us.

51

Robert had grown up in Winter Harbour, Maine. His father was a fisherman who had been lost at sea when Robert was twelve. One night a storm had blown up out of nowhere and six men from the area had been lost. Like me, he was an only child, but the similarities ended there. His mother had devoted her life to him. After her husband's death, she turned her sewing machine into a business and made a living making curtains, working every hour of the day and sometimes long into the night to make a living for herself and her son. Robert says that when he thinks of his mother the same image always appears: Annie Miller bent over her Singer sewing machine, her hands deftly working the fabric through the jumping needle. He had a happy childhood, and his mother even managed to put him through college. He dedicated his first book to her, a history of the fishing communities in Maine. It was well received and he had become a sort of local hero. He married a girl from college when they were both in their twenties, but the marriage ended after a year. Since then there had been a string of girlfriends, but the divorce had made Robert wary of long-term relationships and he never went out with anyone for longer than a couple of months. He figured six months was a good cut-off point.

Of course, I didn't know any of this when I followed him up to Bangor, like a stray dog. We both knew what we were doing was impulsive, and certainly uncharacteristic for me, but it felt right. It wasn't until I had been there a few weeks that the enormity of what I had done came swinging towards me like a wrecking-ball. It was a very hot afternoon and I was alone in the house. It was an apartment on the ground floor of a typical New England clapboard house. Robert had bought it after his divorce and had lived there for eight years. It was old and stuffy and looked like the home of an elderly university professor. In the silence the heaving bookshelves creaked from the weight of their load. Unreturned library books lay strewn about in untidy heaps. Newspapers bought and unread lay in dusty piles. The windows were open but the air outside was as heavy and sticky as the air in the room. I could taste the heat in my mouth every time I took a breath. I walked from room to room, feeling like an intruder. *This is not my home,* I thought as I stood among his things. Robert had gone to Boston to meet his agent, and I was alone in the house for the first time. I had been alone before while Robert went to the store or the bank, but never for a whole day, and it gave me time to think. When we first met that night at the party and talked for hours and hours, I had told Robert all about Grace. But when he asked me about my father I said that he was dead. It just seemed easier at the time. Every day the weight of my lie became heavier. I was annoyed with myself for trying to hide it. Wasn't that what screwed up our lives from the beginning? Trying to cover up the past. I began to worry that I was turning out just like my mother and grandmother. It had sounded so natural: "My father died when I was a baby."

I spent all afternoon preparing dinner, trying to keep myself from thinking too much. When Robert returned, I had set the table out on the porch. He beamed at me as he stepped into the kitchen. "Good news. It's ready for publication; they accepted my second draft."

I smiled nervously and kissed him. I was genuinely happy for him but what was on my mind was more important.

"Well done. Let's eat."

We sat outside and ate, serenaded by the symphony of the frogs croaking in a nearby pond.

The candle on the table flickered in the breeze.

"I lied about my father," I said in a half-whisper.

Robert looked at me without saying anything, waiting for me to continue.

I began my story. I spat the words out, resenting every detail, hating my parents for the life they had handed me. When I finished, I sat still in my chair and waited for Robert to say something.

He let out a long breath and looked at me thoughtfully. "That's some story!" he said as he poured a glass of wine for me. "How can you be so sure of what happened? You tell it as if you were there. As if you know for sure."

"Well, I was told what happened," I said indignantly. "Sarah told me."

"How does she know? She wasn't there either."

I opened my mouth to argue, but stopped. He was right.

"The only way you can ever find out what happened is to talk to your mother or your father about it."

"I can't talk to Grace about it." I couldn't give a reason why. I just knew that I would never talk to Grace about my father again.

"Then find your father and ask him."

I felt a shiver crawl down my spine. "Don't be ridiculous."

"I'm not. It's just. . . how do you know that he didn't fall in love with her?"

I could feel my mouth drying up. I felt angry with him for daring to put another slant on my logic. After all, he knew nothing. "You don't run off without a word of goodbye if you love someone."

"Yes, but maybe he couldn't face telling her who he was."

I got up and walked into the house, banging the screen door behind me.

Robert followed me into the living-room. "Iris. You don't think he did it out of spite?" he asked incredulously.

"Yes, I do!" I snapped. "He was a mean bastard who was out for revenge." Then I felt something inside me crack, like ice melting, and I started to cry.

Ever since Sarah had told me about my father, I had never allowed myself to believe that he was anything but a vindictive monster. Hearing Robert defend him had caught me off guard. My head was swimming.

"What do you know about it anyway?" My voice sounded small and far away.

He came over and put his arms around me. "I know nothing about it," he said, kissing the crown of my head, "but neither do you."

I let my head drop onto his shoulder.

"Iris, I believe you were conceived out of love. How else could you be so beautiful?"

That finished me off. I bawled until his shirt collar was soaked with my tears.

*　*　*

That was the fourth of August 1992. We are not married, but every year we celebrate our anniversary on that date. We did try to have children but didn't succeed. After five years of trying I did conceive, but I had a miscarriage in the fourth month of my pregnancy. I took this to be a warning. I was always acutely aware that my parents' relationship may have left me with some questionable genes and after the miscarriage I got nervous and we stopped trying. It's not too late to try again but I don't feel ready yet. I may never feel ready.

We still live in Bangor and Robert still writes. He also lectures at the university three days a week and we are still very much in love.

Grace sold the house seven years ago. The property company that had bought the land from us offered her an obscene amount of money for the house and remaining lands and Grace decided to get out before it fell down. She bought an apartment overlooking the harbour near Wicklow town. It has two bedrooms, one which she uses as a studio. An art gallery in Wicklow sells several of her paintings every year, which has given her self-confidence a well-deserved boost. Unfortunately she still drinks, and has astounded her doctors by staying alive for so long. I no longer concern myself with her drinking.

In fact we don't talk about it at all. If I happen to call her and she's drunk (I can tell immediately), I just hang up.

Tina and Lisa, the Victory sisters, both ended up marrying very rich men. Tina lives in Connecticut and plays a lot of golf. Lisa married an architect and moved to Los Angeles We still keep in touch.

Andrew remains in good health and runs a successful garden-design business with Kurt, his wonderful partner. They went into business together, but romance soon blossomed (forgive the pun), and they are completely happy. The sword of Damocles hangs over his head, but it has given Andrew a joy for life that he never possessed before his illness. With him, the glass is always half-full. I say a prayer for him every night, and I think someone must be listening. We travelled home together three years ago for Sarah's funeral. Her heart finally gave out, but she had lived into her eighty-sixth year and, as she said herself, enjoyed every one of them. Andrew took her death badly.

I finally decided to spend my money. We bought a house with some land just outside Bangor, and I opened a small bookstore with the money that Grace sent me when she sold the house. It's called Fortune Books and I deal in both new and second-hand books.

I have asked Grace to come over every year since I moved here, but for obvious reasons she won't, so

I try to get back to see her every now and again, when my heart can take it.

The place has changed so much I hardly recognise it. There are so many new houses it makes me feel old, because I can remember when there were only fields. Our old farmhouse was extended and renovated, and it is now a health spa called Natural Springs. They claim that there is a natural water spring under the house, which was news to me. Grace sent me a brochure and, on my last visit home out of curiosity, I booked myself in. Needless to say it looked nothing like the house that was once my home. The floors are limestone with heat coming from underneath. Everything was white. The soothing tunes of Indian music lilted through the speakers of every room. And, they gave me my old room! Well, actually I asked for it. There I was back in my very own room. Except now there were scented candles and fluffy bathrobes. And Grace wasn't moaning in the next room!

But my stay did turn out to be a curious form of therapy. Perhaps it was too many essential oils, but I could feel my grandmother's spirit very close to me. And when I left, I felt a lightness in my soul that I had never experienced. It was as if someone had taken all the unhappiness out of the house and left it in peace, something I had tried to do but failed.

On the last day of my trip I walked into Wicklow town to pick up some things for Robert. Smoked salmon and Tayto crisps were top of my list. The main street was crowded with people, all talking on mobile phones. It's now a recognised national pastime. I walked through a carpark that led to a row of smart new shops. A car engine revved behind me making me jump. I turned around to give the driver a dirty look but he was also on a mobile phone and wasn't even looking at me. He dumped his car at the side of the kerb and got out. I stood there not knowing where to look.

It was too late to walk away. He had seen me. *Larry Doran.*

"Jesus Christ Almighty!" he said, slamming the car door and walking towards me.

"Hi, Larry," I managed to say.

He gave me a warm hug and stood back to take a good look at me. "You're looking great."

He hadn't changed much. His hair was a bit thinner and darker and he carried a few more pounds around his waist. But he looked like the same old Larry. Just for a few seconds he was lost for words, but he soon made up for it and started to talk a mile a minute. Married with three kids. The smart new shops were his. He walked me by each window, showing them off proudly. He insisted we went for coffee, and showed me photos of his children. He even produced photos of his supermarket in Bray. When he stopped to gulp his coffee, I told him a little about my life and Robert.

"Are you happy?"

"I am," I answered, smiling at him.

"Good, 'cos you deserve it. You'd a shite life here and you did right to move away." He leaned over the table towards me and looked around, lowering his voice. "You could have said goodbye though."

"I know. I wasn't thinking straight. I was afraid you might persuade me to stay."

He nodded his head, accepting my explanation. Then he shot a glance around the café again. "You broke my heart, girl."

"I know," I said, feeling my face blush. "I never meant to hurt you."

"I know you didn't." Then his face brightened and he gave a quick laugh. "We probably would have been a fuckin' disaster together!"

"Yes," I agreed, touched by his bluntness. "We probably would have."

We finished our coffee and walked back out to the street.

"Well, Miss Fortune, it was a pleasure as always," he said, leaning over to kiss me.

"Goodbye, Larry."

I watched him walk a few paces and felt a lump in my throat. Some moments are hard to define, and at that moment I had no idea what was happening to me, but I couldn't leave it at that.

"Larry!" I called after him.

He swung around and looked back at me.

449

My hands flapped in the air as I tried to think of what I wanted to say. "Thanks for being such a good pal when I needed you."

"Any time, kiddo," he said, pointing his finger at me like a gun. Then he turned and walked away.

Grace didn't seem to have a clue who Larry Doran was when I told her I had met him. It's probably just as well considering how he had once seen her. Every time I go home she looks worse. The years of drinking and smoking have left her looking decrepit. In recent years she has developed a stutter which makes it hard to have a conversation, not that we ever had many anyway. The path of self-destruction that Grace ploughed for herself is almost at an end. I don't believe she will live for very much longer. Her neighbours are good. They check in on her almost every day to see if she needs anything. Jane Rice is still her doctor and gives her the best care possible, but a body can take only so much.

Jody has remained ever faithful, like a Wicklow collie. Always there for her. I never did find out if there was something going on between them. I figured that if Grace wanted me to know, she would have told me by now. I can't understand why I was so appalled at the idea. I hope they have been together all these years.

I still believe that telling Grace about my father would have been cruel. I will never truly know if I was right to keep it from her, but if you stood in my shoes, you'd see that my heart was in the right place.

Epilogue

I met my father six months ago. It all came about very suddenly. Robert was invited to London by his publishing company and at the last minute I decided to join him. On the second night over dinner he brought it up.

"This could be the one and only chance you have of ever contacting your father," he said casually.

I dropped my knife and fork in shock.

"Surely you have some desire to meet with him, Iris."

He took a piece of paper out of his breast pocket and pushed it towards me. "This is his address in Bath."

My mouth opened but no words came out. Instead I reached for a glass of water and gulped a few mouthfuls. I stared down at the address, fearful that it would jump off the table and bite me.

"Christ, Robert, what brought this on?"

He looked at me squarely, the way he always does when he's trying to reason with people. "He should be told about you, I think you know that. Do you honestly want to end your days knowing that you could have met him but didn't?"

My father's whereabouts had always been something of a pet project to Robert. A couple of years ago, unknown to me at the time, he went through a painstaking process of tracking down a family of Harrisons who owned several paper mills in the Bristol area. He obtained this information from a university in Bristol under false pretences, by telling them it was for a dissertation on British paper mills. When he had finished his investigations, he told me what he had done and what he had discovered. Mainly that the mills had been all shut down by the late 1970's. He also slipped in casually that there was a Tom Harrison of Harrison's paper mills residing in Bath. At the time, I really didn't understand why Robert did it. I felt as if he was trying to poison me with my past. I told him it was prying, that it was no different from going through my underwear drawer when I wasn't looking. My accusations came as a great shock to him and from then on the subject of my father was assiduously avoided by both of us.

I let my eyes rest on the address in Bath, written

in Robert's familiar scrawl.

"How do you know that he'd agree to meet me?"

"I don't. But I do know that he is alive and," he pointed to the piece of paper, "that is where he lives."

When Robert had finished with his publishers, we hired a car and drove to Bath. The hotel we booked into was so old that we felt as if we were staying in a museum. The grand dame at the front desk was straight out of a bygone era. Her blue-rinsed hair was teased into an elaborate bouffant and her lavender perfume filled every corner of the musty lobby. Being surrounded by tiny dainty things like china teacups and embroidered tasselled cushions made me feel like a giant. Even the cucumber sandwiches were cut into minute fingers. I could fit three into my mouth and still keep talking.

Robert made some more enquiries and obtained Tom Harrison's telephone number. For two days I walked the streets of Bath turning the crumpled piece of paper that held my father's address and telephone number, over and over in my hands. I walked past men in cafés and shops and wondered were any of them my father.

On the third morning of our stay I had still not made the call.

"It's your decision," Robert kept saying soothingly.

"So why do I feel there's a gun to my head?" I said, vexed.

Finally, I decided to do it. I waited until Robert had gone out sightseeing just in case I lost my nerve. I dialled the number and almost passed out when I heard the voice on the other end.

"Hello? Tom Harrison," he said in a throaty English accent.

My own voice failed me.

"Hello?"

"My name is Iris. I am related to Grace Fortune and I would like to meet you." I cringed when I heard myself speak. I sounded like a Soviet spy.

The line went quiet. Then, "What about?" he asked sharply.

"I think I may have something to tell you. Can we meet?"

Again he was quiet and for a second I thought he had hung up on me.

"Can't you tell me now?" he asked suspiciously.

"I'd really rather meet you."

His heavy nasal breathing blew down the telephone line as he thought about it.

"One o'clock tomorrow. Do you know where Bentley's restaurant is?"

"I can find it."

"It's beside the train station. I'll see you there tomorrow," he said, and hung up.

I dropped the sweaty receiver and collapsed onto the squeaky bed. I had just had my first conversation with my father and my heart was racing. That evening, as I tried not to think about the following day, something creepy started to happen. I began to fantasise about the father I never had. Maybe he had always longed for a daughter and our meeting would be loving and tearful. My thoughts swung between excited anticipation and downright dread. I hated Robert for dragging me headlong into such a situation and refused to speak to him when he returned from his daytrip. But what really began to alarm me was that, if I was truthful with myself, I had wanted to meet my father for a very long time.

Robert walked me towards the train station the next day, but I insisted on him leaving me to find the restaurant alone. I couldn't find it at first. I wandered up and down the street but couldn't see the place. After a few minutes I located it down a laneway, tucked behind the train station. I made sure that I was ten minutes late before I went in.

Inside, my eyes had to adjust to the dim lighting of the airless basement. The tables were covered in red-and-white-checked cloths and the place had a distinctly seedy atmosphere. I looked around and saw several solitary male diners, but which one was my father? A middle-aged waitress with big hair approached me.

"Do you have a reservation?" she asked. If I hadn't been so nervous I probably would have laughed out loud. The place was almost empty.

"No," I told her politely. "I am meeting a Mr Harrison."

"Oh, Tom's down the back," she said, pointing to the last table.

She went to walk me down but I stopped her. "It's all right. I see him now."

He was sitting in a booth at the end of the restaurant, away from the main dining area, bathed in a swirl of cigarette smoke. He lifted his hand and waved an uncertain salute. I walked slowly towards him, trying desperately not to turn around and charge out of the place. When I got to the table he stood up and extended his hand.

"Hello," he said.

He looked nothing like Andy Williams. But he did bear an unsettling resemblance to my mother. His thick black hair was streaked with gray and oiled back off his face. The eyes were the exact shape and colour as my own, my mother's and my grandmother's. Beneath the thick moustache, a cigarette dangled from his bottom lip. He was dressed in the most appalling Lord of the Manor clothes. A yellow V-neck sweater and cravat were topped off with a tweed jacket that had seen better days. Our handshake was limp and clammy.

"I'm Iris," I said, slipping into the banquette opposite him.

The waitress appeared. "A drink?" she asked with a smile.

I eyed his glass and noticed he was drinking whiskey. I knew I needed something to give me courage so I ordered a white wine. The waitress left and I could feel his eyes boring through me. I looked over and met his gaze but neither of us spoke for a few seconds.

"Who are you?" he asked quietly, his stare becoming more intense.

Out of the corner of my eye I could see the waitress coming back with my wine so I delayed the answer. The glass was set in front of me and we were left alone again. I bit my lip and forced myself to speak.

"My mother is Grace Fortune. I am your daughter." I stared down at the grubby checked tablecloth and waited politely for his reaction. The ice clinked against the side of his glass as he gulped a mouthful of whiskey.

"My God," he said eventually. When I looked at him again his face seemed to have caved inwards. His expression had changed from one of curiosity to sheer disbelief. "Oh dear God!" he groaned, stubbing out his cigarette. He put down his drink and massaged his forehead with both hands. I looked around the restaurant, giving him some time to absorb my words. He looked up at me and went to say something, but stopped.

"What?" I asked.

He grimaced slightly. "What exactly do you know?"

I gave him a long and level look.

"I know that my grandmother gave birth to you and gave you up for adoption. I know that you came back years later and seduced my mother without telling her that you were her half-brother."

His head fell limply, like a condemned man, as I spoke.

"I know that you were engaged to be married to a girl in England, and left before my mother could tell you that she was pregnant."

All the colour had drained from his face leaving him a ghastly shade of gray.

"I don't know what to say. I still to this day can't explain why I acted the way I did." He looked over at me and I could see such sadness in his eyes that I had to look away before I started feeling sorry for him.

"I have never told anyone," he said, emphatically. "You'll have to forgive me; it's such a shock. This is the first time I have ever spoken about it."

I sat perfectly still and waited for him to continue. He looked agitated and beckoned to the waitress, pointing to his now empty glass. Then he turned his attention to me again. "It's haunted me. It's lived with me like a disease." He picked up his packet of cigarettes and shook one out into his trembling hands.

I watched him light it. "Why did you do it?" I asked.

He took the whiskey from the waitress.

"Are you ready to order?" she enquired.

"Not yet," he said dismissively.

Both of us sat in anxious silence.

"Why?" I repeated.

He sighed loudly. "I really can't tell you, because I don't know. I was annoyed and hurt at my mother, your grandmother, for throwing me out the way she did. She told me that it was too late to tell Grace of my existence because it would upset her. How do you think that made me feel?" His voice was choked. He grabbed his fresh whiskey and drank it back. "I hated Grace. I wanted to hurt her," he said angrily. He shut his eyes tightly and his shoulders drooped under the weight of the memory. When he opened his eyes again they had clouded over with despair. "But I fell in love with her."

I felt a well of emotion stirring from deep within, but tried to remain calm on the outside.

His voice grew shaky. "The more I tried to stop myself, the worse it became. I couldn't stay away from her, and I knew," he broke off and exhaled deeply, "*I knew* there was always a chance that I had left her pregnant."

I hung on every word, barely blinking, even though my insides were churning up. The few sips of bitter wine had upset my stomach.

He wiped his forehead with a napkin and shook his head. "I don't expect you to understand all this. *I* certainly don't, and, believe me, I've tried."

I stared into his face. How had Grace not see it?

The eyes, the shape of the nose, the fullness of the mouth. The likeness was so obvious.

He hesitated before his next question. "Did your grandmother tell Grace who I was?"

"No."

A mixture of relief and horror showed on his face. "But she told you?"

"Gran died when I was seventeen and . . ." My throat went dry, I had been fine up until that point, but remembering my gran and who this man was to her made me lose it. At first I thought I could fan my eyes and continue, but as I tried to get the words out I began to sob uncontrollably. "I need the bathroom," I said, jumping up in a panic.

He pointed towards the exit, his face lined with concern, and I stumbled through the restaurant towards the Ladies'. Once inside, I splashed my face with water and took some deep breaths until the delicate springs of my emotions had settled down again. I fixed my hair and put on some lipstick and when I was absolutely sure that I could talk without crying, I walked back to the table where he was still sitting.

"Are you all right?" he asked anxiously.

"Yes, I'm fine now" I said stiffly.

I laced my fingers together and sat up straight. "I needed to see you, just once," I explained. "And I don't want anything from you," I added quickly. "I think it's important that you know I exist. Grace was

never told who you were, and she will never know."
I paused before I spoke the next sentence, eradicating
any traces of self-pity. "She is a chronic alcoholic."

He had torn his napkin into shreds as he listened
to me. "Am I to blame?" he asked softly.

I braced myself for an angry tirade, but nothing
came. I felt emptied of any contempt for the man
sitting before me. "Before I came here I would have
said yes, but now I don't know. I wanted to meet you
today and blame you for everything bad that ever
happened to me. But I can't, because you're not the
depraved person I thought you were."

His eyes filled up with tears but, unlike me, he
managed to blink them back. He cleared his throat
noisily and fell silent for a few minutes.

"Did Grace ever marry?" he asked, snapping out
of his reverie.

"No."

Once again the waitress materialised. "Tom, are
you eating today?" she asked.

"Do you want to eat?" he said, fumbling with a
menu.

The last thing I wanted was food. "Do you mind if
I pass?"

He looked quite relieved and turned to the
waitress. "We'll leave it for today, Betty."

She shrugged her shoulders and walked away. "Is
this a regular haunt of yours?" I asked, looking
around at the other tables.

He gave me a weary smile. "I come here every day for lunch."

The whole place had a tired dreary look. It had probably been fashionable twenty years ago, but it had definitely fallen into decline, along with most of the customers.

"Let's take a walk outside," he suggested.

He threw some notes on the table as we left.

Outside the daylight hurt my eyes and I fumbled in my handbag for sunglasses. We walked through the narrow streets lined with quaint tea-rooms and old English shopfronts. Neither of us spoke for a while; we just walked, each of us engaged in our own private thoughts. It occurred to me that I knew nothing about him.

"Did you marry the girl you were engaged to?" I asked.

"Yes," he said with a wry look. "We had two sons and divorced after eight years."

"No daughters?"

"Not until today," he said, and looked at me remorsefully.

"Did you marry again?"

"Yes. That didn't work out either. No children, but divorced after five years."

"And now. Are you alone?"

He seemed to grow uneasy. "There is someone. It's not very serious."

"Oh," I said blankly, sorry I had asked at all.

"She is a lot younger than I am and she has a child."

I stopped him before he could go any further, raising my hands defensively. "I don't need to know that."

He nodded his head and stopped talking. We walked a bit further until we reached a turning. "I live up there," he said, pointing towards a row of regency houses built in Bathstone. "Will you come in?"

I shook my head vigorously. Entering his home would have meant entering his world and I was certain that I did not want to go there.

He stood looking at me in the thin English sunshine. "You look just like Grace."

My eyes opened wide and I looked at him indignantly, but then realised that he was talking about the Grace he knew before I was born. Not the husk of a woman she was now.

"So do you," I said sarcastically, deflecting his compliment.

"Where do we go from here?" he asked, but I could see in his eyes that he already knew the answer to that question.

"Nowhere," I stated definitely. "I'm leaving tomorrow. I've done what I came to do."

He nodded his head respectfully. "I understand. You know where I am if you ever want to see me again."

We stood at the corner, frozen in time. Neither of us wanting to be the first to walk away.

"Is it too late to say sorry?" he asked doubtfully.

Of course, it was, but his sincerity disarmed me. He stepped closer and looked at me with a fierce intensity. "Iris, please try to forgive me."

Hot angry tears of self-pity ran down my face.

He put his arms around me and I felt the years of hatred and bitterness fall away as he hugged me tightly.

I didn't struggle to break free. Instead, I rested my head on his shoulder and allowed myself time to say goodbye to my father.

The End

Direct to your home!

If you enjoyed this book why not
visit our website:

www.poolbeg.com

and get another book delivered straight
to your home or to a friend's home!

www.poolbeg.com

All orders are despatched within 24 hours.